Tame A Scarred Baron

HISTORICAL REGENCY ROMANCE

Abby Ayles

STARFALL PUBLICATIONS

Copyright © 2024 by Abby Ayles

All rights reserved.

No part of this publication may be reproduced, distributed, or transmitted in any form or by any means, including photocopying, recording, or other electronic or mechanical methods, without the prior written permission of the publisher, except as permitted by U.S. copyright law. For permission requests, contact Starfall Publications info@starfallpublications.com .

The story, all names, characters, and incidents portrayed in this production are fictitious. No identification with actual persons (living or deceased), places, buildings, and products is intended or should be inferred.

Contents

1. Chapter 1 — 1
2. Chapter 2 — 9
3. Chapter 3 — 16
4. Chapter 4 — 23
5. Chapter 5 — 27
6. Chapter 6 — 34
7. Chapter 7 — 42
8. Chapter 8 — 46
9. Chapter 9 — 52
10. Chapter 10 — 60
11. Chapter 11 — 67
12. Chapter 12 — 75
13. Chapter 13 — 80
14. Chapter 14 — 87
15. Chapter 15 — 94
16. Chapter 16 — 99
17. Chapter 17 — 106

18.	Chapter 18	111
19.	Chapter 19	118
20.	Chapter 20	123
21.	Chapter 21	130
22.	Chapter 22	135
23.	Chapter 23	141
24.	Chapter 24	147
25.	Chapter 25	153
26.	Chapter 26	159
27.	Chapter 27	164
28.	Chapter 28	171
29.	Chapter 29	177
30.	Chapter 30	185
31.	Chapter 31	189
32.	Chapter 32	198
33.	Chapter 33	203
34.	Chapter 34	207
35.	Chapter 35	212
36.	Chapter 36	220
37.	Chapter 37	227
38.	Chapter 38	235
39.	Chapter 39	239
40.	Chapter 40	246
41.	Chapter 41	253
42.	Chapter 42	259
43.	Chapter 43	266
44.	Epilogue	272
	Thank you	276

About Starfall Publications 277

Also by Abby Ayles 278

Chapter 1

Lady Evelyn stood in the shadows of Aunt Agnes' bedchamber, her heart heavy with the weight of impending loss. The room, once a sanctuary of warmth and laughter, now felt oppressive, its darkness mirroring the grim reality of Agnes' condition. The heavy curtains, drawn tight against the world outside, seemed to trap the very air within, making each breath a struggle.

Agnes lay still upon her bed, her chest rising and falling in an uneven rhythm. Evelyn's gaze lingered on her aunt's frail form, so different from the vibrant woman who had swept into her life months ago. The silence was broken only by the laboured wheezing that escaped Agnes' lips, a constant reminder of the illness that had stolen her vitality.

Evelyn's mind wandered to the plans they had made, now nothing more than wisps of smoke. America, with its promise of adventure and new beginnings, had seemed so tangible when Agnes first proposed the idea.

They had pored over maps, debating which cities to visit, which sights to see. Agnes had spoken of introducing Evelyn to her circle of friends across the Atlantic, opening doors to a world far removed from the stuffy drawing rooms of London society.

"We'll make quite the pair, you and I," Agnes had declared, her eyes twinkling with mischief. "They won't know what's hit them."

But fate, it seemed, had other plans. Agnes' illness had come swiftly and without mercy, robbing her of the strength to even leave her bed, let alone embark on a transatlantic journey.

Evelyn moved closer to the bed, her fingers whispering over Agnes' hand. Though not bound by blood, their connection ran deep. Agnes had taken her under her wing when

Evelyn was adrift, offering guidance and affection without reservation. She had been more than an aunt; she had been a confidante, a mentor, a friend.

"Oh, Agnes," Evelyn whispered, her voice barely audible. "What I wouldn't give to see you well again."

Agnes' eyes fluttered open at the sound, a ghost of a smile touching her lips. For a moment, Evelyn saw a flicker of the woman she had been—strong, vivacious, unbound by convention. It was gone in an instant, replaced by a look of pain and resignation.

Evelyn swallowed hard, fighting back the tears that threatened to fall. She would be strong for Agnes, just as Agnes had always been strong for her. Yet as she watched her aunt's struggle for each breath, Evelyn couldn't help but mourn for the future they would never share, the adventures left unexplored, the memories unmade.

Evelyn quietly withdrew to a seat in the corner of the room, smoothing her dress softly as she settled into the worn armchair. She cast a final glance at Agnes, relieved to see her aunt's eyes had closed once more, her breathing slightly steadier in sleep.

With a heavy sigh, Evelyn reached into her pocket and pulled out a folded letter. The paper was crisp and its edges slightly worn from the countless times she had taken it out. She read it, and tucked it away again without reply. Amelia's neat handwriting stared up at her, a reminder of the world beyond this sickroom.

Evelyn smoothed the letter on her lap, her eyes skimming over Amelia's warm inquiries about her well-being and tentative questions about her future plans. The caring words brought a lump to her throat. How could she explain the tumultuous events of the past weeks? The excitement of America, dashed by Agnes' sudden illness?

She reached for the small writing desk beside her, pulling out a fresh sheet of paper and a quill. For a moment, she hesitated, the nib hovering above the page. Then, with a deep breath, she began to write.

> "My dearest Amelia,
>
> *I hope this letter finds you well. I apologise for my delayed response; recent events have left me quite overwhelmed.*
>
> *I'm afraid I must share some distressing news. Dear Aunt Agnes has fallen gravely ill...*"

Evelyn paused, her pen trembling slightly. She glanced towards the bed, where Agnes lay motionless save for the shallow rise and fall of her chest. Turning back to her letter, she continued:

> *"Her condition worsens by the day, and I fear... I fear we may not have much time left together. Our plans for America have been set aside. Instead, I find myself playing nurse, watching helplessly as she slips away.*
>
> *Amelia, I confess I am at a loss. Aunt Agnes has been my anchor these past months, guiding me through the stormy waters of society with her wit and wisdom. The thought of a future without her counsel leaves me adrift."*

Evelyn set down her quill, staring at the words she had penned. The ink glistened in the dim light, a stark contrast to the pristine paper. She hesitated, her hand hovering over the letter as if to snatch it back and start anew. The melancholy tone of her missive weighed heavily upon her, and for a moment, she considered tearing it to shreds.

With a sigh, she dusted the letter with sand to dry the ink before folding and sealing it with a drop of wax. It wasn't fair to burden Amelia with such gloom, but the words had poured forth unbidden, a reflection of the fear that gnawed at her very core.

Evelyn's gaze drifted back to Agnes' still form. The steady rise and fall of her aunt's chest offered little comfort. What would become of her when Agnes was gone? The thought sent a shiver down her spine, colder than any winter wind.

She rose from her seat, pacing the room with silent steps. The walls seemed to close in, a physical manifestation of the uncertainty that threatened to suffocate her. America had been a beacon of hope, a chance to escape the suffocating expectations of London society. Now, that dream lay in tatters, as fragile as Agnes' health.

Evelyn's mind wandered to the Judge, his stern visage looming in her thoughts. She could almost hear his voice, cold and unyielding, speaking of duty and family obligation. The mere thought of returning to his household, of being once more under his thumb, made her stomach churn.

She pressed a hand to her mouth, stifling a sob. The fear she had been holding at bay surged forth, threatening to overwhelm her. Where would she go? What would she do? The questions swirled in her mind, each one more daunting than the last.

Evelyn forced herself to take a deep breath, then another. She couldn't afford to fall apart, not now. Agnes needed her, and she would be strong for her aunt's sake. But in the gloom of Agnes' room, with only the sound of thick, syrupy breathing to keep her company, Evelyn allowed herself to acknowledge the truth she had been avoiding.

She was afraid. Terrified, even. The future, once so bright with possibility, now loomed before her like a yawning chasm. At the edge of that chasm stood the Judge, waiting to drag her back into a life she had fought so hard to escape.

A week had passed since Evelyn sent her letter to Amelia, each day blurring into the next as she kept vigil at Agnes' bedside. The inevitable finally came in the early hours of the morning, Agnes slipping away with a quiet sigh that seemed to echo through the now-silent room.

Evelyn sat motionless in the chair beside the bed, her eyes fixed on Agnes' still form. The weight of grief pressed down upon her, threatening to crush her very soul. She had known this moment was coming, had tried to prepare herself, but nothing could have readied her for the stark reality of Agnes' absence.

The world outside continued its relentless march forward, oblivious to the loss that had shattered Evelyn's world. She felt adrift, untethered from all that had anchored her. The future she had once dreamed of with Agnes by her side now seemed a cruel jest, mocking her with its impossibility.

As the morning light crept through the cracks in the curtains, Evelyn's thoughts turned to the Judge. The spectre of her past loomed larger than ever, a dark cloud on the horizon of her uncertain future. She shuddered at the thought of returning to that life, of once again being under his control.

A knock at the door startled Evelyn from her grim reverie. She rose slowly, her limbs heavy with exhaustion and grief. Who could it be at this hour? She hadn't sent word of Agnes' passing to anyone yet. Rather than rouse one of the servants, Evelyn went down to open it herself, groggy from grief and fear.

Evelyn opened the door; her eyes widening in surprise as she beheld the familiar heart-shaped face before her, the calm blue-grey eyes and golden curls peeking out from beneath her bonnet. "Amelia?" she breathed, scarcely believing her eyes.

Without a word, Evelyn threw her arms around her friend, nearly knocking her off balance and clinging to her as if she were a lifeline in a storm-tossed sea. The tears she had been holding back for days finally broke free, and she began to sob, her whole body shaking with the force of her grief.

Amelia gently led Evelyn into the drawing room, her touch a comforting anchor in the chaos of emotions. Evelyn sank onto the settee, her body trembling with exhaustion and grief. Amelia sat beside her, still holding her hand, a silent pillar of support.

"Oh, Amelia," Evelyn whispered, her voice cracking. "I don't know what to do. I just have nowhere to go, nothing to hide behind." She looked down at her hands, clenched tightly into the folds of her skirt. "What if the Judge finds me? What if—"

Amelia reached out and clutched Evelyn's hand, squeezing reassuringly.

"You're not alone, Evelyn," she said softly. "We'll figure this out together."

Evelyn took a deep, shuddering breath, trying to calm herself. Amelia's presence was a balm to Evelyn's raw nerves, her quiet strength a reminder that not all was lost. She continued to fret inwardly, her body still tense as if preparing to flee. Amelia listened to all of her anxieties, murmuring sympathetic sounds.

The first light of dawn was creeping through the windows when Evelyn felt her eyelids growing heavy. She fought against the exhaustion, afraid that if she closed her eyes, she'd wake to find Amelia gone and herself alone once more.

But sleep was a relentless foe. As Amelia's soothing voice washed over her, Evelyn felt herself drifting off, her head coming to rest on her friend's shoulder. Her last conscious thought was one of gratitude for Amelia's unwavering support.

As Evelyn drifted off against the unstoppable tide of sleep, she could just hear Amelia saying, "I may have an idea..."

Evelyn awoke with a start, momentarily disoriented by the unfamiliar surroundings. The events of the previous night came rushing back, and she felt a fresh wave of grief wash over her. Agnes was gone, and the world seemed a colder place for it.

Forcing herself to rise, Evelyn dressed quickly, her movements mechanical. There was work to be done, no matter how much she wished to hide away from the world. Agnes' great-nephew, a man Evelyn had never met, was eager to claim his inheritance. The thought of it made her stomach churn.

As she left the drawing room, she found Amelia already at work, a white dustcloth draped over her arm. The sight of her friend brought a small measure of comfort to Evelyn's aching heart.

"Good morning," Amelia said softly, her eyes filled with concern. "I've begun in the drawing room. How shall we proceed?"

Evelyn took a deep breath, steeling herself for the task ahead. "We'll need to take inventory of everything," she replied, her voice hoarse from crying. "And settle the servants' accounts. The new master of the house will want a clean slate, I'm sure."

They moved through the rooms methodically, Evelyn's heart constricting with each familiar object they catalogued. Every piece of furniture, every trinket, held a memory of Agnes. Amelia worked quietly beside her, offering silent support as she draped dustcloths over chairs and tables.

In Agnes' study, Evelyn paused before her aunt's writing desk. How many letters had Agnes penned here, full of wit and wisdom? How many plans had been made at this very spot? Plans that would now never come to fruition.

"The funeral," Evelyn said suddenly, her voice tight. "It's to be held the day after tomorrow. Far too soon, if you ask me, but the great-nephew insists."

Amelia looked up from the ledger where she'd been noting the contents of the room. "That seems awfully rushed," she agreed, frowning. "Surely he could wait a few days more?"

Evelyn shook her head, bitterness creeping into her voice. "Apparently not. He's eager to take possession of the house. Agnes is barely cold, and already he's counting his inheritance."

She turned away, blinking back tears. The thought of strangers living in Agnes' home, using her things, sleeping in her bed – it was almost too much to bear. But what could she do? She had no claim here, no right to protest.

As they continued their work, Evelyn found herself growing increasingly agitated. The hurried funeral arrangements, the eager great-nephew, the methodical dismantling of Agnes' life – it all felt wrong, disrespectful to the woman who had meant so much to her.

As Evelyn and Amelia worked through the morning, the repetitive nature of their task provided a welcome distraction. Evelyn was trying to focus on each item, carefully noting its description and value, leaving little room for her mind to wander to darker thoughts.

The constant movement from room to room, the scratch of pen on paper, and Amelia's quiet presence beside her created a bubble of focused activity that kept her anxieties at bay.

It wasn't until they paused for a light luncheon that Evelyn's mind began to drift. As they sat in the kitchen, picking at cold meat pies neither of them had much appetite for, Evelyn suddenly remembered Amelia's words from the night before.

"Amelia," she said, setting down her barely touched plate. "Last night, just before I fell asleep, you mentioned something about an idea. What did you mean?"

Amelia's hand paused midway to her mouth, a flicker of uncertainty crossing her face. She lowered the sandwich, her brow furrowing slightly as she seemed to consider her words.

"Well," Amelia began, her tone cautious. "I'm not entirely sure it's a suitable solution, but..." She trailed off, her eyes darting away from Evelyn's gaze.

Evelyn leaned forward, curiosity piqued. "Go on," she encouraged, desperate for any glimmer of hope in her current situation.

Amelia took a deep breath before continuing. "I recently came across a job posting in the newspaper. It's for a governess position in the West Country, at a baron's household."

Evelyn blinked, taken aback. "A governess?" she repeated, the word feeling foreign on her tongue. She had never considered such a role for herself, having been raised to expect a life of leisure and society.

"I know it's not what you're accustomed to," Amelia said quickly, "but it could provide you with a respectable position, away from London and... certain individuals."

Evelyn's mind whirled at the prospect. A governess? The idea seemed almost laughable, yet... The promise of distance from London, from the Judge and whatever lackeys of his might still be lurking there was undeniably tempting.

"I... I don't know, Amelia," she said, her voice hesitant. "I've never even considered such a role. And children? I hardly know the first thing about them."

Memories of her own rigid upbringing flashed through her mind. Stern-faced nannies, endless lessons in etiquette and deportment, the constant pressure to be the perfect little lady. She had never truly experienced childhood as most would understand it.

Amelia leaned forward, her eyes bright with encouragement. "Oh, come now, Evelyn. It's not as daunting as you might think. Besides, how much can a country baron truly expect in terms of manners? I'm sure you're more than qualified to teach a child which fork to use for fish."

Evelyn couldn't help but smile at her friend's enthusiasm. Still, doubt gnawed at her. "But how would I even secure such a position? I have no experience, no references."

A mischievous glint appeared in Amelia's eyes. "Well," she said, lowering her voice conspiratorially, "I could write you a letter of reference. It wouldn't be lying, exactly. Just... embellishing the truth a bit."

Evelyn's eyes widened. "Amelia! You can't be serious."

"Why not?" Amelia replied, her tone light but her eyes serious. "You're intelligent, well-educated, and more than capable of instructing children. The fact that you haven't done so before is merely a technicality."

Evelyn bit her lip, considering. It was a mad idea, surely. And yet... The thought of escaping to the countryside, far from the Judge's reach, was undeniably alluring. Perhaps, in such a setting, she could finally breathe freely, find her footing in a world that had suddenly become so uncertain.

Wordlessly, she nodded, and with a simple gesture, her future was decided. Outwardly, she maintained her calm exterior, but inwardly, her stomach roiled and clenched nervously, the few bites of the meat pie turning to lead. Despite her best efforts, she was once again cast adrift, her future in the hands of others.

Chapter 2

James Ayles, Baron Hastings, stood at the edge of the field, his keen grey eyes surveying the assembled farmers and farmhands. The late summer sun beat down upon them, casting long shadows across the freshly ploughed land. A gentle breeze rustled through the nearby trees, carrying with it the scent of earth and green things.

Before the group, a man in a crisp black suit gesticulated wildly; his voice rising and falling as he expounded upon the virtues of some newfangled drainage method. James observed the dubious expressions on the faces of his tenants, their weathered brows furrowed in scepticism.

"And so, gentlemen, by implementing this innovative system, you'll see a marked improvement in crop yield within the first season!" The man in black concluded with a flourish.

A low murmur rippled through the crowd. James caught fragments of hushed conversations, peppered with words like "nonsense" and "waste of time". He suppressed a sigh, running a hand through his dark hair.

"Any questions?" the suited man asked, his enthusiasm undimmed by the lukewarm reception.

Silence fell over the gathering. James could practically feel the weight of unasked questions hanging in the air. He cleared his throat, drawing all eyes to him.

"Perhaps Mr Hodgson might share his thoughts?" James suggested, nodding towards a grizzled farmer near the front.

Hodgson tugged at his cap, clearly uncomfortable with the attention. "Begging your pardon, m'lord, but we've been draining these fields the same way for generations. Why change now?"

The man in the suit launched into another explanation, but James tuned him out. He studied the faces of his tenants, noting their barely concealed frustration. They were good people, hardworking and loyal. They listened out of respect for him, but their patience was wearing thin.

James felt a familiar tightness in his chest. He wanted to do right by these people, to ensure the estate prospered for the sake of his daughters. But change was a delicate thing, especially in a community as rooted in tradition as this one.

"That's enough for today," James interrupted, his voice carrying across the field. "Thank you for your time, gentlemen. We'll discuss this further in private."

Relief washed over the crowd as they began to disperse. James caught snippets of conversation as they passed.

"Right waste of an afternoon, that was."

"The Baron's a good sort, but this new-fangled nonsense..."

"My granddad would be rolling in his grave if he heard all that rubbish."

James watched them go, a mixture of fondness and frustration warring within him. The estate had to move forward, but how could he convince them when they were so set in their ways?

James watched the last of his tenants disappear into various cottages and barns, their grumbling voices fading into the distance. The weight of responsibility settled on his shoulders like a physical burden, and he exhaled slowly, his eyes scanning the fields stretching out before him.

The land looked parched, even after the recent rains. Two years of poor harvests had left their mark, not just on the soil, but on the faces of his people. James could see the worry etched into their weathered features, the fear of what another bad year might bring.

He ran a hand over his face, feeling the rough texture of his burn scar beneath his fingers. The memory of fire flickered at the edges of his mind, but he pushed it away. There were more pressing concerns than old wounds.

Starvation. Poverty. The words echoed in his head, grim spectres that haunted his every decision. James was no stranger to loss, but the thought of failing those who depended on him sent a chill through his body despite the warmth of the day.

He turned away from the fields, his boots crunching on the dry grass as he made his way back towards the manor. The new drainage system could make all the difference, he knew that. But convincing the farmers to embrace change was like trying to move a mountain with his bare hands.

James's face was clouded with concern as he walked, his mind churning over the problem. He was a man of few words by nature, preferring action to lengthy speeches. But perhaps that was part of the issue. His tenants needed more than just a silent, brooding landlord. They needed reassurance, guidance.

The thought of opening up, of sharing his concerns and hopes with them, made James's stomach clench. He'd kept people at arm's length for so long, it was second nature now. But if it meant the difference between prosperity and ruin for his estate, for his daughters' future...

James paused, looking back over his shoulder at the fields. The sun was setting now, casting long shadows across the land. In the fading light, he could almost see the ghosts of better years past, of abundant harvests and content faces.

With a quiet determination, James set his jaw and continued towards the manor. He had decisions to make, and they couldn't wait. The fate of his people, his legacy, hung in the balance. As was his habit, he walked with his head down and tilted slightly to the side. It was a posture unconsciously done these days to minimize the view of the burned side of his face.

James strode towards the manor, his hands clasped tightly behind his back, lost in thought. The weight of his responsibilities pressed down upon him, each step feeling heavier than the last. He pondered the challenge of convincing his tenants to embrace change, the risks of another poor harvest, and the uncertain future that loomed before them all.

So engrossed was he in his musings that he failed to notice the approaching figure until she was nearly upon him. Mrs Turnbell, his housekeeper, bustled up the path, her face flushed and her usually neat white cap askew.

"My lord," she called out, her voice strained. "I must speak with you at once."

James halted, surprised by her sudden appearance and the clear agitation in her manner. "What is it, Mrs Turnbell?"

The housekeeper drew herself up, her chest heaving with exertion and what James suspected was barely contained frustration. "I regret to inform you, my lord, that your girls are simply unmanageable. I cannot... I will not mind them any longer."

He blinked, momentarily at a loss for words. The girls had always been spirited, yes, but unmanageable? And to have Mrs Turnbell, who had been with the family for years, refuse to look after them...

"Surely it can't be as bad as all that," James said, trying to keep his voice level despite the worry gnawing at his insides.

Mrs Turnbell's eyes flashed. "With all due respect, my lord, it is precisely that bad. You've no idea of the sort of mischief they get into these days. Why, just this morning, I found one of them—well, it won't bear repeating, but suffice to say, if they were my children, I'd—"

"Thank you, Mrs Turnbell, I believe I understand the way of it." James felt a headache building behind his eyes. Reflexively, he turned away slightly, his jaw working. He had known the girls were becoming more difficult to handle, but he had hoped... what? That the problem would simply resolve itself? He suppressed a sigh, acutely aware of Mrs Turnbell's expectant gaze.

James felt his jaw tighten as he considered Mrs Turnbell's words. Surely, this was just a passing phase. The girls were growing, testing their boundaries. It was natural, wasn't it?

"Now, Mrs Turnbell," he began, trying to keep his voice calm and reasonable. "I'm sure it's not as dire as all that. Perhaps if we—"

But the housekeeper cut him off with a sharp shake of her head. "Begging your pardon, my lord, but it is precisely that dire. I have my own duties to consider, and I simply cannot be chasing after your daughters at all hours of the day and night."

James felt his shoulders sag slightly. He knew Mrs Turnbell was right, but the thought of admitting it aloud made his throat constrict. "What would you suggest, then?" he asked, though he feared he already knew the answer.

"A governess, my lord," Mrs Turnbell said firmly. "Someone who can devote their full attention to the girls' education and behaviour."

James drew up short, his whole body tensing at the suggestion. A governess, a stranger in his home, privy to their private lives, to the girls' vulnerabilities? The very idea made his skin crawl.

He opened his mouth to refuse outright, but his eyes caught sight of the bare fields stretching out beyond the manor grounds. The dry, cracked earth seemed to mock him, a stark reminder of all that hung in the balance. His mind began to wander, calculations of crop yields and potential losses clouding his thoughts.

"My lord?" Mrs Turnbell's voice cut through his distraction. "What shall I do about the girls?"

James blinked, forcing himself to focus on the matter at hand. The fields could wait. For now, he had to address this more immediate concern. But even as he tried to formulate a response, he could feel his attention slipping away again, drawn inexorably back to the problems of the estate.

James felt the weight of Mrs Turnbell's words settle upon him like a yoke. His mind raced, torn between the pressing concerns of the estate and the immediate issue of his daughters' behaviour. He opened his mouth to speak, but Mrs Turnbell, her patience clearly at an end, cut him off.

"My lord, if you won't consider a governess, then I'm afraid there's only one other option," she said, her voice firm. "The girls will have to be sent away to finishing school."

The words hit James like a blow to the chest. His breath caught, and a cold, creeping fear gripped his heart. The thought of his daughters leaving, of being sent away from him, was unbearable.

There wasn't much that he feared; the idea, though, of his girls being taken from him, was one that never failed to make him break out into a cold sweat underneath his crisp linen shirt.

He felt his face harden, muscles tensing as he struggled to maintain his composure. The scar on his face pulled a little tightly as he worked to keep his expression blank, a stark reminder of loss and the fragility of life.

With a herculean effort, James forced his features into a mask of stern resolve. When he spoke, his voice was low and controlled, betraying none of the turmoil within.

"Very well, Mrs. Turnbell. I will... consider candidates for a governess."

The words tasted like ash in his mouth, but he knew it was the only way. He would not, could not, send his girls away. The risk was too great, the potential for loss too devastating to contemplate.

Mrs. Turnbell nodded, relief evident in her posture. "A wise decision, my lord. Shall I begin making inquiries?"

James gave a curt nod, not trusting himself to speak further. As Mrs. Turnbell hurried away, he turned his gaze back to the fields, his mind already grappling with this new challenge. A governess. A stranger in his home. But better that than the alternative, he thought grimly. Better that than losing his girls forever.

James made his way back to the manor, his mind still wrestling with the prospect of hiring a governess. As he approached the grand oak doors, he noticed an unusual stillness about the place. No sounds of laughter or running feet echoed through the halls, no shrieks of childish delight rang out from the gardens. The silence was, in his experience, rarely a good sign.

With a weary sigh, he pushed open the door and stepped into the cavernous entrance hall. The quiet seemed to press in on him from all sides, broken only by the soft ticking of the grandfather clock in the corner.

"I hereby declare," James called out, his voice echoing through the house, "that any guilty parties involved in mischief-making who present themselves in my study within the next ten minutes shall be shown leniency."

For a moment, the silence persisted. Then, from somewhere deep within the house, a barely suppressed giggle broke free. James recognised it instantly as Julia's, his lips twitching despite himself. That girl could never quite contain her mirth, even in the direst of circumstances.

"And what terms are you offering for this... amnesty?" Augusta's voice floated down from above, cool and measured. James tilted his head, trying to pinpoint her location, but his eldest daughter remained hidden from view.

"Full amnesty," James replied, his tone firm but not unkind. "No punishment. A clean slate, as it were."

There was a pause, during which James could almost hear the gears turning in Augusta's head. Then, primly, she spoke again. "Very well. We accept your terms, Father."

James sighed heavily as he retreated to his dressing room, his boots echoing on the polished floors. Not bothering to ring for his valet, he shrugged off his brown jacket, still warm from the afternoon sun, and changed into a fresh shirt and waistcoat. The weight of the decision he'd made pressed upon him, but he steeled himself for the conversation ahead.

Returning to his study, James was unsurprised to find his twin daughters standing before his desk, the picture of innocence. Julia fidgeted slightly, her eyes darting around the room, while Augusta stood perfectly still, her gaze fixed on him. They wore matching light blue pinafores with halos of golden-red curls that refused to stay plaited.

He sat behind his desk, eyeing them sternly. "Girls," he began, his voice low and measured, "your behaviour of late has been... concerning."

Julia opened her mouth to protest, but James silenced her with a look. Augusta's eyes narrowed almost imperceptibly.

"Your tendency to act like wild boys rather than young ladies has left me with no choice," James continued. "I've decided to engage a governess to... civilise you."

The words hung in the air for a moment before both girls erupted in protest.

"Father, you can't—" Julia cried.

"This is completely unnecessary—" Augusta began.

James held up a hand, and the room fell silent once more. He met each of their gazes in turn, his expression unyielding. "This is not a discussion," he said firmly. "I am informing you."

Augusta, ever the strategist, spoke first. "You said we wouldn't be punished," she said with just the hint of a pout.

James felt a flicker of pride at her quick thinking, even as he shook his head. "This is not a punishment, Augusta. It's... it's an opportunity. An opportunity to learn, to grow, to become the young ladies I know you can be."

The words tasted hollow in his mouth, and James wondered if he truly believed them himself. He watched as his daughters exchanged glances, a silent conversation passing between them.

"May we go, Father?" Julia asked, her voice uncharacteristically subdued.

James nodded, and the girls filed out of the study, closing the door behind them with a soft click.

Alone once more, James leaned back in his chair, running a hand over his face. He hoped, desperately, that he had been truthful in his words to Augusta; that this governess, whoever she might be, wouldn't be a punishment for all of them.

Chapter 3

The carriage jostled along the rutted road, each bump and sway a stark reminder to Evelyn of how far she was travelling from the familiar streets of London. She gazed out the window, watching as the sprawling city gave way to rolling hills and patchwork fields. The further they went, the tighter her chest felt, a growing knot of anxiety twisting in her stomach.

Evelyn clutched her reticule, her fingers tracing the outline of Amelia's letter within. The offer had seemed a godsend at first—a chance to start anew, to bury the whispers and sidelong glances that had dogged her steps in town. But now, as London faded into the distance, doubt crept in like a chill.

"I say, are you quite all right, miss?"

Evelyn startled, realising she'd been staring unseeing at her fellow passenger. The elderly gentleman peered at her with concern. It was a little unnerving, having a strange man speak to her without an introduction. His eyes, though, crinkled in a friendly manner that put her at ease.

"Perfectly fine, thank you," she managed, forcing a smile. "Just... taking in the scenery."

He nodded, settling back into his seat. "First time to the West Country, is it?"

"Is it that obvious?" Evelyn asked, self-consciously reaching up to adjust her bonnet.

"Oh, most visitors have that same look about them," he chuckled. "Like a fish suddenly finding itself on dry land."

Evelyn's smile faltered. That was precisely how she felt—out of her depth and gasping for air. The thought of being so isolated, so far from the bustle and life of the city, made her heart race. What if she couldn't adapt? What if the quiet drove her mad?

The carriage lurched, and Evelyn gripped the seat. She'd grown up navigating cobblestone streets and crowded markets. How would she manage muddy lanes and open fields? The air already smelled different—earthy and green, lacking the familiar tang of coal smoke and river muck.

As they passed through a small village, Evelyn caught sight of women gossiping by a well. Their curious glances followed the coach. She shrank back, suddenly aware of how her London fashions would stand out. Every eye would be upon her, the newcomer, in a place where everyone knew everyone else's business.

She'd spent a few days with Amelia in London, packing away her finest dresses. However, it was immediately obvious that even the more sedate ones she'd packed would draw attention.

Evelyn took a deep breath, trying to quell her rising panic. She'd made her choice. There was no turning back now. But as the coach rolled on, carrying her deeper into the unknown, she couldn't help but wonder if she'd made a terrible mistake.

Evelyn shook herself from her reverie, chiding herself for her doubts. It was too late for all that now. She'd made her decision, and there was no use in fretting over it. The countryside rolled by, a patchwork of greens and browns that blurred together as the coach rumbled on.

At each stop, more passengers disembarked, until Evelyn was left alone in the carriage. The silence pressed in around her, broken only by the creak of wheels and the steady clip-clop of hooves. She shifted uncomfortably on the hard seat, her body protesting after days of travel.

As the journey stretched on, Evelyn's discomfort grew. Her muscles ached, and her head pounded from the constant jostling. She longed to stretch out, to walk more than the few paces afforded during their brief stops. But she endured, reminding herself that each mile brought her closer to her new life.

Finally, after what felt like an eternity, the coach lurched to a halt. Evelyn peered out the window, her heart quickening as she realised this must be her stop—the last stop on the route. She gathered her belongings with trembling hands, suddenly unsure of what awaited her beyond the carriage door.

As Evelyn stepped down, her legs wobbled beneath her, stiff from the long journey. She steadied herself against the side of the coach, blinking in the bright sunlight. Before she could get her bearings, a loud thud made her jump.

The coach driver had unceremoniously hauled her trunk from the roof, dropping it with a splash into the muddy road. Evelyn let out an involuntary squeak of alarm, her eyes widening at the sight of her precious belongings now sitting in a puddle. The coach driver merely grunted at her distress, shrugged, and disappeared into a small tavern that faced the muddy road.

Evelyn stood rooted to the spot, her gaze darting from one unfamiliar sight to another. The village, if one could call it that, consisted of a mere handful of buildings scattered haphazardly along the muddy road. A weathered sign creaked in the breeze, its faded letters barely legible. The tavern where the coach driver had disappeared seemed to be the only sign of life.

Her heart raced as the reality of her situation sank in. She was utterly alone, with no idea where to go or whom to turn to. The weight of her decision pressed down upon her, threatening to crush what little resolve she had left. Evelyn fought back the urge to cry, knowing it would do her no good.

Just as panic began to set in, the clip-clop of hooves drew her attention. A wagonette rolled to a stop beside her, driven by a sturdy man whose face was hidden beneath the brim of a wide hat. He made no move to look at her directly, seeming content to chew on the piece of straw protruding from his mouth.

Evelyn cleared her throat, hoping to catch the man's attention. "Excuse me, sir. I'm looking for—"

The man cut her off with a grunt, still not meeting her gaze. "You'll be the new governess, then?"

His gruff manner caught Evelyn off guard. She straightened her spine, reminding herself that despite her current circumstances, she was still a lady. "Yes, I am. L—Miss Bane," she said, hurriedly correcting herself, "here to—"

Another grunt interrupted her. The man jerked his thumb towards the back of the wagonette. "Best get in, then."

Evelyn hesitated, eyeing the muddy wheels of the wagonette and her trunk still sitting in a puddle. "My luggage—"

The man turned his face slightly toward her, revealing part of a scarred face. Evelyn took an involuntary step backward. "I'll see to it. You just get yourself settled."

Evelyn eyed the mud-splattered wagonette with growing dismay. The wooden bench, exposed to the elements, bore a patina of grime that made her skin crawl. She hesitated, glancing down at her travelling dress—one of her plainer ones, but still far too fine for such rough accommodations.

With a resigned sigh, she gathered her skirts and gingerly placed her foot on the step. The wagonette creaked ominously as she hauled herself up, and she winced at the thought of what this jarring ride might do to her already aching muscles.

As Evelyn settled onto the hard bench, a horrifying realisation dawned. There was no separate seat for passengers—just this single, narrow perch. She'd have to sit right next to the driver, mere inches from this gruff, scarred stranger.

Her heart began to race. This was improper, indecent even. What would people think, seeing her arrive in such a manner? She'd hoped to make a good first impression, to establish herself as a lady of refinement despite her new position. Instead, she'd be perceived as some common trollop, practically in the lap of the first man she'd encountered.

Evelyn's fingers twisted in her lap as she fought the urge to leap down and flee. But where would she go? She was utterly lost in this strange, muddy village.

The driver finished securing her trunk and climbed back up. Evelyn held her breath as he settled beside her, his bulk causing the bench to shift. She pressed herself against the side of the wagonette, desperate to maintain some semblance of propriety.

The scent of hay and horses filled her nostrils as the driver clicked his tongue, urging the horse forward. Evelyn sat rigidly, her spine straight as a poker, refusing to lean back lest she brush against her silent companion.

As they lurched out of the village, Evelyn's mind raced. What sort of place was she going to, where this was considered an acceptable way to transport a governess? She thought of Amelia's letter, full of warm assurances about the kindness of her new employers. Had her friend been mistaken? Or worse, had she deliberately misled Evelyn about the nature of this position?

Evelyn couldn't help but steal glances at the driver as they rattled along the rutted road. Despite her discomfort, she found herself impressed by his ease with the reins. His hands rested lightly on the leather straps, guiding the horse with the barest of movements. It was clear he knew these roads like the back of his hand.

The man's foot was propped up on the footboard, his posture relaxed despite the constant jostling. Evelyn envied his comfort, acutely aware of her own rigid posture. She shifted slightly, trying to find a position that didn't leave her bouncing like a rag doll with every bump and dip in the road.

As she fidgeted, her skirts rustled against the rough wood of the bench. She winced, imagining the state her dress would be in by journey's end. Another bump sent her lurching sideways, and she barely caught herself before colliding with the driver's solid frame.

"Something wrong, miss?"

The gruff voice startled her. It was the first time he'd spoken since they'd set off. Evelyn straightened, smoothing her skirts with trembling hands.

"No, not at all," she lied, forcing a smile. "I'm simply... adjusting to the ride."

The driver grunted, his eyes never leaving the road ahead. "Not used to country travel, I reckon."

Evelyn felt her cheeks flush. Was her discomfort so obvious? She'd hoped to maintain some semblance of dignity, but it seemed she was failing miserably at every turn.

"I confess, it is rather different from what I'm accustomed to," she admitted, trying to keep her voice steady as they jolted over another rut.

Evelyn bit her lip, trying to regain her composure. The driver's blunt observation stung, but she couldn't deny its truth. She was woefully unprepared for this new world.

"What did you expect, miss?" the driver asked, his tone gruff but not unkind.

The question unleashed a torrent of frustration that Evelyn had been struggling to contain.

"I expected..." she began, her indignity rising. "I expected that a Baron would have at least had the decency to send a proper carriage. Perhaps even a female servant to meet me." The words tumbled out, gaining momentum. "Is this truly how a gentleman of his standing treats his employees? And these roads! They're hardly fit for beasts, let alone people. There's mud everywhere, coating everything. How does anyone manage to keep clean?"

Evelyn knew she was being unladylike, complaining so vociferously to a stranger, but she couldn't seem to stop herself. The discomfort of the journey, the uncertainty of her future, and the shock of her new surroundings all conspired to loosen her tongue.

"I've never seen such a state of affairs," she continued, gesturing at the rutted road before them. "How can anyone live like this? It's barbaric!"

The driver remained silent throughout her tirade, his eyes fixed on the road ahead. His lack of response only fuelled Evelyn's indignation, and she found herself listing every perceived slight and inconvenience she'd encountered since stepping off the coach.

Finally, Evelyn fell silent, her cheeks flushed with emotion and embarrassment. She hadn't meant to lose control like that, but the words had poured out of her like water from a broken dam.

The driver said nothing for a long moment, and Evelyn feared she'd offended him beyond repair. Then, without taking his eyes off the road, he spoke.

"It's the first good rain we've had in weeks, miss," he said, his voice low and steady. "Sorely needed, it was. Might be ruining your hem, but it means the folks around here stand a chance of not starving."

His words hit Evelyn like a physical blow. She felt her face grow hot with shame as the reality of her selfishness sank in. She glanced around, as if seeing the fields dotted with tiny houses for the first time. Here she was, complaining about mud and discomfort, while the people around her were facing the very real threat of starvation.

She'd never been confronted with true privation before. Of course, she knew that people were hungry in London—she wasn't naïve—and of course the infamous rookeries. However, she'd never had to confront true hunger and want before.

Evelyn fell silent, chastened by the driver's words. She stared at her gloved hands, twisting in her lap, as shame washed over her. After a moment, she gathered her courage and decided to change tack.

"I... I see," she said softly. "Perhaps you could tell me, what sort of master is the Baron? I confess, I know little about him."

The driver turned his head slightly, surprise evident in his scarred profile. He chewed on his piece of straw, considering the question.

"Well now," he began, his voice thoughtful. "The Baron, he's... he tries his best to be a fair man, that's certain." He paused, adjusting his grip on the reins. "Looks after his tenants, does what he can to keep 'em from the poorhouse."

Evelyn listened intently, grateful for any insight into her new employer.

"Course," the driver continued, "some might find him a bit rough around the edges. Not one for fancy words or manners, the Baron. But he's got a good heart, underneath it all."

Evelyn pondered this information. A fair man with a good heart was certainly preferable to some of the alternatives she'd imagined during her journey. Still, the phrase 'rough around the edges' gave her pause. What exactly did that mean?

Before she could ask for clarification, the driver spoke again. "He's had his share of troubles, the Baron has. But he does right by his people, and that's what matters most out here."

Evelyn hesitated for a moment, then decided to press further. "And how is the Baron to work for? I imagine you must have some insight, being in his employ."

The driver tilted his head slightly, shifting the brim of the hat a little so that Evelyn caught a glimpse of a sharp profile. He chewed thoughtfully on his piece of straw before answering. "I suppose you'd have to ask one of his servants."

Evelyn's brow furrowed in confusion. *I thought I did just ask one of his servants*, she thought. Then it dawned on her: This man was likely just an outdoor staff member, someone dispatched to pick her up like she was a sack of grain for the horses. He wasn't the coachman at all!

The revelation hit Evelyn like a splash of cold water. Her fingers tightened on the fabric of her skirts as a wave of indignation washed over her. The Baron couldn't even be bothered to send his proper coachman to collect her? Instead, he'd dispatched some common labourer to ferry her to her new position?

She pressed her lips together, fighting to maintain her composure. It wouldn't do to unleash another tirade, not when she'd just made a fool of herself moments ago. But the slight stung, adding to her growing list of grievances against her new employer.

Evelyn turned her face away, staring out at the passing countryside without really seeing it. Her mind raced, conjuring images of the Baron as a neglectful, uncaring master who couldn't be bothered with the comfort or propriety of his staff. Was this how he treated all his employees? Or was she being singled out for such disregard?

Chapter 4

The wagonette jolted over another rut in the road, jarring Evelyn from her brooding thoughts. She winced, her discomfort now compounded by her wounded pride. As they rattled on towards her uncertain future, Evelyn couldn't help but wonder what other unpleasant surprises awaited her at the Baron's estate.

As they crested a small hill, the Baron's manor house suddenly came into view. Evelyn's eyes widened at the sight of the imposing structure, its grey stone walls rising up from the surrounding countryside.

She straightened her spine, preparing herself for the first glimpse of her new home. It was grand enough, but the western wing of the house was blackened and burnt. The sight of it made Evelyn's eyes widen.

To her surprise, the wagonette didn't veer towards the side of the house where she assumed the servants' entrance would be. Instead, it rolled to a stop directly in front of the grand front doors. Evelyn blinked in confusion, certain there must be some mistake.

The driver leapt down from his seat with unexpected agility, landing lightly on his feet. He patted the horse's flank affectionately before moving to collect her trunk from the back of the wagonette.

Evelyn remained perched on her seat, staring pointedly at the driver. She waited, expecting him to offer his hand to help her down as any proper servant would. But the man seemed oblivious to her expectation, focusing entirely on wrestling her trunk from the back of the vehicle.

Frustration bubbled up inside her. Was she to be subjected to one indignity after another? First, the muddy journey in this rickety conveyance, and now she was expected to scramble down on her own like some common farm girl?

Evelyn cleared her throat loudly, hoping to catch the driver's attention. He glanced up at her, his expression blank beneath the brim of his hat. She raised an eyebrow, silently willing him to understand his duty.

Still, he made no move to assist her. Evelyn's cheeks flushed with a mixture of embarrassment and anger. She was a lady, for heaven's sake! How dare this uncouth man leave her stranded atop this wretched wagonette?

Evelyn's patience wore thin as she waited atop the wagonette. With a huff of exasperation, she gathered her skirts and began the precarious descent on her own. Her boots slipped on the muddy step, and she barely caught herself before tumbling ungracefully to the ground.

Heart pounding, Evelyn smoothed her rumpled dress and glared at the driver's back. Was this some sort of test? A way to gauge her mettle before presenting her to her new employer?

"I don't suppose the Baron will be greeting me himself?" she asked, unable to keep the sarcasm from her voice. "Or am I to wander the halls until I stumble upon him by chance?"

The driver paused in his efforts with her trunk, straightening slowly. For the first time, he lifted his chin, allowing Evelyn a clear view of his face. The scar she'd glimpsed earlier ran from his temple to his jaw, lending a fierce cast to his otherwise handsome features. His grey eyes met hers, sharp and penetrating.

"As a matter of fact, Miss Bane," he said, voice still gruff and unyielding, "the Baron has already met you."

Confusion clouded Evelyn's features as she tried to make sense of it. "I beg your pardon?"

Something unreadable passed over his eyes. "I am James Ayles, Baron Hastings. Welcome to the estate," he added as an afterthought.

Evelyn felt the blood drain from her face as the full impact of his words hit her. She refused to be cowed, though—she'd endured too much over the past year to let a simple embarrassment end her now. She tossed her head proudly, daringly meeting the Baron's eyes.

Evelyn watched, her mouth slightly agape, as the Baron effortlessly hoisted her trunk onto his broad shoulder. The mud caking the bottom of it seemed not to bother him in the slightest. Despite her best efforts to maintain her composure, she couldn't help but feel a flicker of admiration for his raw strength and physicality.

Shaking herself from her momentary reverie, Evelyn gathered her wits and hurried after him as he strode towards the house. She had to quicken her pace to keep up with his long strides.

"My lord," she called, slightly breathless, "where are the footmen? Surely it's not proper for you to be carrying my trunk yourself."

The Baron didn't slow his pace, but he did turn his head slightly to address her. "All hands are needed for the spring planting. It can't wait, not with the weather we've had."

Evelyn's eyes flickered with confusion, her brows drawing together at this. It seemed utterly bizarre for a Baron to be doing manual labour, let alone concerning himself with the minutiae of farming. She opened her mouth to question this further but thought better of it.

As they neared the entrance, a new concern struck her. She hesitated, glancing back at the wagonette.

"But what about the horse?" she asked. "Won't it wander off if left unattended?"

The Baron paused at the foot of the steps, turning to face her fully. His grey eyes met hers, a hint of amusement flickering in their depths.

"No," he replied simply, before turning and continuing up the stairs.

Evelyn stood for a moment, stunned by the brevity of his response. She looked back at the horse, which indeed seemed content to stand exactly where it had been left, then hurried to catch up with the Baron once more.

Evelyn followed the Baron up the grand staircase, her bewilderment growing with each step. This was not at all how she'd imagined being shown to her quarters. The opulent surroundings seemed at odds with the mud-splattered man leading the way, her trunk still balanced effortlessly on his shoulder.

They passed several ornate doors before reaching the far end of the house. Evelyn's eyes widened as she realised they were approaching the blackened wing she'd spotted from outside. The Baron pushed open a door just shy of the charred section, revealing a modestly furnished room.

Without ceremony, he deposited her trunk on the floor with a solid thud. Evelyn opened her mouth to speak, but before she could utter a word, the Baron turned on his heel, clearly intending to leave without further ado.

He paused at the threshold, as if suddenly remembering something important. Slowly, he turned back to face her, his hand moving to the brim of his hat. Evelyn held her breath, unsure of what to expect.

As he removed his hat, Evelyn felt her heart skip a beat. The left side of his face was indeed handsome, with chiselled features that wouldn't have looked out of place on a classical statue. But the right side... a web of angry scars stretched from his temple to his jaw, evidence of a horrific burn.

Evelyn stood perfectly still, willing herself not to react. She met his gaze steadily, refusing to look away or show any sign of discomfort. The Baron's grey eyes studied her intently, searching for any hint of revulsion or pity.

Finding none, he inclined his head in a small bow. Without a word, he turned and strode from the room, leaving Evelyn alone with her thoughts and the echo of his retreating footsteps.

Evelyn sank onto the narrow brass bed, her body finally giving in to the exhaustion that had been building throughout the day. The mattress creaked beneath her weight, a far cry from the plush comfort she'd grown accustomed to in London. She stared up at the ceiling, her mind whirling with the events of the past few hours.

What on Earth have I gotten myself into? she thought as she stared up at the plain white ceiling.

Chapter 5

James Ayles, Baron Hastings, shook his head as he strode away from Miss Bane. The woman's incessant chatter and obvious disdain for country life grated on his nerves. He'd hoped for someone more... practical. Someone who understood the gravity of the situation facing his estate and his daughters.

He descended the stairs, his mind already shifting to the pressing matters at hand. The spring planting was far behind schedule, and if they didn't make significant progress soon, his tenants would face a grim winter. The thought of families going hungry under his care twisted his gut.

James pushed open the heavy oak door and stepped out into the weak spring sunshine. The air was thick with the scent of freshly turned earth and the faint tang of desperation. He could see figures dotting the fields, bent low over their work. His footmen were out there too, their fine livery exchanged for rough work clothes.

He strode towards the nearest field, his long legs eating up the distance. As he approached, he recognised young Thomas, a footman barely out of boyhood, struggling with a hoe. The lad's face was red with exertion, his hands already blistering.

"Here, lad," James said gruffly, holding out his hand. "Let me show you."

Thomas looked up, startled. "My lord, I—"

"None of that now," James cut him off, taking the hoe. "Watch."

With practised movements, James demonstrated the proper technique, his muscles remembering the motions from years past. He'd worked these fields alongside his father, learning the rhythms of the land long before he'd inherited the title.

"See?" he said, handing the tool back. "Long, steady strokes. You'll tire less quickly that way. Keep the furrows sharp."

Thomas nodded, a look of determination settling over his young face. "Thank you, my lord."

James clapped him on the shoulder and moved on, his eyes scanning the fields. In the distance, he could see other footmen distributing water to the workers, their usual crisp movements slowed by the unfamiliar terrain.

James scanned the field, his eyes catching on a familiar figure. Nell, one of his most reliable servants, was bent over a row of seedlings, her movements deft and sure. Her wide-brimmed hat, secured by a kerchief, cast a shadow over her face, but he could still see the healthy flush of her cheeks from the sun and honest work.

"Nell!" he called out, his voice carrying across the freshly tilled earth.

She straightened immediately, her face breaking into a warm smile as she spotted him. With a quick brush of her hands against her apron, she hurried towards him, her steps light despite the long hours of labour.

"My lord," she said, dipping into a quick curtsy as she reached him. "How may I be of service?"

James felt a small knot of tension in his chest ease at her eagerness. Here was someone he could rely on, someone who understood the importance of hard work and duty.

"The new governess has arrived," he said, his tone gruff but not unkind. "Could you see to getting her settled in? I fear she's..." He paused as he considered. "Not used to seeing a speck of mud out of place."

Nell's eyes sparkled with amusement, but she quickly schooled her features. "Of course, my lord. I'll see to it immediately. The poor dear must be quite overwhelmed."

James nodded, grateful for her understanding. "Thank you, Nell. Your help is appreciated, as always."

With another quick curtsy, Nell turned and hurried back towards the house, her steps purposeful and her back straight. James watched her go, a small frown creasing his brow. He hoped the new governess would adapt quickly to life at the estate. They needed all hands working together if they were to weather the challenges ahead.

As James stood in the warm spring sun, he grudgingly considered Miss Bane. The woman hadn't fled at the first sight of mud on her skirts, which was more than he'd expected given her obvious discomfort with country life.

He recalled the journey from the coach station, his lips quirking into a wry smile. Miss Bane had chattered incessantly, her crisp London accent pointing out every perceived flaw in the countryside. Yet beneath her complaints, he'd sensed a steely determination. She'd held her head high, even as the rough road jostled her about.

James had stolen glances at her profile as he drove, curiosity getting the better of him. Her dark eyes had flashed with temper and spirit, a stark contrast to the demure governesses he'd interviewed in the past. There was something refreshing about her directness, even if it bordered on impropriety.

He turned away from the field, running a hand through his hair. Perhaps he'd been too hasty in his judgement. Miss Bane might be out of her element, but she hadn't given up at the first hurdle. That, at least, boded well for her ability to handle his spirited daughters.

The sun was beginning to beat down in earnest, and James reached up to swipe at his brow, thoughts still lingering on Miss Bane. Despite her initial shock at his appearance, she hadn't recoiled from him. It was a small mercy, but one he appreciated nonetheless.

He'd seen far too many faces twist in horror at the sight of his scars. He'd agreed to take her on a trial basis, and James was not a man to go back on his word. Besides, sending her away now would only delay the inevitable. His daughters needed a governess, and Miss Bane was here, ready to begin.

A movement in the distance caught his eye. James looked up to see Farmer Giles approaching, accompanied by a man carrying what appeared to be large rolled papers under his arm. The sight made James sigh inwardly. He recognised the man as Mr Wilkins, the surveyor he'd hired to assess the possibility of improving the estate's irrigation system.

James squared his shoulders, pushing thoughts of Miss Bane and household matters aside. He couldn't afford such distractions now, not when the very future of his estate hung in the balance. The farmers needed his full attention if they were to weather this crisis.

He strode forward to meet them, his face settling into the stern mask he wore like armour. As he stepped out to meet Farmer Giles and Mr Wilkins, James silently hoped Miss Bane would prove capable of managing on her own for now. The estate's problems couldn't wait.

James winced as Mr Wilkins pumped his hand with enthusiasm, the man's grip surprisingly strong for one who spent his days poring over maps and figures.

"My lord, I cannot express how thrilled I am to present our findings," Mr Wilkins gushed, his eyes alight with excitement. "We've discovered opportunities that could revolutionise your estate's productivity!"

James extricated his hand, nodding politely. "Indeed? Well, let's hear it then."

Mr Wilkins unfurled his maps with a flourish, spreading them across a nearby wooden table. James leaned in, his brow furrowing as he studied the intricate lines and notations.

"As you can see, my lord, we've mapped out a comprehensive irrigation system that would significantly improve water distribution across your fields," Mr Wilkins explained, his finger tracing the proposed channels. "But that's not all. We've learned that your neighbours to the east are planning a shipping canal. If we act quickly, we could connect to it, opening up new trade routes for your estate's produce."

James felt a twinge of unease. The idea was bold, certainly, but the scale of disruption to his tenants' lives... He glanced at Farmer Giles, noting the older man's furrowed brow.

"It's an intriguing proposal," James said carefully, straightening up. "I'll need time to consider the implications."

Mr Wilkins' face fell slightly, but he nodded. "Of course, my lord. But I urge you not to delay too long. This opportunity won't last forever."

James clasped his hands behind his back, his mind already racing through the potential consequences. The canal could indeed bring prosperity, but at what cost? He thought of the families who had worked this land for generations, their lives intertwined with the rhythms of the estate.

"I appreciate your thoroughness, Mr Wilkins," James said. "I'll review your plans in detail and consult with my tenants. We'll reconvene once I've had time to weigh all factors."

As Mr Wilkins gathered his maps, James turned to Farmer Giles. The old man's weathered face was etched with concern.

"What do you think, Giles?" James asked quietly.

Giles scratched his chin. "It's a big change, m'lord. Might bring good, might bring trouble. Folk 'round here, they don't take to change easy."

James nodded, feeling the weight of responsibility settle heavily on his shoulders. He would need to tread carefully, balancing progress with tradition, the needs of the estate with the lives of those who called it home.

James turned instinctively towards the manor house, its stone walls rising in the distance. His gaze softened as his thoughts drifted to his daughters. They were still young, their laughter echoing through the halls, their mischief keeping the household on its toes. But time was relentless, and soon they would be grown women, in need of security and independence.

The weight of responsibility settled more firmly on his shoulders. He wanted—no, needed—to leave them a legacy they could be proud of, an estate that would provide for them long after he was gone. The thought filled him with renewed determination, steeling his resolve.

James squared his shoulders and turned back to Mr Wilkins, who was still hovering nearby, hope etched on his eager face.

"Mr Wilkins," James said, his voice firm with decision, "I'll need more information before I can make a final choice. Present me with detailed facts and figures. I want to know exactly how much we could ship and what prices we might fetch in better markets. Leave no stone unturned in your analysis."

Mr Wilkins' eyes lit up, and he nodded vigorously. "Of course, my lord! I'll have a comprehensive report on your desk within the fortnight. You won't be disappointed, I assure you."

As the surveyor hurried off, practically tripping over his own feet in his excitement, James allowed himself a small smile. The man's enthusiasm was infectious, even if his ideas were daunting.

James cast one last glance at the manor house, thoughts of his daughters spurring him on. Whatever changes might come, he would face them head-on, for their sake. After all, everything he did was for them—they were all that he had left.

James blinked, realising Farmer Giles had asked him a question. He shook his head, embarrassed at his momentary lapse in attention.

"I beg your pardon, Giles. My mind wandered for a moment. What were you saying?"

The old farmer's weathered face creased with understanding. "No worries, m'lord. I was just askin' about the new seed we tried in the south field. Reckon it's time to check on its progress?"

James nodded, grateful for the farmer's patience. "Yes, indeed. Let's head there now."

As they walked, James tried to focus on Giles's words about crop rotation and soil quality. But his thoughts kept drifting back to his daughters, to the sound of their laughter echoing through the manor's halls.

Unbidden, the memory of smoke filled his nostrils, acrid and choking. James clenched his fists, fighting back the familiar wave of panic that threatened to overwhelm him. He could almost hear the crackle of flames, feel the searing heat on his skin...

"M'lord? You alright there?"

Giles's concerned voice cut through the haze of memory. James realised he had stopped walking, his breath coming in short, sharp gasps.

"I'm fine, Giles," he managed, forcing a smile that felt more like a grimace. "Just... remembering something."

The old farmer's eyes softened with sympathy. He didn't pry, for which James was grateful. Instead, Giles pointed to a nearby field where green shoots were just beginning to push through the soil.

"Look there, m'lord. That new wheat's comin' up strong."

James latched onto the change of subject, grateful for the distraction. He strode towards the field, focusing on the task at hand. Yet even as he bent to examine the tender shoots, part of his mind remained on high alert. It was as if listening for the distant sound of his daughters' cries.

The lingering scent of smoke seemed to follow him, a ghostly reminder of all he had lost and all he still feared to lose.

"Growing strong," James said, running his hand over the tiny green shoots.

James straightened, brushing soil from his hands as he considered Giles's words. Perhaps having Miss Bane in the house wasn't such a terrible notion after all. Another set of watchful eyes could prove useful, especially with his daughters' penchant for mischief.

"Aye, m'lord," Giles continued, a sly grin creeping across his weathered face. "Speakin' of new arrivals, I hear there's a fresh face up at the manor. A new governess, is it?"

James nodded, his expression neutral. "Indeed. Miss Bane arrived just this afternoon."

Giles chuckled, his eyes twinkling. "A comely lass, is she? The young lads about the estate will be right pleased to have another pretty face to admire, I'd wager."

James opened his mouth to dismiss the notion, but found himself pausing. He hadn't really considered Miss Bane in those terms. His mind drifted back to their first encounter, recalling her appearance with a newfound awareness.

Dark eyes, flashing with spirit and indignation, chestnut curls that seemed barely contained beneath her bonnet, skin so pale it seemed to glow in the afternoon sun, a stark contrast to the muddy lane they'd travelled...

"I suppose," James conceded reluctantly, "the young men might find her pleasing to look upon. She's certainly... striking."

Giles's grin widened, but James quickly added, "Not that it matters. She's here to educate my daughters, not to catch the eye of every farmhand and stable boy."

Despite his stern words, James found his thoughts lingering on Miss Bane's appearance. He shook his head, annoyed at himself for such frivolous musings. There were far more pressing matters at hand than the new governess's looks.

James turned away from Giles, pretending not to notice the knowing look in the old farmer's eyes. He focused intently on the young wheat shoots, running his fingers over their delicate stalks again, testing to see how they sprang back.

"We should check the drainage in the lower field," he said gruffly, desperate to change the subject. "With all this rain on the dry soil, I worry about flooding."

But even as he spoke, James found his thoughts drifting. Miss Bane's face swam before his mind's eye, unbidden and unwelcome. He saw again those dark eyes, wide and startled like a doe's when she'd realised who he was. The memory of her indignation, the flush of colour in her cheeks, stirred something in him he thought long dead.

James clenched his jaw, irritated by his own foolishness. He'd locked away such thoughts years ago, after the fire. His heart was not his to give; it belonged to his daughters and to the estate. There was no room for pretty governesses with flashing eyes and sharp tongues.

And yet...

He shook his head forcefully, as if to dislodge the image of Miss Bane from his mind. It was ridiculous, this fixation. She was here to teach his girls, nothing more. He had no business thinking of her in any other capacity.

"My lord?" Giles's voice cut through his reverie. "Are you quite alright?"

James realised he'd been standing still, staring blankly at the wheat field. He cleared his throat, embarrassed by his lapse.

"Perfectly fine, Giles," he said, his voice perhaps a touch too stern. "Now, about that drainage issue..."

As they walked towards the lower field, James silently berated himself. He was the Baron of Hastings, not some lovesick youth. He had responsibilities, duties that required his full attention. He couldn't afford to be distracted by a pair of dark eyes, no matter how bewitching they might be.

Chapter 6

Evelyn knelt before the empty grate, her fingers hovering uncertainly over the unfamiliar iron tools. The chill of her journey still clung to her bones, seeping through her travelling dress despite the relative warmth of the day outside. She had never built a fire before, always relying on servants to tend to such matters. Now, faced with the prospect of warming herself, she felt woefully unprepared.

She picked up the poker, its weight foreign in her hand. How did one even begin? Surely there must be kindling of some sort. Her gaze darted around the sparse room, seeking anything that might serve. A stack of newspapers caught her eye, tucked neatly beside the fireplace.

"Well," she murmured to herself, "I suppose that's a start."

Evelyn reached for the papers, her movements hesitant. She crumpled one sheet, then another, arranging them in what she hoped was a suitable formation within the grate. The iron tools clinked together as she fumbled with them, the sound seeming to mock her inexperience.

"Now for the wood," she said, eyeing the small stack beside the hearth. She selected a few pieces, trying to recall how she had seen fires laid in the past. As she placed them atop the paper, doubt crept in. Was this correct? Would it even catch?

A sharp knock at the door startled her, nearly causing her to drop a log on her foot. Evelyn straightened, brushing her hands against her skirts as she rose.

"Yes?" she called, her voice betraying a hint of relief at the interruption.

"It's Nell, miss," a voice called through the door. "His lordship thought I might help get you settled."

Evelyn felt a wave of relief wash over her. "Please, do come in," she called, smoothing her skirts and willing the colour in her cheeks to fade.

The door creaked open, and Nell stepped inside. Her warm smile immediately put Evelyn at ease, dispelling some of the tension that had built up since her arrival.

"Welcome to Aylesbury Manor, Miss Bane," Nell said, dipping into a small curtsy. "I hope your journey wasn't too taxing?"

Evelyn couldn't help but notice how pretty the maid was, in a rural sort of way. Her flax-blonde hair was neatly tucked beneath her cap, and her dark blue eyes sparkled with a hint of mischief.

"It was... eventful," Evelyn replied, her mind flashing back to the uncomfortable ride with the Baron. She pushed the thought aside, focusing on the present. "I'm grateful for your assistance."

Nell's gaze drifted to the fireplace, and Evelyn felt a fresh wave of embarrassment. The maid's lips twitched, but she maintained her composure.

"You must be worn out from your travels, miss," Nell said kindly. "Why don't you have a seat? I'll tend to the fire for you."

Evelyn hesitated, torn between relief and a desire to prove herself capable. "I wouldn't want to impose—"

"Nonsense," Nell interrupted, already moving towards the hearth. "It's my job, after all. And between you and me, miss, I've had plenty of practice."

As Nell set about arranging the kindling and logs, Evelyn sank into a nearby chair, watching with a mixture of curiosity and admiration. The maid's movements were swift and sure, her hands deftly manipulating the tools that had seemed so foreign to Evelyn moments ago.

"There we are," Nell said, striking a match and touching it to the paper. The flame caught quickly, licking up the kindling and spreading to the logs. "It'll be nice and warm in here in no time."

"Thank you," Evelyn murmured, genuinely grateful. "I'm afraid I'm not terribly accustomed to... well, to much of anything here, it seems."

Nell turned, her expression softening. "Don't you worry, miss. We'll have you settled in before you know it."

Evelyn watched as Nell moved easily towards the trunk at the foot of the bed. The maid's efficiency was a stark reminder of Evelyn's own inexperience, and she felt a twinge of unease settle in her stomach.

"Shall I help you unpack, Miss Bane?" Nell asked, her fingers already working at the clasps.

"That would be most kind," Evelyn replied, rising from her chair. She hesitated, unsure whether to assist or simply observe.

As Nell began to remove Evelyn's carefully folded gowns, she glanced up with a curious expression. "If you don't mind me asking, miss, did you come from a large household? With many servants, I mean?"

Evelyn's breath caught for a moment. She had never outright lied about her circumstances, but neither had she been entirely forthcoming. "Yes," she said carefully, "I did. Quite a large household, in fact."

It wasn't untrue, she reasoned. Aunt Agnes's home had been sizeable, with a full complement of staff, and the Judge's household before that had been ostentatiously grand. The fact that Evelyn had been raised in such circumstances need not be mentioned.

Nell nodded slowly, her brow furrowing slightly as she continued to unpack. "That explains it, then," she said, more to herself than to Evelyn.

"Explains what?" Evelyn asked, curiosity overriding her caution.

Nell looked up, a faint blush colouring her cheeks. "Oh, I didn't mean... It's just, well, it explains why a governess wouldn't know how to tend a fire, is all."

Evelyn felt her own face grow warm. "I suppose it does," she admitted, forcing a small laugh. "I'm afraid I'm rather useless when it comes to practical matters."

To her surprise, Nell's expression softened. "Don't worry yourself about it, miss. We all have to start somewhere."

Evelyn found herself relaxing slightly. "You're very kind," she said. "I must admit, I'm a little jealous of your practical knowledge. I do hope I'll gain some of my own soon."

Nell's smile brightened as she continued to help Evelyn unpack. Her deft hands moved swiftly, removing each garment with care and laying it out on the bed. As she lifted a pale blue dress with pleated trim at the hem and delicate lace at the neckline, her eyes widened in admiration.

"Oh, Miss Bane," Nell breathed, her fingers tracing the intricate lacework. "This is beautiful. Your last mistress must have been very generous indeed."

Evelyn felt a pang of guilt at the maid's words. Thoughts of Aunt Agnes flashed through her mind – the woman who had taken her in, treated her as family and insisted on a new wardrobe for her new life away from the Judge. It wasn't entirely a lie to agree, was it?

"Yes," Evelyn said softly, pushing aside her discomfort. "She was very kind to me."

Nell held the dress up against Evelyn's face, her eyes sparkling with approval. "This colour suits you perfectly, miss. It brings out your eyes." She paused, a mischievous grin playing at her lips. "I'd wager you left a string of broken hearts behind you in London."

Evelyn couldn't help but laugh at the notion. If only Nell knew how close to the truth that was. "I'm afraid not," she replied, shaking her head. "My life has been rather… sheltered."

As Nell continued to unpack, chattering away about the manor and its inhabitants, Evelyn felt warming to the young maid. There was something refreshingly genuine about her, a warmth that cut through the uncertainty and fear that had plagued Evelyn since her arrival.

For the first time since setting foot in Aylesbury Manor, Evelyn felt a glimmer of hope. Perhaps she wasn't entirely alone in this strange new world. Perhaps, in Nell, she might find a friend.

Evelyn watched as Nell continued to unpack, her movements efficient and practised. The maid's hands paused as she lifted another gown, her brow furrowing slightly as she glanced back at Evelyn.

"Oh, Miss Bane," Nell exclaimed, a hint of embarrassment colouring her cheeks. "I'm terribly sorry. You're still in your travelling dress. Would you like some help changing?"

Evelyn hesitated, suddenly aware of her rumpled appearance. "I… perhaps I should," she murmured, then paused. A thought occurred to her, and she bit her lip uncertainly. "But shouldn't I greet my new charges first? I wouldn't want to be a complete surprise to them."

To her surprise, Nell let out an unladylike snort. "I'd wager they've already seen you, miss, even if you haven't seen them."

Evelyn blinked, puzzled by the cryptic reply. She opened her mouth to ask what Nell meant, but the maid had already turned away, busying herself with explaining the household laundry system.

"The servants will collect your clothes for washing," Nell said, her voice muffled as she bent to retrieve a stray stocking. "You needn't worry about that."

Evelyn's curiosity about Nell's earlier comment gnawed at her, but she found no opportunity to ask as the maid continued her efficient unpacking. Instead, she watched as Nell's gaze lingered once more on the pale blue dress, a wistful expression crossing her face.

"If I may say so, miss," Nell said softly, her fingers ghosting over the delicate lace, "you might not want to trust the servants with such fine work. It's... well, it's not something we see often here."

Evelyn felt a pang of sympathy for the young maid. "It is rather lovely, isn't it?" she said gently.

Nell nodded, her eyes still fixed on the dress. "I hope one day I'll have a dress so beautiful," she murmured, almost to herself. Then, as if remembering her place, she straightened and offered Evelyn a bright smile. "Now then, miss, shall we get you changed?"

Evelyn stood still as Nell's nimble fingers worked at the fastenings of her travelling dress. The fabric, stiff with dried mud, clung stubbornly to her skin. She felt a twinge of embarrassment at her dishevelled state, but Nell's cheerful chatter put her somewhat at ease.

"There we are, miss," Nell said, easing the dress over Evelyn's shoulders. "Let's get you into something more comfortable."

The tea gown Nell selected was a soft, dove-grey light wool that whispered against Evelyn's skin as she slipped it on. The warmth from the crackling fire began to seep into her bones, chasing away the last of the chill from her journey.

"I'll have one of the kitchen maids bring up a tray for you later," Nell promised, smoothing the gown's folds. "You must be famished after your travels."

Evelyn nodded gratefully, sinking into a chair by the fire. As Nell turned to leave, a question that had been nagging at Evelyn's mind since her arrival bubbled to the surface.

"Nell," she called softly, causing the maid to pause at the door. "I was wondering... how close are we to the burnt-out West Wing, and all of that..."

Nell's expression softened. "Oh, you needn't worry about that, miss. The house is as sturdy as a fortress. You're quite safe here."

Evelyn hesitated, then lowered her voice. "What... what happened there?"

For the first time since their meeting, Nell's face went blank, her usual warmth replaced by a hardness that startled Evelyn. "We don't talk about that, miss," Nell said, her tone clipped.

Evelyn felt her cheeks burn with embarrassment. She looked down at her hands, twisting in her lap. "I'm sorry, I didn't mean to pry."

As quickly as it had appeared, the hardness vanished from Nell's face, replaced once more by her cheerful demeanour. "No harm done, miss. Why don't you get some rest? I'll be back with your food later."

With that, Nell slipped out of the room, leaving Evelyn alone with her thoughts and the crackling fire. There was something ghoulish about it, sitting and taking such comfort from a fire when part of her new home lay in ruins from a fire just a few steps away.

***

The Baron sat hunched over his desk, the flickering candlelight casting long shadows across the study. His eyes strained to make out the figures in the ledger before him, the rows of numbers blurring into an indecipherable mess. He pinched the bridge of his nose, trying to ward off the headache that threatened to overtake him.

The agricultural reports were grim. The new methods he'd been pushing hadn't taken hold as quickly as he'd hoped, and now his tenants faced the very real possibility of a lean harvest. James felt the weight of their livelihoods pressing down upon his shoulders, a burden he'd never asked for but couldn't bring himself to shirk.

His mind drifted to the tense dinner he'd endured earlier. The girls had barely touched their food, their faces set in stubborn scowls that spoke volumes about their feelings towards the new governess. James had tried to engage them in conversation, but his efforts had been met with sullen silence or monosyllabic responses.

He sighed, running a hand through his unkempt hair. The arrival of Miss Bane had stirred up a hornet's nest, and he wasn't entirely sure he had the energy to deal with the fallout. Her incessant chatter during the drive from the coach station still rang in his ears, a stark contrast to the quiet solitude he'd grown accustomed to.

A sharp knock at the study door startled him from his reverie. James straightened in his chair, his shoulders tensing instinctively.

"Come in," he called, his voice rough from disuse.

The door creaked open, and James found himself hoping it wasn't Miss Bane. He wasn't prepared to face another barrage of questions or complaints about country life. Not tonight, when his patience was already worn thin.

James looked up as Nell entered the study, her familiar presence a welcome respite from his troubled thoughts. She hesitated at the threshold, her usual confidence replaced by an uncharacteristic nervousness.

"Begging your pardon, my lord. I didn't mean to disturb you," Nell said, her eyes darting to the scattered papers on his desk. "You look exhausted. Perhaps we could speak tomorrow instead?"

James waved away her concern, gesturing for her to approach. "Nonsense, Nell. You're here now. What's on your mind?"

Nell stepped closer, wringing her hands. James frowned, unaccustomed to seeing her so ill at ease. She'd been a steady presence in the household for years, her cheerful demeanour a balm to his own melancholy. To see her troubled now only added to his unease.

"Well, sir, it's about Miss Bane," Nell began, her voice lowered as if afraid the very walls might overhear. "I know she's only just arrived, and I don't want to speak out of turn..."

James leaned back in his chair, a weariness settling over him that had nothing to do with the late hour. "Go on," he prompted, bracing himself for whatever fresh complication the new governess had introduced to his already chaotic household.

Nell took a deep breath, her resolve visibly strengthening. "It's just... I'm concerned about how she'll fit in here, my lord. She seems rather... unsuited to country life."

James couldn't help but let out a dry chuckle. "That much was evident from the moment she stepped off the coach, Nell. But surely it's too soon to judge?"

"Perhaps, sir," Nell conceded, though her furrowed brow suggested she wasn't entirely convinced. "But I fear her... unfamiliarity with our ways might cause more upheaval than the girls can handle. They've been through so much already."

James felt a pang of guilt at the mention of his daughters. He'd been so consumed with the estate's troubles that he'd barely given thought to how they might be adjusting to Miss Bane's presence. He rubbed his temples, trying to ward off the headache that threatened to overwhelm him.

"What exactly has Miss Bane done to worry you so, Nell?" he asked, dreading the answer.

James felt his muscles tense as he waited for Nell's response. The maid's hesitation only heightened his concern.

"Well, my lord," Nell began, her voice barely above a whisper, "I showed Miss Bane to her room earlier, and I noticed she seemed... unfamiliar with the hearth."

James leaned forward, his brow furrowing. "Unfamiliar? How so?"

Nell wrung her hands, clearly uncomfortable with what she was about to say. "She didn't seem to know how to light a fire, sir. Or how to tend one safely."

James's blood ran cold. He stood abruptly, his chair scraping against the wooden floor. The memory of flames licking at the walls of his home, the acrid smell of smoke, the screams... He shook his head, forcing the memories away.

"Are you certain, Nell?" he asked, his voice hoarse.

Nell nodded solemnly. "I am, my lord. I wouldn't have mentioned it if I wasn't sure. I know how important fire safety is to you... to all of us."

James paced behind his desk, his mind racing. The entire household knew the strict protocols in place regarding fire safety. It wasn't just a matter of practicality; it was a matter of survival. The thought of someone so careless with fire being responsible for his daughters sent a chill down his spine.

Thank you for bringing this to my attention, Nell," he said, his voice tight with suppressed emotion. "I'll speak with Miss Bane first thing in the morning. We can't afford to take any risks, not with..."

He trailed off, unable to finish the sentence. Nell's eyes softened with understanding.

Of course, my lord. Is there anything else you need?"

James shook his head, suddenly feeling every bit of his thirty-five years. "No, thank you, Nell. You may go."

As the door closed behind her, James sank back into his chair, his head in his hands. The arrival of Miss Bane had already complicated matters more than he'd anticipated. Now, with this new information, he found himself questioning whether he'd made a grave mistake in bringing her to Hastings Manor.

Chapter 7

Evelyn stood before the looking glass, her fingers nervously smoothing down the front of her plain grey dress. The fabric felt coarse beneath her touch, a far cry from the silks and muslins she'd once worn.

She tilted her head, examining the neat braids at her temples that led into a simple chignon at the nape of her neck. It was a style that spoke of practicality rather than fashion, but she hoped it would strike the right balance between respectability and approachability.

Her reflection stared back at her, pale and wide-eyed. Evelyn took a deep breath, willing her racing heart to slow. The enormity of what lay ahead threatened to overwhelm her. These girls, strangers to her, would now be her charges. Their education, their comportment, their very futures would rest in her hands.

"You can do this," she whispered to her reflection. "You must."

The looking glass offered no reassurance. Evelyn's gaze drifted to the small hearth in her room, a reminder of her near-disaster the night before. Heat crept up her neck at the memory of fumbling with the fire irons, grateful that the maid had shown her the basics. It was but one of many skills she'd need to master if she were to maintain this charade.

Evelyn squared her shoulders, lifting her chin. She may not have been born to this life of service, but she'd be damned if she'd let that stop her from excelling at it. With one final glance at her reflection, she turned towards the door.

Her hand hesitated on the latch. Beyond lay a world utterly foreign to her—a world of early mornings and hard work, of children's laughter and lessons. A world where she was no longer Lady Evelyn, but simply Miss Bane, the governess.

"Forward," she murmured, echoing her father's favourite command. "Always forward."

Evelyn descended the grand staircase, her hand gliding along the polished banister. Each step felt like a descent into the unknown, her stomach fluttering with a mixture of anticipation and dread. The house was deathly silent, almost tomb-like.

As she approached the drawing room, Evelyn paused to smooth her dress one final time. She took a deep breath, steeling herself for the encounter that would shape her future. With a trembling hand, she reached for the door handle.

The moment the door swung open, chaos erupted. Two enormous dogs bounded towards her in a chaotic tumble of shaggy grey fur, their paws scrabbling against the polished wooden floor. Before Evelyn could react, she found herself engulfed in a whirlwind of fur and slobber.

"Oh!" she squeaked, stumbling backward against the wall as the enthusiastic beasts vied for her attention. Their rough tongues lapped at her face and hands, leaving trails of warm saliva in their wake. Evelyn's carefully arranged hair came loose, wisps falling about her face as she tried to fend off the overzealous greeting.

Evelyn's heart raced as she heard muffled giggling from within the drawing room. Her cheeks burned with embarrassment, but a spark of indignation flared in her chest. This was no accident—it was a test, and one she refused to fail.

Gathering what remained of her dignity, Evelyn pushed herself away from the wall. She stood as tall as her petite frame would allow, fixing the enormous beasts with a stern glare.

"Down!" she commanded, her voice ringing out with surprising authority. "Leave off at once!"

To her astonishment, the dogs obeyed. Their tails drooped, and they circled each other, whining softly. Evelyn felt a pang of guilt at their crestfallen expressions, but she pushed the feeling aside. She was here to be a governess, not to coddle overgrown puppies.

With trembling hands, Evelyn attempted to smooth her hair back into place. She dabbed at her face with her handkerchief, grimacing at the traces of dog saliva. Her neat grey dress was now adorned with pawprints and tufts of grey fur.

She'd never encountered dogs of such immense size before, let alone been accosted by them. The largest dog she'd ever seen had been her cousin's pampered spaniel, a far cry from these shaggy behemoths.

Taking a deep breath, Evelyn straightened her spine and lifted her chin. She may look a fright, but she would face whatever lay beyond that door with all the poise she could muster. Her expression was hard and would have parted a sea by the time she regained the doorway to the drawing room.

Evelyn stepped into the drawing room, her eyes immediately falling upon two young girls who stood side by side, their faces a picture of feigned innocence. Despite their best efforts, the mischievous glint in their eyes betrayed them.

"Miss Augusta and Miss Julia, I presume?" Evelyn asked drily, arching an eyebrow at the pair.

The girls exchanged a quick glance, their lips twitching as they fought to suppress their smiles. Evelyn opened her mouth to address them further, but the sound of heavy booted footsteps echoing through the house made her pause.

The sisters' eyes widened in unison. "Uh oh," they muttered, their earlier bravado evaporating in an instant. They moved as one, attempting to sidle past Evelyn towards the door.

Evelyn, however, was quicker. She shifted her stance, effectively blocking their escape. Her expression hardened into a dour look that brooked no argument. The girls froze, caught between their new governess and the approaching storm. The footsteps grew louder, more insistent. Evelyn's heart quickened, but she kept her face impassive. She would not show weakness, not now.

The Baron marched into view, his face like thunder. He came to an abrupt halt, taking in the scene before him: Evelyn, dishevelled and covered in dog hair; his daughters, trapped and guilty; and the two enormous hounds, who had the good sense to slink behind a chaise longue.

Evelyn met the Baron's stormy gaze, refusing to flinch under his scrutiny. She may have looked a fright, but she would not cower. Whatever came next, she was determined to face it with all the dignity she could muster...if one could be said to have dignity with a tuft of dog fur in one's hair like a courtier's ostrich plume.

Evelyn watched as the Baron's face darkened, his grey eyes stormy with anger. His gaze swept over his daughters, who seemed to shrink under his scrutiny. The girls' earlier mischief had vanished, replaced by a palpable tension that filled the room.

Augusta and Julia stared resolutely at the floor, their shoulders hunched as if bracing for the impending reprimand. Evelyn felt a sudden, unexpected pang of sympathy for the pair. She remembered all too well the sting of disappointment from her own father, the weight of expectations that could crush a young spirit.

Before she could second-guess herself, Evelyn stepped forward, plastering a bright smile on her face. She turned to the Baron, her voice light and airy.

"My lord, I must thank your daughters for their thoughtfulness," she said, ignoring the startled looks from both the girls and their father. "They were kind enough to introduce me to your magnificent dogs. I've never had the pleasure of being around such fine animals before."

A puzzled frown formed on the Baron's face, his gaze shifting from his daughters to Evelyn. She could see the confusion in his eyes, warring with the anger that still simmered beneath the surface.

Evelyn pressed on, her smile unwavering. "I must admit, I was quite taken aback at first. But Miss Augusta and Miss Julia were most helpful in showing me how to properly greet such large dogs. It was quite the...educational experience." She turned back to face the girls and quirked an eyebrow at them.

Evelyn watched as understanding dawned on the girls' faces. They quickly caught on to her ruse, nodding enthusiastically.

"Oh yes, Father," Augusta chimed in, her voice a touch too bright. "We thought Miss Bane should meet Brutus and Caesar straight away."

Julia nodded vigorously. "We wanted to show her how friendly they are, didn't we, Augusta?"

The Baron's gaze flicked between his daughters and Evelyn, his expression still clouded with doubt. Evelyn could see the wheels turning in his mind, weighing the likelihood of this tale against his daughters' usual antics.

Seizing the moment, Evelyn turned to face him fully, summoning every ounce of charm she possessed. She tilted her head slightly, allowing a few stray wisps of hair to frame her face, and gave him her most dazzling smile. It was a look that had once captivated half the ton, and she prayed it would work its magic now.

The effect was immediate. The Baron's stern demeanour faltered, his eyes widening slightly as he took in her radiant expression. For a moment, he seemed at a loss for words, his earlier anger dissipating like morning mist. Evelyn held his gaze, her heart hammering in her chest. She'd gambled everything on this moment, and now she waited, breath held, to see if it would pay off.

Chapter 8

After what felt like an eternity, the Baron cleared his throat. "Well," he said, his voice gruff but no longer thunderous, "I suppose that's... thoughtful of you girls." He turned to his daughters, who were doing their best to look angelic. "Take Brutus and Caesar back outside now. They've had quite enough excitement for one morning."

The girls nodded quickly, relief evident on their faces. They scurried towards the chaise longue, coaxing the two enormous dogs out from their hiding place.

"Come on, Brutus," Augusta called softly.

"Here, Caesar," Julia added, patting her leg.

The dogs emerged, tails between their legs, looking as sheepish as their young mistresses. The motley procession shuffled towards the door, the girls shooting grateful glances at Evelyn as they passed.

Evelyn watched as the girls and dogs disappeared from view, a small smile playing at her lips. She felt a sense of triumph, having navigated her first challenge as governess with unexpected grace. The girls' grateful glances hadn't escaped her notice, and she hoped this shared secret might form the foundation of a bond between them.

Her satisfaction was short-lived, however, as she became acutely aware of the Baron's intense gaze upon her. Evelyn turned to face him, smoothing her rumpled dress as best she could. She lifted her chin, meeting his eyes with a mixture of deference and quiet confidence.

"Your daughters seem quite... spirited, my lord," she ventured, her tone carefully neutral.

The Baron's expression remained inscrutable, his grey eyes searching her face. He let her comment pass without acknowledgement, the silence stretching between them like a taut wire.

Just as Evelyn began to feel her composure slipping, the Baron spoke. "I'm glad to have this moment alone with you, Miss Bane."

Evelyn's eyebrows rose involuntarily, surprise flickering across her features. She hadn't expected such a direct approach, especially not so soon after her arrival. A thousand possibilities raced through her mind, each more alarming than the last.

Had he seen through her charade already? Was she to be dismissed before she'd even begun? She had only been taken on a trial basis, after all, and could be summarily dismissed without notice.

She swallowed hard, forcing her expression into one of polite inquiry. "Indeed, my lord?" she asked, her voice remarkably steady despite the nervous flutter in her chest.

Evelyn felt her heart quicken as the Baron straightened, his imposing figure casting a shadow across the room. His grey eyes, usually so inscrutable, now bore into her with an intensity that made her want to shrink back. She steeled herself, refusing to show any outward sign of discomfort.

"Miss Bane," he began, his voice low and grave, "I wish to address the matter of my daughters' education."

Evelyn nodded, relief washing over her. This, at least, was familiar territory. She had been thoroughly educated as a lady, and while she might not have experience as a governess, she certainly knew what was expected of young ladies of quality.

"Of course, my lord," she replied, her voice steady and assured. "I assure you, I have every intention of moulding Miss Augusta and Miss Julia into accomplished young ladies. By the time I've finished with them, they'll have their pick of suitors at every ball in London."

Evelyn smiled, certain she had said exactly what any father would want to hear. She could already picture the girls, resplendent in silk gowns, dancing with handsome young men at Almack's. It was the future she herself had once dreamed of, before... well, before everything had changed.

To her surprise and dismay, the Baron's expression didn't soften at her words. Instead, his brow furrowed deeper, his jaw clenching visibly. The air in the room seemed to grow colder, and Evelyn felt a chill run down her spine.

"Miss Bane," the Baron said, his voice tight with barely suppressed emotion, "I believe there has been a grave misunderstanding."

Evelyn's smile faltered, confusion and a hint of fear creeping into her mind. She had been so certain she knew what he wanted to hear. What could she have possibly said wrong?

Evelyn felt as though the ground had shifted beneath her feet. She stared at the Baron, certain she must have misheard him. His words echoed in her mind, each repetition more startling than the last.

"I... I beg your pardon, my lord?" she managed, her voice barely above a whisper.

The Baron's expression remained stern, but there was a flicker of something in his eyes—determination, perhaps, or a hint of vulnerability. "You heard me correctly, Miss Bane. I have no desire to see my daughters paraded about like prize mares at a county fair. Their worth is not measured by their ability to secure a wealthy husband."

Evelyn's mind reeled. This was utterly unprecedented. In all her years in society, she had never encountered a father who didn't view his daughters' marriages as a matter of utmost importance. It went against everything she had been taught, everything she had believed about a woman's place in the world.

And yet...

As the initial shock began to fade, Evelyn felt a strange stirring in her chest. It was a feeling she couldn't quite name—a mixture of curiosity, excitement, and something that felt dangerously close to hope.

"You wish for them to be... independent?" she asked, carefully choosing her words.

The Baron nodded, his gaze never leaving her face. "I want them to be capable of standing on their own two feet, Miss Bane. To have minds of their own and the skills to support themselves, should the need ever arise."

Evelyn found herself nodding along, almost unconsciously. The idea was radical, even scandalous, but there was something undeniably appealing about it. She thought of her own situation, how different things might have been if she had been prepared for a life beyond the ballrooms and drawing rooms of London.

"I see," she said slowly, her mind racing with possibilities. "I confess this is not what I expected when I took the posting."

Evelyn's mind whirled with the implications of the Baron's words. She opened her mouth to speak, but thinking better of it, fell into silent contemplation again. The Baron seemed to take her silence as hesitation. He nodded, a flicker of understanding crossing his face.

"I realise this is not what you expected, Miss Bane," he said, his voice softening slightly. He gestured towards the door with one arm. "If this arrangement is unacceptable to you, you may leave without any stain on your character. I'll ensure you have a glowing reference for your next position."

Evelyn's eyes widened. Leave? When things had suddenly become so intriguing? She held up a hand, surprising herself with her boldness.

"My lord, I'm not disagreeing with you," she said quickly. "I'm merely... surprised. Your views are quite progressive."

The Baron's eyebrows rose slightly, but he remained silent, waiting for her to continue. Evelyn took a deep breath, knowing she was about to overstep the bounds of propriety, but unable to contain her curiosity.

"If I may be so bold," she began, her heart racing, "how will the young ladies live once you're... that is to say, ladies can't inherit titles. How will they manage?"

For a moment, Evelyn feared she had gone too far. The Baron's face remained impassive, and she braced herself for a stern rebuke. To her surprise, he merely nodded, as if he had been expecting this question.

"You're quite right, Miss Bane," he said. "The title is entailed to a distant cousin. However, I took steps long ago to separate the estate from the title." Evelyn's eyes widened as the implications of his words sank in. The Baron continued, his voice matter-of-fact. "My daughters will inherit the estate in its entirety. They will be very wealthy women, Miss Bane, with no need to rely on a husband for their security."

Evelyn felt as though the world had tilted on its axis. Everything she had believed about a woman's place in society, about the importance of making a good match, suddenly seemed less certain. The idea was shocking, almost scandalous, and yet... intriguing.

Evelyn turned away from the Baron, her gaze drifting to the ornate fireplace. Her mind wandered unbidden to darker times, to the suffocating confines of her marriage to the Judge.

The memories washed over her like a cold wave: the constant fear, the bruises hidden beneath long sleeves, the desperate struggle to break free from his iron grip. She remembered the night she had finally escaped, how she had run through the rain-slicked streets of London, her heart pounding in her chest. The terror of being caught, of being dragged back to that gilded cage, had haunted her for months afterwards.

As these painful recollections swirled in her mind, a new realisation began to dawn: Augusta and Julia would never face such a fate. They would never be trapped, never be forced to endure what she had. The Baron's unconventional approach to their upbringing would ensure they always had choices, always had the means to chart their own course in life.

A smile began to spread across Evelyn's face, slow at first, then blossoming into something radiant and genuine. She turned back to face the Baron, allowing the full force of her joy to shine through.

The effect on the Baron was immediate and striking. He blinked rapidly, clearly taken aback by the transformation in her countenance. For a moment, he seemed at a loss for words, his usual stern demeanour cracking ever so slightly.

"My lord," Evelyn said, her voice warm and filled with newfound determination, "I believe we shall get along quite well indeed."

The Baron simply nodded, apparently still struggling to find his voice. He turned abruptly and made his way towards the door. As he reached the threshold, he paused, glancing out the window.

"Good luck, Miss Bane," he said gruffly, before disappearing into the hallway.

Evelyn moved to the window, curiosity piquing as she wondered what had caught the Baron's attention. Outside, she spied Augusta and Julia engaged in a boisterous game with Brutus and Caesar. The girls were laughing, their hair flying wildly as they tumbled about on the lawn, the enormous dogs bounding around them with joyful abandon.

Despite her misgivings about the appropriateness of such behaviour, Evelyn couldn't help but laugh softly to herself. She was beginning to feel like there might be a place for her here after all.

She gazed out at the girls thoughtfully. Though she approved of the Baron's demand for an unconventional education, Evelyn realised with a start that she hadn't the faintest clue as to what that actually meant.

Evelyn watched the girls from the window, a small smile playing on her lips as she observed their carefree antics. The sight of Augusta and Julia romping with the dogs was a far cry from the prim and proper young ladies she had expected to find. There was something refreshing about their unbridled joy, even if it did fly in the face of societal expectations.

Her musings were interrupted by the sound of hushed voices in the hallway. Curiosity piqued, Evelyn moved closer to the door, careful not to make a sound. She recognised the voices as belonging to some of the household staff.

"I give her a fortnight, tops," one voice declared with a snicker. "You saw how she looked when she arrived, all fancy frocks and airs. She'll be running back to London before the month's out."

"Nah," another voice chimed in, "the young misses'll see to her before then. Remember the last one? Didn't even make it a week before she was in tears."

Evelyn felt her cheeks grow hot, indignation rising in her chest. She pressed her ear closer to the door, straining to catch every word.

"Well, I heard from Cook that the Baron himself doesn't think she'll last a week," a third voice added, barely containing her glee at sharing such juicy gossip. "Said he'd never seen anyone less suited to country life."

The servants' laughter echoed in the hallway, each guffaw stoking the fire of Evelyn's determination. She straightened her back, chin lifting defiantly. City princess, indeed! She'd show them all what she was made of.

As the servants' voices faded away, Evelyn turned back to the window, her gaze falling once more on Augusta and Julia. She watched as they tumbled about, their laughter carried on the breeze, and felt a fierce protectiveness wash over her. These girls needed her, whether they knew it yet or not. And she'd be damned if she'd let a few snide comments or country discomforts drive her away.

Chapter 9

Evelyn surveyed the two girls before her, their hair windswept and cheeks flushed from their outdoor exertions. With some wrangling, she'd managed to herd them back indoors. She smoothed her own skirts, trying to project an air of calm authority she didn't quite feel.

"Well then, with the day's dosage of shenanigans out of the way," Evelyn said with an eyebrow arched significantly, "perhaps we might try doing something a little more productive? Perhaps you might show me the schoolroom?"

Augusta—at least, Evelyn assumed it was Augusta, the more serious of the pair—straightened her posture. "We don't have a schoolroom, Miss Bane."

Evelyn blinked, momentarily taken aback. Her gaze caught Augusta's eyes flicking towards what she assumed was the West Wing, but the girl's expression remained carefully neutral. Evelyn decided not to press the matter for now.

"I see," she said, her mind racing to adapt. "In that case, perhaps you'd be so kind as to show me your favourite room in the house? I'm still finding my bearings, you understand."

Julia's face lit up. "Oh! Mine's the kitchen! Cook lets me lick the spoon when she makes pudding!"

Augusta shot her sister a quelling look. "That's hardly proper, Julia."

Evelyn hid a smile. "I'm rather fond of sweets, myself," she said, leaning in conspiratorially toward Julia. "Still, Cook probably wouldn't appreciate us taking up so much space in her kitchen, would she? Let's have a bit of a look around, shall we? I'd love to see the parts of the house that are special to you."

As they set off, Evelyn carefully observed the girls' interactions. Augusta moved with a quiet grace, while Julia practically bounced along beside her. Though their faces were identical, the contrast between them was striking.

"This is the music room," Augusta announced, pushing open a heavy oak door. "Father says it hasn't changed since our grandmother's day."

Evelyn stepped inside, taking in the faded grandeur. Heavy velvet curtains framed tall windows, and portraits of stern-faced ancestors gazed down from the walls. A pianoforte stood near the darkened fireplace, half-covered in a white dropcloth. In one corner stood a beautiful harp, its strings gleaming in the afternoon light.

"Do either of you play?" Evelyn asked, gesturing towards the instruments.

A flicker of something – pride, perhaps? – crossed Augusta's face. "I do," she said softly. "Father says I have a talent for it."

Julia rolled her eyes. "She's always plucking away at that thing. It's dreadfully dull."

"And what do you prefer, Julia?" Evelyn asked, sensing an opportunity to draw her out.

Julia's eyes sparkled. "The piano!" she announced.

Evelyn smiled warmly at the girls. "I'd be delighted to hear you play. Would you mind giving me a little performance?"

Augusta nodded, her movements graceful as she approached the harp. She settled herself on the small stool, her back straight and shoulders relaxed. As her fingers touched the strings, Evelyn marvelled at the girl's poise. Augusta's eyes closed, a look of serene concentration settling over her features.

The first notes rang out, clear and crisp. Augusta's hands moved with precision, each pluck of the strings deliberate and controlled. The melody that emerged was hauntingly beautiful, speaking of hidden depths beneath the young girl's reserved exterior.

When Augusta finished, Evelyn was blinking back unexpected tears. "That was lovely," she murmured.

Julia, not to be outdone, bounded over to the pianoforte. "My turn!" she announced, whipping off the dropcloth with a flourish that sent dust motes dancing in the air.

Where Augusta had been all careful control, Julia was pure exuberance. Her fingers flew over the keys, the tempo wild and erratic. She hit wrong notes here and there, but her enthusiasm was infectious. Evelyn was tapping her foot, caught up in Julia's joy.

As the last echoes of Julia's spirited performance faded, both girls turned expectant faces towards their new governess.

"Do you play, Miss Bane?" Augusta asked, her tone polite but curious.

Evelyn's smile turned wistful. "I did, once upon a time," she admitted. "The pianoforte, actually. But it's been... oh, many years since I last touched the keys."

"Why'd you stop?" Julia asked, her head tilted to one side.

Evelyn paused, memories of her marital home flitting through her mind. "Life has a way of changing our paths," she said carefully. "Sometimes the things we loved in our youth get left behind."

Julia wrinkled her pert little nose at that, clearly finding the idea of giving up something she loved preposterous. Augusta, however, tilted her head thoughtfully, considering Evelyn carefully.

Evelyn glanced at the ornate clock on the mantelpiece, suddenly aware of how much time had passed. She clapped her hands together, drawing the girls' attention.

"Come now, we've much more to learn if you're to be accomplished young ladies. Music is but one facet of a well-rounded education."

Augusta's brow furrowed, her lips pursing in a way that reminded Evelyn startlingly of the Baron. The girl cast a longing look at her beloved harp as she rose from the stool.

"I fail to see what could be more important than perfecting one's art," Augusta said, her tone clipped.

Evelyn bit back a smile. How like herself Augusta was at that age—so certain, so focused. "There's much a young lady must know to enter society—"

"Surely you don't mean to teach us how to flutter fans and arrange flowers for dinner parties?" Augusta scoffed, her disdain palpable.

The vehemence in the girl's voice caught Evelyn off guard. She'd expected some resistance, but this level of scorn towards social graces was surprising. Before she could formulate a response, Julia piped up.

"Oh, but that sounds rather fun!" Julia's eyes sparkled with interest. "Do you know all about London society, Miss Bane? Have you been to grand balls?"

Evelyn's chest tightened at the eager curiosity in Julia's voice. Memories of glittering chandeliers and swirling gowns threatened to overwhelm her, but she pushed them aside.

"I've attended my fair share," she said carefully. "But there's more to being a lady than just socialising. It's about carrying oneself with grace and dignity in all situations."

Augusta's frown deepened. "Father says we're not to concern ourselves with such frivolities."

Evelyn's heart skipped a beat as Julia leaned forward, eyes shining with curiosity. "Did you dance with many gentlemen at the balls, Miss Bane? Were they terribly handsome?"

The eager question caught Evelyn off guard. She glanced at Augusta, noting the girl's sharp gaze fixed upon her. It was clear that each sister sought very different answers, and Evelyn knew she must tread carefully.

"Well," Evelyn began, choosing her words with care, "I did, but you know, there's so much more to those events than just dancing with gentlemen."

Julia's face fell slightly, but Augusta's posture relaxed a fraction.

Evelyn continued, "In fact, some of the most interesting conversations I had were with other ladies. We'd discuss books, art, and even politics on occasion."

"Politics?" Augusta's eyebrows rose, a flicker of interest crossing her face.

"Of a sort," Evelyn nodded, seizing the opportunity. "For instance, let's say that you must host a dinner with the great and good of the county. Who do you seat closest to you? Who will be offended by being seated far away? Who do you allow to escort you into the dining room? All of these things mean something in society—if you offend the wrong person, well, maybe they'll simply snub you. Or," she said, fixing each girl with a pointed look, "perhaps they will refuse to buy any of the produce from your estate; what will that mean for your tenants?"

The twins exchanged a look, clearly never having considered such a thing before. Evelyn, sensing their shift in perspective, pounced. "A well-rounded education prepares you for all manner of situations. Which is why," she added, inspiration striking, "I propose a bit of an exchange."

Both girls looked at her quizzically.

"You see," Evelyn explained, "I'm woefully unprepared for country life. Perhaps we could learn from each other? I'll teach you about the wider world, including how to navigate social situations—whether you choose to engage with them or not. In return, you can help me understand more about life here in the countryside."

Julia bounced on her toes. "Oh, yes! We can show you how to gather eggs without getting pecked!"

Augusta's lips twitched in what might have been the ghost of a smile. "I suppose there's merit in understanding social conventions, even if one chooses not to participate."

Evelyn felt a wave of relief wash over her. "Excellent. Then we have an agreement. Now, shall we start with a tour of the grounds? I'd love to see where you spend your time outdoors."

As they headed towards the door, Evelyn caught Augusta studying her once more, a thoughtful expression on her face. It seemed she'd passed some unspoken test, at least for now.

***

James slumped in his chair, the weight of the day pressing down on his broad shoulders. His study, once a sanctuary, now felt like a prison. The ledgers before him swam with figures, each one a reminder of the mounting challenges facing his estate.

He scrubbed at his face, the rough skin of his scarred hand catching on his stubble. The fire crackled in the hearth, but its warmth failed to reach him. Outside, the sun was sinking, painting the sky in hues that called to him like a siren's song.

"Blast it all," he muttered, pushing away from the desk. His boots echoed on the polished floor as he strode to the window. The rolling hills of his land stretched before him, verdant and inviting. His fingers twitched, longing for the feel of a horse's reins or the smooth wood of a walking stick.

A knock at the door interrupted his brooding.

"Enter," he barked, not turning from the view.

"Begging your pardon, my lord," came the hesitant voice of his steward. "But there's been another setback with the new planting methods. Some of the tenants are threatening to abandon the experiment altogether."

James's jaw clenched. Of course. Another problem to add to the growing pile. He turned, fixing the man with a steely gaze.

"Tell them I'll meet with them personally tomorrow. We can't afford to lose ground on this."

The steward nodded his greying head and retreated, leaving James alone once more. He paced the length of the study, restless energy thrumming through his veins. The walls seemed to close in around him, suffocating in their opulence.

His eyes fell on the portrait of his late wife, her smile frozen in time. A familiar ache bloomed in his chest, mingling with the ever-present fear for his daughters' futures. He'd sworn to protect them, to keep them safe from the pain he'd endured. But at what cost?

The laughter of children drifted through the open window, and James found himself drawn back to it. In the fading light, he could just make out the forms of his girls in the garden, the new governess hovering nearby. Miss Evelyn, with her city airs and endless chatter.

He'd been certain she'd have fled back to London at the first splatter of mud, but she seemed to be a stubborn little thing.

James leaned against the window frame, one arm above his head, his gaze fixed on the scene unfolding in the garden below. His daughters, Augusta and Julia, darted across the lawn, their laughter carried on the evening breeze. The sight of them so carefree should have warmed his heart, but a familiar knot of anxiety tightened in his chest.

He expected Miss Bane to intervene at any moment, to call the girls to order with stern words about proper behaviour. It was what their previous governess would have done, what any sensible woman charged with their care and education ought to do. But as he watched, Miss Bane merely smiled, her face softening with an indulgent expression as the girls tumbled about with his hunting dogs.

James frowned, perplexed. This wasn't at all what he had anticipated from the prim and proper Londoner who had arrived on his doorstep. He'd been certain she'd try to mould his wild country girls into refined young ladies, all airs and graces with no substance. Yet here she was, allowing them their freedom, their joy.

As if sensing his scrutiny, Miss Bane glanced up towards his study window. Their eyes met for a brief moment, and James felt an unexpected jolt. He stepped back, out of sight, his heart racing as if he'd been caught doing something unseemly.

When he dared to look again, Miss Bane was moving to follow the girls across the uneven ground of the kitchen garden. Her step faltered, and she stumbled slightly, catching herself with a grace that belied her city upbringing. The girls turned back, concern evident in their postures. They said something to their governess, and to James's surprise, Miss Bane threw back her head and laughed.

The sound carried up to him, clear and unrestrained. It was a far cry from the nervous chatter that had filled his wagonette on the day of her arrival. For a moment, James felt a pang of something he couldn't quite name. Envy, perhaps, at the easy rapport she seemed to be developing with his daughters. Or maybe...

He shook his head, banishing the thought before it could fully form. Despite his best efforts, James found his gaze drawn back to Miss Bane once again. Her bonnet had come loose and was hanging down her back, revealing thick chestnut hair that gleamed in the setting sun. This irritated James further for some reason he couldn't quite name.

He clenched his jaw, fingers tightening on the window frame. What business did she have looking so... so carefree? So at ease in a world that was meant to be foreign to her? And why in God's name did it matter to him?

James turned abruptly from the window, determined to put the vexing governess out of his mind. He strode back to his desk, each step feeling heavier than the last. The ledgers awaited him, a mountain of figures and responsibilities that demanded his attention.

He lowered himself into his chair, the leather creaking beneath him. His hand reached for the quill, but his eyes refused to focus on the columns before him. Instead, they kept straying to the window, to the fading laughter outside.

James growled in frustration, running a hand through his unkempt hair. This was ridiculous. He was a grown man, a baron with an estate to manage and daughters to protect. He had no time for... for whatever this distraction was.

Yet even as he berated himself, he found his body betraying him. He half-rose from his chair, drawn inexorably back towards the window and the scene beyond. It took every ounce of his considerable willpower to force himself back down, to pick up the quill and bend his head over the ledgers.

The numbers swam before his eyes, meaningless squiggles that refused to resolve into anything coherent. James gritted his teeth, determined to focus, to lose himself in the familiar rhythm of accounts and projections. But the memory of Miss Bane's laugh, of her hair catching the light, lingered at the edges of his mind like a persistent ghost.

James's gaze drifted from the ledgers, settling on a letter tucked beneath a stack of papers. He pulled it out, recognising it as Miss Bane's acceptance of the governess position. Her handwriting caught his eye—clean and precise, yet with a distinctly feminine flourish to the loops and curves.

He ran a calloused thumb over the words, noting how she had agreed to his stipulation of a trial period. A month, he'd insisted upon. Surely that would be enough time to determine if she was a good fit for his household, for his girls.

James leaned back in his chair, the leather creaking softly. He tried to focus on the practicalities of the arrangement, to view Miss Bane as nothing more than an employee. Yet unbidden, the image of her laughing in the garden rose in his mind.

He shook his head, irritated with himself. This wouldn't do at all. If the woman proved too much of a distraction, he need only dismiss her at the end of the trial. It was a simple solution, one that should have eased his mind.

Instead, James found himself frowning at the thought. The girls seemed to be warming to her, and despite his initial misgivings, Miss Bane appeared to be determined to adapt to their household.

He folded the letter, creasing it perhaps more sharply than necessary. No, he mustn't allow himself to become entangled in such thoughts. The trial period was a safeguard, nothing more. If Miss Bane's presence continued to unsettle him, he would simply have to...

James paused, realising he had no idea how to finish that thought. The prospect of dismissing her no longer held the reassurance it once did.

Chapter 10

Evelyn sat at the head of the dining table, her back straight and her hands folded neatly in her lap. Augusta and Julia flanked her on either side, their faces a mix of curiosity and mild boredom.

"Now, girls," Evelyn began, her voice soft but firm, "when engaging in conversation with a gentleman at the table, one must strike a delicate balance. You wish to be engaging without appearing overly eager."

A look of confusion crossed Augusta's face. "But why should we care what they think of us?"

Evelyn suppressed a smile. "It's not about their opinion of you, my dear. It's about maintaining your own dignity and reputation."

Julia leaned forward, her eyes sparkling. "How does one appear interesting without being too forward?"

"An excellent question," Evelyn replied. "The key is to—"

The door swung open with a creak, cutting off Evelyn's words. Baron Hastings strode into the room, his tall frame filling the doorway. His eyes darted from Evelyn to his daughters, a frown etching deep lines around his mouth.

"What's all this, then?" he asked, his voice gruff.

Evelyn's heart quickened, but she kept her composure. "Good afternoon, Baron. We were just discussing the finer points of dinner conversation."

The Baron's eyebrows shot up. "Dinner conversation? Is this what you are spending your time on?"

"Of course, Father," Julia chimed in. "Miss Bane was about to tell us how to speak with gentlemen without appearing too forward."

The Baron's frown deepened. "Gentlemen? What gentlemen?"

Evelyn felt a flush creep up her neck. "It's merely a hypothetical situation, Baron. I assure you, we're not planning any mixed dinner parties."

"See that you don't," he growled. His gaze lingered on Evelyn for a moment longer than necessary, and she felt a strange flutter in her chest.

Evelyn lifted her chin, refusing to be cowed by the Baron's intimidating presence. A spark of defiance ignited within her, overriding her sense of decorum. "I beg your pardon, Baron, but this is an important part of a young lady's education."

The Baron's eyes flashed. "It won't be a part of these young ladies' education."

"You're not allowing me to do my job," Evelyn retorted, her voice rising slightly. She was acutely aware of how improper her behaviour was, but she couldn't seem to stop herself.

"You had specific instructions," the Baron fired back, his jaw clenching.

Augusta and Julia's heads swivelled back and forth between their father and governess, their eyes wide with fascination. The tension in the room crackled like static electricity.

Evelyn stood, her hands braced against the table. "And those instructions were to prepare them for independence. How can they be truly independent if they can't navigate social situations?"

The Baron took a step forward, his presence looming. "They won't need to navigate those situations if they never enter them."

"That's utterly unrealistic," Evelyn scoffed, her cheeks flushed with emotion.

"It's my decision," the Baron growled, his voice low and dangerous.

Evelyn opened her mouth to argue further, but caught herself. She glanced at the girls, who were watching the exchange with rapt attention, and realised how far she'd overstepped. She closed her mouth sharply with a click of her teeth. The Baron, clearly taking this as a sign of victory, straightened with a slightly smug tilt to his chin.

Evelyn watched as the Baron turned on his heel, preparing to leave the dining room. His broad shoulders were set in a rigid line, radiating an air of superiority that made her blood simmer. The way he carried himself, as if his word was law and not to be questioned, struck a raw nerve within her.

Memories of the Judge's controlling manner flashed through her mind, and something inside Evelyn snapped. She would not be cowed by another man, not ever again. Without thinking, she hurried after the Baron, her nostrils flaring and eyes flashing.

"Baron Hastings," she called, her voice sharper than she'd intended. "A word, if you please."

He paused at the threshold, turning slowly to face her. His grey eyes were stormy, but Evelyn refused to be intimidated. She lifted her chin, meeting his gaze squarely.

"I believe we have more to discuss regarding your daughters' education," she said, her tone clipped and formal despite the anger coursing through her veins.

The Baron's jaw tightened. "I thought we had settled the matter, Miss Bane."

"Settled?" Evelyn let out a short, incredulous laugh. "Hardly. You cannot simply dictate terms without considering the consequences."

She was dimly aware that she was overstepping her bounds, that her position hung by a thread, but she couldn't seem to stop herself. The words tumbled out, fuelled by a righteous indignation she hadn't known she possessed.

"Your daughters deserve a complete education, one that prepares them for all aspects of life. You cannot shelter them forever, my lord."

The Baron's eyes narrowed dangerously, and he turned his face more fully toward her, giving her an unobstructed view of the scars that ran up the side of his face. It was clearly meant to intimidate her, but to her credit, Evelyn stood her ground. "I can, and I will. You forget your place, Miss Bane."

His dismissive tone only served to stoke the flames of Evelyn's anger. She took a step closer, her hands clenched at her sides.

"My place?" she hissed, her voice low but intense. "My place is to educate and guide your daughters to the best of my ability. If you cannot see the value in that, then perhaps it is you who has forgotten his place as a father."

Evelyn's heart pounded in her chest as the silence stretched between them. She wondered if she had truly gone too far this time, her words hanging in the air like a challenge. Inwardly, she felt a twinge of regret for her sharp tongue, but outwardly, she kept her face set in a mask of determination.

The Baron stared at her, his grey eyes unreadable. Evelyn could almost see the thoughts churning behind his stern visage, weighing the merits of continuing their argument. She braced herself for another verbal assault, her chin lifted defiantly.

"I have bigger problems to attend to at the moment," he said at last, as if that were the sword that cut off their argument with finality. He strode away from Miss Bane and was at the front door before she gathered herself up and hurried after him once again.

Evelyn hurried after the Baron, her skirts rustling as she caught up to him at the front door. A footman was already there, handing him his hat and a sturdy walking stick. She felt a flicker of frustration at his dismissive attitude.

"My lord," she said, her voice firm despite her racing heart, "we are not finished with this discussion. There's more to settle on this score."

The Baron paused, one hand on the doorknob. He turned to face her, his grey eyes unreadable beneath the brim of his hat. For a moment, they stood in silence, the tension palpable between them.

Finally, he spoke, his voice low and measured. "Miss Bane, I hope you can argue and walk at the same time, because I cannot devote any more time to this discussion while standing still."

Without waiting for her response, he strode out onto the gravel drive. Evelyn blinked in surprise, then gathered her skirts and hurried after him. She was not about to let this matter drop so easily.

As she fell into step beside him, Evelyn realised she had never been this close to the Baron before. His long strides forced her to walk at a brisk pace, and she could smell the faint scent of leather and tobacco that clung to his coat. It was oddly distracting, but she pushed the thought aside, focusing on the task at hand.

"My lord," she began, slightly breathless from the exertion, "I understand your concerns for your daughters' welfare, but surely you can see the importance of a well-rounded education?"

The Baron kept his gaze fixed ahead, his jaw set in a stubborn line. "I see the importance of keeping them safe, Miss Bane. The world is not kind to young women who are unprepared for its harsh realities."

Evelyn felt a pang of empathy at his words, recognising the fear that lay beneath his gruff exterior. Yet she pressed on, determined to make him understand.

Evelyn took a deep breath, steeling herself for the argument ahead. She could feel the Baron's stubbornness radiating off him in waves, but she refused to back down.

"My lord," she began. Her voice was steady despite her racing heart. "I must point out that if we don't teach the girls how to interact with gentlemen, they will be wholly unprepared when the time comes that they must do so."

The Baron's frown deepened, etching harsh lines around his mouth. He stopped abruptly, turning to face her with a thunderous expression. "They won't ever need to, Miss Bane. It's a waste of time."

Evelyn felt a flicker of frustration at his obstinance. She opened her mouth to argue further, but he cut her off with a sharp wave of his hand.

"If you're so pressed for ideas on lessons, spend more time on mathematics," he growled. "I don't want them wasting any time on silly nonsense, like dancing or how to hold a parasol."

His dismissive tone made Evelyn's cheeks flush with indignation. She took a step closer, her eyes flashing with determination. "With all due respect, Baron, those skills are not 'silly nonsense'. They are essential for young ladies to navigate society, regardless of whether you wish them to or not."

The Baron's jaw clenched, and Evelyn could see the muscle ticking in his cheek. She knew she was treading on dangerous ground, but she couldn't let this go. The girls' future was at stake.

"Society," he spat the word as if it left a bad taste in his mouth. "What society do you think there is to be had out here?" he said, gesturing broadly with a sweep of his arm. Evelyn glanced about herself, realising that the Baron's brisk walking had led them farther than she had thought. In a field across the lane, a pair of cows watched them with lipid eyes, chewing great mouthfuls of grass lazily.

Evelyn watched as the Baron nodded triumphantly, a self-satisfied smirk playing at the corners of his mouth. He clearly thought he'd made an irrefutable point about the girls' isolation. Without another word, he set off again, his long strides carrying him swiftly towards the cows' enclosure.

Evelyn's eyes widened as she watched him approach the stile. Surely he didn't expect her to—

But he did. With practised ease, the Baron stepped up and over the wooden structure, landing gracefully on the other side. He turned back to her, his eyebrows raised in challenge. The message was clear: he thought this would be too much for her, that she'd turn back now, effectively ending their argument.

A spark of defiance ignited in Evelyn's chest. She'd be damned if she let him win so easily. Gathering her skirts in one hand, she approached the stile with determination. It was higher than she'd anticipated, and for a moment, doubt crept in. But the sight of the Baron's smug expression steeled her resolve.

Taking a deep breath, Evelyn placed one foot on the first step. Her shoes, more suited to London drawing rooms than country fields, offered little purchase on the worn wood.

She wobbled slightly but pressed on, gripping the top of the stile with white-knuckled hands.

With an ungainly movement, she swung her leg over the top. For a terrifying moment, she teetered precariously, certain she would topple over in an undignified heap. But then, with a final push, she made it to the other side.

Her landing was far from graceful. Her feet slipped on the damp grass, and she stumbled forward, arms windmilling as she fought to keep her balance. By some miracle, she managed to stay upright, though her heart pounded wildly in her chest.

Straightening up, Evelyn met the Baron's astonished gaze. His eyes were wide with surprise, clearly not having expected her to follow. A small, triumphant smile tugged at her lips as she brushed a stray lock of hair from her face.

"You were saying, my lord?" she asked, her voice steady despite her breathlessness.

Evelyn watched as the Baron set off again, his long strides carrying him down the field with grim determination. The ground beneath her feet grew softer with each step, and she silently cursed her choice of footwear. Her delicate shoes, more suited to London drawing rooms than muddy country fields, sank into the earth with alarming ease.

Still, she refused to be deterred. Gathering her skirts higher, she hurried after the Baron, her mind racing as she tried to formulate her next argument. The squelching sound of her shoes in the mud was most undignified, but she pressed on, unwilling to let him win this battle of wills.

"My lord," she called out, slightly breathless from the exertion, "surely there must be occasions for socialising, even out here in the country?"

The Baron's response was a derisive snort, tossed over his shoulder without breaking his stride.

Evelyn's face tightened in focus. Her brows slightly furrowed as she picked her way through the increasingly treacherous terrain. Her eyes darted between the ground and the Baron's retreating back, trying to find the safest path while keeping up with his relentless pace.

Suddenly, an idea struck her. "What about harvest festivals?" she asked, her voice carrying across the field. "Or country fairs? Surely such events are common in these parts?" She resorted to hopping from foot to foot, trying not to sink deeper into the mud as she followed him.

Evelyn noticed the Baron's pace slowing, and a flicker of triumph sparked within her. She had struck a chord, and she wasn't about to let this advantage slip away.

Carefully picking her way through the muddy field, she pressed on. "My lord, what about tenant suppers after the harvest? I've heard it's quite a common celebration among country estates. Surely your daughters would be expected to attend such gatherings?"

The Baron's shoulders stiffened, but he didn't turn to face her. Evelyn took his silence as encouragement to continue.

"And if your daughters are to inherit the estate one day," she ventured, her voice growing more confident despite her precarious footing, "wouldn't it be their duty to host such events? To maintain good relations with the tenants and oversee the running of the estate?"

She watched as the Baron's steps faltered slightly, his hand tightening on his walking stick. Evelyn held her breath, waiting for his response. She knew she was treading on delicate ground, both literally and figuratively, but she couldn't back down now.

"That's... different," the Baron finally grumbled, his voice low and reluctant.

Evelyn sensed an opening and pressed on, her words coming out in a rush. "But it's not, my lord. These are precisely the sort of social situations the girls need to be prepared for. They'll need to know how to converse with people from all walks of life, how to manage a household, how to host gatherings. These skills are essential, whether they marry or not."

The Baron came to a complete stop, turning to face her with a conflicted expression. Evelyn could see the internal struggle playing out across his features, a deep line formed on his forehead as he considered his thoughts

Evelyn watched the Baron's face intently, searching for any sign of concession. To her surprise, his expression softened slightly, the harsh lines around his mouth easing. For a moment, she dared to hope that she had finally broken through his stubborn resolve.

But then, something shifted in his eyes. The corners of his mouth twitched, and a bemused look spread across his features. Evelyn felt her earlier triumph evaporate, replaced by a prickle of defensiveness.

Chapter 11

"What, pray tell, are you smiling at, my lord?" she demanded, her chin lifting in defiance.

The Baron said nothing, his grey eyes twinkling with barely suppressed mirth. Instead, he glanced pointedly downward, his gaze settling on Evelyn's feet.

Confused, Evelyn followed his line of sight. Her eyes widened in horror as she realised her predicament. While she had been so focused on their argument, her feet had been steadily sinking into the muddy field. Her once-pristine shoes were now completely submerged, the hem of her dress dangerously close to the muck.

A small, undignified squeak of alarm escaped her lips as she tried to lift one foot, only to find it firmly stuck in the thick, glutinous mud. The more she struggled, the deeper she seemed to sink. A small sound like a breathy chuckle escaped from the Baron, and Evelyn turned a dour look on him, her eyes narrowed.

"Don't you dare laugh," she said, her voice low and dangerous. "These shoes are from Madame Lucine's, and made from custom duchesse satin."

Evelyn felt her cheeks burn with embarrassment as the Baron's grin widened. His amusement at her predicament was infuriating, and she bristled at the thought of appearing foolish before him. When he extended his hand to help her, she pointedly turned away, determined to extricate herself from this mess without his assistance.

Gathering her strength, Evelyn gritted her teeth and yanked her right leg upward with all her might. The mud released her foot with a horrible squelching sound that echoed across the field. She wobbled precariously, fighting to maintain her balance on her one free leg.

To her dismay, she realised her shoe had remained firmly lodged in the muck. Evelyn glanced up at the Baron, her face flushed with exertion and frustration. He leaned casually on his walking stick, looking for all the world as if he had nowhere else to be but here, watching her struggle.

His nonchalant attitude only served to fuel her determination. Evelyn refused to give him the satisfaction of seeing her defeated by a patch of mud. With a defiant lift of her chin, she placed her stockinged foot down on a nearby clump of weeds, wincing slightly at the dampness that immediately seeped through the delicate fabric.

Using this precarious foothold, Evelyn braced herself to free her other foot. She could feel the Baron's eyes on her, but she refused to meet his gaze. Instead, she focused all her energy on the task at hand, silently vowing that she would rather ruin every stitch of clothing she owned than admit defeat.

Evelyn gritted her teeth, determined to free her left foot. With a mighty heave, she wrenched it from the mud's grasp. The sudden release caught her off guard, and she felt herself losing balance. Her arms windmilled frantically as she teetered backwards, her heart leaping into her throat.

Time seemed to slow as she fell, the sky above her spinning lazily. Then, with a sickening squelch, she landed flat on her back in the thick, cold mud. The impact knocked the wind from her lungs, leaving her gasping like a fish out of water.

For a moment, Evelyn lay there, stunned and struggling to breathe. The earthy smell of mud filled her nostrils, and she could feel it seeping through her dress, coating her hands and face. She blinked rapidly, trying to clear her vision as muddy droplets trickled down her forehead.

Suddenly, the Baron's face appeared above her, his expression transformed from amusement to genuine concern. He extended his hand, leaning down to offer assistance.

"Miss Bane, are you all right? Here, let me help you up," he said, his voice tinged with worry.

Evelyn glared up at him, acutely aware of how ridiculous she must look. Mud splattered her once-fine dress, caked her hands, and smeared across her face. Her carefully arranged hair had come loose, plastered to her head with muck. The urge to accept his help warred with her wounded pride.

Drawing in a shaky breath, she fixed the Baron with a steely gaze. "Not. A. Word," she ground out between clenched teeth, her voice low and dangerous.

Despite her fierce warning, Evelyn found herself reaching for the Baron's outstretched hand. His grip was strong and sure as he pulled her to her feet, the mud releasing her with a series of undignified sloppy sounds. She stumbled slightly, her stockinged feet slipping on the slick ground, and found herself steadied by the Baron's firm grasp on her elbow.

As she regained her footing, Evelyn dared to glance up at her employer. The Baron's face was a study in forced solemnity, his lips pressed into a thin line that twitched at the corners. She could see the mirth dancing in his grey eyes, barely contained beneath his serious expression.

"Miss Bane," he said, his voice remarkably steady, "I must say, you wear the countryside well."

Evelyn felt her cheeks burn with a mixture of embarrassment and indignation. She shot him a look that could have curdled milk, silently daring him to continue.

Undeterred, the Baron pressed on, his tone dripping with exaggerated sincerity. "In fact, I don't believe I've ever seen you look more fetching."

Evelyn glared at the Baron, her anger flaring hot and bright for a moment. How dare he mock her in this state? But as she looked down at herself, taking in the full extent of her muddy predicament, something shifted inside her. The absurdity of the situation struck her all at once, and before she could stop herself, a bubble of laughter escaped her lips.

The sound of her own mirth startled her, but once it started, she found she couldn't stop. Evelyn laughed, a full, rich sound that echoed across the field. She caught sight of the Baron's face, his expression one of utter bewilderment, which only made her laugh harder.

When she finally caught her breath, Evelyn grinned up at him, her eyes sparkling with mirth. "You know, my lord," she said, still chuckling, "all the ladies in London talk of going on great scenery tours of the English countryside, but I rather doubt any of them meant quite like this."

The Baron blinked, clearly taken aback by her sudden change in demeanour. Evelyn pressed on, emboldened by his surprise. "In fact," she added, gesturing to her mud-caked form, "I've heard tell of ladies at Bath who put mud on their skin to improve their complexions. Perhaps I've stumbled upon a new beauty treatment?"

To Evelyn's astonishment, the Baron's stern façade cracked. The corners of his mouth twitched, and then, to her utter amazement, he smiled. It was a genuine smile that transformed his entire face, softening the harsh lines and bringing a warmth to his grey eyes that she had never seen before.

"Well, Miss Bane," he said, his voice tinged with amusement, "if that's the case, I daresay you won't age for years to come."

Evelyn's laughter faded as she caught the Baron's eye, a curious warmth spreading through her chest. His smile, so rare and unexpected, transformed his face entirely. The skin marred by the burn scar softened, and his grey eyes sparkled with an unfamiliar light. For a moment, she forgot her muddy state, captivated by this glimpse of the man beneath the stern exterior.

Then, as if forgetting himself, the Baron reached up and swiped some mud off Evelyn's face. His calloused thumb grazed her skin, almost brushing across her lips. The touch, rough yet gentle, sent a jolt through her body. They both froze at the contact, the Baron's hand paused by Evelyn's chin.

Evelyn stared up into his eyes, suddenly aware that she was breathing hard as if she'd been running. Her heart thundered in her chest, and she felt a flush creeping up her neck that had nothing to do with embarrassment. The Baron stared right back at her, his eyes burning with an intensity that made her breath catch in her throat.

Time seemed to stand still. The cold mud seeping through her clothes, the squelch of the field beneath her feet, even the gentle breeze - all faded away. There was only the Baron's burning gaze and the warmth of his hand near her face. Evelyn felt herself teetering on the edge of something vast and unknown, both thrilling and terrifying.

She watched as the Baron's eyes flickered to her lips for the briefest moment, and she felt a rush of heat course through her body. The air between them crackled with tension, thick and heavy. Evelyn's mind raced, torn between the urge to step closer and the instinct to pull away.

Evelyn felt the moment shatter as the Baron's expression suddenly hardened. The warmth in his eyes vanished, replaced by a cold, almost angry look. It was as if a wall had slammed down between them, leaving her breathless and confused.

Flustered, she glanced down at her feet, only to realise with dismay that they were once again sinking into the thick mud. She shifted uncomfortably, unsure how to extricate herself from this predicament without further embarrassment.

Before she could formulate a plan, the Baron let out a frustrated sigh. Without warning, he bent down and scooped her up into his arms as if she weighed no more than a feather. Evelyn gasped, her hands instinctively grasping at his shoulders for balance.

"My lord!" she exclaimed, her voice pitched higher than usual. "This is most improper! Put me down at once!"

She wriggled in his arms, trying to free herself, but his grip remained firm. The Baron's jaw clenched, and he fixed her with a stern glare that made her breath catch in her throat.

"Hold still, Miss Bane," he snapped, his voice gruff and brooking no argument. "Unless you'd prefer I drop you right back into that mud?"

Evelyn stilled immediately, her cheeks burning with a mixture of indignation and embarrassment. She was acutely aware of the strength in his arms, the warmth of his body seeping through her mud-soaked clothes. Despite her discomfort, she couldn't help but feel a treacherous flutter in her stomach at their proximity.

Evelyn reluctantly wrapped her arms around the Baron's neck, acutely aware of their improper closeness. She held herself as still as possible, trying to ignore the warmth of his body against hers and the strength in his arms as he carried her effortlessly across the field.

To her surprise, the Baron didn't simply deposit her on slightly drier ground. Instead, he strode purposefully towards the distant fence line, his long legs eating up the distance with ease. Evelyn was torn between relief at being rescued from the mud and mortification at being carried like a child.

Desperate for a distraction from her current predicament, Evelyn craned her neck to look back at the muddy quagmire they were leaving behind. She sighed at the mucky mess that had once been her shoes, still firmly embedded in the thick, gluey mud.

"Oh, my shoes," she lamented softly, unable to keep the sadness from her voice.

Evelyn felt the Baron's muscles tense beneath her as he strode across the field. His jaw was set, a hard line that spoke volumes about his irritation. She could feel the rumble of his voice in his chest as he spoke, his words clipped and dismissive.

"They're just shoes, Miss Bane. Surely a woman like yourself must have more than one pair."

Evelyn stiffened in his arms, her eyes narrowing as she glared up at him. The casual disregard in his tone ignited a spark of indignation within her.

"They are not 'just shoes', my lord," she said sharply, her voice cutting through the air between them. "Did you even see them?"

The Baron's stride faltered for a moment, clearly taken aback by the vehemence in her tone. Evelyn pressed on, her words tumbling out in a rush of frustrated passion.

"They were royal blue silk, with the most delicate pink pleated trim around the ankle. The heel was small, in the Italian style." Her voice softened slightly as she continued, a note of wistfulness creeping in. "They were unique to me, carefully chosen to be as flattering as possible and to match a specific dress."

Evelyn felt her frustration mounting as the Baron carried her across the field. His dismissive attitude towards her shoes had struck a nerve, and she found herself unable to hold back the tide of emotions that washed over her.

"I don't think men have the slightest idea how much work goes into being a woman," she said, her voice tight with exasperation. "You only see powder puffs and soft smiles and think it's easy."

The Baron's eyebrows rose slightly, but he remained silent, his eyes fixed ahead as he continued to walk. Emboldened by his silence, Evelyn pressed on.

"We agonise over picking just the right dress, the best shoes, the most flattering ribbon to tie about our waists," she explained, her words tumbling out in a rush. "And for what? Do men like you even notice, or understand how much work it is?"

She glanced up at the Baron's face, searching for any sign of comprehension. His expression remained impassive, but she thought she detected a flicker of something—surprise, perhaps?—in his grey eyes.

"Every choice we make, every accessory we select, is carefully considered," Evelyn continued, warming to her subject. "The colour of a gown must complement our complexion, the cut must flatter our figure, the fabric must be appropriate for the occasion. And shoes—oh, the shoes! They must be the perfect height, the ideal shape, the most becoming colour."

She paused, taking a breath before adding, "And all of this effort, all of this painstaking attention to detail—it's not merely vanity, my lord. It's an art form, a language of its own. One that I fear most men are utterly incapable of understanding."

Evelyn felt a flicker of surprise as the Baron's steps slowed, his pace becoming more measured. She couldn't see his face fully from her position in his arms. She could see his sharp jawline, but she suspected that her words were sinking in, prompting him to consider her perspective more deeply.

Emboldened by this subtle change, Evelyn softened her tone, her voice taking on a gentler, more persuasive cadence. "I understand that you might think all of this feminine nonsense is pointless, my lord," she said, choosing her words carefully. "But it's a valuable tool, one that your daughters might turn to their advantage."

She paused, letting her words hang in the air between them for a moment before continuing. "You can teach them to shoot and ride and whatever else you deem important," she acknowledged, her voice filled with a quiet conviction. "But shouldn't they have every tool at their disposal that they might need?"

Evelyn glanced up at the Baron's face, trying to gauge his reaction. His expression remained inscrutable, but she thought she detected a flicker of consideration in his grey eyes, as if he were turning her words over in his mind.

"The world is changing, my lord, but not fast enough for them," she pressed on, her voice soft but insistent. "The skills that served women in the past may not be enough in the future, God willing, but until that day, your daughters will need to navigate a complex social landscape. That's one where the right dress, the perfect shoes, can open doors and create opportunities."

She took a breath, her next words coming out in a rush of earnest passion. "I'm not suggesting that we neglect their other education, far from it. But shouldn't we give them every advantage, every weapon in their arsenal, to face whatever challenges lie ahead?"

Evelyn fell silent, her heart pounding in her chest as she waited for the Baron's response. She knew she was treading on dangerous ground, challenging his long-held beliefs about what was proper and necessary for his daughters. But she couldn't shake the feeling that this was a crucial moment, a chance to plant a seed that might, in time, blossom into a new understanding between them.

Evelyn waited, her heart pounding, for the Baron's response, but it never came. He remained silent, his face turned away from her as he carried her across the field. The lack of reaction left her feeling deflated, as if all her impassioned words had simply drifted away on the breeze.

As they neared the fence, Evelyn felt a twinge of disappointment settle in her chest. Had she overstepped? Perhaps her argument had fallen on deaf ears after all.

With surprising gentleness, the Baron set her down on the ground near the stile. Evelyn's feet sank slightly into the damp grass, a stark reminder of her bedraggled state. She attempted to catch his eye, searching for any hint of how her words had landed. The Baron, though, kept the wide brim of his hat tilted low, obscuring his face from view.

Shoulders slumping, Evelyn turned towards the stile. She began to climb over carefully, acutely aware of her ruined stockings. The rough wood caught at the delicate fabric, threatening to unravel it further. She sighed softly, mourning the loss of yet another item from her wardrobe.

As she reached the top of the stile, Evelyn steeled herself for an ungraceful descent on the other side. To her surprise, she saw the Baron's hand appear before her, palm up in a gentlemanly offer of assistance. She hesitated for a moment, taken aback by this unexpected courtesy.

Cautiously, Evelyn placed her hand in his. The Baron's grip was firm and steady as he helped her down from the stile, his touch deliciously warm against her mud-chilled skin.

Evelyn was on the other side of the fence, her dress a ruined mess of mud and grass stains. She made a half-hearted attempt to brush off the worst of it, but quickly realised it was a lost cause.

Her hair, which had come loose during her misadventure, hung in damp, muddy tendrils around her face. She reached up to tuck a particularly bothersome strand behind her ear, only to grimace as she felt the grit of dried mud against her skin.

With a sigh of defeat, Evelyn glanced up, expecting to find herself alone. To her surprise, the Baron still stood on the other side of the fence, his tall figure casting a long shadow in the late afternoon light. His presence made her acutely aware of her dishevelled state, and she felt a flush of embarrassment creep up her neck.

Determined to salvage what little dignity she had left, Evelyn straightened her spine and offered the Baron a dismissive wave. "I've taken up quite enough of your valuable time today, my lord," she said, injecting a note of forced lightness into her voice. "I assure you, I can find my way back to the house on my own."

She expected him to leave then, to turn on his heel and stride away as he so often did. To her bewilderment, the Baron remained rooted to the spot, his grey eyes fixed upon her with an intensity that made her breath catch in her throat.

Evelyn felt unable to look away, caught in his gaze like a moth drawn to a flame. The Baron's face, usually so stern and impassive, now held a curious mix of emotions. There was warmth there, a softness she had never seen before, but it warred with something else—conflict, perhaps, or uncertainty.

The moment stretched between them, taut with unspoken words and unfamiliar tension. Evelyn felt her heart begin to race, responding to something in the Baron's gaze that she couldn't quite name.

Then, as suddenly as it had begun, the moment shattered. The Baron turned abruptly, his familiar brisk gait carrying him swiftly away across the field. Evelyn watched him go, her mind whirling with confusion and a strange, unexpected sense of loss. Startlingly alone, Evelyn began to limp her way home with as much of her tattered dignity as she could.

Chapter 12

Evelyn limped into her room, leaving a trail of mud and grass in her wake. Her entire body ached, and she longed for nothing more than to sink into a hot bath and wash away the evidence of her misadventure. With trembling fingers, she reached for the bell pull, giving it a firm tug.

Moments later, a soft knock at the door heralded Nell's arrival. Evelyn called for her to enter, bracing herself for the maid's reaction.

As Nell stepped into the room, her eyes widened comically, taking in Evelyn's bedraggled appearance. The maid's hand flew to her mouth, barely concealing the spark of amusement that danced in her eyes.

Evelyn couldn't help but chuckle softly at herself. "I'm afraid I've made rather a mess of things, Nell," she said, gesturing ruefully at her mud-caked dress and tangled hair.

Nell's lips twitched, fighting a smile. "That you have, miss," she agreed, her voice tinged with barely suppressed laughter. "Shall I draw you a bath?"

"Please," Evelyn sighed gratefully. "I fear I'll need to soak for hours to get all this mud off."

As Nell bustled about preparing the bath, she wrangled a couple of footmen to carry the small hip bath into her room. She also enlisted some scullery maids to fill it. Meanwhile, Evelyn attempted to peel off her ruined stockings. The fabric clung stubbornly to her skin, and she winced as she tugged at a particularly stubborn bit.

"Here, let me help you with that, miss," Nell offered, kneeling beside her. With deft fingers, she gently eased the stockings off, revealing Evelyn's mud-streaked legs.

"I don't suppose there's any hope for these?" Evelyn asked, holding up the tattered remains of her stockings.

Nell pursed her lips, examining the fabric critically. "I'm afraid not, miss. They're beyond saving, I'd say."

Evelyn sighed, tossing the ruined stockings aside. "I'm beginning to fear that this position will be harder on my wardrobe than I had considered."

A look of confusion crossed Nell's face at Evelyn's words. "Begging your pardon, miss, but didn't you have a proper governess wardrobe already? Most in your position would have clothes suited for country life."

Evelyn's heart skipped a beat. She'd slipped up, revealing more than she'd intended. Thinking quickly, she forced a rueful smile. "I wasn't always a governess, Nell. I'm afraid I've always had a weakness for pretty things. Practicality wasn't my strong suit."

The maid's expression softened, a hint of understanding in her eyes. "Ah, I see. Well, we'll have to remedy that, won't we? Can't have you ruining all your nice things."

As the last of the servants filed out, leaving the bath steaming invitingly, Evelyn rose from her chair. A sudden chill swept through her, and she shivered, wrapping her arms around herself.

Nell noticed immediately. "Oh, you're freezing, miss! Let's get that fire going properly."

Evelyn watched in silent admiration as Nell knelt before the hearth. With practised ease, the maid coaxed the embers back to life, adding kindling and logs until a cheerful blaze crackled in the grate. The warmth began to seep into the room, and Evelyn felt a pang of envy at Nell's skill.

"There we are," Nell said, dusting off her hands as she stood. "That should warm you up nicely while you bathe."

"Thank you, Nell," Evelyn murmured, her gaze still fixed on the dancing flames. "I must confess, I'm rather in awe of how easily you managed that."

Nell's eyes widened in surprise. "It's nothing special, miss. Just a bit of practice, that's all."

Evelyn nodded, trying to hide her embarrassment. She'd revealed yet another gap in her supposed experience, and she couldn't afford many more such slips.

Evelyn sank into the hot water with a grateful sigh, feeling the warmth seep into her aching muscles. The gentle lapping of the water against the copper tub soothed her frazzled nerves, and she closed her eyes, allowing herself a moment of pure bliss.

"Would you like me to help wash your hair, miss?" Nell's voice broke through her reverie.

Evelyn's eyes fluttered open. "Oh, yes, please. That would be lovely."

As Nell's nimble fingers worked through her tangled locks, Evelyn felt herself relax further. The maid's touch was gentle yet efficient, which made Evelyn feel grateful for the unexpected kindness.

"You've got such beautiful hair, miss," Nell remarked, her voice tinged with admiration. "So thick and such a lovely chestnut colour."

Evelyn hummed in acknowledgement, her mind racing. Here was an opportunity to learn more about the family without arousing suspicion. She chose her words carefully. "That's very kind of you to say, Nell. The twins have rather striking hair as well, don't they?"

"Oh, yes," Nell agreed enthusiastically. "It's quite something to see, especially when the sun catches it just so."

Sensing an opening, Evelyn pressed on. "I wonder, did they inherit that from their mother?"

Nell's hands stilled for a moment before resuming their task. "They did indeed, miss. The late Lady Hastings had the most beautiful hair you've ever seen. A proper halo of red-gold curls, she had."

A small giggle escaped Nell's lips, and Evelyn tilted her head slightly, curious. "What's so amusing?"

"Oh, it's nothing really," Nell said, her voice dropping to a conspiratorial whisper. "It's just... Well, from stories I've heard of his youth, the Baron has always seemed to prefer fair hair, you see."

Evelyn's breath caught in her throat, her mind immediately flashing to the moment the Baron had reached out to brush the mud from her face. She forced herself to keep her voice light and casual. "That's fortunate indeed." She paused, focusing on scrubbing at herself to remove the mud on her neck. "Was it a love match between them, then?"

Evelyn waited, her heart inexplicably racing as Nell paused, considering her question.

"Oh, it was a true romance, miss," Nell sighed wistfully. "The sort you read about in novels. Lady Hastings, she was something special. A true country lass, she was."

Evelyn's fingers tightened imperceptibly on the edge of the tub. "How so?"

"She could speak to the farmers about their crops one moment. Then, she would turn around and charm the finest lords and ladies in a drawing room the next," Nell explained, her voice warm with admiration. "Never put on airs, she didn't. Always had time for everyone, no matter their station."

A curious heaviness settled in Evelyn's chest, her mood souring for reasons she couldn't quite fathom. She frowned, trying to untangle the knot of emotions that had suddenly formed within her.

"I see," she murmured, her voice barely audible over the gentle lapping of the bathwater.

Nell continued to work her fingers through Evelyn's hair, rinsing away the last traces of mud. "There we are, miss. Shall I rinse it once more?"

Evelyn nodded, closing her eyes as Nell poured clean water over her head. The coolness was a welcome distraction from her tumultuous thoughts.

"Thank you, Nell," Evelyn said at last, forcing a smile. "I believe I can manage from here."

"Of course, miss. I'll send the footmen up later to remove the bath," Nell replied, gathering up the soiled clothing. "Is there anything else you need?"

Evelyn shook her head. "No, thank you. You've been most helpful."

As the door closed behind Nell, Evelyn rose from the bath, wrapping herself in a soft robe. She padded across the room to the small mirror perched atop her dresser, sinking onto the stool before it.

Her reflection stared back at her, pale and drawn. Droplets of water clung to her skin, and her damp hair hung in tangled waves around her face. With a sigh, Evelyn reached for her brush, beginning to work through the knots.

As Evelyn brushed her hair, her mind wandered back to the earlier encounter with the Baron. Her hand slowed, the brush hovering mid-stroke as she recalled the way he had looked at her before departing. There had been something in his eyes, a flicker of... what? Concern? Interest? She couldn't quite place it, but the memory made her pulse quicken.

She found herself reliving the moment he had lifted her effortlessly from the mud. His strength had surprised her, his hands firm yet gentle as he'd set her back on her feet. Evelyn's cheeks warmed at the recollection.

Then there was that instant when he'd reached out, his calloused fingers brushing away the mud from her face. The touch had been brief, fleeting, but Evelyn's stomach did a little flip as she remembered it. His grey eyes had locked with hers, and for a heartbeat, the world had seemed to stand still.

Evelyn shook herself, resuming her brushing with renewed vigour. "Don't be foolish," she muttered to her reflection. She'd sworn off men completely, and for good reason. It had been easy enough to keep that vow, especially after giving up Richard.

At the thought of Richard, a familiar ache bloomed in her chest. The pain might have dulled over time, but it hadn't disappeared entirely. Evelyn set down her brush, her hands clenching into fists in her lap.

"Never again," she whispered fiercely, renewing her vow to keep men out of her heart. She'd learned her lesson the hard way, and she wouldn't make the same mistake twice...thrice. No matter how intriguing the Baron might be, she couldn't afford to let her guard down.

That night, as she was preparing for bed, there was a small sound outside of her door. Evelyn, tucked safely into her bed, was reluctant to leave it again. The old manor house was always creaking and groaning as if it were alive, the wind moaning around the corners. It had Evelyn constantly on edge enough as it was. Still, she picked up the small candlestick next to her bed and cautiously set out to investigate.

On opening her door and peering into the hallway, Evelyn saw nothing at first. She was preparing to close the door again when she happened to look down. There, placed carefully just beyond the threshold, were her beautiful blue shoes. They were perfectly cleaned with only a slight dulling of the silk to suggest they were anything other than new.

Chapter 13

Evelyn closed the ledger with a satisfied snap, her eyes flicking between Julia and Augusta. The girls wore matching expressions of bewilderment, though Augusta's brow was furrowed in concentration.

"Well done, both of you," Evelyn said, her voice warm. "Balancing a household budget is no small feat, but you've made excellent progress."

Julia groaned, flopping dramatically onto the settee. "It's dreadfully dull, Miss Bane. When will we ever need to know such things?"

"More often than you might think," Evelyn replied, a wry smile tugging at her lips. She thought of the countless hours she'd spent poring over the Judge's accounts, carefully concealing his less savoury transactions. "A well-managed household is the foundation of a comfortable life."

Augusta straightened in her chair, grey eyes sharp with interest. "Is it very different from managing an estate's finances, Miss Bane?"

"The principles are similar, though the scale is rather different," Evelyn answered, gathering up the papers. "Now, I believe your father has requested you take your afternoon constitutional."

The girls rose, Julia with considerably more enthusiasm than her sister. As they departed, Evelyn tucked the ledger under her arm and made her way towards the housekeeper's domain.

The corridors of Hastings Manor still felt like a maze to Evelyn, but she was slowly learning her way around. She rounded a corner, only to find herself face-to-face with an unfamiliar tapestry. Frowning, she backtracked, trying to retrace her steps.

After several wrong turns, Evelyn finally found herself in the right wing of the house. She knocked on the housekeeper's door, relief washing over her as Mrs. Thorne's voice bade her enter.

"Ah, Miss Bane," the housekeeper said, looking up from her desk. "I trust the lesson went well?"

Evelyn nodded, handing over the ledger. "The girls are making progress, though I fear Julia finds it less than enthralling."

Mrs. Thorne chuckled, a knowing glint in her eye. "That one would rather be outdoors, chasing butterflies or climbing trees. Speaking of which, I believe the Baron mentioned taking them riding this afternoon."

"Yes, he's quite insistent on their physical education," Evelyn replied, a hint of admiration in her voice. "I must admit, I agree with him on that point, even if I'm still adjusting to country life myself."

The housekeeper's expression softened. "It takes time, Miss Bane. You'll find your footing soon enough."

Evelyn chuckled wryly, her mind drifting back to a few days prior. The memory of slipping in the mud, her skirts sodden and heavy, flashed vividly before her eyes. She could almost feel the squelch of wet earth beneath her palms, smell the rich scent of damp soil.

"Find my footing indeed," she muttered, and the housekeeper gave her a knowing look—everyone in the house had seen the muddy footprints and the silty bathwater. "At least I can be grateful the girls didn't witness that particular misadventure," she said, shaking her head. "I'm not sure I could have maintained any semblance of dignity after such a display."

Mrs. Thorne's lips twitched, her eyes glinting with something Evelyn couldn't quite decipher. "I wouldn't be so certain of that, Miss Bane. Just because you didn't see them doesn't mean they didn't see you."

Evelyn blinked, heat rising to her cheeks. "I beg your pardon?"

The housekeeper leaned forward, her voice dropping to a conspiratorial whisper. "Those twins, Miss Bane, they're professionals when it comes to hiding. They know every nook and cranny of this estate, every hedge and hollow. I'd wager they've seen far more than anyone suspects."

"Good heavens," Evelyn murmured, her mind racing. How many times had she thought herself alone, only to have an audience? She cleared her throat, attempting to regain her composure. "Well, I... I appreciate you sharing this information, Mrs. Thorne. It seems I have much to learn about my charges."

The housekeeper nodded, a hint of sympathy in her eyes. "Don't fret, Miss Bane. You'll get the measure of them soon enough."

Evelyn hurried to her room, her mind still reeling from Mrs. Thorne's revelation. She changed into her walking boots, lacing them tightly and smoothing her plain blue day dress. As she made her way to the front door, she steeled herself for whatever the afternoon might bring.

Julia and Augusta were already there, bouncing on their heels with barely contained excitement. Evelyn's heart warmed at their enthusiasm, but it froze when she caught sight of the Baron standing beside them.

"Good afternoon, Miss Bane," he said, his voice gruff.

Evelyn nodded, certain her surprise showed on her face. She'd scarcely seen the man since their muddy encounter, and she'd begun to suspect he was deliberately avoiding her. The thought had brought a mixture of relief and... something else she dared not examine too closely.

"I'll be joining you on your walk today," the Baron announced, his tone brooking no argument.

Evelyn blinked. "That's really not necessary, my lord. I'm quite capable of—"

"I insist," he interrupted, his grey eyes fixed on her. "We can't have you falling down a well or some such nonsense, can we?"

Evelyn stared at him, unsure if he was jesting or not. His face remained impassive, save for a slight twitch at the corner of his mouth. Was that... amusement?

"I assure you, my lord, I have no intention of—"

"Intentions matter little when it comes to accidents, Miss Bane," he said, cutting her off once more. "Shall we?"

He gestured towards the door, and Evelyn was at a loss for words. The girls giggled, clearly delighted by this turn of events, and Evelyn resigned herself to an afternoon of awkward silences and muddy paths.

When she took the girls on her own, they were content to stick to gravel paths and country lanes. Evelyn suspected that the Baron's idea of a walk was very different from her own. As they stepped out into the crisp air, Evelyn couldn't shake the feeling that this walk would be anything but ordinary.

Evelyn watched as Julia and Augusta scampered ahead, their laughter drifting back on the breeze. She envied their carefree spirits, especially as she found herself walking beside the Baron, his presence as imposing as the oak trees lining the path.

"You're dawdling, Miss Bane," the Baron said, his voice gruff. "One would think you've never taken a proper walk before."

Evelyn bit back a sharp retort. "I assure you, my lord, I'm quite capable of keeping pace. Perhaps if you weren't so intent on finding fault with every step I take—"

"Fault?" He arched an eyebrow. "I'm merely observing. Your gait is uneven, and you're not utilising the walking stick properly."

She glanced down at the stick he'd thrust into her hands before they'd left. "I wasn't aware there was a proper way to use a walking stick, my lord."

"Of course there is," he scoffed. "You're holding it all wrong. Here, allow me to demonstrate."

Before Evelyn could protest, the Baron's large hand closed over hers, adjusting her grip on the stick. His touch, though brief, sent an unexpected jolt through her.

"There," he said, stepping back. "Now you won't look like a complete novice."

Evelyn bristled. "I appreciate your concern, my lord, but I assure you I'm quite capable of managing a simple walk without your constant critique."

The Baron's eyes narrowed. "Is that so? Then perhaps you'd care to explain why you're breathing so heavily? We've barely covered a mile."

Evelyn felt heat rise to her cheeks, acutely aware of her quickened pulse. "The air is rather thick today," she said, lifting her chin. "And I'm not accustomed to such... vigorous exercise."

"Clearly," he muttered. "We'll have to remedy that. Can't have you collapsing from exhaustion every time you venture outside the house."

"I have not collapsed once since arriving here," Evelyn protested, her patience wearing thin.

The Baron's lips twitched. "No, but you did take quite a tumble in the mud not long ago. I'd hate for a repeat performance."

Evelyn's steps faltered, her cheeks burning at the memory. "That was... an unfortunate incident. One I don't intend to repeat."

"See that you don't," he said, his tone softening slightly. "The girls have grown quite fond of you. It would be a shame if you were to injure yourself and have to leave."

Evelyn let the Baron's comment pass, but she couldn't help casting a sideways glance at him. His profile was stern, yet there was something almost... protective in his stance. She shook her head, banishing the thought.

As they continued along the path, Evelyn was trying to reconsider her approach. Perhaps she had been too hasty in dismissing his advice. After all, this was his domain, and she was still very much a stranger to country life.

"My lord," she began, her voice softer than before, "I... perhaps I spoke too hastily. I admit, I could use more guidance when it comes to navigating the countryside safely."

The Baron's eyebrows rose, surprise evident in his grey eyes. "Is that so, Miss Bane? I thought you were quite content with your current level of expertise."

Evelyn bit back a retort, forcing herself to remain calm. "The girls have been most helpful, pointing out which plants to avoid and which might cause a rash. But I'm aware there's still much for me to learn."

"Indeed," he nodded, his expression thoughtful. "Very well, Miss Bane. If you're willing to learn, I'm willing to teach."

As they walked, the Baron began pointing out various plants and explaining their properties. Evelyn listened intently, surprised by the depth of his knowledge. She found herself genuinely interested, asking questions and absorbing the information.

"This one here," he said, gesturing to a cluster of delicate white flowers, "is meadowsweet. It's quite useful for treating headaches and fevers."

Evelyn leaned closer, careful not to touch. "It's beautiful. I had no idea so many of these plants had medicinal properties."

The Baron nodded, a hint of approval in his eyes. "There's much to learn from nature, Miss Bane. It's not all about avoiding dangers."

As they continued their walk, Evelyn was starting to relax as the tension between them became easing. She realised that perhaps there was more to the Baron than she had initially thought.

Evelyn's curiosity got the better of her as they walked along the winding path. She glanced at the sturdy walking stick in her hand, then at the Baron's own.

"My lord, if I may ask, why do you insist on carrying these sticks? Surely they're not necessary for every outing?"

The Baron's lips quirked into what might have been a smile. "Ah, Miss Bane, you'd be surprised at their utility." He turned suddenly, calling out to the girls who were skipping ahead. "Julia! Augusta! Come here a moment. Show Miss Bane how one properly uses a good stick."

The twins' faces lit up with excitement. They darted off into the nearby copse, returning moments later with sticks of their own.

"Watch this, Miss Bane!" Julia cried, bounding ahead.

Evelyn watched, bemused, as the girls demonstrated. Augusta planted her stick firmly on the ground, using it to navigate a particularly rocky stretch of path.

"See?" she explained, her voice steady despite the uneven terrain. "It helps keep your balance when the ground's not cooperating."

Julia, meanwhile, had wandered into a nearby meadow. She poked her stick into the lush grass, prodding here and there with surprising care.

"And this," she called back, "is how you find hidden bogs! You don't want to step in one of those by accident—bogs'll swallow you up faster than a poor man with a bowl of soup!"

Evelyn's eyes widened as she watched Julia's stick sink several inches into what had appeared to be solid ground. "Good heavens," she murmured. "I had no idea."

The Baron nodded approvingly at his daughters. "Well done, girls. You see, Miss Bane? These sticks are far more than mere accessories. They're tools for survival in the countryside."

Evelyn looked at her own stick with newfound respect. "I stand corrected, my lord. It seems I have much to learn about country life."

Evelyn's steps faltered as they rounded a bend in the lane. Ahead, a cluster of woolly bodies blocked their path, their bleating filling the air. She instinctively took a step back, her grip tightening on the walking stick.

"Is something the matter, Miss Bane?" the Baron asked, his voice tinged with amusement.

Evelyn swallowed hard, trying to mask her discomfort. "Not at all, my lord. I simply... wasn't expecting to encounter a flock of sheep on our walk."

The Baron's lips twitched. "Ah, yes. Another valuable lesson in country living. These sticks aren't just for walking, you know. They're quite useful for moving along disagreeable animals."

Before Evelyn could respond, the Baron strode forward, gently poking at the nearest sheep with his stick. To her amazement, the animal shuffled aside with little fuss.

"You see?" he called back. "No need for alarm. A firm but gentle touch is all that's required."

Julia and Augusta, who had been watching with barely contained excitement, seized the opportunity. They darted forward, brandishing their sticks like swords.

"Come on, Miss Bane!" Julia cried. "It's ever so much fun!"

Evelyn watched, equal parts horrified and impressed, as the girls fearlessly ran at the sheep. They waved their sticks, urging the animals along with surprising efficiency.

"Hup! Hup!" Augusta called, her usually reserved demeanour forgotten in the excitement of the moment.

The sheep bleated in protest but moved nonetheless, parting like a woolly sea before the twins' determined advance. Evelyn was caught between admiration for their boldness and concern for their safety.

"My lord," she began, her voice tight with worry. "Is it quite safe for them to—"

The Baron cut her off with a chuckle. "They've been doing this since they could walk, Miss Bane. The sheep are more afraid of them than they are of the sheep, I assure you."

As if to prove his point, the last of the flock scurried off the path, leaving it clear for their passage. Julia and Augusta returned, flushed with exertion and triumph.

"Did you see, Miss Bane?" Julia asked, her eyes shining. "That's how it's done in the country!"

Chapter 14

Evelyn couldn't help but chuckle as she watched Julia and Augusta scamper ahead, their walking sticks now transformed into imaginary swords. The girls lunged and parried, their laughter echoing through the countryside.

As Julia swung her stick particularly close to Augusta's head, Evelyn instinctively opened her mouth to chastise them. But she hesitated, her words dying on her lips as she reconsidered.

The Baron, ever observant, raised an eyebrow. "Why did you hesitate, Miss Bane? Surely you don't approve of such reckless behaviour?"

Evelyn took a moment to gather her thoughts, her eyes still on the girls as they continued their mock battle. When she spoke, her voice was quiet but firm.

"I've just realised, my lord, that there might be more than one kind of disagreeable animal out here when they're alone." She turned to face the Baron, meeting his gaze steadily. "Animals that could benefit from a good whacking."

Her eyes flickered meaningfully, and she saw understanding dawn on the Baron's face. His expression shifted, a mix of surprise and something else—perhaps respect?—crossing his features.

"I see," he said, his voice low. "You believe the girls should be prepared to defend themselves?"

Evelyn nodded, relieved that he had grasped her meaning so quickly. "Precisely, my lord. While I would never encourage violence, I believe there's wisdom in being prepared for... unexpected encounters." Instinctively, Evelyn pulled at her sleeves, ensuring that her arms were fully covered—a remnant from her time with the Judge, when her daily life was a struggle to keep evidence of his misdeeds hidden.

The Baron was silent for a moment, his gaze thoughtful as he watched his daughters. When he spoke again, there was a new note of approval in his voice.

"You continue to surprise me, Miss Bane. I'm beginning to think you might have more country sense than I initially gave you credit for."

Evelyn and the Baron walked in silence for a moment, the only sounds the crunch of gravel beneath their feet and the distant laughter of the girls. The quiet stretched between them, not entirely uncomfortable but laden with unspoken thoughts.

Finally, Evelyn gathered her courage and broke the silence. "My lord, does this mean you've reconsidered your stance on the girls' education?" She held her breath, hoping she hadn't overstepped.

The Baron didn't answer immediately. He seemed to be weighing his words carefully. When he did speak, his question caught Evelyn off guard.

"Tell me, Miss Bane, are the girls able to calculate yearly income from tenant leases yet? Or understand how interest on credit works?"

Evelyn blinked, taken aback by the unexpected query. "I... well, we haven't quite reached those topics yet, my lord. But I assure you, they're coming along nicely in their studies."

The Baron's grey eyes fixed on her, his gaze intense. "And how, Miss Bane, can you think social graces are even remotely as important as these more practical matters?"

Evelyn felt her cheeks warm under his scrutiny. She hadn't expected such a direct challenge to her teaching methods. She took a deep breath, gathering her thoughts before responding.

Evelyn took a deep breath, steeling herself for the conversation ahead. She turned to face the Baron, her chin lifted slightly in defiance.

"My lord, if you found so much fault with the way I walked down a country lane, would you want your daughters exposed to the same sort of ridicule when they entered a London drawing room, or when they were presented?"

She watched as the Baron's expression hardened, his jaw clenching visibly. For a moment, she thought he might simply walk away, ending the conversation before it began. But then he spoke, his voice low and firm.

"The girls aren't ever going to London, Miss Bane. And they definitely won't be presented at court."

Evelyn blinked, taken aback by the finality in his tone. She had expected resistance, certainly, but not this outright refusal. She opened her mouth to argue, then closed it again, realising she needed to choose her words carefully.

"But surely, my lord, you can't mean to keep them isolated forever," she said, her voice gentle but insistent. "How will they find husbands, have families?"

Evelyn froze, her words dying on her lips as the Baron stopped abruptly. His face had gone pale, his eyes haunted by some unseen spectre.

"They won't ever marry," he said, his voice sharp as a knife.

Evelyn blinked, certain she had misheard. "I beg your pardon, my lord?"

The Baron's gaze snapped to her, his grey eyes burning with an intensity that made her take a step back. "You heard me, Miss Bane. My daughters will not marry. Not now, not ever."

Confusion and shock warred within Evelyn. She had known the Baron was protective of his girls, but this... this was beyond anything she had imagined. "But... why?" she asked, her voice trembling slightly. "Surely you don't mean to keep them from experiencing love, from having families of their own?"

The Baron's face twisted, a mixture of pain and anger flashing across his features. When he spoke, his words were clipped, each one seeming to cost him dearly. "Because mothers die, Miss Bane. Having children is just too perilous. I won't allow them to take such a risk."

Evelyn felt her blood boiling, her fingers clenching around her walking stick. She took a deep breath, willing herself to remain calm, but the Baron's words had struck a nerve she couldn't ignore.

The Baron turned abruptly, striding away as if the matter was settled. Evelyn wasn't about to let him off so easily. She hurried forward, her skirts swishing as she stepped in front of him, forcing him to meet her gaze.

"My lord," she said, her voice trembling with barely contained fury, "you cannot make such unilateral decisions for your daughters as if they were farmers you can order about, telling them what to plant and how to plough their fields."

The Baron's eyes flashed dangerously. "I can and I will, Miss Bane. I am their father and the lord of this estate."

Evelyn felt her composure slipping. She knew she was overstepping, but she couldn't stop herself. "Being their father and the lord of the estate doesn't make you the master of their entire lives!"

"It does, Miss Bane," the Baron retorted, his voice as cold and unyielding as stone. "It most certainly does."

Evelyn stared at him, aghast. Her heart pounded in her chest, a mixture of fury and disbelief coursing through her veins. She knew she was treading on dangerous ground, but she couldn't stop herself. The words tumbled out before she could rein them in.

"You're not being a father, you're being a tyrant!" she shouted, her voice echoing across the empty field.

As she glared at the Baron, his face seemed to shift and blur. Suddenly, she was no longer looking at James Ayles, but at her own father, his stern countenance etched with disappointment. Then, just as quickly, it morphed into the cruel visage of the Judge, his eyes cold and unforgiving. Evelyn blinked hard, forcing herself back to the present.

"The twins deserve the chance to live their own lives," she continued, her voice thick with emotion. "Not just the narrow path you've set out for them. They should be free to make their own choices, to experience love and loss, joy and heartbreak. That's what living truly means!"

The Baron's face hardened, his grey eyes glinting like steel. "They'll live however I believe best for their survival," he growled. "I won't have them risking their lives for some foolish notion of romance or adventure. You don't understand the dangers, Miss Bane. You can't possibly comprehend what's at stake."

Evelyn felt tears pricking at her eyes, but she blinked them back furiously. Her chest heaved with the effort of containing her emotions, words of defiance dancing on the tip of her tongue.

She wanted to shout at the Baron, to tell him he had no idea what she understood, what she had endured. But the revelation would be too much, too dangerous. She clenched her fists, nails digging into her palms as she fought to keep her secrets locked away.

The Baron glowered at her, his grey eyes stormy with anger and something else—perhaps a flicker of pain? For a moment, they stood frozen, locked in a silent battle of wills.

Suddenly, the Baron's gaze shifted, looking past her. Evelyn turned, following his line of sight. Her heart sank as she spotted Julia and Augusta standing a short distance down the lane, hands clasped tightly together. Their eyes were wide with shock and confusion, darting between their father and their governess.

Evelyn's anger drained away, replaced by a wave of shame. How much had the girls heard? What damage had she done with her outburst? She opened her mouth, desperate to say something, anything, to ease the tension that crackled in the air.

But before she could speak, Julia's voice, small and trembling, broke the silence. "Papa? Miss Bane? Why are you shouting?"

Augusta, ever the more perceptive of the two, tightened her grip on her sister's hand. Her clear grey eyes, so like her father's, were filled with a mixture of worry and understanding far beyond her years.

Evelyn glanced at the Baron, unsure of how to proceed. The anger had faded from his face, replaced by a look of weariness that made him seem suddenly older. He ran a hand through his hair, a gesture that spoke volumes of his inner turmoil.

Evelyn took a deep breath, forcing her emotions under control. She turned back to the Baron, her voice low and steady. "My lord, I would be happy to continue this discussion at another time, but perhaps not in front of the girls. If you're here just to quarrel, we'll be fine without your company."

The Baron blinked, clearly caught off guard by her sudden change in demeanour. For a moment, he seemed unsure how to respond to being so summarily dismissed by a governess. His brow furrowed, and Evelyn half-expected him to argue. But then, to her surprise, he gave a curt nod.

"Yes, quite right," he muttered, his voice gruff. He cleared his throat, addressing the girls. "Julia, Augusta, I need to check on Farmer Hawkins' progress. Miss Bane will see you back to the house."

Without another word, he turned on his heel and strode away. Evelyn watched him go, her anger still simmering beneath the surface. It was infuriating how he could walk away from a heated argument with such grace. His broad shoulders and trim waist cut a handsome figure against the rolling countryside.

She clenched her fists, willing herself not to stare. It wouldn't do to let her gaze linger, especially not with the girls watching. Evelyn turned back to Julia and Augusta, forcing a smile onto her face.

"Come along, girls," she said, her voice only slightly strained. "Let's proceed with our day."

***

James strode across the fallow field, his boots sinking into the soft earth with each determined step. The encounter with Miss Bane still echoed in his mind, her sharp words cutting through his usual stoic demeanour. He clenched his jaw, irritation and something else—something he refused to name—warring within him.

'If you're here just to quarrel, we'll be fine without your company.'

The governess's parting shot rang in his ears. James shook his head, trying to dislodge the memory of her flashing eyes and the defiant tilt of her chin. How had she developed such a razor-sharp tongue? And where did she find the audacity to use it on him, of all people?

He paused atop a small rise, surveying his lands. The spring air was warm and heavy, carrying the scent of fresh earth and new growth. It should have calmed him, as it always did, but today it only served to remind him of Miss Bane's earlier tumble into the mud. The corner of his mouth twitched involuntarily at the memory of her indignant expression.

James frowned, catching himself. This was precisely the problem. Despite her argumentative nature—or perhaps because of it—he found himself seeking out her company at every turn. It was maddening. He had far more important matters to attend to than sparring with an impertinent governess.

And yet...

He couldn't deny the spark of life her presence ignited within him. Their verbal jousts left him feeling more invigorated than he had in years. It was as if she saw through his carefully constructed façade of stern indifference, challenging him at every turn.

James removed his hat and ran a hand through his hair, frustrated by the direction of his thoughts. He needed to focus on his estate, on ensuring his tenants' welfare. Not on deciphering the enigma that was Miss Evelyn Bane.

James sighed heavily, his broad shoulders sagging under the weight of his responsibilities. He turned his gaze to the bottom of the sloping field, where a patch of stubborn weeds awaited his attention. The land there had long been a thorn in his side, its low-lying nature making it prone to waterlogging and difficult to cultivate.

He began his descent, each step deliberate and measured. The soft earth clung to his boots, a constant reminder of the challenges that lay ahead. As he reached the boggy area, James crouched down, running his calloused fingers through the tangle of weeds and damp soil.

Focus, man, he chided himself silently. *This land won't clear itself.*

Determined to banish all thoughts of Miss Bane from his mind, James set to work, measuring the dampness of the soil. His irritation was only compounded because Farmer

Hawkins was meant to be meeting him here, but the man was nowhere to be seen. Company would have been a welcome distraction from the mental torment that Miss Bane inflicted on him.

So engrossed was he in his labour that James failed to notice the sun was not shining as brightly. He toiled on, oblivious to the gathering storm clouds on the horizon, building into a dark, ominous column.

Chapter 15

Evelyn watched the Baron's retreating figure with a mixture of frustration and relief. His constant presence had been both vexing and oddly comforting. She shook her head, banishing such thoughts, and turned her attention back to the girls.

"Miss Evelyn, look how far we've come!" Julia exclaimed, her cheeks flushed with exertion.

Evelyn glanced around, surprised to find herself in unfamiliar surroundings. The path they'd taken wound through a copse of ancient oaks, their gnarled branches stretching overhead. She realised with a start that they had indeed ventured further than ever before.

"I hadn't noticed," she admitted, a hint of pride creeping into her voice. Perhaps she was becoming more accustomed to country life than she'd thought.

Augusta, ever observant, pointed to a gap in the trees. "We're near the canal worksite. Father mentioned they've built a temporary dam."

"Oh, can we go see it?" Julia bounced on her toes, eyes shining with excitement. "Please, Miss Evelyn?"

Evelyn hesitated. The Baron hadn't expressly forbidden them from visiting the worksite, but she wasn't certain he'd approve. Still, it seemed a harmless enough diversion.

"Well, I suppose we could—"

A sudden gust of wind cut her off, whipping her skirts about her legs. Evelyn looked up, her heart sinking as she saw dark clouds gathering on the horizon. The air had taken on that peculiar stillness that often preceded a storm.

"I'm afraid not, girls," she said firmly. "We need to head back immediately."

"But Miss Evelyn—" Julia began to protest.

"No arguments," Evelyn interrupted, her tone brooking no dissent. "Those clouds look ominous, and I'd rather not explain to your father why we're all soaked to the skin."

She ushered the twins back onto the path, quickening their pace. The wind picked up, carrying with it the scent of rain. Evelyn silently cursed her own distraction. How had she not noticed the changing weather?

As they hurried along, she found herself wishing the Baron had stayed with them after all. His steady presence would have been reassuring in the face of the approaching storm. Evelyn shook her head, willing that thought away—she refused to rely on him for something so menial as just making their way home.

Evelyn quickened her pace, urging the girls along as the wind whipped around them with increasing ferocity. The hem of her skirt was already dusted with dirt, but she paid it no mind; her focus solely on getting her charges back to the safety of the manor.

A flash of lightning illuminated the darkening sky, followed by a low rumble of thunder. Julia let out a small yelp, clutching at Evelyn's arm.

"It's all right," Evelyn soothed, though her own heart raced. "We'll be there before you know it."

As they rounded a bend in the lane, Evelyn spotted two figures in the distance, approaching swiftly. Her breath caught in her throat, instinct taking over as she pulled the girls behind her. Who could be out in such weather?

She squinted against the wind, relief flooding through her as recognition dawned. "It's all right, girls," she called over the rising gale. "It's Mr. Smith and Thomas from the house."

The Baron's steward and one of the footmen hurried towards them, concern etched on their faces. Mr. Smith, a thin man with greying whiskers, reached them first. They were both out of breath, clearly having run the whole way from the manor. When they reached Evelyn and the twins, they both bent over double, drawing in great panting breaths. Thomas recovered first, looking behind Evelyn for something.

Evelyn's relief at seeing Mr. Smith and Thomas quickly turned to confusion as Thomas glanced behind her, his brow furrowing.

"Where's the Baron, Miss? Didn't he go walking with you?" Thomas asked, his voice raised to be heard over the wind.

Evelyn frowned, a twinge of guilt pricking at her. She'd been so focused on getting the girls back safely that she'd forgotten about their earlier disagreement. "He'd gone... somewhere," she replied, suddenly realising she had no idea where the Baron had wandered off to. "I'm not entirely sure where."

Augusta stepped forward, shielding her eyes against the grit blown up by the wind. "Father said he was going to Farmer Hawkins' lower field," she stated matter-of-factly.

Evelyn watched as Thomas and Mr. Smith exchanged an alarmed look, their faces paling. The sudden tension in their postures sent a chill down her spine that had nothing to do with the approaching storm.

"What is it?" Evelyn asked, her voice sharp with concern. "What's wrong?"

Evelyn's heart lurched as Mr. Smith cleared his throat, his eyes darting between her and the girls. The wind whipped around them, carrying the first drops of rain.

"Miss Bane," Mr. Smith began, his voice strained, "the dam upstream—it's not holding. Heavy rains have swelled the canal beyond what it can bear."

Evelyn's eyes widened, her mind racing to understand the implications. "But what does that—"

"The Baron," Mr. Smith cut in, his words tumbling out in a rush. "He's down in Hawkins' lower field, right in the path of—" He broke off, casting a worried glance at the girls.

Evelyn's breath caught in her throat as understanding dawned. The Baron was in danger, and he had no idea. She looked at Augusta and Julia, their faces a mixture of confusion and growing fear.

"We need to warn him," Evelyn said, her voice steadier than she felt. "How much time do we have?"

Mr. Smith shook his head, his expression grim. "Not long. The workmanship was shoddy—it could give way any moment."

Evelyn's mind raced. She couldn't leave the girls, but the Baron needed to be warned. She turned to Thomas and Mr. Smith, decision made. "Take the girls back to the house, quickly. I will find the Baron."

"But Miss Evelyn—" Julia began to protest.

"Miss, you don't know the way—"

"Surely you can't—"

"No arguments," Evelyn said firmly, her tone leaving no room for debate. "Go with Thomas and Mr. Smith. Now. You two," she said, turning to Thomas and Mr. Smith. "You can scarcely breathe, let alone run that far. Point me in the right direction, and get the girls back to the house at once."

Thomas and Mr. Smith exchanged a weary look, but knew better than to argue with the steely resolve in Evelyn's eyes. Mr. Smith stepped forward, pointing a shaking finger down the muddy lane.

"Follow this path until you reach the fork, then bear left," he instructed, his voice rasping. "Hawkins' lower field butts up against the canal, just past the old willow stand."

Evelyn committed the directions to memory with a sharp nod. Every second mattered.

Thomas, perhaps sensing the gravity of the situation more keenly than the girls, rallied his spirits. "Well now, which of you young ladies fancies a ride back to the house?" he asked, forcing a jovial tone.

Julia looked uncertainly between Evelyn and Thomas, her eyes wide with fear. Augusta simply stared at Evelyn, her expression unreadable.

"Go on, both of you," Evelyn urged, giving them what she hoped was a reassuring smile. "I'll find your father and we'll be along directly."

With a final nod to Mr. Smith and Thomas, Evelyn turned and took off at a brisk trot down the path, her skirt bunched in her fists. Dimly, Evelyn was aware that she was flashing an awful lot of ankle, but such frivolity didn't matter at the moment. The first fat drops of rain spattered against her face, the wind whipping her hair into a frenzy.

Her heart pounded in her ears, the gravity of the situation crashing over her like the impending storm. The Baron was in grave danger, unaware of the peril bearing down upon him. Evelyn's steps faltered for the briefest moment as the reality of it struck her—if the dam burst, the deluge could easily sweep him away.

Gritting her teeth, she pressed on, her pace increasing to a flat-out run. The path grew muddier underfoot, the rain falling in thick sheets now. Evelyn's breathing came in ragged gasps, her lungs burning, but she dared not slow.

A flash of lightning cracked across the sky, momentarily illuminating her surroundings in stark relief. She squinted against the downpour, finally spying the fork in the road ahead. Veering left as Mr. Smith had instructed, she followed the path as it curved through a dense copse of trees.

The old willow stand loomed ahead, its twisted branches swaying violently in the wind. Evelyn's steps faltered as she spotted the dark shape of the canal cutting across the field beyond. Even from this distance, she could see the swollen waters churning angrily, straining against the makeshift dam.

"Baron!" she screamed, her voice nearly drowned out by the howling storm. "Baron Hastings!"

There was no response, no sign of movement amidst the sheets of rain. Fear gripped her heart in an icy vice. Where was he?

Chapter 16

Evelyn's eyes darted frantically across the rain-lashed field, her heart pounding in her chest. Suddenly, she spotted a figure kneeling in the sodden grass, seemingly oblivious to the tempest raging around him. Relief flooded through her, quickly followed by a surge of frustration.

"James!" she cried out, her voice hoarse from exertion and fear. The use of his Christian name startled her, but there was no time for propriety now.

The Baron's head snapped up at the sound, his expression bewildered as he caught sight of Evelyn racing down the hill towards him. He rose to his feet, his forehead creased in confusion.

Evelyn's feet slipped and slid on the muddy slope as she hurtled towards him. Her lungs burned, her skirts were a sodden mess, but none of that mattered. She had to reach him, had to warn him.

"James!" she called again, her voice cracking. "The dam—it's going to burst!"

As she neared him, her foot caught on a hidden root. Evelyn stumbled, careening towards the Baron with alarming speed. She braced herself for impact, but instead felt strong hands grasping her arms, steadying her.

The Baron held her firmly, his grey eyes wide with surprise and concern. "Miss Bane? What on earth—"

"We have to leave, now!" Evelyn gasped, clutching at his coat. "The dam upstream—it's not holding. This field will be underwater any moment!"

Evelyn felt the Baron's grip tighten on her hand as comprehension dawned in his eyes. Without a word, he turned and began pulling her up the steep incline. The urgency of the moment struck her anew as she stumbled after him, her sodden skirts clinging to her legs, her petticoat completely soaked.

The rain lashed at them mercilessly, turning the ground beneath their feet into treacherous mud. Evelyn's heart pounded in her chest, her breath coming in ragged gasps as they struggled against the slope. She slipped, her feet sliding out from under her, but the Baron's firm grip kept her upright.

"Hold on!" he shouted over the howling wind, his voice barely audible above the storm.

Evelyn gritted her teeth, pushing herself to keep pace with his longer strides. The Baron moved with surprising agility, his powerful frame seemingly unhindered by the challenging terrain. She marvelled at his strength as he hauled them both up the slippery bank, his hand never loosening its hold on hers.

A deafening crack rent the air, causing Evelyn to falter. She glanced back instinctively, though the dam was acres away. A strange silence seemed to follow for a moment.

"Don't look back!" he commanded, his voice gruff with exertion. "Keep moving!"

Evelyn turned her attention back to the treacherous climb, her legs burning with the effort. The Baron's steady presence beside her was oddly comforting, despite the dire circumstances. She found herself grateful for his unwavering strength as they scrambled up the muddy slope, the roar of the impending flood growing louder behind them.

Evelyn's lungs burned as she and the Baron finally crested the hill. Her legs gave way beneath her, and she collapsed onto the sodden grass, gasping for air. Beside her, she heard the Baron's laboured breathing as he too sank to the ground.

For a moment, all Evelyn could focus on was the pounding of her heart and the rain pelting her face. Then, a deep rumbling sound caught her attention. She pushed herself up onto her elbows, her eyes widening in disbelief.

A massive wall of murky water came crashing through the field below, obliterating everything in its path. The sheer force of it was terrifying, uprooting trees and sweeping away fences as if they were mere twigs. Evelyn watched, transfixed, as the torrent engulfed the very spot where the Baron had been standing just minutes ago.

The enormity of what they'd just escaped hit her like a physical blow. She turned to look at the Baron, who was staring at the destruction with an unreadable expression. His hair was plastered to his forehead, rivulets of water running down his face and neck.

Evelyn opened her mouth to speak, but found she had no words. The roar of the flood and the pounding rain filled the silence between them. She felt a sudden, overwhelming exhaustion wash over her, and she flopped back onto the grass.

The rain continued to pour down, soaking her to the bone, but Evelyn found she didn't care. They were alive. That was all that mattered. She closed her eyes, letting the rain wash over her face, too drained to even consider moving.

Evelyn lay on the sodden grass, her chest heaving as she tried to catch her breath. The roar of the flood still echoed in her ears, a stark reminder of how close they'd come to disaster. She turned her head, blinking away the raindrops that clung to her lashes, to find the Baron staring at her with an expression she couldn't quite decipher.

"You saved me," he said, his voice barely audible above the storm. There was a note of disbelief in his tone, as if he couldn't quite fathom what had just transpired.

A sudden wave of relief washed over Evelyn, bringing with it an unexpected bout of giddiness. She felt laughter bubbling up in her chest, born of sheer joy at being alive. Before she could stop herself, a small chuckle escaped her lips.

"Well, I could hardly let anything happen to you, could I?" she said, her voice light despite her exhaustion. "I'd have to find a new job otherwise."

For a moment, the Baron simply stared at her, his grey eyes wide with surprise. Then, to Evelyn's astonishment, a huff of laughter escaped him. It was a short, gruff sound, but it transformed his face entirely. The usual stern set of his jaw softened, and the lines around his eyes crinkled in a way she'd never seen before.

"I suppose you would," he replied, a hint of amusement in his voice.

Evelyn felt a warmth bloom in her chest at the sight of his lightened expression. It occurred to her that she'd never heard him laugh before, and the effect was rather striking. The scar on his face seemed less pronounced, his features softer and more approachable.

For a moment, they simply lay there, gazing at each other in delighted relief. The rain continued to pour down, soaking them to the bone, but Evelyn found she didn't mind. There was something surprisingly intimate about this shared moment of survival, their usual barriers washed away by the storm.

The Baron's grey eyes locked onto hers, and Evelyn inhaled sharply, unable to breathe for a moment. His gaze was intense, filled with an emotion she'd never seen in him before. He tilted slightly towards her, eyes fixed on her lips, which she licked reflexively. He followed the motion and his pupils dilated slightly. For a heart-stopping moment, she thought he might kiss her. More alarming still was the realisation that she wanted him to.

Her heart pounded, a heady mixture of lingering danger and sudden excitement coursing through her veins. A wild, inappropriate thought flashed through her mind—if he were to kiss her, she knew she would grasp him by the collar, pulling him closer. The very idea sent a shiver down her spine that had nothing to do with her drenched clothes.

The moment stretched, taut with possibility. Evelyn was holding her breath, caught between propriety and desire. But then, as quickly as it had come, the moment passed. The Baron blinked, seeming to come back to himself. He cleared his throat, the sound barely audible over the pounding rain.

Instead of the kiss that Evelyn had half-feared, half-hoped for, the Baron pushed himself to his feet. He extended a hand to her, his expression once again unreadable.

"We should get back to the house," he said, his voice gruff. "The girls will be worried."

Evelyn nodded, trying to ignore the twinge of disappointment that tugged at her heart. She placed her hand in his, allowing him to help her to her feet. As she stood, she found herself mere inches from him, close enough to see the droplets of rain clinging to his eyelashes.

The Baron's dark hair curled slightly in the rain, falling just over his collar in a way that was utterly charming to Evelyn. Beneath his sharp nose, his lips curved perfectly, sharp as if they'd been cut with a sculptor's knife.

Swallowing hard, Evelyn pulled back, her heart still racing from the intensity of the moment. She averted her gaze, focusing on the sodden grass beneath her feet as they began to turn towards the manor. The adrenaline that had propelled her down the hill seemed to have deserted her entirely, leaving her limbs feeling like lead.

As they took their first steps, Evelyn's legs gave a little wobble. She gritted her teeth, determined not to show any further weakness. The Baron, however, noticed her unsteadiness immediately. Without a word, he offered his arm, his grey eyes watching her with an expression that bordered on concern.

Evelyn stared at the proffered arm dubiously. Part of her bristled at the idea of being seen as some delicate flower in need of assistance. She was no wilting violet, after all, but as she gazed up at the long trek back to the house, practicality won out over pride. With a small nod of acquiescence, she placed her hand on his elbow.

The Baron seemed pleased by her acceptance, a ghost of a smile tugging at the corners of his mouth. To Evelyn's surprise, he gently covered her hand on his elbow with one of his own. The warmth of his palm seeped through her rain-soaked glove, sending an unexpected shiver down her spine.

As they began their slow ascent, Evelyn was hyper-aware of every point of contact between them. The solid strength of his arm beneath her hand, the gentle pressure of his palm atop hers, the occasional brush of his coat against her side as they walked. It was a curiously intimate arrangement, one that left her feeling both comforted and slightly flustered.

As they trudged up the muddy path, the rain slowly easing to a gentle patter, the Baron broke the silence. "I must say, Miss Bane, I'm rather astonished," he said, his voice a low rumble. "I never imagined you'd come all that way to save me. I didn't think you had it in you."

Evelyn felt a flash of indignation at his words. She turned her head to look at him, narrowing her eyes. "Oh, really? And why is that, my lord? Because I'm some delicate flower from London who can't handle a bit of mud?"

The Baron's eyebrows rose, clearly taken aback by her sharp retort. Evelyn pressed on, unable to contain herself. "You always act as if I'm some damsel in distress, incapable of handling the slightest difficulty. But if I recall correctly, it was you who was the damsel in distress today, not I."

For a moment, the Baron stared at her, his grey eyes wide with surprise. Then, to Evelyn's astonishment, a deep chuckle rumbled from his chest. It was a rich, warm sound that sent an unexpected thrill through her.

"I suppose you're right," he admitted, a hint of amusement in his voice. "I was indeed the damsel in this particular scenario. And you, Miss Bane, were my most unlikely knight in shining armour."

Evelyn felt a surge of triumph at his words, along with a peculiar warmth in her chest. She lifted her chin, unable to suppress a small smile. "Well," she allowed, magnanimous in her triumph, "a knight in sodden cotton at any rate."

Evelyn's legs felt like lead as she trudged alongside the Baron, their pace slowed to accommodate her exhaustion. Despite her earlier bravado, the adrenaline had long since faded, leaving her drained and aching. She was grateful for the Baron's consideration, though she'd never admit it aloud.

The rain had eased to a light drizzle, but the air remained heavy with moisture. Thunder rumbled ominously in the distance, a reminder that their reprieve might be short-lived. Dark clouds loomed overhead, threatening to unleash another deluge at any moment.

For a while, they walked in companionable silence. Evelyn felt oddly comforted by the Baron's steady presence beside her. His arm remained a solid support under her hand, his grip on her fingers firm but gentle. She stole a glance at his profile, noting the set of his jaw and the distant look in his eyes. He seemed lost in thought, perhaps contemplating the near-disaster they'd just escaped.

Evelyn shivered suddenly, a chill running through her despite the warm spring day. Her sodden clothes clung to her skin, making her feel clammy and uncomfortable. She tried to suppress the tremor, not wanting to appear weak or fragile in front of the Baron.

But James noticed. Without a word, he stopped walking and began to shrug off his jacket. Evelyn's eyes widened in surprise.

"My lord, what are you doing? You needn't—"

He ignored her protests, draping the garment around her shoulders. The jacket was massive on her petite frame, enveloping her in warmth. It was a light wool with a satin lining, mercifully dry on the inside. More importantly, it radiated heat from the Baron's body, instantly chasing away the chill that had settled in her bones.

Despite her initial objections, Evelyn found herself snuggling into the jacket gratefully. The scent of sandalwood and something uniquely James surrounded her, oddly comforting. She pulled it tighter around herself, relishing the warmth.

When she glanced up at the Baron, she found him watching her with a decidedly smug expression. His grey eyes sparkled with amusement, a small smirk playing at the corners of his mouth. Evelyn felt her cheeks warm, and she wasn't entirely sure it was just from the jacket.

Evelyn tried to keep her gaze fixed on the muddy path ahead, but her eyes seemed to have a mind of their own. They kept darting towards the Baron, now clad only in his waistcoat and shirtsleeves. She chided herself for her impropriety, yet found it increasingly difficult to look away.

The residual rain had begun to dampen his linen shirt, causing it to cling to his broad shoulders and well-muscled arms. Evelyn caught herself admiring the way the fabric draped over his arms, showing the solid muscles beneath as he walked, revealing hints of the strength that lay beneath. She quickly averted her eyes, heat rising to her cheeks.

But her resolve was weak, and soon enough, she found herself stealing another glance. The Baron's dark hair was tousled by the wind and rain, giving him a roguish appearance that was quite at odds with his usual stern demeanour. A droplet of water traced a path down his neck, disappearing beneath his collar, and Evelyn found herself following its journey with far too much interest.

She bit her lip, suppressing a smile at her own audacity. Who would have thought that the countryside could offer such... admirable scenery? The thought nearly made her laugh out loud, and she had to disguise the sound as a cough.

The Baron turned to her, concern etched on his features. "Are you all right, Miss Bane?"

Evelyn nodded quickly, not trusting herself to speak. She pulled his jacket tighter around herself, partly for warmth, but mostly to hide her flushed cheeks. As they continued their trek back to the house, Evelyn couldn't help but think that perhaps country life had its merits after all.

Chapter 17

As the manor finally came into view, Evelyn felt a wave of relief wash over her. The sight of the grand house, with its sturdy stone walls and inviting windows, was a balm to her weary soul. Even from this distance, she could see the front door standing wide open, a beacon of warmth and safety.

Mrs. Turnbell, the housekeeper, stood at the threshold, waving the edge of her apron in a gesture of welcome. Evelyn's heart swelled with gratitude at the sight. The promise of warm tea and dry, clean clothing was such a relief that Evelyn felt renewed vigour as she walked.

She glanced at the Baron, wondering if he felt the same. His expression was inscrutable as always, but she thought she detected a hint of relief in the set of his shoulders. Perhaps he, too, was grateful for the sight of home.

The moment they reached the door, Mrs. Turnbell's eyes widened, taking in their bedraggled state. "Good heavens!" she exclaimed, then turned to shout into the house. "Mary! Fetch hot water for baths at once! Thomas, bring tea to the drawing room! And someone find dry clothes for Miss Bane!"

The house erupted into a flurry of activity, servants scurrying to and fro in response to Mrs. Turnbell's barked orders. Evelyn felt a rush of gratitude for the efficiency of the household staff.

Before she could fully process the commotion, a blur of movement caught her eye. Julia and Augusta came bounding down the stairs, their faces alight with relief and joy.

"Father! Miss Bane!" Julia cried, her voice trembling with emotion. "We were so worried!"

Augusta, usually more reserved, was close on her sister's heels. "What happened? Are you both all right?"

Evelyn felt a warmth bloom in her chest at the sight of the girls. Despite her exhaustion, she managed a smile. "We're quite all right, dears. Just a bit wet and muddy."

The Baron, to Evelyn's surprise, opened his arms to his daughters. They rushed into his embrace, and for a moment, Evelyn saw a softness in his expression that took her breath away. It was gone in an instant as he gently but firmly disentangled himself from the girls.

"Now, off you go," he said, his tone brooking no argument. "Miss Bane and I need to get dry and warm. We'll explain everything later."

The girls nodded, casting one last concerned look at Evelyn before hurrying away. As they disappeared up the stairs, Evelyn felt a twinge of longing. How lovely it must be, she thought, to have such affection waiting for you at home.

Evelyn began to shrug off the Baron's jacket, her fingers fumbling from the cold. Before she could remove it, however, the Baron's hand shot out, gently catching her wrist.

"Keep it on until you get upstairs," he said, his voice gruff but not unkind. "My valet can retrieve it later."

Warmth bloomed in Evelyn's chest at this unexpected kindness. She offered him a small, grateful smile, feeling suddenly shy. "Thank you, my lord," she murmured, pulling the jacket closer around her shoulders.

Turning towards the grand staircase, Evelyn began to trudge upwards, her sodden skirts heavy and clinging around her legs. She had only managed a few steps when the Baron's voice stopped her abruptly.

"Miss Bane," he called, his tone oddly hesitant. "You were wrong, you know."

Evelyn froze, disbelief coursing through her. Surely he didn't want to argue at a moment like this? She turned back, an incredulous look on her face, ready to deliver a sharp retort.

To her surprise, the Baron's expression was not one of confrontation. Instead, he seemed to be fighting back a smile, his grey eyes twinkling with barely suppressed amusement.

"I never thought you were a damsel in distress," he said, his lips quirking upwards. "A distressing damsel, perhaps, but never one in distress."

Evelyn's mouth fell open in shock, her tired mind struggling to process this unexpected jest. For a moment, she simply stared at him, utterly flabbergasted. Then, despite her exhaustion and the lingering tension of their near-disaster, she felt laughter bubbling up inside her.

***

James trudged up the stairs, his boots leaving a trail of muddy water in his wake. He pushed open the door to his dressing room, where Johnson, his valet, awaited him with an expression of barely concealed horror.

"My lord! You're soaked to the bone!"

James grunted in response, allowing Johnson to fuss over him as he peeled off his sodden coat. His mind whirled with the day's events, replaying the moment Evelyn had appeared on the crest of the hill, her hair wild and her eyes blazing with determination.

Johnson tutted as he wrestled with James's waterlogged boots. "What on earth possessed you to be out in such weather, my lord?"

James barely heard him. He was lost in the memory of Evelyn's voice, urgent and breathless as she warned him of the impending flood. The way she'd grabbed his arm, her fingers digging into his sleeve as she pulled him to safety.

"My lord?" Johnson's voice cut through his reverie. "Are you quite all right?"

James blinked, realising he'd been staring blankly at the wall. "Yes, yes. Just... thinking."

He shook his head, trying to clear it of the image of Evelyn's face, flushed with exertion and rain. He'd never seen anyone look so... alive. So magnificent. The thought made him uncomfortable, a warmth spreading through his chest that had nothing to do with the dry clothes Johnson was now helping him into.

"I've never seen anything like it," he muttered, more to himself than to Johnson.

"Like what, my lord?"

James waved a hand dismissively. "Nothing. It's been a long day."

As Johnson continued to fuss over him, James found his thoughts drifting back to Evelyn. He'd underestimated her, he realised. She was made of sterner stuff than he'd given her credit for. The way she'd raced across the fields, heedless of the danger to herself...

He frowned, a strange mixture of admiration and unease settling in his stomach. It was... unsettling, this newfound respect for her. He wasn't sure what to make of it.

James paced his bedroom restlessly once he was safely in his quilted dressing gown. The fire had been made up and flickered warmly behind the screen. His mind kept returning to the image of Evelyn, hair plastered to her face, eyes wild with urgency as she'd warned him of the impending danger.

He'd been wrong about her. Damnably, infuriatingly wrong.

A wry smile tugged at his lips. If a pampered London lady could show such unexpected mettle, perhaps he ought to consider yielding a little himself. Clearly, Evelyn wasn't the weak, simpering woman he'd initially taken her for.

James paused by the window, gazing out at the rain-lashed grounds. There was more to her than met the eye, he was certain of it now. No ordinary governess would have risked life and limb as she had. But whatever secrets she might be harbouring, he found himself disinclined to pry. For now, at least.

A sudden thought struck him, and James felt the blood drain from his face. If not for Evelyn's actions, his daughters might well be orphans at this very moment. The realisation hit him like a physical blow, leaving him breathless.

He owed her a debt he could never hope to repay. The thought was unsettling, to say the least. James Ayles, Baron Hastings, was not a man accustomed to owing anyone anything.

And yet...

The magnitude of what might have been weighed heavily upon him. His girls, left alone in the world, just as he had been. The very idea sent a shudder through him.

James stood at the window, his reflection ghostly in the rain-streaked glass. The storm raged on, but his thoughts were consumed by the woman who had braved its fury to save him.

Evelyn. She was an enigma, this governess who had arrived on his doorstep with her London airs and seeming distaste for country life. Yet beneath that polished exterior lay a core of steel he hadn't anticipated. A woman who valued her independence, who wasn't afraid to speak her mind or take action when it mattered most.

He admired that about her, he realised with a start. It was a quality he hadn't encountered often in the women of his acquaintance, who were more concerned with social niceties and finding suitable matches. Evelyn was different. She had come here to make her own way in the world, to earn her own living. And now, she had saved his life without a moment's hesitation.

James's hands clenched at his sides. He owed her everything, and the weight of that debt sat uneasily upon his shoulders. As he watched the rain lash against the windowpane, a resolve began to form within him. He would find a way to repay her, no matter how long it took.

It wasn't just about settling a debt; it was about acknowledging the worth of a woman who had proven herself far more capable and courageous than he had ever given her credit for.

The question was, how? What could he possibly offer that would be commensurate with what she had done? Money seemed crass, a mere pittance in the face of such bravery. No, it would have to be something more meaningful, something that spoke to the independent spirit he now recognised in her.

James turned from the window, his mind whirling with possibilities. Whatever form his repayment took, he was determined to see it through. Evelyn deserved no less.

Chapter 18

Over the next few days, Evelyn noticed a marked change in the Baron's demeanour. His customary gruffness seemed to have softened, replaced by a gentler manner that caught her off guard.

When they passed in the hallways, he no longer averted his gaze but offered a nod of acknowledgement. He invited Evelyn to dine with him and the girls, a shocking thing for a servant, but a welcome change to eating alone in her room.

This shift both pleased and puzzled Evelyn. She found herself warming to his newfound kindness, though a part of her remained wary, unsure of its permanence. Still, she decided to seize the opportunity to bridge the gap between them.

One afternoon, as she prepared for her literature lesson with Julia and Augusta, Evelyn took a deep breath and approached the Baron in his study.

"My lord," she began, her voice steady despite her nerves, "I wondered if you might like to observe our lesson today. We're studying Shakespeare's 'Julius Caesar'."

The Baron looked up from his papers, surprise evident in his grey eyes. After a moment's hesitation, he nodded. "I'd be... interested to see how you conduct your lessons, Miss Bane."

In the music room, Julia and Augusta's eyes widened at the sight of their father. Evelyn gave them an encouraging smile as she began the lesson.

"Now, girls, let's continue where we left off. Augusta, would you read Brutus's soliloquy?"

As Augusta's clear voice filled the room, Evelyn glanced at the Baron. His face was impassive, but his eyes were fixed intently on his daughter.

Julia, ever the performer, threw herself into the dramatic scenes with gusto. When it came time to act out Caesar's assassination, she brandished an imaginary dagger with such enthusiasm that Evelyn couldn't help but laugh.

"Et tu, Brute?" Julia cried, collapsing to the floor with theatrical flair.

Even the Baron's lips twitched in amusement.

Augusta, for her part, seemed more interested in the historical aspects. "Miss Bane, is it true that the real Caesar was stabbed twenty-three times?"

"Indeed it is," Evelyn replied, impressed by Augusta's curiosity. "The play takes some liberties with history, but that detail is accurate."

As the lesson progressed, Evelyn found herself stealing glances at the Baron. His presence, once intimidating, now felt almost... comfortable. When their eyes met, she saw something warm and approving in his gaze that made her heart skip a beat.

Evelyn couldn't help but notice the Baron leaning towards her, his voice low as he spoke. "I've always admired Roman history," he confided, a rare spark of enthusiasm lighting his eyes.

She turned to him, one eyebrow arched in amusement. A wry smile tugged at the corners of her mouth as she regarded him. "I never would have guessed, my lord," she replied, her tone dry as dust. "Your daughters are named Julia and Augusta, your dogs are Brutus and Caesar, and I have it on good authority that your favourite stallion is named Nero."

The Baron blinked, taken aback by her astute observation. For a moment, Evelyn feared she'd overstepped, but then a low chuckle rumbled from his chest. It was a rich, warm sound that sent an unexpected shiver down her spine.

"You're more observant than I gave you credit for, Miss Bane," he said, his grey eyes twinkling with amusement. "I suppose I'm not as subtle as I thought."

"Perhaps not, my lord," she agreed, her own smile widening. "But it's refreshing to see such passion for history. It's a subject often overlooked in favour of more... fashionable pursuits."

The Baron nodded, his expression growing thoughtful. "Indeed. There's much to be learned from the past, Miss Bane. Triumphs and follies alike."

Their eyes met, and Evelyn felt a sudden spark of connection. For a brief moment, the barriers between them—of class, of circumstance, of their respective roles—seemed to fade away. They were simply two people sharing a mutual interest, a fleeting understanding. Strangely, Evelyn felt as if he were inviting her to confide something, to clear the murkiness of her own past. Even stranger was that Evelyn was sorely tempted to do so.

There was a sudden silence in the music room, which drew Evelyn back to reality. Turning her attention back to the girls, Evelyn clapped politely, and the Baron followed suit.

"Miss Bane," Julia chirped, her eyes bright with excitement, "we're still going to read Antony and Cleopatra next, aren't we? You promised!"

Evelyn's smile faltered as she felt the Baron's gaze boring into her. She turned to meet his eyes, her chin lifting slightly. "Of course," she said, her voice steady. "It's an important part of history, after all."

She hoped the emphasis on the historical aspect would appease the Baron, but his frown only deepened. Evelyn's heart sank, but she refused to show her discomfort.

Julia, oblivious to the tension, twirled around the room, her arms outstretched. "I've heard it's terribly romantic," she sighed dreamily. "Oh, I hope to have a great romance like that one day!"

Augusta rolled her eyes. "It's hardly romantic if everyone dies," she pointed out pragmatically.

Evelyn opened her mouth to respond, but the Baron's voice cut through the room, low and controlled. "Miss Bane, a word in the hall, if you please."

Evelyn's stomach clenched, but she nodded gracefully. "Of course, my lord," she said, following him out of the room.

As the door closed behind them, Evelyn steeled herself for the confrontation. She'd known this moment would come eventually, but she'd hoped to have more time to prove herself before facing the Baron's disapproval. Now, standing in the dim hallway, she felt acutely aware of the precariousness of her position.

Evelyn's heart raced as she faced the Baron in the dimly lit hallway. His grey eyes, which had been so warm mere moments ago, now held a steely glint that made her breath catch in her throat. She straightened her spine, determined not to show any weakness.

The Baron took a deep breath, his nostrils pinched. When he spoke, his voice was low and controlled. "Miss Bane, I must ask you: why do you feel the need to blatantly disregard my instructions on filling my daughters' heads with romantic nonsense?"

Evelyn felt her cheeks flush with indignation. She lifted her chin, meeting his gaze squarely. "With all due respect, my lord, I am not filling their heads with anything. Your daughters are intelligent, thoughtful young women, fully capable of forming their own opinions."

The Baron's eyebrows shot up, clearly taken aback by her forthright response. Evelyn pressed on, her voice gaining strength. "I am merely providing them with a well-rounded education, which includes literature and history. It would be remiss of me to exclude such important works simply because they contain elements of romance."

She watched as the Baron's expression shifted, a mix of frustration and something else—perhaps grudging respect—flitting across his features. Evelyn held her ground, her heart pounding in her ears as she awaited his response.

Evelyn watched as the Baron's mouth opened, then closed again without a word. His brow furrowed, and she sensed his internal struggle. Seizing the moment of hesitation, she pressed on, her voice steady despite her racing heart.

"My lord, I fear you're fighting a losing battle. You cannot keep your daughters sheltered forever, nor can you protect them from the realities of life by simply withholding information."

The Baron's eyes narrowed, but Evelyn refused to back down. She took a deep breath and continued, her words measured and clear.

"The more rigid and controlling you are, the more likely you are to lose them entirely. They will forge their own paths when they're able, with or without your blessing."

She watched as surprise flickered across the Baron's face, his stern expression faltering. Evelyn felt a surge of courage, emboldened by his silence.

"Consider this, my lord: How will you stop your daughters from simply eloping when they decide that's the only way to get what they want?"

The Baron's eyes widened, and Evelyn pressed onward. "Listen to me," she said with her voice lowered, but a bit of a glint in her eye. "As the daughter of a strict father, I left home at the first opportunity that presented itself, and I regretted it bitterly very quickly. I had nowhere to turn because I'd burned my bridges."

Evelyn's heart pounded as she realised the weight of her words. She'd revealed far more than she'd intended, and now the Baron's piercing gaze seemed to see right through her carefully constructed façade.

The Baron tilted his head, his grey eyes narrowing as he considered her words. The silence stretched between them, thick and heavy. Evelyn felt her cheeks grow warm under his scrutiny, her earlier boldness evaporating like morning dew.

She pressed her lips together, determined not to let any more slip. The urge to explain herself, to justify her past actions, bubbled up within her, but she ruthlessly suppressed it. She'd already said too much.

The Baron's expression remained unreadable, but there was a new intensity in his gaze that made Evelyn's skin prickle. She felt exposed, as if he could see every secret she'd been trying so desperately to hide.

Evelyn shifted her weight from one foot to the other, fighting the urge to fidget under his unwavering stare. The hallway suddenly felt too small, too confining. She longed to flee, to retreat to the safety of her room and compose herself, but she knew she couldn't. Not without the Baron's dismissal.

As the silence stretched on, Evelyn found herself unable to meet his eyes any longer. She lowered her gaze to the floor, studying the intricate pattern of the carpet as if it held the answers to all her problems.

Evelyn held her breath, waiting for the Baron's response. The silence stretched on, each second feeling like an eternity. Just as she thought she might burst from the tension, the Baron finally spoke.

"Miss Bane," he said, his voice low and measured, "I thank you for speaking your mind, as always. Your opinion is... duly noted."

Evelyn's heart leapt at his words, hope blossoming in her chest. Perhaps he had truly listened, perhaps he would—

"However," the Baron continued, his tone cooling, "I think we've all had quite enough learning for one day. Your services are not required further this afternoon. You are free to go."

The dismissal stung like a physical blow. Evelyn felt her cheeks flush with a mixture of embarrassment and disappointment. She had dared to hope, for one brief moment, that she had made a breakthrough. That the Baron had seen the wisdom in her words. But no—he was sending her away, brushing off her concerns as easily as one might swat away an irritating fly.

Evelyn swallowed hard, fighting to maintain her composure. She would not let him see how deeply his dismissal had affected her. With a stiff nod, she turned away, her back straight and her head held high.

As she walked down the hallway, each step echoing in the oppressive silence, Evelyn felt a weight settle in her chest. She had overstepped, revealed too much of herself, and for what? To be dismissed like a recalcitrant child? The urge to look back, to see if the

Baron was watching her retreat, was almost overwhelming. Evelyn resisted, keeping her gaze fixed firmly ahead. She would not give him the satisfaction of seeing her falter.

Evelyn made her way to her room, her steps heavy and her mind in turmoil. The Baron's dismissal echoed in her ears, a stinging reminder of her precarious position. She felt off-kilter, as if the ground beneath her feet had suddenly shifted.

As she reached for the door handle, Evelyn took a deep breath, trying to compose herself. She longed for the solitude of her room, a moment to gather her thoughts and steady her nerves.

The door swung open, and Evelyn nearly jumped out of her skin. There, perched on her bed like two inquisitive birds, sat Julia and Augusta. Evelyn blinked, momentarily stunned. How on earth had they managed to beat her here?

Before she could voice her surprise, Julia launched herself across the room. The girl's arms wrapped around Evelyn's waist, nearly knocking the wind out of her.

"Miss Bane!" Julia cried, her voice muffled against Evelyn's dress. "We were so worried!"

Evelyn instinctively brought her arms up to return the embrace, her heart warming despite her tumultuous emotions. She looked over Julia's head to Augusta, who remained seated on the bed, her grey eyes—so like her father's—fixed intently on Evelyn's face.

"Are you in trouble, Miss Bane?" Augusta asked, her voice quiet but direct.

Evelyn felt a lump form in her throat. She gently disentangled herself from Julia's embrace and moved further into the room, closing the door behind her. How could she answer Augusta's question when she wasn't entirely sure herself?

"I'm not certain," Evelyn admitted, sinking into the chair by her small writing desk. "Your father and I had a... disagreement about your education."

Evelyn watched as Julia and Augusta exchanged a meaningful glance, their young faces suddenly serious. She felt a flicker of unease at the shift in their demeanour.

Julia bit her lip, hesitating for a moment before speaking. "Miss Bane, Father... he's been different ever since the fire."

Evelyn blinked, taken aback by this unexpected turn in the conversation. Her mind raced, trying to process this new information. She leaned forward, lowering her voice instinctively. "How so?" she asked, her curiosity overriding her usual caution.

The twins shared another look, a silent communication passing between them. Evelyn felt a pang of envy at their closeness, even as she waited with bated breath for their response.

It was Augusta who finally spoke, her grey eyes - so like her father's - filled with a sadness that seemed far too old for her young face. "Before, he always smiled, especially at Mother. Now..." She trailed off, her brow furrowing as she searched for the right words.

"Now, Father is so serious. He has no time for stories or anything fun," Julia finished for her sister, her usually cheerful voice subdued.

Evelyn felt her heart constrict at the girls' words. The image of the stern, aloof man she'd come to know clashed with the one they described - a smiling, easy-going father.

Evelyn's heart ached for the girls, their words painting a vivid picture of the man their father had once been. She longed to know more, to unravel the mystery of what had changed him so dramatically. But as she opened her mouth to ask, she caught herself. It wouldn't be right to pry into such personal matters, especially not from the Baron's own children. Moreover, she didn't want them to relive anything traumatic.

Instead, she took a deep breath and smiled gently at Julia and Augusta. "Your father loves you both very much," she said softly, her voice filled with conviction. "Everything he does, every decision he makes, is because he wants what's best for you. Even if we don't always understand or agree with his methods."

The girls looked at her, their young faces a mixture of hope and uncertainty. Evelyn reached out, giving each of their hands a gentle squeeze. "Now, I think it's best if you two run along. I'm sure you have other lessons to attend to."

With a bit of reluctance, Julia and Augusta nodded and made their way out of the room. As the door closed behind them, Evelyn let out a long, weary sigh. She sank back into her chair, her mind whirling with all she'd learned.

Chapter 19

The afternoon stretched on, long and quiet. Evelyn tried to occupy herself with reading, but found she couldn't focus on the words. Her thoughts kept drifting back to the Baron, to the fire, to the man he'd been before. She found herself watching the clock, waiting for the usual summons to dinner.

But as the hands of the clock ticked on and the sky outside her window darkened, no summons came. The realisation settled over her like a heavy blanket. Evelyn sat heavily on the edge of her bed, her shoulders slumping. She'd pushed too far, said too much. Now, it seemed, she was to be excluded from the family meal.

Evelyn's thoughts were interrupted by a gentle knock at the door. Her heart leapt, hoping for a moment that it might be the Baron, come to apologise or at least explain.

She sprang to her feet eagerly, but when she called out, "Come in," it was Nell who entered, bearing a tray of food. The sight of the tray confirmed Evelyn's fears. She was being excluded from the family dinner. Her stomach twisted, and she felt her eyes prick with unshed tears.

Nell set the tray down on the small table by the window, then turned to Evelyn with a concerned look. "Is everything all right, Miss Bane? You look quite upset."

Evelyn tried to smile, but it felt more like a grimace. "I'm fine, Nell. Thank you for bringing the tray."

Nell wasn't fooled. She stepped closer, her brow furrowed with worry. "Begging your pardon, Miss, but you don't look fine at all. Has something happened?"

Evelyn hesitated, torn between maintaining her composure and the desperate need to confide in someone. Nell's kind face and genuine concern broke through her resolve.

"Oh, Nell," Evelyn sighed, sinking onto the edge of her bed. "I fear I've made a terrible mistake. I spoke out of turn to the Baron, and now..." She gestured helplessly at the tray.

Nell's eyes widened in understanding. She sat down beside Evelyn, propriety forgotten in the face of the governess's distress. "There, there, Miss," she said softly, patting Evelyn's hand. "The Baron can be a difficult man, to be sure. But he's not unreasonable. Whatever's happened, I'm sure it'll blow over soon enough."

Evelyn shook her head, feeling the weight of her words pressing down on her. "I'm not so certain, Nell. I revealed things about myself that I shouldn't have. I challenged his authority over his own children. I..." She trailed off, unable to voice her deepest fear - that she'd ruined everything, that she'd be sent away.

Nell listened patiently, her face a picture of sympathy. When Evelyn finished speaking, the maid gave her hand a gentle squeeze. "Do you really feel that you've erred in your behaviour?"

Evelyn nodded, her eyes downcast. "Yes, I do," she admitted, her voice barely above a whisper. "I fear I've made a terrible mistake, not just in speaking up, but in coming to the Baron's house at all." The words tumbled out, heavy with regret and uncertainty.

As soon as the words left her lips, Evelyn saw something pass over Nell's face—a flicker of hurt, perhaps, or disappointment. Realising how her statement must have sounded, Evelyn hurriedly added, "Oh, but Nell, I could never regret meeting you, or the girls. Never that."

The maid's expression softened slightly, but a troubled look remained in her eyes. Nell stood up, smoothing her apron as if to leave. Evelyn felt a pang of loneliness at the thought of being left alone with her tumultuous thoughts.

But as Nell reached the door, she stopped, her hand resting on the handle. She turned back to face Evelyn, her forehead creased as he delved into deep thought.

Evelyn watched as Nell's expression shifted, her earlier sympathy giving way to a more serious demeanour. The maid's hand fell from the doorknob as she turned back to face Evelyn fully.

"Miss Bane," Nell began, her voice low and measured, "I've been a servant for a long time now. Seen a lot of people come and go, I have." She paused, her eyes searching Evelyn's face. "And dismissals, well, they tend to follow a pattern."

Evelyn felt her heart skip a beat at the word 'dismissals'. She swallowed hard, trying to maintain her composure as Nell continued.

"Have you ever been dismissed before, Miss?" Nell asked, her tone gentle but direct.

Evelyn shook her head, feeling her chest tightened, struggling to find her breath. She'd never imagined she'd be a servant, so she was utterly unprepared for this moment. It felt strange and terrible to have fallen so far from such a privileged upbringing, to be living so far outside of the gilded life she'd once enjoyed.

Nell nodded grimly, her lips pressed into a thin line. "I thought as much," she said softly. "Well, Miss, if you don't mind me saying so, it's best not to be taken by surprise in these situations. You should... prepare for the worst."

The words hit Evelyn like a physical blow. She felt the colour drain from her face as the full weight of Nell's warning settled over her. Prepare for the worst. The phrase echoed in her mind, each repetition bringing with it a fresh wave of anxiety.

Nell seemed to sense Evelyn's distress. She took a step forward, as if to offer comfort, but then thought better of it. Instead, she gave a small, sad smile. "I'm sorry, Miss. I don't mean to upset you. I just... well, I thought you ought to know."

With that, Nell turned and left the room, closing the door softly behind her. Evelyn remained frozen in place, staring at the spot where Nell had stood, her mind reeling from the maid's words.

Evelyn sat on the edge of her bed, Nell's warning echoing in her mind. The urge to push the thought away, to pretend everything would sort itself out, was overwhelming. It was how she'd always coped before, wasn't it? Letting life sweep her along, never taking control of her own fate.

With a start, Evelyn realised this was exactly how she'd ended up in that ill-fated affair with Richard, how she'd wound up marrying the Judge with no forethought. She'd drifted into it, never considering the consequences, never taking charge of her own choices. The memory of those days filled her with shame and regret.

No, Evelyn thought, straightening her spine. She wouldn't live like that again. She'd promised herself she would be different, stronger, more in control of her own destiny. Even if that destiny now included being a servant.

The thought struck her like a bolt of lightning. She was a servant now, wasn't she? Her life, her future, they were no longer entirely her own. She was at the mercy of others' whims, their decisions. Evelyn's hands clenched in her lap, her nails digging into her palms.

The realisation was bitter, but she forced herself to face it head-on. This was her reality now. She had to be prepared for whatever came next, even if that meant dismissal.

With a deep breath, Evelyn stood up. She would face this challenge as she should have faced so many others in her past - with clear eyes and a steady heart. She might be a servant, but that didn't mean she had to be passive. She could still make choices, still shape her path, even within the confines of her new station.

Evelyn stood, her movements measured and deliberate. She crossed the room to the large trunk that had been sitting at the foot of her bed since her arrival. For a moment, her hand hesitated on the lid, but she steeled herself and lifted it open.

The familiar scent of cedar wafted up, stirring memories she quickly pushed aside. Evelyn reached for her dresses, folding each one with precise, careful movements. She smoothed out every wrinkle, her fingers lingering on the fabric as if committing its texture to memory.

One by one, she placed her belongings into the trunk. Books were stacked neatly in one corner, their spines aligned perfectly. Her writing case, a gift from Aunt Agnes, was tucked safely between layers of clothing. Each item was a piece of her life, now being tidily packed away.

Evelyn worked methodically, her face a mask of concentration. She refused to let her mind wander, focusing solely on the task at hand. When her hands trembled as she folded a particular dress, she paused, took a deep breath, and continued.

She moved around the room, gathering her few possessions. The small trinkets she'd acquired since arriving at the manor were wrapped carefully in soft cloth before being nestled into the trunk: a seashell from Augusta, an uneven piece of tatted lace from Julia, a piece of sealing wax. Evelyn's movements were unhurried, almost ritualistic in their precision.

As she worked, Evelyn kept her thoughts firmly tethered to the present moment. She wouldn't allow herself to think of Julia's infectious laughter or Augusta's keen observations. She pushed away the image of the Baron's stern face softening into a rare smile. Instead, she counted each item as it went into the trunk, letting the numbers fill her mind.

Evelyn closed the trunk with a soft click, her fingers lingering on the brass latch for a moment. She straightened, surveying the room one last time. It looked bare now, stripped of her personal touches. The few items she'd decided to leave out—her nightgown, a change of clothes for the morning, her hairbrush—seemed lonely on the dresser.

With a deep breath, Evelyn turned and sat on the edge of her bed. Her hands, now idle, found each other in her lap, fingers interlacing. She felt oddly calm, a stark contrast to the tumult of emotions she'd experienced earlier.

The room was quiet, save for the gentle ticking of the clock on the mantelpiece. Evelyn let her gaze drift to the window, where the last vestiges of daylight were fading into dusk. She watched as the shadows lengthened, creeping across the floor towards her feet.

In the gathering darkness, Evelyn's mind was clear, her thoughts ordered. She'd done what she could to prepare for the worst, as Nell had advised. Now, all that remained was to face whatever tomorrow might bring.

Evelyn's spine straightened, her chin lifting slightly. She'd weathered storms before, hadn't she? Perhaps not quite like this, but she was no stranger to adversity. If dismissal came, she would face it with dignity. And if, by some chance, she was allowed to stay, she would embrace the opportunity with renewed determination.

A small smile tugged at the corners of her mouth. Whatever happened, she would not be caught unawares again. She was ready—ready to stand on her own two feet, ready to carve out her own path, whatever form it might take.

As night settled fully over the manor, Evelyn remained seated, her posture straight, her gaze steady. She was prepared to meet her future head-on, come what may.

Chapter 20

Evelyn's eyes flew open, her heart racing as she jerked awake. Sunlight streamed through the window, painting the room in a warm glow. She blinked, disoriented, realising she had fallen asleep atop the covers, still fully dressed.

Her gaze fell on the small table near the window, where a tray of breakfast sat waiting. The sight of it made her stomach churn. How long had it been there? Who had brought it? The thought of someone entering while she slept, seeing her in such a vulnerable state, made her cheeks burn.

Evelyn forced herself to rise, smoothing her wrinkled dress with trembling hands. She approached the tray, eyeing its contents: a pot of tea, a small plate of toast, and a dish of preserves.

The tea had long since gone cold. She poured herself a cup anyway, more out of habit than desire. The china rattled slightly as she lifted it to her lips, her nerves making her hands unsteady. The tepid liquid did little to soothe her anxiety.

Evelyn picked up a piece of toast, turning it over in her hands. The mere thought of eating made her feel ill, her stomach a tight knot of apprehension. What would the day bring? Would she be packing her trunk in earnest, forced to leave the manor and the girls she had grown so fond of?

She took a small bite, the toast dry and tasteless in her mouth. Evelyn chewed mechanically, her mind racing. Perhaps she should seek out the Baron, plead her case. But no, that would be unseemly. She was a governess now, not a lady of leisure. She would wait to be summoned, to learn her fate.

The toast sat like lead in her stomach. Evelyn set the remainder aside, unable to force down another bite. She sipped at her tea instead, willing her nerves to settle.

A sharp rap at the door startled Evelyn from her anxious reverie. She nearly spilt her tea, hastily setting the cup down with a clatter.

"Come in," she called, her voice sounding strained to her own ears.

The door creaked open, revealing one of the footmen. His face was a mask of polite indifference as he delivered his message. "Miss Bane, the Baron requests your presence in his study."

Evelyn's heart plummeted. This was it, then. The moment she'd been dreading since their argument the day before. She nodded, not trusting her voice, and the footman withdrew.

For a moment, Evelyn sat frozen, her mind racing. She smoothed the bodice of her dress as she stood, acutely aware of how rumpled it was from her night spent atop the covers. There was no time to change, no way to make herself more presentable. She would have to face whatever came as she was.

Taking a deep breath, Evelyn stepped out into the corridor. The manor seemed unnaturally quiet, the usual bustle of servants and children conspicuously absent. Her footsteps echoed hollowly as she made her way towards the stairs.

Each step felt heavier than the last as Evelyn descended. The portraits of stern-faced Ayles ancestors seemed to glare down at her, their painted eyes full of judgement. She fought the urge to quicken her pace, to run back to her room and hide.

The journey to the Baron's study stretched interminably. Evelyn's legs felt like lead, her chest tight with dread. She found herself counting her steps, anything to distract from the hammering of her heart.

At last, she stood before the heavy oak door of the study. Evelyn raised her hand to knock, then hesitated. She closed her eyes, drawing in a steadying breath. Whatever lay beyond that door, she would face it with dignity.

Evelyn rapped her knuckles against the solid oak, the sound echoing in the quiet corridor. She steeled herself, squaring her shoulders as she heard the Baron's muffled voice bid her enter.

The study door swung open with a creak, revealing the Baron standing behind his imposing desk. His face was a mask of impassivity, giving no hint as to his thoughts or intentions. Evelyn felt her heart skip a beat, but she refused to let her trepidation show. She mirrored his stiff demeanour, clasping her hands before her to still their trembling.

"You wished to see me, my lord?" Evelyn's voice came out steadier than she'd dared hope, betraying none of the anxiety churning within her.

The Baron's grey eyes met hers, his gaze piercing. "Indeed, Miss Bane. Please, come in."

Evelyn stepped into the study, the scent of leather-bound books and tobacco smoke enveloping her. She stood before the desk, her back ramrod straight, chin lifted ever so slightly in defiance. If this was to be her dismissal, she would face it with dignity.

The Baron's scarred face remained inscrutable as he studied her. The silence stretched between them, heavy with unspoken words. Evelyn fought the urge to fidget under his scrutiny, instead meeting his gaze with a calm she did not feel.

"I've been considering our...discussion from yesterday," the Baron finally spoke, his tone carefully neutral.

Evelyn inclined her head slightly, not trusting herself to speak. She watched as the Baron's fingers drummed once, twice on the polished surface of his desk—the only outward sign of any inner turmoil.

"It is sometimes...difficult for a party that has been incorrect to admit this, and to rectify it," the Baron continued, his voice clipped and precise.

Evelyn stared at the Baron, her brow furrowing slightly as she processed his words. The tension in his jaw, the careful precision of his speech—it dawned on her that he was struggling to apologise. A flicker of surprise passed through her, quickly replaced by a cautious hope.

The Baron cleared his throat, his gaze dropping momentarily to the papers on his desk before meeting her eyes once more. "Miss Bane, it has become... apparent to me that your actions and convictions stem from a genuine desire for the well-being of my family."

Evelyn's breath stilled, trapped in her chest. She remained silent, scarcely daring to move lest she break the fragile moment.

"Even when we find ourselves at odds," the Baron continued, his voice growing firmer, "I cannot deny that your intentions are... commendable. You have shown a level of dedication to my daughters that goes beyond mere duty."

A warmth bloomed in Evelyn's chest, chasing away some of the cold dread that had gripped her since their argument. She allowed herself to relax slightly, her shoulders losing some of their rigidity.

"While I may not always agree with your methods," the Baron said, a hint of his usual gruffness returning to his tone, "I cannot fault your motivations. It is... refreshing to encounter someone so invested in the girls' futures."

Evelyn felt a small smile tugging at the corners of her mouth. She inclined her head slightly, acknowledging his words. "Thank you, my lord. I assure you, the girls' well-being is my utmost priority."

The Baron nodded, a flicker of something—approval, perhaps?—passing across his features. "Indeed. It is for this reason that I have decided..."

Evelyn's heart leapt into her throat as the Baron reached into his desk drawer. Her eyes widened as he withdrew a familiar piece of paper—her letter of acceptance. The sight of it made her blood run cold, memories of penning those words flooding back. She had been so eager, so hopeful then. Now, that same letter might spell her doom.

The Baron held the letter between his fingers, his gaze flicking between it and Evelyn. She stood rooted to the spot, scarcely daring to breathe. This was it, then. He would invoke the terms of her trial period, send her packing back to London in disgrace.

"Miss Bane," the Baron's voice cut through the silence, "I have decided to dispense with the trial period."

Evelyn blinked, certain she had misheard. The Baron's face remained impassive as he turned towards the nearby candle, its flame flickering softly. With deliberate slowness, he held the corner of the letter to the flame.

The parchment caught quickly, orange tongues licking up its edges. Evelyn watched, transfixed, as the words she had so carefully crafted disappeared into ash. The Baron held the burning letter until the last moment, then dropped it into a metal wastebasket where it smouldered into nothing.

"Your position here is no longer conditional," the Baron said, turning back to face her. "You have proven yourself more than capable, Miss Bane. I trust you will continue to serve this household with the same dedication you have shown thus far."

Evelyn's mind reeled, struggling to process this unexpected turn of events. Relief washed over her in waves, mingled with a surge of pride. She had done it. Against all odds, she had earned her place here.

"Thank you, my lord," she managed, her voice barely above a whisper. "I... I am honoured by your trust. I assure you, I will not disappoint you."

Evelyn stood before the Baron, her heart still racing from the unexpected turn of events. She watched as a hint of satisfaction played across his features, his grey eyes softening ever so slightly. The tension that had hung between them seemed to dissipate, replaced by a tentative warmth.

"I trust this arrangement is satisfactory to you as well, Miss Bane?" the Baron inquired, his voice carrying a note of approval she had rarely heard before.

"Yes, my lord," Evelyn replied, a genuine smile gracing her lips. "I am most grateful for your confidence in me."

For a moment, Evelyn allowed herself to bask in the glow of her success. She had done it—she had secured her position, proven her worth. The sense of accomplishment swelled within her chest, a heady feeling of triumph.

But as quickly as it had come, the elation began to fade. A sobering thought crept into her mind, dampening her spirits. Evelyn's smile faltered, her brow furrowing slightly as the realisation struck her.

She had sought independence, had relished the idea of earning her own wage, yet here she stood, her future once again in the hands of a man. The Baron's word may have secured her position for now, but it could just as easily take it away. One misstep, one disagreement, and she could find herself cast out with nowhere to turn.

Evelyn's gaze dropped to the metal wastebasket where the ashes of her acceptance letter still smouldered. The sight of it, once a symbol of her newfound security, now seemed to mock her. She had traded one form of dependence for another, exchanging the constraints of her old life for the precarious position of a governess.

The weight of her situation settled upon her shoulders like an unwelcome lead shawl, heavy and unyielding. Evelyn forced herself to meet the Baron's eyes once more, maintaining her composure even as doubt gnawed at her insides. She was grateful, yes, but the price of her gratitude was a stark reminder of her vulnerability.

The Baron's brow furrowed as he observed her. "Miss Bane, is something amiss?"

Evelyn startled, realising her inner turmoil must have shown on her face. She quickly schooled her features into a mask of polite neutrality. "No, my lord. It's nothing of consequence."

She turned to leave, eager to escape the suffocating confines of the study and sort through her jumbled thoughts in private. Before she could take a step, she felt a gentle pressure on her arm. The Baron's hand rested there, light yet firm, halting her retreat.

"Miss Bane," his voice was softer now, tinged with concern. "I assure you, if something troubles you, I would hear of it."

For a moment, Evelyn struggled to find her breath. The warmth of his hand seeped through the fabric of her sleeve, a stark contrast to the chill of uncertainty that gripped her heart. She turned back to face him, her eyes meeting his. The genuine concern she saw there made her resolve waver.

For a moment, Evelyn considered confiding in him, laying bare her fears and frustrations. But the words caught in her throat. How could she explain the paradox of her situation? That his very act of kindness had only served to highlight her lack of true independence?

Evelyn hesitated, caught between her desire to maintain a professional distance and the unexpected warmth in the Baron's gaze. His hand remained on her arm, a gentle anchor in the storm of her thoughts. She took a deep breath, steeling herself.

"My lord, I... I am truly grateful for your trust and the security you've offered," Evelyn began, her voice low and sincere. "But I find myself in a rather perplexing situation."

The Baron's brow furrowed slightly, but he remained silent, waiting for her to continue.

"You see, I came here seeking independence, a chance to make my own way in the world," Evelyn explained, her words gaining strength as she spoke. "And while I've found great satisfaction in my work with the girls, I've realised that my position is still... precarious."

She glanced down at the wastebasket, where the ashes of her letter lay. "My future, my very livelihood, still rests in the hands of another. In your hands, my lord. And while I don't doubt your integrity, the fact remains that I am still beholden to the whims of... of a man."

Evelyn felt her cheeks flush as she spoke, but she pressed on. "What I truly crave, what I've always longed for, is true independence. The ability to stand on my own two feet, to make my own choices without fear of... of losing everything at a moment's notice."

She looked up, meeting the Baron's gaze once more. His expression was unreadable, but his eyes remained fixed on her, attentive.

"I know it may sound ungrateful, especially after your kindness," Evelyn continued, her voice softening. "But I hope you can understand. It's not about you, my lord. It's about... about having control over my own destiny."

Evelyn's heart raced as the Baron remained silent, his grey eyes fixed upon her. She fought the urge to fidget under his intense gaze, her breath hitching suddenly. Had she overstepped? The silence stretched between them, taut as a bowstring.

Just as Evelyn opened her mouth to apologise, to take back her words, the Baron's expression shifted. The stern lines of his face softened, replaced by a look of thoughtful consideration. He gestured towards the chair across from his desk, his movements deliberate and unhurried.

"Please, Miss Bane, sit."

Chapter 21

Evelyn hesitated for a moment, then lowered herself into the offered seat. The leather creaked softly beneath her as she perched on the edge, her back ramrod straight. She watched as the Baron settled into his own chair, the high-backed leather affair that seemed to dwarf even his imposing frame.

The Baron leaned forward, resting his elbows on the polished surface of his desk. His fingers steepled before him, and Evelyn was captivated by the shafts of sunlight that tilted in through the window across his scarred features. When he spoke, his voice was low and measured.

"Please, Miss Bane, continue."

Evelyn's was momentarily breathless, her chest seizing up. She waited, scarcely daring to move, waiting to see if the Baron was sincere.

Evelyn hesitated, her gaze flickering between the Baron's expectant face and her own clasped hands. The weight of her past pressed down upon her, a burden she'd carried in silence for so long. Could she truly trust this man with even a fraction of her story?

She drew in a deep breath, steadying herself. The Baron's grey eyes remained fixed upon her, patient and attentive. There was something in his gaze—a flicker of understanding, perhaps—that gave her courage.

"My lord," Evelyn began, finding the words as she spoke, "I find myself in a rather... delicate position. You see, in my youth, I..." She paused, swallowing hard against the lump in her throat. "I found myself with very few options."

The Baron remained silent, his expression neutral. Evelyn pressed on, her words carefully measured.

"There was a time when I found myself in... in a rather difficult situation. I had nowhere to turn, no one to rely upon." Evelyn's gaze dropped to her hands, her fingers twisting together in her lap. "It was a dark period in my life, one that taught me the value of independence."

She looked up, meeting the Baron's eyes once more. "I don't mean to burden you with the details, my lord. But perhaps you can understand why the idea of true independence holds such appeal for me."

The Baron leaned back in his chair. A thoughtful crease marked his forehead as he sank into deep thought. Evelyn held her breath, waiting for his response, hoping she hadn't revealed too much or too little.

Evelyn held her breath, watching the Baron's face for any sign of his reaction. His expression remained inscrutable, those grey eyes fixed upon her with an intensity that made her want to squirm in her seat. She resisted the urge, forcing herself to meet his gaze steadily.

After what felt like an eternity, the Baron spoke. "Miss Bane, I... I understand."

Evelyn blinked, certain she had misheard. "My lord?"

"And I am grateful for your insight," he continued, his voice low and measured. "Truly."

Surprise coursed through Evelyn, mingled with a wave of relief so profound it nearly took her breath away. She hadn't realised how tightly wound she had been until that moment, when the tension began to seep from her shoulders.

The Baron leaned forward, his elbows resting on the desk. "In fact, Miss Bane, I understand more than you might give me credit for. Your dilemma—the very situation you find yourself in—it is precisely what I hope my own daughters will be able to avoid in their future."

Evelyn's eyes widened, her mind racing to process his words. "I... I don't quite understand, my lord."

A ghost of a smile played at the corners of the Baron's lips. "You speak of independence, of the desire to stand on your own two feet. It is a noble aspiration, one I share for Augusta and Julia. I do not see why you should be any different from them, that is, able to secure your own future and livelihood."

Evelyn felt as though the ground beneath her feet had shifted. She had expected anger, perhaps even dismissal. Instead, she found herself faced with understanding, even approval. It was almost too much to comprehend.

Evelyn watched as the Baron's expression shifted, a mix of sympathy and resignation settling across his features. He leaned back in his chair, his fingers drumming a thoughtful rhythm on the desk.

"Miss Bane," he began, his voice tinged with a hint of regret, "while I sympathise with your position, I'm afraid I cannot change the very fabric of our society. The world we live in is not always just, nor is it easily altered."

He paused, his grey eyes meeting hers with unexpected warmth. "As much as I might wish to offer you the independence you seek, the fact remains that I am your employer. Our positions, as dictated by society, cannot be easily overcome."

Evelyn nodded, a sigh escaping her lips. She had known, of course, that her situation could not be so easily remedied. Still, the Baron's words, though not unexpected, carried a weight that settled heavily upon her shoulders.

"I understand, my lord," she replied, her voice soft but steady. "And I appreciate your candour."

A thought struck her then, unbidden and perhaps unwise to voice. Yet, emboldened by the Baron's unexpected sympathy, Evelyn started speaking before she could reconsider.

I cannot help but wonder," she mused, her gaze drifting to the window where the grounds stretched out beyond. "Would things be different if more women were able to be employers themselves?"

The words hung in the air between them, a challenge to the very foundations of their society. Evelyn held her breath, uncertain how the Baron would respond to such a radical notion.

Evelyn watched as the Baron's expression shifted, a slow, sad smile spreading across his face. His grey eyes held a mixture of amusement and something deeper, more contemplative.

"Miss Bane," he said, his voice tinged with a hint of wonder, "I find you terribly modern. Shocking, even."

Evelyn's heart skipped a beat, fearing she had overstepped. But as she searched his face, she saw no anger or disapproval. Instead, there was a glimmer of admiration in his eyes that took her by surprise.

"And yet," the Baron continued, his smile widening slightly, "I find I cannot disapprove. Your thoughts, while unconventional, are not without merit."

Relief washed over Evelyn, and she felt her own lips curving into a smile. It was as if a bridge had been built between them, spanning the chasm of their different stations and experiences. For the first time since her arrival at the manor, she felt truly seen and understood.

"Thank you, my lord," she said softly. "I'm glad we've come to a new understanding."

As the words left her mouth, a sudden realisation struck her. Without thinking, she mused aloud, "I suppose Lady Rosalind must have rubbed off on me more than I thought."

Evelyn's heart skipped a beat as she realised her mistake. The name had slipped out unbidden, a fragment of her past she'd fought so hard to keep hidden. She watched as the Baron's eyes narrowed, his expression shifting from open curiosity to something more guarded.

"Lady Rosalind?" he asked, his voice low and measured. "I don't believe you've mentioned her before, Miss Bane."

Evelyn's mind raced, searching for a way to explain without revealing too much. She clasped her hands tightly in her lap, willing them not to tremble. The silence stretched between them, thick with unspoken questions.

"I... she was..." Evelyn began, stumbling over her words. She took a deep breath, steadying herself. "Lady Amelia, Rosalind is her younger sister."

The Baron nodded slowly. "I see—you were in Lady Amelia's household, yes? And she had two younger sisters, if I recall." His gaze flicked momentarily to the waste basket, as if realising for the first time that he had burnt a whole letter.

Evelyn felt a wave of relief wash over her, though it was tinged with a twinge of guilt for the lie. She had always prided herself on her honesty, but in this moment, self-preservation won out.

"Yes, my lord," she confirmed, her voice steady despite her racing heart. "Lady Amelia does indeed have two sisters."

The Baron leaned forward, his interest piqued. "And how did you come to be in their household, Miss Bane? It seems an unusual arrangement for someone of your... personality."

Evelyn's mind whirred, crafting a story that skirted as close to the truth as she dared. "I knew the family, my lord," she began, choosing her words carefully. "Lady Harrington, Amelia's mother, had tragically passed away at a young age. The family was in need of assistance, and I was fortunate enough to be in a position to help.

As soon as the words left her mouth, Evelyn noticed a change come over the Baron's face. His brow furrowed, and a shadow seemed to pass across his eyes. The mention of Lady Harrington's untimely death had clearly struck a chord with him.

"I see," he said, his voice low and grave. "A tragic loss indeed."

Evelyn watched as the Baron's expression darkened further, his gaze distant as if lost in thought. She could almost see the wheels turning in his mind, connecting her words to his own fears and experiences. The atmosphere in the room had shifted, becoming heavy with unspoken concerns.

Evelyn's heart raced as the silence stretched between them. The weight of her deception pressed down upon her, each passing moment making her feel increasingly wretched. She watched the Baron; his expression grew intense, a furrow appearing as he was absorbed in thought. His eyes were distant and unfocused. The ticking of the clock on the mantelpiece seemed to grow louder with each second, a relentless reminder of her dishonesty.

She longed to speak, to fill the oppressive silence with explanations or apologies, but fear kept her lips sealed. What if he saw through her half-truths? What if he pressed for more details she couldn't provide?

The Baron's expression remained troubled, his mind clearly grappling with thoughts far removed from their conversation. Evelyn seized upon his distraction, desperate for an escape from the suffocating atmosphere of the study.

"My lord," she ventured, her voice barely above a whisper, "perhaps I should attend to the girls now. They'll be expecting their lessons."

For a moment, Evelyn wasn't sure he had heard her. The Baron's gaze remained fixed on some point beyond her, his thoughts clearly elsewhere. Then, with a slight start, he seemed to come back to himself.

"Yes, of course," he murmured, waving a hand absently. "You may go, Miss Bane."

Evelyn rose from her chair, relief flooding through her even as guilt gnawed at her conscience. She curtsied quickly, not daring to meet the Baron's eyes, and hurried towards the door. As she reached for the handle, she hesitated, glancing back over her shoulder. The Baron had already turned away, his attention focused once more on the papers strewn across his desk.

With a quiet sigh, Evelyn slipped out of the study, closing the door softly behind her. Though she had avoided disaster this time, Evelyn felt as if she were living beneath a precariously balanced axe—it was only a matter of time before it would fall.

Chapter 22

Evelyn's footsteps echoed through the empty corridor as she hurried away from the Baron's study, her heart still pounding in her chest. Relief washed over her like a cool breeze, but it was tinged with the acrid taste of guilt. She had narrowly avoided disaster, but at what cost?

As she rounded the corner towards her chamber, Evelyn's mind whirled with the implications of her deception. She had always prided herself on her honesty, yet here she was, weaving half-truths and omissions like a skilled seamstress. The weight of her lies pressed down upon her shoulders, threatening to crush her beneath their burden.

Reaching her door, for the second time in as many days, Evelyn let out a startled yelp as she realised someone was within her room. Nell, clearly taken by surprise as well, let out her own small shriek of alarm as Evelyn burst through the door.

Evelyn's hand flew to her chest, her heart racing from the sudden fright. "Nell! Goodness, you scared me half to death!"

Nell clutched Evelyn's dress to her bosom, her eyes wide. "Me? You're the one who came bursting in like the hounds of hell were after you!"

Evelyn leant against the doorframe, catching her breath. Her brow furrowed as she took in the scene before her. Her trunk lay open on the floor, its contents partially strewn about. Nell stood in the middle of the chaos, one of Evelyn's favourite day dresses held aloft by the shoulders. "What on earth are you doing in here?"

Nell's surprise melted into a knowing smile. "Why, unpacking your trunk, of course. I knew you'd be staying."

"But... how could you possibly know that?" Evelyn asked, her voice barely above a whisper.

Nell's smile widened, showing more of her teeth. "Oh, Miss Bane, I never believed for a moment that the Baron would dismiss you. Not after everything that's happened--Himself is clearly fond of you."

Evelyn stepped into the room, closing the door behind her. She sank onto the edge of her bed, her legs suddenly weak. "I'm glad you at least had faith--I was certain he'd send me packing."

Nell carefully laid the dress across the back of a chair and moved to sit beside Evelyn. "The Baron may be a stubborn old goat at times, but he's not a fool. He knows a good thing when he sees it...even if it takes him some time to recognise it."

Evelyn felt a blush creep up her neck. "I wouldn't go that far."

Nell shrugged, her eyes twinkling with mischief. "I've known the Baron longer than you have, Miss Bane. You'll just have to take my word for it."

Evelyn conceded the point with a nod. "I suppose you're right. Still, I can't help but feel I'm on shaky ground here."

As she spoke, Evelyn's gaze drifted downward, and she froze. There, stark against the polished wooden floorboards, were a series of sooty footprints. Her brow furrowed as she traced their path from the hearth to where Nell now sat.

"Nell," Evelyn began, her voice low and hesitant, "what's happened here?"

The maid followed Evelyn's gaze, her eyes widening as she took in the mess. "Oh, blimey," she muttered, jumping to her feet. "I'm ever so sorry, Miss Bane. I was in such a hurry to make sure that you'd be all unpacked--I wanted to surprise you."

Evelyn stood, moving closer to inspect the damage. The footprints were small, clearly belonging to Nell, but they were numerous. It seemed the maid had been pacing back and forth across the room, leaving a crisscrossing pattern of black smudges in her wake.

"Well, you certainly managed that," Evelyn said with a wry smile.

Nell looked over at Evelyn, her round cheeks lifting in another smile. "Perhaps next time I can repay the fright you gave me," she said, her tone mischievous.

Evelyn sighed and flopped backward. "I sincerely hope not."

Nell only laughed in response.

***

Evelyn felt as though she were walking through a dream. The world around her seemed slightly out of focus, colours muted and sounds distant. She blinked rapidly, trying to shake off the strange sensation that had clung to her since her narrow escape in the Baron's study.

As she attempted to guide the girls through their French lesson, Evelyn was stumbling over words she normally spoke with ease. A look of confusion crossed Augusta's face, while Julia's eyes sparkled with barely concealed amusement.

"Miss Bane, are you quite all right?" Augusta asked, her tone more curious than concerned.

Evelyn forced a smile. "Of course, dear. Now, where were we?"

She turned back to the blackboard, chalk poised to write, but her mind went blank. The French verb conjugations she had planned to review seemed to have vanished from her memory, replaced by a swirling fog of anxiety and guilt.

Julia giggled softly. "I think we were about to conjugate 'être', Miss Bane."

"Ah, yes. Thank you, Julia," Evelyn murmured, though she made no move to write.

The chalk trembled in her hand. Evelyn stared at it, watching as a fine white powder dusted her fingertips. She felt a sudden, irrational urge to wipe it on her dress, to rid herself of its clinging presence.

With a start, she realised both girls were watching her intently. Evelyn cleared her throat. "Perhaps we should end our lessons early today. I'm feeling a bit... under the weather."

Augusta's eyes narrowed. "But it's not even lunchtime yet."

"I know, but..." Evelyn trailed off, unable to formulate a reasonable excuse. "Well, consider it a reward for your hard work this week. Why don't you go enjoy the sunshine?"

Julia needed no further encouragement. She leapt from her chair with a whoop of delight, grabbing her sister's hand. "Come on, Gus! Let's go see if we can find any new frog spawn in the pond!"

"You know I hate it when you call me Gus!" Augusta groused as the pair of them disappeared out the door.

As the girls raced from the schoolroom, Evelyn sank into her chair, her head in her hands. She felt utterly drained, as though she had run for miles rather than simply taught a short lesson.

Evelyn sank onto the settee, her fingers tracing the intricate floral pattern of the upholstery. She closed her eyes, willing her racing thoughts to slow. The room felt stifling, despite the open windows that allowed a gentle breeze to rustle the curtains.

She inhaled deeply, trying to centre herself. The faint scent of lavender from the garden mingled with the musty odour of old books that permeated the music room-turned-schoolroom. It was a comforting smell, one that usually brought her peace. Today, however, it did little to calm her frayed nerves.

The creak of the door startled her from her reverie. Evelyn's eyes flew open, and she leapt to her feet as though scalded. The Baron stood in the doorway, his imposing figure filling the frame.

"Miss Bane," he said, his voice gruff. "I was looking for the girls. Have you seen them?"

Evelyn's heart hammered in her chest. She smoothed her skirts, acutely aware of how dishevelled she must appear. "They're out of doors, my lord. I... I dismissed them early today."

The Baron's eyebrows rose, his scarred face twisting into an expression Evelyn couldn't quite decipher. Was it surprise? Disapproval? She found herself unable to meet his gaze, her eyes instead fixing on a point just over his shoulder.

"I see," he said after a moment. "And may I ask why?"

Evelyn swallowed hard, her mouth suddenly dry. "I... I wasn't feeling quite myself, my lord. I thought it best to end the lesson before I made any... errors in their education."

Evelyn's heart continued to race as she watched the Baron's expression soften. He turned towards the window, his gaze sweeping over the sun-dappled grounds.

"It is a very fine day," he mused, almost to himself. "Far too fine for the girls to be cooped up inside all day."

Evelyn released a breath she hadn't realised she'd been holding. Perhaps he wasn't cross with her after all. She watched as he shifted his weight, clearly about to take his leave. But then he paused, his hand resting on the doorframe.

The Baron turned back to face her, his grey eyes meeting hers with an intensity that made her breath catch. "Miss Bane," he began, his voice low and surprisingly gentle. "Sometimes when I have a hard time thinking, a good walk will help to clear my head."

Evelyn blinked, caught off guard by the unexpected suggestion. Was he offering her advice? Or perhaps... an invitation? She found herself unable to look away from his steady gaze, searching for some hint of his true meaning.

"I... that's very kind of you to suggest, my lord," she managed to stammer out, her fingers twisting nervously in her skirts.

The Baron nodded, a ghost of a smile playing at the corners of his mouth. "The path along the eastern field is particularly pleasant this time of year. The wildflowers are in bloom." He paused for a moment, then said, "There are a number of beehives out there that I should like to inspect, too."

There was another silence. Evelyn tilted her head, not sure she understood what was happening. The Baron continued to stare at her expectantly, drumming his fingers a little on the doorframe.

Evelyn's heart skipped a beat as realisation dawned. The Baron wasn't merely offering advice—he was inviting her to join him. She blinked, momentarily stunned by the unexpected turn of events.

"Oh," she breathed, a faint blush colouring her cheeks. "You mean... together?"

The Baron cleared his throat, his fingers still drumming an uneven rhythm on the doorframe. "If you're amenable, of course. I wouldn't want to impose."

Evelyn hesitated, her mind racing. They'd hardly spent any time alone, just the two of them. The prospect was both thrilling and terrifying. She glanced up at him, intending to politely decline, but the words died on her lips.

The Baron's usually stern countenance had softened, his grey eyes holding a hint of vulnerability she'd never seen before. There was something almost boyish in his hopeful expression, which made Evelyn feel utterly charmed.

"I... I would be delighted, my lord," she heard herself say, surprising even herself with the warmth in her voice.

The Baron's face lit up, a genuine smile transforming his features. "Excellent," he said, gesturing forward with one arm. "Shall we?"

Evelyn took a deep breath. "I'll fetch my bonnet," she said. As she brushed past him, she caught the faint scent of leather and bare earth—a scent she was beginning to associate with him. She quickly nipped up to her room, putting a simple straw bonnet on her head and tying the light green ribbon loosely beneath her chin.

They made their way out of the house in companionable silence, the warm spring air enveloping them as they stepped onto the gravel path. Evelyn found herself sneaking glances at the Baron, marvelling at how different he seemed outside the confines of the house. He seemed to stand a little taller, his face was a little lighter. Evelyn realized with a start that he probably moved through the house constantly on edge. He was likely afraid of hitting a doorway with his broad shoulders or striking his head on one of the ancient beams that held up the ceiling.

Evelyn's mind whirled as they walked along the path, her thoughts a jumble of anxiety and curiosity. The Baron strode beside her, his long legs easily matching her shorter steps. She glanced up at him, noting the way the sunlight caught the silver threads in his dark hair.

"It's a lovely day, isn't it?" she ventured, wincing inwardly at the banality of her words. The Baron merely nodded, his eyes fixed on the path ahead.

Evelyn bit her lip, searching for something more substantial to say. "I've noticed the wildflowers blooming. They're quite beautiful. Do you know their names?"

The Baron grunted noncommittally, gesturing vaguely towards a patch of yellow blooms. Evelyn's shoulders slumped slightly. She'd hoped this walk might provide an opportunity to clear the air between them, but his reticence was proving a formidable obstacle.

"I suppose the bees must be quite busy with all these flowers," she tried again, her voice betraying a hint of the strain she felt. "Do you tend to the hives yourself, or—"

The Baron stopped abruptly, turning to face her. Evelyn nearly stumbled in her haste to halt beside him, her words trailing off as she met his gaze.

"Miss Bane," he said, his voice surprisingly gentle. "You needn't feel obligated to fill every moment with conversation. Sometimes, silence can be... companionable."

Evelyn blinked, taken aback by his perceptiveness. "I... I'm sorry, my lord. I thought perhaps you expected..."

He shook his head, a small smile tugging at the corners of his mouth. "I invited you on this walk to clear your head, not to tax it further. Please, feel free to simply... be." The Baron looked about for a moment. "Just...take a moment to enjoy where you are. Look. Listen."

Evelyn took a deep breath, letting the Baron's words sink in. She closed her eyes for a moment, feeling the warmth of the sun on her face and the gentle breeze rustling her skirts. When she opened them again, it was as if she were seeing the world anew.

Chapter 23

The fields stretched out before them, a patchwork of vibrant greens and golds. Wildflowers dotted the landscape, their delicate petals swaying in the breeze. Evelyn's gaze was drawn to a patch of brilliant blue cornflowers, their colour as vivid as a summer sky. Nearby, a cluster of scarlet poppies nodded their heads, their petals as fine as silk.

She turned slowly, taking in the full panorama. The young wheat was already knee-high, its tender stalks dancing in the wind. In the distance, she could see the neat rows of vegetables in the kitchen gardens, their leaves a rich, dark green against the tilled earth.

Evelyn closed her eyes again, this time focusing on the sounds around her. The gentle rustle of leaves in the breeze was punctuated by a symphony of birdsong. She could hear the cheerful twittering of sparrows, the melodious warble of a thrush, and the distant caw of a crow.

As she listened more intently, another sound reached her ears. Carried on the wind was the faint melody of human voices. Evelyn opened her eyes, searching for the source. In a far-off field, she could just make out the figures of farm workers, their voices raised in song as they went about their labour.

The beauty of it all nearly took her breath away. Evelyn turned to the Baron, her eyes shining with wonder. "It's magnificent," she breathed, her voice barely above a whisper. "I've never truly seen it before, not like this."

Evelyn looked up at the Baron gratefully, her heart skipping a beat as she found him gazing down at her with unexpected warmth. His grey eyes, usually so stern, now held a glimmer of pleasure at her newfound appreciation for his world. The corners of his mouth lifted in a subtle smile that transformed his scarred face, softening the hard lines and making him appear years younger.

They began walking again, this time veering off the main lane onto a narrow dirt path that wound its way through a meadow thick with wildflowers. The trail was barely wide enough for one person, forcing them to walk so close that their arms nearly brushed with each step.

Evelyn was acutely aware of the Baron's presence beside her, the warmth radiating from his body and the faint scent of leather and earth that clung to him.

As they navigated the uneven ground, Evelyn was occasionally stumbling on hidden roots or loose stones. Each time, the Baron's hand would shoot out to steady her, his touch firm yet gentle on her elbow or the small of her back. The contact, brief as it was, sent a thrill through her that she struggled to suppress.

The path dipped into a small hollow, sheltered on either side by gnarled old oak trees. Here, the wildflowers grew in even greater profusion, creating a riot of colour that seemed almost dreamlike in its beauty. Bees hummed busily among the blooms, their steady drone a soothing counterpoint to the rustle of leaves overhead.

Evelyn paused for a moment, closing her eyes to breathe in the heady scent of flowers and sun-warmed earth. When she opened them again, she found the Baron watching her, an unreadable expression on his face.

Evelyn's gaze followed the Baron's as he gestured towards a secluded corner of the hollow. Hidden amongst the lush foliage, she spied a collection of woven straw beehives, their dome-like shapes blending seamlessly with the natural surroundings.

"I'd like to check on how they're progressing," the Baron said, his voice tinged with enthusiasm. "It's been a fortnight since I last inspected them."

Evelyn felt a flutter of apprehension in her chest. "Aren't you afraid of being stung?" she asked, eyeing the hives warily.

To her surprise, the Baron chuckled, a warm, rich sound that made her stomach flutter. "Most things that sting or bite do so because they're afraid," he explained, his grey eyes twinkling with amusement. "If I'm slow and deliberate, they won't pay me much mind."

Evelyn watched, both fascinated and nervous, as the Baron approached the hives. His movements were indeed slow and measured, each step placed with careful consideration. As he drew nearer, she could hear the low, steady hum of the bees intensify.

The Baron crouched beside the nearest hive, his large hands surprisingly gentle as he examined the structure. Evelyn was holding her breath, half-expecting a swarm of angry bees to descend upon him at any moment. But true to his word, the insects seemed largely unperturbed by his presence.

"Would you like to come closer?" the Baron asked, glancing over his shoulder at her.

Evelyn hesitated, her heart racing. The thought of approaching the hives filled her with trepidation, yet she felt an inexplicable urge to prove herself brave in the Baron's eyes.

Evelyn wavered, her heart racing as she eyed the buzzing hives. The Baron extended a hand to her without turning back around, his attention on the beehive in front of him. It was an invitation and a reassurance all at once. For a moment, she wrestled with propriety, keenly aware of how improper it would be to accept his bare hand. Her curiosity made her push aside her reservations.

Taking a deep breath, Evelyn stepped forward, her ungloved hand slipping into his. The contact sent a jolt through her, his skin warm and calloused against her own. She marvelled at how small her hand looked, enveloped in his much larger one.

Gently, the Baron drew her closer, his movements slow and careful. Evelyn found herself inching forward, her eyes darting between his face and the hives. As she neared, the buzzing grew louder, but it wasn't the angry sound she'd expected. Instead, it was a steady, almost soothing hum.

"That's it," the Baron murmured, his voice low and encouraging. "Nice and easy."

Evelyn's felt a lump form in her throat, making it hard to breathe as she realised how close they now stood. The Baron's presence enveloped her, solid and reassuring. She could feel the warmth radiating from his body, smell the earthy scent that clung to him. Her pulse quickened, and she wasn't sure if it was from proximity to the bees or to him.

Automatically, clearly without really thinking about what he was doing, the Baron wrapped one long arm around Evelyn's waist, holding her steady on the uneven ground as she knelt next to him. The Baron's arm was like a steel band, but not restricting in any way, surprisingly gentle despite his immense strength.

Evelyn held her breath as the Baron carefully lifted the top of the hive further, revealing the intricate world within. She had expected chaos, a frenzied swarm of angry insects ready to attack. Instead, she found herself mesmerised by the orderly bustle before her.

The bees moved with purpose, each seeming to know its precise role in the complex dance of the hive. Workers scurried along the honeycomb, their bodies heavy with pollen. Others tended to the developing larvae, their movements gentle and deliberate. In the centre, surrounded by attendants, Evelyn caught a glimpse of the queen, her larger body unmistakable among her subjects.

"It's... extraordinary," Evelyn breathed, her earlier fear forgotten in the face of such marvellous efficiency. She leaned in closer, captivated by the intricate patterns of the honeycomb and the steady hum of thousands of tiny wings.

The Baron's voice was low and warm near her ear. "They each have a purpose, a place. Every bee knows exactly what it must do for the good of the hive."

Evelyn nodded, unable to tear her eyes away from the scene. She watched as a worker bee landed on the edge of the hive, its legs coated with bright yellow pollen. With practiced movements, it began to groom itself, storing the precious cargo in the pollen baskets on its legs.

"I had no idea they were so... organised," Evelyn admitted, her voice filled with wonder. "I always imagined it would be utter bedlam inside a hive."

The Baron chuckled softly, the sound rumbling through his chest. "Nature often surprises us with its inherent order. These little creatures have much to teach us about cooperation and purpose."

As they watched, a scout bee returned to the hive, performing an intricate dance that Evelyn couldn't quite follow. Other bees gathered around, seeming to pay close attention to the performance.

"What's it doing?" Evelyn asked, her curiosity overcoming her lingering nervousness.

"Ah," the Baron said, a note of excitement in his voice. "That's the waggle dance. It's telling the others where to find a new source of nectar."

Evelyn huffed out a small laugh, marvelling at the intricate dance of the bees. She watched, transfixed, as the Baron gently reached into the hive. His large hands moved with surprising delicacy, carefully pinching off a small piece of honeycomb. With practised ease, he brushed the bees off, ensuring none were harmed in the process.

The Baron turned to her, offering the golden morsel. "Here," he said, his voice low and warm. "Try this."

Evelyn hesitated, eyeing the sticky chunk dubiously. She'd never tasted honey straight from the comb before. Gingerly, she accepted it, feeling the waxy texture between her fingers.

"Go on," the Baron encouraged, a hint of amusement in his grey eyes.

Taking a deep breath, Evelyn brought the honeycomb to her lips and took a small bite. The moment the honey touched her tongue, her eyes widened in surprise and delight. It was unlike anything she'd ever tasted before - sweet, yes, but with complex floral notes that danced across her palate. The freshness was astonishing, so different from the processed honey she was accustomed to.

A laugh bubbled up from her chest, bright and genuine. "Oh!" she exclaimed, her face lighting up with pleasure. "It's absolutely divine! It's warm--I didn't think it would be warm!"

The Baron's lips quirked into a small smile, his eyes crinkling at the corners as he watched her reaction. Evelyn felt a warmth bloom in her chest that had nothing to do with the honey and everything to do with the way he was looking at her.

Evelyn laughed again, feeling a delightful sense of mischief, as if she were a child who had snuck a sweet from the kitchen. The honeycomb's rich flavour burst across her tongue once more as she took another bite, savouring the complex notes of wildflowers and summer sunshine.

The Baron watched her, his grey eyes alight with an unexpected warmth. A smile played at the corners of his mouth, softening the hard lines of his face. "You've got a bit of honey there," he said, his voice low and tinged with amusement.

Evelyn was acutely aware of every point of contact between them - his hand on her cheek, the warmth of his body so close to hers, the intensity of his gaze holding her own. Time seemed to slow as their eyes met. Evelyn was unable to look away, captivated by the intensity of the Baron's gaze. His hand lingered on her cheek, warm and calloused against her soft skin. She was acutely aware of how close they were standing, of the steady rise and fall of his chest, of the faint scent of leather and earth that clung to him.

The buzzing of the bees faded into the background as they knelt there, frozen in a moment that felt both endless and fleeting. Evelyn's heart raced, her pulse thundering in her ears. She saw something flicker in the Baron's eyes - a vulnerability, a longing that mirrored her own unexpected feelings.

Evelyn was momentarily breathless as she realised the Baron's touch had lingered far beyond what was necessary to remove the honey. His calloused thumb traced a gentle arc across her cheekbone, sending a shiver down her spine. She remained perfectly still, afraid that even the slightest movement might shatter this fragile moment.

Time seemed to slow, the world narrowing to just the two of them. The steady hum of the bees faded into the background, replaced by the thundering of her own heartbeat. Evelyn was acutely aware of every point of contact between them - his hand on her cheek, the warmth of his body so close to hers, the intensity of his gaze holding her own.

She searched his face, noting how the usual stern set of his jaw had softened, how his grey eyes held a kind of wonder she'd never seen before. The scar that marred one side of his face seemed less harsh in this light, a testament to his strength rather than a flaw.

Evelyn felt herself leaning into his touch, almost imperceptibly. Her lips parted slightly, though no words came. She was afraid to speak, to move, to do anything that might break this spell that had fallen over them.

The air between them seemed to crackle with unspoken tension. Evelyn's mind raced, a jumble of conflicting thoughts and emotions. She knew she should pull away, that this was highly improper, yet she couldn't bring herself to end the moment. Instead, she remained frozen, caught in the Baron's gaze, her skin tingling where his hand rested.

Chapter 24

The distant sound of a dog barking shattered the moment, startling both Evelyn and the Baron. His hand dropped away from her cheek, leaving her skin tingling where his touch had been. Evelyn's heart raced as she struggled to regain her composure, acutely aware of the impropriety of what had just transpired.

"Thank you," she managed to say, her voice barely above a whisper. "Both for... ensuring I was presentable, and for showing me the bees. It's truly fascinating."

The Baron nodded, his expression once again guarded as he turned back to the hive. "It was an overdue trip anyway," he said gruffly, carefully replacing the top of the beehive.

Evelyn tilted her head, curiosity overcoming her lingering embarrassment. "Overdue? Why is that?"

The Baron's hands stilled for a moment, and when he spoke, his voice held a note of hesitation. "It's... well, it's a bit of a superstition, I suppose. Beekeepers are meant to tell their bees about all changes."

"Changes?" Evelyn prompted, intrigued by this unexpected glimpse into the Baron's world.

He straightened up, brushing his hands on his trousers. "Aye. Births, deaths, marriages... any significant event in the beekeeper's life. It's said that if you don't keep the bees informed, they might leave the hive or stop producing honey."

Evelyn was smiling at the quaint tradition. "And what changes have you been remiss in sharing with your little friends?"

The Baron's gaze met hers, and for a moment, Evelyn saw a flicker of something unreadable in his grey eyes. "Your arrival, Miss Bane. I've neglected to inform them of our new governess."

Evelyn's heart fluttered as the Baron extended his hand to help her up. She hesitated for a moment, acutely aware of the lingering tension between them, before placing her hand in his. His grip was firm yet gentle as he effortlessly pulled her to her feet.

She took a moment to brush the errant dirt and leaves from her dress, finding with a slight twitch of amusement that she wasn't nearly so fussed about that as she was when she first arrived.

As they began to walk back towards the manor, Evelyn felt hyper-aware of the Baron's presence beside her. The silence between them felt charged, filled with unspoken words and emotions. She stole a glance at his profile, noting the way that his eyes roved over the landscape, catching every detail.

Curiosity gnawed at her, and before she could stop herself, Evelyn broke the silence. "What would you have told the bees about me?" she asked, her voice softer than she'd intended. "If I hadn't been here to meet them myself, I mean."

The Baron's stride faltered for a moment, and Evelyn saw a flicker of surprise cross his face. He seemed to consider her question carefully before responding.

"I suppose," he began, his deep voice rumbling low, "I would have told them that a new governess had arrived at the manor. That she was..." He paused, searching for the right words. "That she was unlike anyone I had expected."

Evelyn felt her cheeks warm at his words. "How so?" she pressed, unable to quell her curiosity.

The Baron's grey eyes met hers, and for a moment, Evelyn saw a vulnerability there that made her breath catch. "I would have told them that she was stubborn and opinionated," he said, a hint of amusement in his tone. "That she wasn't afraid to challenge me, even when it might have been wiser to hold her tongue."

Evelyn opened her mouth to protest, but the Baron continued before she could speak. "And I would have told them that she cared for my daughters with a fierceness that surprised me. That she was bringing life and laughter back into our home in a way I hadn't realised we needed." A pause. "That she was brave," the Baron added softly. "Braver than a governess has any right to be."

Evelyn felt her cheeks warm at the Baron's words. She had never considered herself brave before, and hearing him describe her thus stirred something within her. She ducked her head, both pleased and flustered by the unexpected praise.

They walked in companionable silence for a while, their footsteps crunching softly on the gravel path. Evelyn found her mind wandering, turning over the events of the past weeks like puzzle pieces that refused to fit together. There was something nagging at her, a persistent feeling that she was missing some crucial detail.

She glanced at the Baron, studying his profile as he gazed out over the rolling hills of his estate. His words about telling the bees of changes echoed in her mind, mingling with fragments of conversations and half-formed thoughts. The pieces were there, she was certain, but she couldn't quite make sense of them.

Evelyn frowned slightly, frustrated by her inability to pinpoint the source of her unease. Was it the Baron's unexpected softness towards her? The strange tension that had arisen between them at the beehives? Or was it something else entirely, some detail she had overlooked?

She thought back to her arrival at the manor, to the girls' lessons, to the storm and her mad dash across the fields. Each memory seemed to hold a clue, yet the full picture remained stubbornly out of reach.

As they drew nearer to the house, Evelyn found herself stealing glances at the Baron, wondering if he held the key to this puzzle she couldn't solve. But his face remained impassive, giving away nothing of his thoughts.

The nagging feeling persisted, like an itch she couldn't quite reach. Evelyn sighed softly, resigning herself to the fact that for now, at least, the mystery would remain unsolved.

Evelyn's brow furrowed as they continued their walk back to the manor. The nagging feeling of something amiss persisted, gnawing at the edges of her thoughts. She tried to shake it off, to focus on the beauty of the countryside around her, but the sensation refused to dissipate.

The Baron glanced at her, his grey eyes narrowing slightly. "You seem troubled, Miss Bane. Is something the matter?"

Evelyn hesitated, unsure how to articulate the vague unease that had settled over her. "I... I'm not entirely certain," she admitted, her voice soft. "There's something I can't quite put my finger on. It's as if I'm missing a crucial piece of information, but I've no idea what it might be."

The Baron nodded thoughtfully, his gaze sweeping over the rolling hills of his estate. "I understand the feeling," he said after a moment. "When I find myself in such a state, unable to work something out, I've found it best to simply focus on the things I can do."

Evelyn tilted her head, intrigued by his perspective. "How do you mean?"

"Well," the Baron continued, his voice taking on a contemplative tone, "sometimes it's best to be like the bees we just observed. They don't fret over the grand design of things or worry about what they can't control. They simply attend to their task in life, and more often than not, things work out as they should."

Evelyn considered his words, finding a certain wisdom in them. "I suppose there is something to be said for focusing on one's duties," she mused.

The Baron's lips quirked into a small smile. "Indeed. The bees don't question their purpose or worry about what might come tomorrow. They simply do what needs to be done, day after day. And in doing so, they create something rather extraordinary, don't they?"

The Baron paused and nodded out towards a field of wheat that waved lazily in the warm summer breeze. "I can't do anything about not enough rain, or bad market prices, but I can do something about that field right over there—I can make sure it gets harvested. There's joy and beauty in that fact."

Evelyn couldn't help but smile at the Baron's unexpected philosophical turn. On impulse, she nudged him playfully with her elbow, her eyes sparkling with mischief.

"My, my, Baron Hastings," she teased, her voice light. "That's awfully romantic for a country lord. I never took you for a poet."

The Baron waved her off, but Evelyn caught the hint of amusement in his eyes. His lips twitched, fighting a smile he seemed determined not to show.

"Hardly poetry, Miss Bane," he grumbled, though there was no real bite to his words. "Merely practical observations."

Evelyn laughed softly, shaking her head. As they approached the manor, she turned to face him, suddenly aware of how much she had enjoyed their unexpected outing.

"Thank you for the walk, Baron," she said, her voice warm with sincerity. "And for sharing your bees with me. It was truly fascinating."

The Baron nodded, his expression softening almost imperceptibly. "You're welcome, Miss Bane."

With a final smile, Evelyn entered the manor, her mind still buzzing with thoughts of honey and hidden depths. She made her way to the grand staircase, her hand trailing lightly along the polished banister as she began to ascend.

Halfway up, a sudden impulse seized her. Evelyn paused, turning to look back down at the entry hall. Her chest tightened, and she struggled to find her breath.

The Baron stood at the foot of the stairs, his grey eyes fixed upon her. There was an intensity in his gaze that made Evelyn's heart skip a beat. For a moment, neither of them moved, caught in a tableau of unspoken emotions.

Evelyn's heart raced as she stood frozen on the stairs, caught in the Baron's intense gaze. The moment stretched between them, warm with unspoken emotions and possibilities.

Suddenly, the steward's voice cut through the silence. "My lord, there's an urgent matter requiring your attention."

The spell broken, Evelyn seized her chance. She whirled around and dashed up the remaining stairs, her cheeks burning. As she reached the landing, she nearly collided with Nell, who gave her a curious look.

"Miss Bane? Is everything alright?" the maid asked, her eyes filled with concern.

Evelyn mumbled a hasty excuse and hurried past, retreating to the sanctuary of her room. She closed the door behind her and leaned against it, her breath coming in quick gasps. She put the backs of her hands on her cheeks, feeling how flushed they were.

What was happening to her? She pressed a hand to her chest, feeling the frantic beating of her heart. The Baron's gaze had stirred something within her, something she thought long buried after she had given up Richard.

Evelyn crossed to the window, staring out at the rolling countryside without really seeing it. She had promised herself she would never again be at the mercy of a man's whims. She had vowed to live for herself, to carve out her own path in the world.

And yet... the way the Baron had looked at her, the gentleness of his touch as he wiped away the honey, the unexpected depth he had revealed during their walk - it all threatened to unravel her carefully constructed defences.

Evelyn closed her eyes, conflicted. She had worked so hard to keep her secrets, to maintain her independence. But the growing warmth she felt in the Baron's presence was becoming harder to ignore. It both thrilled and terrified her.

She thought of Richard, of the pain his betrayal had caused. Could she risk opening her heart again? And what of her position here? If the Baron knew the truth about her past, would he cast her out?

Evelyn sank onto the edge of her bed, her mind a whirlwind of conflicting emotions. She knew she stood at a crossroads, torn between the safety of her secrets and the tantalising possibility of something more.

Chapter 25

James sat at his desk, poring over maps and ledgers with his steward, Mr. Hawkins. The failed canal project on the neighbouring estate had thrown their plans into disarray, and they were now scrambling to find alternative routes to market for the estate's grain.

"What about the old road through Millbrook, sir?" Mr. Smith suggested, tracing a winding line on the map with his finger.

James shook his head. "Too narrow for our wagons. We'd lose half the crop before we even reached the main road."

He leaned back in his chair, rubbing his temples. The constant worry over the estate's finances was beginning to wear on him. His eyes drifted to the window, where he caught a glimpse of Evelyn walking with the girls in the garden. For a moment, he allowed himself to be distracted by the sight of her, her laughter carrying faintly through the glass.

"My lord?" Mr. Smith's voice snapped him back to attention.

"Yes, sorry," James muttered, forcing his gaze back to the papers before him. "What about the river? Could we use barges?"

The steward frowned. "It's possible, but it would require significant investment in equipment and men skilled in river navigation."

James drummed his fingers on the desk, weighing the costs against the potential benefits. The estate's future hung in the balance, and he couldn't afford to make the wrong decision.

"We need to consider every option," he said finally. "Draw up a detailed proposal for the river route, including all associated costs. And see if you can find out what our neighbours to the east are planning. Perhaps we could share resources."

Mr. Smith nodded, gathering up the papers. "Very good, my lord. I'll have the report ready for you by tomorrow afternoon."

As the steward left, James found his gaze drawn once again to the window. Evelyn was now kneeling beside Augusta, examining something in the flower beds. He watched as she gently guided the girl's hand, explaining something with animated gestures.

James forced his attention back to the papers strewn across his desk, but the numbers and figures blurred before his eyes. He reached for a map of the local waterways, tracing the sinuous lines of rivers and streams with his finger. The idea of transporting crops by river had merit, but as he studied the routes, his mind betrayed him once more.

The rushing water on the map morphed into the torrent that had nearly swept him away that fateful day. And there was Evelyn, racing across the fields to warn him, her skirts hitched up and her face flushed with exertion.

James closed his eyes, but the image only grew more vivid. He saw her again as she'd looked after they'd scrambled to safety: rain-soaked and dishevelled, her hair a wild tangle about her face. But it was her eyes that haunted him most—wide and determined, filled with a fierce light he'd never seen before.

He shook his head, trying to dislodge the memory. It was folly to dwell on such things. He was a widower with responsibilities, not some lovesick youth. And yet...

The scent of damp earth and rain filled his nostrils, a phantom from that day. He could almost feel the warmth of her body as they'd huddled together on the embankment, their breath coming in ragged gasps.

"Damn it all," James muttered, pushing back from his desk. He stood and paced the length of his study, willing his traitorous mind to focus on the task at hand. But every time he glanced at the map, he saw only Evelyn's face, rain-streaked and beautiful.

With a frustrated growl, James turned to the window. In the gardens below, Evelyn was now showing Julia how to prune a rosebush. Her movements were graceful, her smile warm as she guided the girl's hands. James found himself leaning closer, drinking in the sight of her.

James watched from his study window as Evelyn and the girls crouched near a flowering shrub. Julia's excited squeal carried across the garden, and he saw her carefully pluck something from a leaf. Even from this distance, he could see the triumphant grin on her face as she turned to Evelyn.

He tensed, anticipating Evelyn's reaction. Surely a London lady would recoil from whatever creepy-crawly Julia had discovered. He'd seen it countless times before—governesses who claimed to love the outdoors, only to shriek at the first sign of an insect.

To his astonishment, Evelyn held out her hand without hesitation. Julia gently deposited her find—a plump, fuzzy caterpillar—onto Evelyn's palm. James leaned closer to the window, fascinated by the scene unfolding outside.

Evelyn's laughter floated to him on the languid summer breeze, light and melodious. She bent her head, examining the caterpillar as it inched across her skin. The expression on her face made James's breath catch in his throat. It was the same look of wonder and delight he'd seen when she'd first encountered the beehive—a mixture of curiosity and joy that transformed her entire countenance.

He found himself captivated by the sight. Evelyn's eyes sparkled as she pointed out the caterpillar's markings to the girls, who clustered around her, equally entranced. Her cheeks were flushed with excitement, and a stray lock of hair had escaped its pins, curling against her neck.

James realised he was gripping the windowsill, his knuckles white. He forced himself to relax, but couldn't tear his gaze away from Evelyn. She was so different from what he'd expected—so much more. The way she engaged with his daughters, encouraging their curiosity about the world around them, stirred something long dormant within him.

As he watched, Evelyn carefully transferred the caterpillar back to a leaf. She knelt beside the girls, pointing out where it might build its cocoon. Her enthusiasm was infectious, and James found himself smiling despite his best efforts to maintain his usual stern demeanour.

Like a great dog, James shook himself all over and at last managed to pull back from the window. Inwardly, he cursed himself without any real conviction for insisting that his study be in a room so near the gardens, thinking that it would be a comfort on days he was trapped indoors.

James finally surrendered to the restlessness that had been plaguing him. With a sigh, he pushed back from his desk and rose to his feet. The sudden movement caught the attention of his two hunting dogs, Brutus and Caesar, who had been dozing near the fireplace. Their heads lifted in unison, eyes bright with anticipation.

"Easy, lads," James murmured, crossing the room to where they lay. He knelt beside them, running his hands over their sleek heads. Brutus, the older of the pair, pushed his muzzle into James's palm, while Caesar's tail thumped eagerly against the floor.

The familiar warmth of their fur beneath his fingers soothed James, grounding him in a way that poring over ledgers and maps never could. He scratched behind Brutus's ears, eliciting a contented groan from the old dog.

"What do you say we stretch our legs, eh?" James asked, his voice low and conspiratorial. Both dogs perked up at the suggestion, Caesar rising to his feet with youthful exuberance.

James stood, his knees protesting slightly. He realised with a start how long he'd been hunched over his desk, lost in a maze of figures and worries—and distracting thoughts of Evelyn. The dogs pressed close to his legs, their excitement palpable.

As he reached for his walking stick, James's gaze was drawn once more to the window. The afternoon sun bathed the gardens in a warm, golden light. He could just make out Evelyn and the girls in the distance, still engrossed in their explorations of the natural world.

A part of him longed to join them, to share in their wonder and laughter. But he pushed the thought aside, reminding himself of the countless tasks that demanded his attention. Still, as he turned towards the door, dogs at his heels, James couldn't quite shake the image of Evelyn's radiant smile from his mind.

James strode across the fields towards the Wilkins' farm, his boots sinking into the soft earth with each step. Brutus and Caesar loped ahead, their noses to the ground as they searched for interesting scents. The crisp spring air carried the promise of new life, a reminder that lambing season was fast approaching.

Absently, James plucked a sturdy stick from the ground and tossed it ahead. Caesar bounded after it, while Brutus, ever the more dignified of the pair, merely watched his younger companion with what James could have sworn was a look of disdain.

As he walked, James's mind wandered. He found himself thinking of Evelyn, as he so often did these days. The way she'd looked in the garden, her face alight with wonder as she showed the girls a caterpillar. It was a far cry from the prim London lady who'd first arrived at his estate.

He shook his head, trying to dislodge the image. There were more pressing matters at hand. The upcoming lambing season would be crucial for the estate's finances. With the failed canal project and the uncertainty in the grain markets, a successful lambing could mean the difference between a prosperous year and a lean one.

Caesar returned with the stick, dropping it at James's feet with an expectant look. James obliged, throwing it again, this time towards a copse of trees in the distance. As he watched the dog race after it, he couldn't help but envy the animal's single-minded focus. How simple life must be when one's only concern was the next throw of a stick.

The Wilkins' farm came into view, a tidy collection of stone buildings nestled in a small valley. James could see old Tom Wilkins in the yard, checking the fences of the lambing pen. The farmer waved as James approached, and James raised a hand in greeting.

He needed to focus on the task at hand. The estate, his tenants, his daughters—these were the things that should occupy his thoughts. Not a pair of bright eyes and a laugh that seemed to chase away the shadows that had cloaked his heart for so long.

James approached the field where Farmer Wilkins stood, his eyes scanning the flock of sheep grazing contentedly. A sense of satisfaction washed over him as he took in the sight of the ewes, their sides swollen with the promise of new life.

"Good afternoon, my lord," Wilkins called out, touching his cap in greeting. "Come to check on our woolly friends, have you?"

James nodded, his gaze still fixed on the sheep. "They're looking well, Tom. Heavy with lambs, I see."

Wilkins beamed with pride. "Aye, that they are. Should be dropping soon, if I'm not mistaken. It's been a good year for feed, and it shows in the flock."

"Mmm," James murmured absently, his mind already racing ahead to calculations of potential profits and the impact on the estate's finances.

The farmer's voice cut through his musings. "The young ladies will be pleased, I reckon. Nothing quite like seeing the little ones frolicking about."

James blinked, caught off guard by the mention of his daughters. For a moment, he saw them as they had been years ago, squealing with delight at the sight of newborn lambs. The memory brought an unexpected pang of nostalgia.

"Yes, I suppose they will," he replied, his voice gruff to mask the sudden emotion. He cleared his throat, forcing his thoughts back to the practical matters at hand. "What's your estimate for this year's crop, Tom?"

As Wilkins launched into a detailed assessment of the expected lambing numbers, James found his attention wandering once more. He couldn't help but wonder how Evelyn might react to the sight of the newborn lambs. Would she share in the girls' excitement, or would she maintain the prim demeanour of a proper London lady?

The image of Evelyn, her face alight with wonder as she cradled a tiny lamb, rose unbidden in his mind. James pushed the thought away, irritated by his own distraction. He had more important matters to consider than the fancies of a governess.

James abruptly cut off Farmer Wilkins mid-sentence, his patience wearing thin. "Thank you for your time, Tom. I'll be in touch about the lambing arrangements."

Without waiting for a response, he turned on his heel and strode away, leaving the bewildered farmer in his wake. Brutus and Caesar fell into step beside him, sensing their master's agitation.

As he made his way back across the fields, James found his thoughts in disarray. He'd come out here to clear his head, to focus on the estate's needs, but instead, he felt more scattered than ever. The upcoming lambing season, the grain shipments, the estate's finances—all of it seemed to blur together in his mind, overshadowed by thoughts of...

James shook his head forcefully, as if he could physically dislodge the image of Evelyn from his mind. This was becoming intolerable. He couldn't afford such distractions, not with so much at stake.

But as he walked, a realisation slowly dawned on him. Perhaps the reason for his distraction was not what he'd initially thought. It wasn't some foolish infatuation—no, it was simpler than that. He still owed Evelyn a debt for saving his life during the flood. The weight of that unpaid obligation was what was truly bothering him.

James felt a surge of relief at this revelation. Of course, that was it. He was a man who prided himself on meeting his obligations, and this unresolved debt was gnawing at him, throwing him off balance.

Well, there was a simple solution to that. He would repay Evelyn for her bravery, and then everything would return to normal. He'd be able to focus on his work again, free from this constant distraction.

As he approached the manor, James's stride lengthened, fuelled by his newfound determination. He would settle this debt, and then he'd finally be at peace. Everything would go back to the way it was supposed to be.

He ignored the small voice in the back of his mind that whispered doubts about this plan. After all, what could he possibly offer that would adequately repay someone for saving his life?

James strode back towards the manor, his mind racing with newfound purpose. The solution had come to him like a bolt from the blue—the only gift truly worthy of Evelyn's actions was the chance at a new life. It was so obvious now that he wondered how he hadn't seen it before.

Chapter 26

As he approached the house, James slowed his pace, considering the implications of his idea. Doubt crept in as he mounted the steps to the front door. Would Evelyn see this as the generous offer it was meant to be, or would her independent spirit be offended? James frowned, realising the delicacy of the situation.

He paused in the entrance hall, removing his hat and gloves as he pondered his next move. The more he thought about it, the more he realised he needed expert advice. This wasn't a matter to be handled lightly or without proper consideration of all potential outcomes.

"I'll need to speak with Jones," James muttered to himself, referring to his long-time solicitor. The man had a keen understanding of both legal matters and social niceties. He would know how to structure such an offer in a way that wouldn't cause offence or misunderstanding.

Decision made, James headed towards his study to pen a letter requesting an urgent meeting with Mr Jones. As he walked, he found himself both excited by the prospect of repaying his debt to Evelyn and oddly unsettled by the thought of her leaving Thornfield.

James paced the length of his study, his steps quick and purposeful. The late hour did nothing to dampen his enthusiasm. If anything, the quiet of the house only fuelled his anticipation. He felt a surge of energy coursing through him, a vitality he hadn't experienced in years.

He paused by the window, gazing out at the moonlit grounds. The prospect of settling his debt with Evelyn filled him with an unfamiliar excitement. He could already imagine the look of surprise on her face, the way her eyes would light up when he presented his offer.

James ran a hand through his hair, a restless gesture he'd thought long abandoned. He felt almost boyish in his eagerness, a feeling both thrilling and disconcerting. Part of him wanted to seek her out immediately, to share his plans and see her reaction.

But no, he reminded himself. This required finesse, proper planning. He couldn't rush in like an overeager schoolboy. Still, the thought of making Evelyn happy, of giving her a chance at a new life, sent a warm rush through him.

He moved to his desk, fingers drumming an impatient rhythm on the polished wood. Perhaps he could at least hint at his intentions, gauge her reaction. The idea of waiting until everything was perfectly arranged suddenly seemed unbearable.

Before he could talk himself out of it, James strode towards the door. He'd find Evelyn, just for a moment. A brief conversation to set the stage for what was to come. His heart raced as he stepped into the hallway, filled with an anticipation he hadn't felt in years.

James took the stairs two at a time, his heart pounding with a mixture of excitement and nervous energy. The quiet of the house at this late hour barely registered in his mind as he focused solely on reaching Evelyn's room. The impropriety of his actions never crossed his thoughts; all that mattered was sharing his plans with her.

As he reached the landing, James paused for a moment, catching his breath. He ran a hand through his hair, attempting to smooth it into some semblance of order. His fingers brushed against the rough texture of his scar, but for once, he paid it no mind.

James continued up the stairs, his footsteps muffled by the thick carpet. As he rounded the corner, he stopped short, surprised to see Nell standing in the hallway. The maid was dusting the ornate frame of a portrait, her movements slow and almost reverent.

His gaze shifted to the painting itself, and James felt a familiar ache in his chest. The late Baroness Ayles looked down at him; her strawberry blonde hair cascading over her shoulders, her blue eyes seeming to sparkle even in the stillness of oil and canvas. It was the same hair that graced his daughters' heads, a constant reminder of what he'd lost.

Nell's face was turned towards the portrait, and even in the dim light of the hallway, James could see the sheen of unshed tears in her eyes. The maid's usual cheerful demeanour was absent, replaced by an expression of wistful melancholy.

Concern furrowed James's brow. He'd known Nell since she was a girl, and it was unlike her to appear so affected. "Nell," he said softly, not wanting to startle her. "Is all well?"

Nell turned, hastily wiping at her eyes. "Oh! My lord, I didn't hear you approach," she said, her voice slightly unsteady. She glanced back at the portrait, a sad smile tugging at her lips. "I was just... remembering, I suppose."

James nodded, understanding all too well the power of memories. He looked up at his late wife's face, feeling a complex mix of emotions swirling within him. "She had that effect on people," he murmured, more to himself than to Nell.

"Forgive me, my lord," Nell said with a watery smile. "I suppose she must never be far from your thoughts."

James felt a sudden jolt, as if the floor had shifted beneath his feet. The realisation struck him like a slap to the face: he hadn't thought of his late wife in... how long? Days? Weeks? The absence of her memory in his recent thoughts was a gaping void he hadn't even noticed until this moment.

Guilt crashed over him like a wave, threatening to drag him under. How could he have forgotten her, even for a moment? And worse, he knew exactly what—or rather, who—had occupied his mind instead. Evelyn's face flashed before his eyes, and James felt a surge of shame so intense it made him physically recoil.

He swallowed hard, forcing himself to meet Nell's gaze. "Yes," he said, his voice rougher than he'd intended. "Yes, of course. She's... she's never far from my thoughts."

The lie tasted bitter on his tongue, but James couldn't bring himself to admit the truth. Not to Nell, not to himself. He glanced up at the portrait again, willing himself to feel the familiar ache of loss, the constant companion he'd lived with for so long.

But even now, with his late wife's image before him, James found his thoughts drifting back to Evelyn. The contrast between the two women—one a cherished memory, the other a living, breathing presence that had somehow woven herself into the fabric of his daily life—left him feeling adrift and uncertain.

James felt a tightness in his chest as he looked at Nell, her eyes still glistening with unshed tears. He cleared his throat, trying to find his voice. "Do you... do you think of her often, Nell?"

The maid's gaze softened, a wistful smile playing at her lips. "I do, my lord. It's hard not to, especially when I'm tending to the house." She paused, her fingers tracing the edge of her apron. "Sometimes I can't help but wonder what the Baroness would have thought of all the changes on the estate, and in the house itself."

James felt his stomach drop, guilt washing over him anew. He'd made so many changes in recent years, driven by necessity and his own restless desire to move forward. Had he inadvertently erased her presence from their home?

Nell sighed, her eyes drifting back to the portrait. "And I wonder..." she hesitated, as if unsure whether to continue. "I wonder what she would have thought of a stranger raising her children. The Baroness was such a devoted mother, after all."

That made James's veins turn to ice. He'd been so caught up in his plans for Evelyn, in the excitement of offering her a new life, that he'd forgotten the most important thing: his daughters. His late wife's daughters. How could he have even considered bringing in someone else to raise them, to shape their futures?

He stared at the portrait, at the familiar curve of his wife's smile, the sparkle in her painted eyes. For the first time in years, James felt truly lost, adrift in a sea of conflicting emotions and forgotten loyalties.

James stood rooted to the spot, his gaze fixed on the portrait of his late wife. The familiar ache in his chest had returned, but now it was tinged with a sharp edge of guilt. He felt torn between the past and the present, between duty and desire.

It's... comforting to know that you'll always be here, Nell," he said, his voice rough with emotion. "To remember her, to keep her memory alive in this house."

Nell smiled softly, her eyes still glistening. "Of course, my lord. The Baroness was... she was special to all of us." She paused, then added gently, "If you'll excuse me, I should finish my rounds."

James nodded absently, barely registering Nell's quiet departure. His attention remained fixed on the portrait, on the familiar features of the woman he'd loved and lost. He found himself searching her painted eyes, as if hoping to find some guidance, some answer to the turmoil in his heart.

The silence of the hallway pressed in around him, broken only by the soft ticking of a distant clock. James felt the weight of the years since her passing, the slow healing that had begun to take place without his even realising it. And now, faced with her image, he felt caught between two worlds.

He thought of Evelyn, of the plans he'd been so eager to share just moments ago. The excitement he'd felt now seemed distant, overshadowed by a renewed sense of loss and confusion. James ran a hand over his face, feeling the rough texture of his scar beneath his fingers.

What would you have me do?" he whispered to the portrait, knowing full well no answer would come. Yet he stood there, waiting, as if the painted canvas might somehow impart some wisdom, some direction for the path ahead.

James pulled out his pocket watch, the smooth gold case cool against his palm. The delicate hands pointed to just past eight o'clock. If he hurried, he might catch Evelyn in the hallway as she prepared the girls for bed.

His gaze drifted down the corridor towards Evelyn's room and the girls' chambers. He could almost hear the soft murmur of their voices, the gentle rustling of bedclothes being turned down. For a moment, he felt an overwhelming urge to join them, to be part of that quiet, domestic scene.

But then his eyes shifted to the opposite end of the hallway, where his own room lay in solitary silence. The portrait of his late wife seemed to watch him, her painted eyes holding a question he couldn't quite decipher.

James stood frozen, caught between two paths. His hand tightened around the watch, its steady ticking a counterpoint to his racing thoughts. He took a half-step towards Evelyn and the girls, then hesitated, glancing back at his own room.

The weight of his earlier guilt pressed down on him, making each potential step feel leaden. He wavered, indecision rooting him to the spot. The excitement that had propelled him up the stairs now felt distant, replaced by a confusing mix of longing and uncertainty.

James looked down at the watch again, watching the seconds tick by as he stood paralysed in the hallway, unable to choose which way to go.

Chapter 27

Evelyn watched with amusement as Julia and Augusta darted about the meadow, their laughter echoing across the sun-dappled grass. She'd devised a scavenger hunt as a way to combine their lessons with some much-needed outdoor exercise, and the girls had taken to it with surprising enthusiasm.

"I've found the acorn!" Julia shouted, holding up her prize triumphantly.

Augusta, not to be outdone, emerged from behind a nearby oak tree. "And I've got the bird's feather."

Evelyn smiled, ticking off the items on her list. "Well done, girls. Now, can either of you spot something that starts with the letter 'M' that is neither animal nor mineral?"

The twins exchanged a glance before dashing off in opposite directions. Evelyn leaned back against the rough bark of the tree, relishing the warmth of the spring sun on her face. She'd never imagined she'd find such joy in teaching, let alone in the countryside she'd once dreaded.

"Miss Bane! Miss Bane!" Julia's excited voice pulled her from her reverie. "Is this what you meant?" She held up a small, delicate mushroom, her eyes shining with pride.

"Excellent work, Julia," Evelyn praised, unable to keep the warmth from her voice. "And Augusta, have you found—"

"Moss," Augusta interrupted, appearing at her sister's side with a clump of green fuzz in her hand. "It also starts with 'M'."

Evelyn chuckled. "Indeed it does. You're both doing splendidly."

As the girls continued their search, Evelyn was marvelling at how far they'd come. Augusta's quiet intelligence had blossomed, while Julia's exuberance had found a productive outlet. And she, too, had changed. The London lady who'd arrived at Ayles Manor seemed a stranger now.

"Miss Bane?" Augusta's voice was uncharacteristically hesitant. "What's the next item?"

Evelyn consulted her list. "Something that reminds you of happiness."

The girls paused, their brows furrowed in thought. Evelyn watched them, curious to see what they'd choose. After a moment, Julia's face lit up, and she raced towards a patch of wildflowers.

Evelyn's gaze followed Julia as she darted towards the wildflowers, her golden hair streaming behind her like a banner. A sudden prickling sensation at the nape of her neck made Evelyn turn, and she nearly jumped out of her skin to find the Baron standing mere feet away.

"My lord!" she exclaimed, pressing a hand to her chest. "I didn't hear you approach."

The Baron stood as tall and sturdy as one of the ancient oaks that dotted the meadow, his broad shoulders casting a shadow over her. Despite her startlement, Evelyn was unconsciously angling towards him, as if drawn by some unseen force.

"My apologies, Miss Bane," he said, his voice a low rumble. "I didn't mean to startle you."

Evelyn's heart, which had been racing from the shock, now seemed to quicken for an entirely different reason. She cleared her throat, willing herself to maintain her composure.

"Not at all, my lord. We were just in the middle of a scavenger hunt. The girls are searching for something that reminds them of happiness."

The Baron's grey eyes swept over the meadow, lingering on his daughters as they scoured the grass and flowers. "And what would you choose, Miss Bane?"

The question caught her off guard. Evelyn was staring up at him, struck by the way the sunlight caught the silver threads in his dark hair. She opened her mouth to respond, but no words came.

"Papa!" Augusta's voice broke the moment. "Have you come to join our lesson?"

The Baron's lips twitched in what might have been the ghost of a smile. "I'm afraid I'm woefully unprepared for Miss Bane's clever challenges."

Julia bounded up, clutching a handful of buttercups. "Look, Miss Bane! These remind me of happiness. They're so bright and cheerful!"

Evelyn tore her gaze from the Baron, focusing on her young charge. "That's a lovely choice, Julia. And you, Augusta?"

The other twin held up a small, smooth stone. "This reminds me of the ones we used to skip across the pond with Mama."

A heavy silence fell, and Evelyn saw the Baron stiffen beside her. She ached to reach out, to offer some word of comfort, but propriety held her back.

Evelyn watched as Julia's eyes lit up, her gaze fixed on the small stone in Augusta's hand.

"Oh! Can we go skip stones on the pond, Miss Bane? Please?" Julia pleaded, bouncing on her toes.

Augusta, usually more reserved, nodded eagerly. "It's been so long since we've done that."

Evelyn glanced at the Baron, uncertain how he would react to the mention of an activity they'd once shared with their mother. To her surprise, he gave a slight nod.

"Very well," Evelyn said, smiling at the girls. "But mind you don't get your dresses wet."

The twins dashed off towards the pond, their laughter carried back on the breeze. Evelyn was falling into step beside the Baron as they followed at a more sedate pace.

The silence between them felt charged, like the air before a storm. From the corner of her eye, Evelyn noticed the Baron's hands clenching and unclenching at his sides. His jaw worked as if he were chewing on words he couldn't quite spit out.

"The girls seem to be thriving under your tutelage, Miss Bane," he said at last, his voice gruff.

Evelyn felt a flush of pride. "Thank you, my lord. They're remarkable young ladies."

The Baron nodded, then fell silent once more. Evelyn could almost hear the gears turning in his mind, sense the tension radiating off him in waves. She longed to ask what troubled him, but held her tongue, acutely aware of the line between governess and employer.

As they neared the pond, the sound of splashing and giggles reached them. Evelyn saw the Baron's shoulders relax a fraction, a ghost of a smile tugging at his lips as he watched his daughters.

Evelyn watched the girls skipping stones across the pond's surface, a sense of contentment settling over her. The gentle splashing of water and the girls' laughter created a soothing melody, one that seemed to ease the tension that had been building between her and the Baron.

Suddenly, the Baron turned to face her, his grey eyes intense. "Miss Bane, I... I realise I haven't properly thanked you for your bravery that day."

Evelyn blinked, caught off guard by the abrupt change in conversation. Her mind raced back to that harrowing afternoon when she'd raced across the fields to warn him of the impending flood. The memory of rain-soaked clothes and the thundering of her own heartbeat flooded her senses.

"My lord, I..." she began, fumbling for words. "It was nothing, truly. Anyone would have done the same."

The Baron shook his head, a hint of frustration creasing his brow. "No, Miss Bane. Not anyone would have risked their life as you did. I've been remiss in not acknowledging it sooner."

Evelyn felt her cheeks warm under his intense gaze. She clasped her hands tightly in front of her, unsure how to respond to this unexpected show of gratitude. The Baron's usual gruff demeanour had softened, and she found herself captivated by this rare glimpse of vulnerability.

"I... I'm glad I was able to help, my lord," she managed, her voice barely above a whisper. "Your safety, and that of the girls, is of utmost importance to me."

The Baron opened his mouth as if to say more, but hesitated. Evelyn held her breath, acutely aware of the charged atmosphere between them. The sounds of the girls' play seemed to fade into the background, leaving only the rustle of leaves and the pounding of her own heart.

Evelyn's heart fluttered as the Baron's intense gaze held hers. His usual stern demeanour had softened, revealing a vulnerability that both intrigued and unsettled her.

"I would still like to thank you properly, Miss Bane," he said, his voice low and earnest. "Your actions that day were... extraordinary."

She swallowed hard, fighting the urge to look away. "My lord, I assure you, it's not necessary—"

"It is," he interrupted, then seemed to catch himself. "At least, I feel it is. And... there's something else."

Evelyn waited, watching as he struggled to find the right words. It was a rare sight, the usually decisive Baron Hastings at a loss.

"I would like to ask a favour of you, Miss Bane," he finally managed, his words coming out in a rush.

Evelyn couldn't help herself. She arched an eyebrow, a teasing smile playing at the corners of her mouth. "My lord, do you intend to thank me by asking me for a favour?"

The Baron's eyes widened for a moment, and Evelyn feared she'd overstepped. But then, to her surprise and delight, a chuckle escaped him—a rich, warm sound that sent a shiver down her spine.

"I suppose it does sound rather contradictory when put that way," he admitted, the hint of a smile softening his features.

Evelyn was momentarily breathless as she waited for the Baron to continue. His usual stern demeanour had softened, and she found herself captivated by the warmth in his grey eyes.

"I would like to ask if you would consider acting as hostess at the tenants' luncheon," he said, his words coming out in a rush. "If you were to attend, it would mean the tenants' wives could join as well. It would make them very happy."

Evelyn blinked, surprised by the request. She had heard whispers of the annual luncheon from the staff, but never imagined she would be invited to play such a prominent role. As she pondered the invitation, she couldn't help but notice the eager expression on the Baron's face. It was clear that this request meant more to him than he was letting on.

"I... I'm honoured by your request, my lord," Evelyn said, her mind racing. "But surely there must be someone more suitable? Perhaps one of the local gentry ladies?"

The Baron shook his head, a flicker of something—disappointment?—crossing his features. "There's no one I would trust more with this task, Miss Bane. Your kindness and intelligence would be most welcome."

Evelyn felt a warmth bloom in her chest at his words. She glanced towards the pond, where Julia and Augusta were still engrossed in their game, then back to the Baron's hopeful face. In that moment, she realised how much she wanted to attend, not only to help the Baron, but for the chance to be on his arm.

Evelyn's heart fluttered at the Baron's words, but a knot of uncertainty tightened in her stomach. She longed to accept his invitation, to stand by his side at the luncheon, yet doubt gnawed at her resolve.

"My lord, I'm deeply honoured by your request," she began, her voice soft. "But I fear I may not be the right choice. I've never attended such an event, let alone acted as hostess. I wouldn't know what to do or say."

The Baron's brow furrowed, and for a moment, Evelyn thought she saw a flicker of disappointment in his eyes. But then his expression softened, and he took a step closer to her.

"Miss Bane," he said, his voice low and earnest, "I have no doubts that you will do splendidly. You need only be yourself."

Evelyn's breath was stilled at his proximity. She could smell the faint scent of leather and pine that clung to him, a scent she had come to associate with safety and strength.

"But what if I make a mistake?" she whispered, voicing her deepest fear. "What if I embarrass you or offend the tenants?"

The Baron's lips quirked into a small smile. "I assure you, Miss Bane, that is impossible. Your kindness and genuine nature will win them over, just as they have..." He trailed off, clearing his throat. "Just as they have endeared you to the girls."

Evelyn felt her cheeks warm at his words. She glanced towards the pond, where Julia and Augusta were still engrossed in their game, then back to the Baron's hopeful face. For just a moment, Evelyn caught a glimpse of the man that he had been before the great tragedy that seemed to divide his life in two.

Evelyn's heart raced as she contemplated the Baron's request. The warmth of his gaze and the sincerity in his voice made her want to accept on the spot. However, before she could formulate a response, a loud splash and a shriek of laughter from the pond caught her attention.

She turned to see Julia waist-deep in the water, her dress soaked through, while Augusta stood at the edge, trying to coax her sister back to dry land.

"Oh, goodness," Evelyn muttered, her cheeks flushing with embarrassment. She'd been so caught up in her conversation with the Baron that she'd neglected her charges. "I'm terribly sorry, my lord, but I must attend to the girls before they catch their death of cold."

The Baron nodded, a hint of amusement playing at the corners of his mouth. "Of course, Miss Bane. We wouldn't want that."

Evelyn took a step towards the pond, then paused, turning back to face him. "As for your request, my lord... might I have some time to consider it? It's a significant responsibility, and I wouldn't want to give you an answer without proper thought."

It was impossible to miss the way the Baron's face fell, though it was nearly imperceptible to anyone not well-acquainted with him. "Of course."

With a grateful nod, Evelyn hurried towards the pond, calling out to Julia and Augusta. As she approached, a mix of emotions swirled within her. She felt excitement at the prospect of attending the luncheon, nervousness about her ability to fulfill such a role, and a lingering warmth from the Baron's unexpected praise..

As Evelyn herded the girls back towards the house, her mind whirled with thoughts of the Baron's unexpected invitation. Julia's dress dripped steadily, leaving a trail of puddles in her wake, whilst Augusta tutted and fussed over her twin. Evelyn barely registered their chatter, her attention focused inward.

She imagined herself at the tenants' luncheon, seated across from the Baron at a long table laden with fine china and sparkling silverware. In her mind's eye, she saw herself engaging in witty conversation, drawing smiles from the usually stern-faced man. The thought sent a flutter through her chest.

Then, unbidden, another image formed. She pictured herself standing beside the Baron, her hand resting lightly on his arm as they greeted the tenants and their wives. She could almost feel the solid warmth of him beneath her fingers, the strength in his arm as he guided her through the crowd.

Evelyn felt her cheeks warm at the direction of her thoughts. She glanced guiltily at the girls, but they were still absorbed in their own conversation, oblivious to their governess's wandering mind.

As they neared the house, Evelyn was liking the idea of attending the luncheon more and more. It would be a chance to see a different side of the Baron, to stand beside him as an equal rather than just an employee. The prospect both thrilled and terrified her.

She pictured herself in her best dress, her hair carefully arranged, ready to face the scrutiny of the tenants and their wives. Would they accept her in this role? Would the Baron be pleased with her performance?

Evelyn shook her head slightly, trying to clear away the fanciful thoughts. She was getting ahead of herself. She hadn't even accepted the invitation yet. But as she ushered the girls inside, she couldn't quite shake the warmth that had settled in her chest at the idea of standing arm-in-arm with the Baron.

With a sudden jolt, Evelyn's pleasant musings about the luncheon came to an abrupt halt. A cold dread washed over her, replacing the warmth she'd felt moments before. Her steps faltered as the realisation struck her like a physical blow.

She didn't know if she was truly free.

Chapter 28

The thought of her husband, the cruel Judge Banfield, loomed in her mind like a spectre. Her chest tightened, and she struggled to find her breath as she struggled to recall the last she'd heard of him. Had there been news of his death? Or had she simply fled, leaving her past behind without a backward glance?

The weight of her forgotten identity pressed down upon her. She'd been Miss Bane for so long now, slipping into the role of governess with such ease that she'd momentarily forgotten her true self. Lady Evelyn Banfield, a woman with a past shrouded in uncertainty and fear.

Her hands trembled as she helped Julia out of her wet dress, her mind racing. How could she have forgotten something so crucial? The possibility that she might still be bound in marriage to that monstrous man sent a shiver down her spine.

Evelyn's thoughts whirled in a dizzying spiral. If the Judge was still alive, still her husband in the eyes of the law, what did that mean for her current situation? For her growing feelings towards the Baron? The very idea of accepting the Baron's invitation to the luncheon now seemed fraught with danger.

She felt as though she were standing on the edge of a precipice, her carefully constructed new life threatening to crumble beneath her feet. The simple joy she'd felt at the Baron's request now seemed like a distant memory, overshadowed by the looming spectre of her past.

Evelyn's hands shook as she helped Julia into dry clothes, her mind racing with fragmented memories. She tried to steady her breathing, focusing on the task at hand while her thoughts whirled like autumn leaves caught in a gale.

Suddenly, a conversation with Aunt Agnes surfaced from the depths of her memory. It had been shortly after her arrival at Agnes' house, when she was still trembling with fear at every knock on the door.

"What became of him, Aunt Agnes?" Evelyn had asked, her voice barely above a whisper. "The Judge... after his crimes were exposed to the ton?"

Aunt Agnes had paused in her needlework, her weathered face creasing with concern. She'd set aside her embroidery and taken Evelyn's hands in her own, her touch warm and comforting.

"My dear," she'd said, her voice gentle but firm, "all you need to know is that the Judge won't be able to trouble you anymore."

At the time, Evelyn had been too relieved to press for details. She'd allowed herself to be soothed by her aunt's assurances, desperate to believe that her nightmare was truly over.

Now, standing in the nursery of Hastings Manor, Evelyn felt a chill run down her spine. What had Aunt Agnes meant? Had the Judge been imprisoned? Exiled? Or had something more permanent befallen him?

The uncertainty gnawed at her. She'd been so focused on building her new life, on becoming Miss Bane the governess, that she'd pushed aside all thoughts of her past. But now, with the Baron's invitation hanging in the air, she couldn't ignore the question any longer.

Evelyn realised she needed answers. She couldn't move forward, couldn't even consider accepting the Baron's request, until she knew for certain what had become of Judge Banfield. The thought of writing to Amelia crossed her mind. Perhaps her friend could discreetly make enquiries in London.

Evelyn gathered the girls' wet clothes, her mind still reeling from the sudden resurgence of her past. She made her way down the stairs, intending to deliver the sodden garments to the laundry. As she rounded the corner, she nearly collided with the Baron.

"Oh! My lord, I beg your pardon," she stammered, clutching the damp bundle to her chest.

The Baron steadied her with a gentle hand on her elbow. "No harm done, Miss Bane. Are you quite all right? You look a bit pale."

Evelyn forced a smile, acutely aware of the warmth of his touch. "I'm fine, thank you. Just a bit flustered after the girls' misadventure at the pond."

The Baron's eyes lingered on her face, concern etched in his features. He opened his mouth as if to speak, then closed it again. The unasked question hung heavy in the air between them.

Evelyn felt her heart constrict. She knew he was waiting for her answer about the luncheon, could see the hopeful glimmer in his eyes. The weight of her secret pressed down upon her, making it difficult to breathe.

"My lord," she began, her voice barely above a whisper, "about your invitation..."

The Baron's posture stiffened, his hand falling away from her arm. "Yes?"

Evelyn swallowed hard, guilt gnawing at her insides. "I... I promise to give you my answer this evening, after I've had more time to consider. If that's agreeable to you?"

Relief washed over the Baron's face, followed quickly by a guarded optimism. "Of course, Miss Bane. I look forward to hearing your thoughts on the matter."

As Evelyn watched him walk away, she felt a wave of shame crash over her. She had given him hope, however small, when she knew full well that she might not be free to accept his invitation. The truth of her identity burned within her, threatening to consume the life she had built as Miss Bane.

***

The clock on the mantelpiece chimed midnight, its soft tones echoing through the silent study. James Ayles, Baron Hastings, sat hunched over his desk, a lone candle casting flickering shadows across the papers strewn before him. He rubbed his eyes, weary from hours of poring over ledgers and agricultural reports.

His gaze drifted to the window, where moonlight filtered through a gap in the heavy curtains. A sigh escaped his lips as he realised how late it had grown. Surely Miss Bane would be fast asleep by now, nestled in her bed like his daughters.

James felt a twinge of disappointment settle in his chest. He'd hoped—expected, even—that she would have sought him out before retiring for the night. The invitation to preside over the tenants' luncheon was no small matter, after all. It was the closest thing to an olive branch he could offer, a gesture of goodwill after their recent disagreements.

He pushed back from the desk, the legs of his chair scraping against the wooden floor. Restless energy propelled him to his feet, and he found himself pacing the length of the study. His mind wandered, replaying their earlier conversation. Had he been too abrupt? Too presumptuous? Perhaps she found the idea distasteful, or worse, insulting.

James paused by the fireplace, absently running his fingers along the smooth marble of the mantel. He caught sight of his reflection in the mirror above, the flickering candlelight casting strange shadows across his scarred face. A rueful smile tugged at his lips. What a fool he was, to think she might...

He shook his head, banishing the thought before it could fully form. It wouldn't do to dwell on such fancies. Miss Bane was his daughters' governess, nothing more. Her opinion of him shouldn't matter beyond her ability to perform her duties.

And yet...

James froze, his hand still resting on the mantel. Had he heard footsteps in the hallway? He held his breath, straining to catch the faintest sound. The house creaked and settled around him, but there was nothing else.

He exhaled slowly, shaking his head at his own foolishness. Of course there was no one about at this hour. He was letting his imagination run wild, conjuring up false hopes like a lovesick schoolboy.

James turned back to his desk, determined to put such nonsense out of his mind. He'd just settled into his chair when he heard it again—the unmistakable sound of soft footfalls on the carpet outside his study.

His heart quickened, but he forced himself to remain calm. It was probably just one of the servants making their nightly rounds. Or perhaps Augusta had woken with another of her nightmares. There was no reason to think—

A gentle knock on the door cut through his musings.

James stood, his legs suddenly unsteady beneath him. He crossed the room in three long strides, his hand hovering over the doorknob for a moment before he grasped it firmly.

Taking a deep breath to steady himself, he opened the door just enough to peer into the dimly lit hallway beyond.

James's breath caught in his throat as he beheld Evelyn standing in the hallway. The flickering candlelight cast a warm glow across her face, illuminating her dark eyes that seemed to shine with an inner fire.

Her hair, usually so neatly arranged, was haphazardly pinned up, as if she'd taken it down and hastily attempted to restore order. He was nearly overcome with the urge to reach forward and slide one or two pins out, to let it tumble free, to lose his hands in her thick locks...

He found himself utterly transfixed, unable to tear his gaze away from her. The soft light played across her features, accentuating the curve of her cheek, the gentle slope of her neck. James's heart thundered in his chest, a rhythm so loud he was certain she must hear it.

"Miss Bane," he managed, his voice rougher than he'd intended. He cleared his throat, trying to regain his composure. "I... Is everything all right?"

Evelyn's lips parted as if to speak, but no words came. James watched, mesmerised, as she drew in a shaky breath. The candle flame wavered, casting dancing shadows across her face.

Time seemed to stretch between them, each second an eternity. James stood frozen, his hand still gripping the doorknob, afraid that any movement might shatter this moment. He drank in every detail of her appearance, committing it to memory.

A lock of hair finally slipped free, falling to brush against Evelyn's cheek. James's fingers twitched with the overwhelming urge to reach out and tuck it back into place. He clenched his fist at his side, fighting against the impulse.

James stood transfixed, his breath caught in his throat as Evelyn's lips curved into a soft smile. Her eyes, though troubled, held a warmth that made his heart skip a beat.

"I would be honoured to accept your invitation, my lord," she said, her voice barely above a whisper.

The Baron felt a rush of relief wash over him, mingled with something else he couldn't quite name. He opened his mouth to respond, but before he could form the words, Evelyn had already turned away. Her skirts rustled softly as she retreated down the darkened hallway, leaving James alone with the lingering scent of lavender and the echo of her footsteps.

He closed the study door and leaned against it, his mind whirling. The tension that had knotted his shoulders all evening suddenly eased, replaced by an unfamiliar lightness. James pressed a hand to his chest, startled by the rapid beating of his heart.

As he crossed back to his desk, a strange sensation bloomed within him. It was more than mere contentment or satisfaction. With a jolt of surprise, James realised he was experiencing something he hadn't felt in years: anticipation. He was looking forward to the tenants' luncheon with an eagerness that both thrilled and unsettled him.

The Baron sank into his chair, a bemused smile playing at the corners of his mouth. He glanced down at the papers strewn across his desk, agricultural reports and ledgers that had consumed his thoughts for so long. Yet now, they seemed less pressing, less all-encompassing.

Instead, his mind wandered to the upcoming luncheon. He pictured Evelyn seated beside him at the head table, her presence bringing a warmth and vitality that had been absent for far too long. The image filled him with a quiet joy, unexpected but not unwelcome.

He was also filled with a new sort of confidence. Surely, if she had accepted this invitation, then she would also agree to the other offer he intended to make her at the luncheon...

Chapter 29

The day of the luncheon dawned bright and clear, a perfect summer's day. Evelyn smoothed her hands over her dress, a wine-coloured calico, nervously as she made her way across the lawn to where the trestle tables had been set up. The air was thick with the scent of freshly cut grass and the gentle buzz of insects.

As she approached, she caught sight of the Baron standing at the head table, deep in conversation with a ruddy-faced farmer. He glanced up, his eyes meeting hers for a brief moment, leaving Evelyn breathless for a moment. She chided herself silently for such a foolish reaction.

"Miss Bane," the Baron called, gesturing her over. "Allow me to introduce you to Mr Hawkins and Mr Fairfax."

Evelyn nodded politely to the two farmers as she took her seat across from the Baron. Mr Hawkins, a portly man with a jovial smile, immediately launched into a detailed description of his prize-winning pigs. On her other side, Mr Fairfax, a thin, weather-beaten man, listened with a slight frown.

The table groaned under the weight of the food - roasted meats, fresh bread, and an array of vegetables from the estate's gardens. Evelyn's mouth watered at the sight, but she hesitated, unsure of the proper etiquette.

"Go on, Miss Bane," the Baron said, his voice low. "I assure you, our farmers have hearty appetites. You needn't stand on ceremony here."

Evelyn nodded, reaching for a slice of bread. As she did so, her eyes met the Baron's again, and she was surprised to see a hint of warmth there. She quickly looked away, focusing on her plate.

"So, Miss Bane," Mr Hawkins boomed, "what do you make of our little corner of the world? Quite different from London, I'd wager!"

Evelyn opened her mouth to respond, but found herself at a loss for words. How could she explain the complex emotions she felt about her new home?

Evelyn hesitated, acutely aware of the Baron's gaze upon her. She took a deep breath, composing her thoughts.

"I must confess," she began, her voice soft but clear, "I never imagined the countryside to hold so much beauty."

Mr Hawkins let out a hearty chuckle, his ruddy cheeks growing even redder. "Aye, miss, I'd wager your fancy London education didn't prepare you for the likes of this!"

Mr Fairfax nodded in agreement, a rare smile cracking his weathered features. "City folk often don't know what to make of our little slice of heaven."

Evelyn felt a flush creep up her neck, but she managed a small laugh. "You're quite right, gentlemen. I've been on a steep learning curve ever since I arrived."

She glanced at the Baron, expecting to see disapproval in his eyes. Instead, she found a glimmer of something that looked almost like pride. It made her heart flutter in a most disconcerting way.

"But," she continued, emboldened, "I find myself enjoying the challenge. Each day brings new discoveries."

Mr Hawkins beamed at her. "That's the spirit, miss! You'll be a proper country lass in no time."

Evelyn smiled, feeling a warmth spread through her chest. For the first time since her arrival, she felt truly at ease among these people. She caught the Baron's eye again, and this time, she didn't look away.

Evelyn became the centre of attention as the farmers' wives gathered around her, their eyes alight with curiosity. Mrs Hawkins, a plump woman with rosy cheeks, leaned in eagerly.

"Oh, Miss Bane, do tell us about the London fashions! Are they as scandalous as we've heard?"

Evelyn shifted in her seat, acutely aware of the Baron's presence just a few feet away. "I'm afraid I'm not the best person to ask about such matters," she demurred with a gentle smile.

Another woman, whom Evelyn recognised as Mrs Fairfax, chimed in. "Surely you must have attended grand balls and soirées? What are they like?"

Evelyn's mind flashed to her last ball in London, the suffocating crush of bodies, the whispers and pointed looks. She suppressed a shudder. "They can be quite... overwhelming," she said carefully.

The women exchanged glances, clearly unsatisfied with her vague responses. Mrs Hawkins pressed on, "Don't you ever wish you were back there, Miss Bane? All those handsome gentlemen and exciting entertainments?"

Evelyn felt a sudden tightness in her chest. Without meaning to, her eyes sought out the Baron. He was engaged in conversation with Mr Fairfax, but as if sensing her gaze, he looked up. Their eyes met across the table, and for a moment, the chatter around her faded away.

Turning back to the expectant faces of the farmers' wives, Evelyn took a deep breath. "To be perfectly honest," she said, her voice soft but steady, "I have no desire to ever go back there."

The women fell silent, surprise evident on their faces. Evelyn felt a weight lift from her shoulders as she spoke the truth aloud for the first time. London, with all its glittering façades and hidden dangers, held no allure for her now.

Here, among the rolling hills and open skies, she had found something she never knew she was missing: a simplicity that offered much contentment, and a sense of security she'd never known.

Evelyn's admission hung in the air for a moment, the farmers' wives exchanging glances of surprise and curiosity. Mrs Hawkins was the first to recover, her face breaking into a warm smile.

"Well then, Miss Bane," she said, her eyes twinkling, "if you're to be a true country lass, you ought to learn how we have our fun too!"

The other women nodded enthusiastically, a chorus of agreement rising around Evelyn.

"Oh, yes!" Mrs Fairfax chimed in. "We must show you our games. It's only proper."

Before Evelyn could fully process what was happening, she found herself being ushered away from the table, the women chattering excitedly around her. They led her to a small enclosure where several piglets were rooting about in the dirt.

"Now, Miss Bane," Mrs Hawkins explained, "the game is simple. We'll see who can hold a piglet the longest without it squealing. The winner gets to keep the little darling!"

Evelyn's eyes widened. "Oh, I couldn't possibly—" she began, but her protests were cut short as Mrs Fairfax scooped up a wriggling piglet and deposited it unceremoniously into Evelyn's arms.

The moment the piglet touched her, it let out an ear-piercing squeal. Evelyn, startled by the sudden noise and the warm, squirming bundle in her arms, burst into laughter. The sound of her own mirth mingled with the piglet's squeals, creating a cacophony that drew curious glances from across the lawn.

As Evelyn struggled to contain both her laughter and the squirming piglet, she caught sight of the Baron watching from a distance. His usually stern face bore an expression she'd never seen before – a mixture of amusement and something softer, almost tender. The sight made her heart skip a beat, and she nearly dropped the piglet in her distraction.

"Pickier than a Mayfair mam fielding suitors," Mrs Hawkins tutted, taking the squealing piglet from Evelyn.

Evelyn's cheeks ached from laughter as she handed the piglet back to Mrs Hawkins. She smoothed her hands over her dress, still chuckling, when Mrs Fairfax let out a gasp.

"Oh, Miss Bane! Your lovely dress!"

Evelyn glanced down to see a smudge of mud across her skirt where the piglet had nestled. For a moment, she felt a flash of her old self—horrified at the thought of a ruined garment. But as she looked up at the concerned faces of the farmers' wives, something shifted within her.

"Well," Evelyn said, her eyes twinkling with mirth, "I suppose I've received a love token from my porcine suitor."

The women stared at her for a heartbeat before erupting into peals of laughter. Mrs Hawkins clutched her sides, tears streaming down her ruddy cheeks.

"Oh, Miss Bane," she wheezed between guffaws, "you're a treasure, you are!"

Mrs Fairfax, wiping her eyes, chimed in, "It's more of a love token than I've seen in years, that's for certain!"

"Speak for yourself, Martha," another woman teased. "Some of us still have a bit of romance left in our lives!"

"Ha!" Mrs Fairfax retorted. "If you call Bert falling asleep in his chair every night 'romance', then I suppose you're right!"

The women dissolved into laughter once more, and Evelyn found herself swept up in their camaraderie. For the first time since arriving at the estate, she felt truly at ease, accepted not as a curiosity from London, but as one of their own.

As the laughter subsided, Evelyn caught sight of the Baron watching from across the lawn. His expression was unreadable, but she thought she detected a hint of approval in his eyes.

For just a moment, she let herself look back at him just as Evelyn—not Miss Bane, not Lady Evelyn with her secrets—just Evelyn. Something tangible but unknowable passed between her and the Baron as they locked eyes, and for a moment, Evelyn could swear that the Baron was trying to silently ask her something.

***

James stood at the edge of the lawn, his eyes fixed on the lively gathering before him. The farmers' wives had taken to Evelyn with unexpected warmth, and now they beckoned her towards another of their peculiar games. He watched as they produced small, misshapen balls—homemade soap, he realised—and wooden laundry bats.

"Come now, Miss Bane," one of the older women called. "Let's see how far you can whack it!"

Evelyn's laugh carried across the grass, light and unrestrained. James felt an odd tightness in his chest at the sound.

"Why, it's almost like cricket," Evelyn remarked, accepting a bat with a bemused smile.

The women exchanged glances, their faces a mix of amusement and indignation.

"Cricket?" scoffed Mrs Hodges, her ruddy cheeks puffing out. "Bless you, miss, but we came up with this long before any toff thought to make a proper game of it."

"Aye," another chimed in. "Our grandmothers were batting soap balls when your lot were still prancing about in rouge and powdered wigs."

James expected Evelyn to bristle at the impertinence, but to his surprise, she threw her head back and laughed even harder.

"Well then," she said, hefting the bat with unexpected determination, "you'll have to teach me the proper way, won't you?"

As he watched Evelyn take her stance, James found himself unable to look away. She swung the bat with more force than grace, sending the soap ball soaring in a wild arc. The women cheered, and Evelyn's face lit up with genuine delight.

For a moment, James forgot about the estate's troubles, the constant worry over crops and tenants. He forgot about the weight of responsibility that seemed to press down on him day and night. All he could see was Evelyn, her hair coming loose from its pins, her cheeks flushed with exertion and joy.

James leaned against the cider table, his eyes still fixed on Evelyn as she attempted another swing at the soap ball. He barely registered the approach of several farmers until they were at his elbow, helping themselves to mugs of the strong, amber liquid.

"Fine day for it, my lord," old Tom Cobbett remarked, his weathered face creasing into a smile.

James grunted in agreement, not quite ready to tear his gaze away from the scene before him.

"That Miss Bane," another farmer—Giles, James thought—said casually. "She's a right bright spot on the estate, ain't she?"

James felt his shoulders tense slightly. He turned to face the men, his expression carefully neutral. "Is that so?"

"Oh, aye," Tom nodded, taking a long swig of cider. "Livened up the whole place, she has. The missus says she's never seen the young ladies so cheerful."

"Proper lady, but not afraid to get her hands dirty," Giles added. "Saw her out in the kitchen garden t'other day, learning about herbs from old Mrs Potts."

James found himself at a loss for words. He'd known, of course, that Evelyn had been making an impact on his daughters, but he hadn't realised how far her influence had spread.

"She's got a way about her," another farmer chimed in. "Makes you feel like you matter, even if you're just a tenant."

The Baron's throat felt oddly tight. He reached for a mug of cider, using the moment to collect himself.

"Well," he said at last, his voice gruffer than he'd intended. "I'm... pleased to hear she's settling in so well."

The farmers exchanged knowing glances, but James pretended not to notice. He turned back to watch Evelyn, who was now attempting to teach one of the farmers' wives how to curtsy properly. The sight brought an unbidden smile to his face.

James sipped his cider, his eyes still drawn to Evelyn as she laughed with the farmers' wives. He barely registered the conversation around him until old Tom's words cut through his distraction.

"Surprised no one's snapped up a woman like Miss Bane yet," Tom mused, his tone deceptively casual. "Seems a right shame, that does."

James frowned, turning to face the group of farmers. "What do you mean by that?"

Giles chuckled, elbowing Tom in the ribs. "Well, my lord, just that she's a fine lady, ain't she? Clever and kind, good with the young'uns."

"Aye," another farmer chimed in, his eyes twinkling. "Would be a lucky man indeed to have her for a wife."

James felt a strange tightness in his chest at their words. He opened his mouth to respond, but found himself at a loss. The farmers exchanged glances, their expressions a mix of amusement and exasperation.

"Course," Tom added, his voice lowered conspiratorially, "reckon she'd need a man who could keep up with her. Someone steady, like. With a good head on his shoulders."

The Baron's brow furrowed deeper. He couldn't shake the feeling that he was missing something important. The farmers were looking at him expectantly, their gazes heavy with meaning he couldn't quite decipher.

"I... suppose that's true," James said slowly, his mind struggling to catch up. "Miss Bane is certainly... capable."

Giles let out a snort of laughter, quickly disguised as a cough. Tom shook his head, a bemused smile playing at the corners of his mouth.

"Aye, my lord," he said, clapping James on the shoulder. "That she is. That she is indeed."

James stood rooted to the spot, his eyes still fixed on Evelyn as she laughed with the farmers' wives. The conversation around him faded to a distant hum, but snippets of the farmers' words managed to pierce through his distraction.

"If nothing else," old Tom mused, stroking his chin, "Miss Bane's a great beauty, ain't she? Be an ornament at any table, that one."

Giles nodded sagely. "Aye, and she's got lovely eyes. Never seen their like before, like being stared at by a doe."

James said nothing, his gaze unwavering as Evelyn attempted another swing at the soap ball. Her hair had come loose from its pins, a few errant strands framing her flushed face. The farmers exchanged knowing glances, barely suppressing their amusement.

"What do you think, my lord?" Tom asked, his voice tinged with barely concealed mirth. "Wouldn't you agree Miss Bane's a right beauty?"

James barely registered the question, his mind still caught up in the sight of Evelyn's radiant smile. Before he could stop himself, he murmured, "Yes, she is."

The farmers erupted into poorly disguised snickers behind his back. James blinked, suddenly aware of what he'd just said. He turned to face the group, his cheeks burning with embarrassment.

"I mean," he stammered, trying to regain his composure, "Miss Bane is... certainly... presentable."

But it was too late. The farmers were already exchanging triumphant looks, their eyes twinkling with mischief.

James felt as though he'd been struck by lightning. The farmers' knowing glances, their pointed remarks—it all suddenly clicked into place. They weren't just praising Evelyn; they were trying to push him towards her.

He grunted, a noncommittal sound that neither confirmed nor denied their suspicions. The farmers' eyes gleamed with triumph, and James knew he'd given himself away.

Desperate to escape their scrutiny, he reached for the cider jug and refilled his mug. Without a word, he turned and strode away, his face burning with a mix of embarrassment and something else he couldn't quite name.

Chapter 30

As he put distance between himself and the group, James found his thoughts in turmoil. He couldn't deny the truth in what the farmers had said. Evelyn was indeed a fine woman—intelligent, kind, and undeniably beautiful. And today had proven beyond doubt that she possessed a natural grace when it came to dealing with the tenants.

James took a long swallow of cider, barely tasting it as his mind raced. The idea of remarrying had never truly crossed his mind before, not since... He pushed the painful memory aside. But now, watching Evelyn laugh with the farmers' wives, he couldn't help but see the sense in it.

An estate like his needed a mistress, someone to manage the household and tend to the social obligations he'd long neglected. And his daughters—they deserved a mother figure, someone who could guide them through the intricacies of womanhood that he was ill-equipped to handle.

James found himself at the edge of the gathering, his eyes once again drawn to Evelyn. She was attempting another swing at the soap ball, her face alight with determination and joy. Something stirred in his chest at the sight, a feeling he'd thought long buried.

He shook his head, trying to clear it. It was madness to even consider such a thing. And yet...

James stood at the edge of the lawn, his mind reeling from the revelation that had struck him like a thunderbolt. He'd always assumed that if he ever remarried, it would be a purely practical arrangement—a union of convenience to provide his daughters with a mother figure and his estate with a capable mistress. Love had never entered into the equation.

Yet here he was, his heart racing as he watched Evelyn laugh with the farmers' wives. The warmth that spread through his chest at the sight of her smile was unmistakable, and utterly unexpected.

When had his thoughts turned so fondly towards her? James couldn't pinpoint the exact moment. Perhaps it had been gradual, like the changing of seasons—so subtle he hadn't noticed until he found himself in the midst of it.

He took another swig of cider, barely tasting it as his mind grappled with this newfound awareness. The very notion of love—of opening his heart again—was terrifying. He'd sealed that part of himself away after the tragedy, convinced that such happiness was no longer meant for him.

But Evelyn... She'd brought light back into his home, joy to his daughters' faces. And now, it seemed, she'd awakened something in him he'd thought long dead.

James watched as Evelyn attempted another swing at the soap ball, her face a picture of determined concentration. The sight made his breath catch, a mixture of admiration and something deeper, something he was only now beginning to recognise.

Love. The word echoed in his mind, both thrilling and frightening. He hadn't allowed himself to consider the possibility of a second love match, not in all these years. Yet here he was, his heart quickening at the mere thought of Evelyn's smile.

James watched with a mixture of amusement and unease as the farmers produced their instruments. The lively strains of a country dance filled the air, and soon impromptu lines of dancers formed between the tables. His eyes narrowed as he saw one of the younger farmers approach Evelyn, extending a hand in invitation.

A sharp pang of jealousy shot through him, surprising in its intensity. James tensed, ready to intervene if necessary. But Evelyn's laugh carried across the lawn, light and carefree. She accepted the farmer's hand with a graceful nod, allowing herself to be led into the dance.

James found himself unable to look away as Evelyn attempted to follow the unfamiliar steps. She moved with an innate elegance, even as she stumbled over the more complex figures. Her face was alight with laughter, cheeks flushed with exertion and mirth.

The sight of her, so at ease among his tenants, stirred something deep within him. James realised with a start that he'd never seen her quite like this before—unguarded, joyful, free from the constraints of her position.

As the dance ended, James noticed a crowd of young farm hands gathering behind Evelyn. They jostled each other, each vying for the chance to claim the next dance. The Baron felt his jaw clench, an irrational surge of possessiveness rising within him.

He took a step forward, unsure of what he intended to do. But before he could intervene, Evelyn turned to the group of eager young men with a gracious smile. She said something James couldn't hear, but her words seemed to placate the crowd. They laughed good-naturedly, and one lucky lad stepped forward to lead her into the next set.

James remained rooted to the spot, his emotions in turmoil. He couldn't deny the fierce pride he felt at seeing Evelyn so effortlessly charm his tenants. Yet the sight of her in another man's arms, even in so innocent a context, left him feeling oddly bereft.

James stood at the edge of the gathering, his mind a whirlwind of conflicting emotions. The lively music and laughter seemed distant, muffled by the roar of his own thoughts. He watched Evelyn as she twirled through another dance, her face alight with joy. The sight both warmed his heart and filled him with an inexplicable sense of longing.

As the sun began to dip below the horizon, casting long shadows across the lawn, James felt as though he stood on the precipice of something momentous. A decision he hadn't even realised he'd been grappling with loomed before him, demanding his attention.

His eyes swept over the assembly, taking in the scene of merriment. Suddenly, he caught sight of Nell in the crowd. She was watching him intently, her gaze knowing. With a slight nod, she made her way towards him, weaving through the revellers with practised ease.

"My lord," Nell said softly as she approached. "You seem troubled."

James grunted, unsure how to respond. Nell's perceptiveness had always been uncanny.

"How long have we known each other, Nell?" he asked, his voice gruff.

She tilted her head, a small smile playing at her lips. "Why, I've been at the estate since I was a girl, my lord. You know that."

"Precisely," James nodded, his gaze drifting back to Evelyn. "And in all that time, I don't think I've ever been able to hide anything from you."

Nell followed his line of sight, her expression softening. "I can tell when you're in turmoil, my lord. It's written all over your face."

James sighed, running a hand through his hair. "Is it that obvious?"

"Only to those who know you well," Nell replied gently. She paused, her eyes searching his face.

James found himself strangely comforted by Nell's presence. Her familiar face and steady gaze grounded him amidst the tumult of his thoughts. Without quite meaning to, he blurted out a question that had been nagging at him.

"Nell, what do you do when you're troubled?" he asked, his voice gruff with barely concealed emotion. "You always seem so... light. So cheerful. As if nothing ever bothers you."

Nell's eyes widened slightly, surprised by the personal nature of his query. She tilted her head, considering her response carefully.

"Well, my lord," she began, her voice soft but clear, "my mam always told me something that's stuck with me all these years."

James raised an eyebrow, silently urging her to continue.

Nell's lips curved into a gentle smile. "She said that if something's troubling me so much, then it's not the right thing to do. The right thing, she always said, feels easy and without any doubt."

James felt as though the wind had been knocked out of him. He stared at Nell, his mind racing to process her words. The simplicity of the advice struck him deeply, challenging everything he'd been grappling with.

"Without any doubt," he repeated softly, more to himself than to Nell. "Has that worked for you?"

"It has, my lord," Nell said with surprising conviction. "My life's without much in the way of regrets."

"How fortunate you are," James said with a small smile, slightly tinged with sadness. With a bow, he excused himself.

James retreated from the lively gathering, his mind a tempest of conflicting thoughts. He found himself in the quiet solitude of his study, the muffled sounds of merriment filtering through the closed door. With a heavy sigh, he sank into the worn leather of his chair, his fingers absently tracing the familiar grooves in the armrests.

As he sat there, contemplating the events of the day and the unexpected stirrings in his heart, James's hand drifted to his pocket. His fingers brushed against something cool and metallic, and he froze. Slowly, he withdrew the object, holding it in his palm.

Was he truly doing what was right for his daughters? For his estate? For himself?

Chapter 31

As the evening wore on, Evelyn was caught up in the warm glow of merriment that filled the manor's front lawns. The farmers and their wives had proven to be delightful company, their rough-hewn manners a refreshing change from the stilted propriety she'd known in London. She made an attempt to put her hair back in order, still marvelling at how comfortable she felt among these country folk.

Her eyes scanned the gathering, searching for the Baron's tall figure, but he seemed to have vanished. A twinge of disappointment flickered through her, quickly pushed aside. She'd hoped to share a moment with him, to see if his eyes held the same warmth she'd glimpsed during their dance earlier.

Instead, her gaze landed on Nell across the crowded hall. The maid's face lit up with a smile, and she raised her hand in a small wave. Evelyn returned the gesture, grateful for the friendly face amidst the sea of revellers.

The air had grown thick with pipe smoke and the heady scent of spilled ale. Several of the farmers swayed on their feet, red-faced and grinning as they bellowed out snatches of bawdy songs. Their long-suffering wives began to appear at their elbows, tugging at sleeves and whispering urgently about the lateness of the hour.

"Come along now, Tom," one woman chided, her voice carrying over the din. "The cows won't milk themselves come morning, drunk or no."

Evelyn bit back a laugh as she watched the exodus begin. Bleary-eyed men were steered towards the door by determined spouses, a few protesting weakly about "one more for the road".

She found herself oddly touched by the simple affection evident in these exchanges, so different from the cold marriages of convenience she'd witnessed in her previous life. The wives here didn't hesitate to lay their heads on their husbands' shoulders, and the husbands eagerly wrapped their arms about their wives' waists.

Evelyn lingered by the front door, watching the last of the guests depart. The cool night air whispered against her flushed cheeks, a welcome respite from the stuffy warmth inside. As the sound of laughter and creaking wagon wheels faded into the distance, she found herself alone with her thoughts.

The evening had left her feeling oddly content, yet a restlessness stirred beneath the surface. She wandered towards the gardens, her steps slow and aimless. The simple joy she'd witnessed between the farmers and their wives had awakened something within her—a longing she'd pushed aside for far too long.

Her mind drifted to Richard, and the whirlwind romance they'd shared. It had been intoxicating at the time, a heady rush of stolen moments and passionate declarations. But now, with the perspective of distance, she saw it for what it truly was: a tempest without substance.

Evelyn paused by a rose bush, its blooms silvered by moonlight. She reached out, gently tracing the velvet curve of a petal. What she'd witnessed tonight was different—a steady flame rather than a consuming blaze. The farmers and their wives shared a companionship built on years of shared joys and hardships, a love tempered by time and understanding.

A pang of emptiness echoed through her chest. For all the excitement of her affair with Richard, they'd never truly known each other. There had been no quiet moments of companionship, no shared dreams of a future together. It had been a fantasy, as insubstantial as morning mist.

Evelyn sighed, wrapping her arms around herself. The contentment of the evening had faded, leaving her acutely aware of the void in her life. She yearned for something real, something lasting. Not just passion, but partnership. Understanding. Trust.

Evelyn startled as a shadow fell across the rose bush. She turned to find the Baron standing beside her, his tall figure silhouetted against the deepening twilight. Her heart quickened, though she couldn't quite say why.

"My lord," she said, offering him a small smile. "I trust you found the day a success?"

The Baron's face was difficult to read in the fading light, but there was a tension in his shoulders that hadn't been there earlier. He cleared his throat, seeming uncharacteristically ill at ease.

"Miss Bane," he began, then paused. "Evelyn," he ventured, looking as if he were tasting her name like a food he had just encountered. When Evelyn didn't correct him, the lines on his face lifted upward. "I wonder if I might impose upon you for a walk?"

Evelyn glanced towards the horizon, where only the faintest sliver of sun still clung to the edge of the world. "At this hour? Surely it's growing rather late..."

"Please."

The word hung between them, startling in its simplicity. In all their time together, Evelyn couldn't recall the Baron ever uttering that particular phrase. There was something in his voice, a note of... vulnerability, perhaps? It stirred something within her, a mixture of curiosity and concern.

"Very well," she found herself saying, even as her mind raced with questions. "Lead on, my lord."

Evelyn fell into step beside the Baron, their footsteps crunching softly on the gravel path. The night air was cool against her skin, carrying the sweet scent of late-blooming flowers. She was acutely aware of the Baron's presence, his arm mere inches from her own. The silence between them felt charged, yet not uncomfortable.

As they walked, Evelyn stole glances at her companion. The Baron's brow was furrowed, his jaw clenched as if wrestling with some internal struggle. Several times, he drew in a breath as if to speak, only to release it in a quiet sigh. Evelyn was curious about what weighed so heavily on his mind, but she resisted the urge to pry.

In London, she might have felt compelled to fill such a silence with idle chatter. Here, surrounded by the gentle rustling of leaves and the distant call of a nightingale, words seemed unnecessary. There was a peacefulness to this moment that Evelyn was loath to disturb.

Their path took them past a small pond, its surface a mirror of starlight. The Baron paused, his hand twitching as if he might reach for her. Evelyn's heart quickened, but he merely gestured for her to precede him along a narrower section of the path.

As they continued their stroll, Evelyn found her thoughts drifting. She wondered what the Baron had wanted to discuss that required such privacy. Was it about her position as governess? The girls' education? Or perhaps...

She pushed that last thought aside, chiding herself for entertaining such fanciful notions. Whatever the Baron's reasons, she would wait for him to broach the subject in his own time.

Evelyn's curiosity grew as the Baron led her along a winding path through a copse of trees. The moonlight filtered through the leaves, casting dappled shadows on the ground. As they emerged from the grove, a small red brick cottage came into view, nestled in a clearing.

The sight took Evelyn's breath away. The cottage looked as if it had stepped out of a fairy tale, its weathered bricks softened by climbing roses and ivy. A freshly painted door, a cheerful shade of blue, stood out against the deep red of the bricks. Flowers of every hue imaginable spilled from window boxes and lined the neat garden path.

"It's beautiful," Evelyn murmured, unable to keep the wonder from her voice.

The Baron nodded, a hint of pride in his eyes. "It's been on the estate for... I frankly don't know how long," he said with a slight crease between his brows. "It's housed a number of tenants and distant relations, though it's been quite empty of late."

As they drew closer, Evelyn noticed more details. A cosy porch swing hung from sturdy beams, inviting lazy summer afternoons. The windows glowed with warm, golden light, hinting at the comfort within.

The evening air was alive with magic. Fireflies began to appear, their soft lights blinking on and off like earthbound stars. They danced around the cottage, weaving between the flowers and casting fleeting glimmers across the ivy-covered walls.

Evelyn felt as if she'd stepped into another world. The worries and uncertainties that had plagued her earlier seemed to melt away in the face of such simple beauty. She turned to the Baron, a question forming on her lips, but the words died as she caught sight of his expression.

The moonlight cast soft shadows across his features, smoothing the harsh lines that usually creased his brow. For the first time since she'd known him, he looked... vulnerable. His eyes, usually so guarded, held a warmth that made her heart skip a beat.

"Miss Bane," he began, his voice low and uncertain. "Evelyn. I... This cottage is yours."

Evelyn blinked, sure she must have misheard. "I beg your pardon, my lord?"

The Baron cleared his throat, a faint flush colouring his cheeks. "The cottage. It's yours, if you want it."

Evelyn's mind whirled, struggling to make sense of his words. "I... I don't understand. What do you mean, it's mine?"

She watched as the Baron's hand slipped into his pocket, withdrawing something small that glinted in the moonlight. He held it out to her, and Evelyn saw that it was a key - old and slightly tarnished, but unmistakably a brass house key.

Evelyn eyed it warily; in London, it was common practice for wealthy men to offer their mistresses small homes or apartments. A key passing between them was the sign of a woman being offered carte blanche.

She couldn't begin to imagine that the Baron would offer such a thing, however. Evelyn looked up at the Baron, her eyes questioning, pulling back a little.

"I mean exactly that," he said, his voice growing steadier. "This cottage is yours, to do with as you please. You may live here for as long as you like, even...even if you leave your position."

Evelyn stared at the key in his outstretched hand, her thoughts a jumble of confusion and disbelief. "But... why? I don't understand, my lord. What does this mean?"

Evelyn's heart raced as she stared at the key in the Baron's outstretched hand. His words seemed to echo in the still night air, each one sending a fresh wave of shock through her.

The Baron's eyes softened, a hint of understanding flickering in their depths. "I believe I comprehend more than you might think, Miss Bane," he said, his voice low and earnest. "Your desire for independence... it's not so different from what I've always wanted for my daughters."

Evelyn's breath caught in her throat. Could he truly understand? She searched his face, looking for any sign of mockery or condescension, but found only sincerity.

"This cottage," he continued, gesturing to the charming structure behind them, "it's in your name now. There are some documents back at the manor that need your signature, but the property is yours."

Evelyn's mind whirled with possibilities. Her own home, a place that was truly hers. The thought was almost too much to comprehend.

The Baron cleared his throat, a hint of awkwardness creeping into his manner. "And if you wish... you could even rent it out. For additional income, you understand. It would be entirely up to you. It will always be yours, even if you—you don't live here anymore." A cloud passed over the Baron's face as he said this last bit.

Evelyn's eyes widened at this. Not only was he offering her a home, but a potential source of income as well? It seemed too good to be true. Yet as she looked into the Baron's eyes, she saw no deceit there, only a mixture of hope and nervousness.

"My lord," she began, her voice barely above a whisper, "I...I don't—"

The Baron reached out and gently took her wrist, his hand dwarfing hers. Without another word, the Baron placed the brass key in her hand, the weight of it surprising. Evelyn stared down at it for a moment, unable to comprehend it all.

Evelyn's fingers curled around the key, its weight anchoring her to the moment. She stared at it, unable to fully comprehend the magnitude of what the Baron had just offered her. A home. Independence. Freedom.

Her eyes stung with unshed tears as she looked up at the Baron, his face a mixture of hope and uncertainty in the moonlight. In that instant, she saw him not as her employer or as a nobleman, but as a man who had given her something no one else ever had: a choice.

All her life, men had sought to control her. The Judge had seen her as a pretty bauble to be locked away, a trophy to be displayed at his convenience. Even Richard, for all his talk of rescue and romance, had treated her like a package to be shuttled from one hiding place to another.

But this... this was different.

The Baron wasn't asking for anything in return. He wasn't trying to keep her tethered to him or to anyone else. Instead, he had given her the means to stand on her own two feet, to make her own decisions about her future.

Evelyn's heart swelled with a rush of emotion so intense it nearly took her breath away. Gratitude, yes, but also a profound sense of possibility. For the first time in her life, she felt truly seen, truly understood.

Evelyn's heart raced, her emotions overwhelming her usual sense of propriety. Without thinking, she flung her arms around the Baron's neck, pulling him close. She felt him stiffen for a moment, clearly taken aback by her impulsive action. But then, just as she'd instinctively known he would, his strong arms encircled her waist, steadying her.

The warmth of his body against hers sent a shiver down her spine. Evelyn breathed in his scent - a mixture of leather, pipe tobacco, and something uniquely him. She felt safe, anchored in a way she'd never experienced before.

As the initial rush of emotion began to subside, Evelyn became acutely aware of their position. The Baron's chest rose and fell against hers, his breath warm against her hair. His arms, while gentle, held her securely, as if he were afraid she might slip away.

Evelyn's cheeks flushed, realising the impropriety of her actions. Yet she couldn't bring herself to pull away just yet. There was something comforting, something right about being held by him. It was a feeling she'd never known she was missing until this moment.

She tilted her head back slightly, intending to apologise for her forwardness. The words died on her lips as she met the Baron's gaze. His eyes, usually so guarded, were filled with a mixture of surprise and something else - something that made throat constricted, cutting off her breath.

Time seemed to stand still as they looked at each other, the moonlight casting soft shadows across their faces. Evelyn felt her heart pounding, aware of every point of contact between them. The Baron's hands at her waist, her arms around his neck, their bodies pressed close.

She could see the desire in his eyes, the longing that mirrored her own. Yet he made no move, allowing her the freedom to choose.

In that moment, Evelyn felt a rush of gratitude and affection for this man who had given her so much. Not just a home, but the power to make her own decisions. She appreciated his restraint, his willingness to let her set the pace.

Taking a deep breath, Evelyn gathered her courage. Slowly, cautiously, she leaned in, her lips brushing against his. The Baron's breath hitched, but he remained still, letting her lead.

Emboldened by his response, Evelyn pressed her lips more firmly against his. The Baron's arms tightened around her waist as he returned the kiss, his touch gentle and reverent. Evelyn's eyes fluttered closed, losing herself in the warmth of his embrace.

As the kiss deepened, the Baron's initial hesitance gave way to growing enthusiasm. His hand moved to cup her cheek, his thumb caressing her skin with surprising tenderness. Evelyn sighed softly against his lips, her fingers threading through his hair.

The world around them seemed to fade away, leaving only the two of them in this perfect moment. Evelyn felt a warmth spreading through her chest, a sense of rightness that she had never experienced before.

The Baron pulled back at last, his eyes wide with surprise at his own boldness. Evelyn saw a flush rising in his cheeks as he drew in a breath, no doubt to offer some stuttering apology.

She wouldn't give him the chance.

With a soft smile curving her lips, Evelyn leaned in and captured his mouth in another swift kiss. The Baron's eyes fluttered closed as he exhaled a low, rumbling laugh against her lips. When she pulled back, his gaze had regained some of its usual composure, though a glimmer of something new and heated danced in their depths.

"We should return to the house," he murmured, his voice husky. One corner of his mouth quirked upwards. "Unless you'd prefer to stay here... in your new home?"

Evelyn felt a fresh wave of warmth flood her at the thought of the little cottage - her cottage. Her own safe haven, a place that was truly hers. Yet even as the idea beckoned, another part of her longed for the comfort and familiarity of the manor.

Squeezing the Baron's hand, she smiled up at him. "I think I'd like to go home," she said softly. "To the manor, that is."

A low chuckle rumbled in the Baron's chest. "In that case," he said, his tone taking on a teasing lilt, "you may wish to release me, my lady."

"I would be delighted to," she said, arching one brow playfully, "if you would put me down, my lord."

The Baron blinked at Evelyn for a moment. Without even realising it, he had swept her clean off her feet, which now dangled above the ground somewhere near his calves. He looked down as if disbelieving that he had done so. The Baron chuckled again, the rich sound warming Evelyn from the inside out. With an exaggerated sigh of regret, he bent and gently set her back on her feet.

As her slippers met the soft earth, Evelyn couldn't resist one last impish jab. "There now," she said lightly, patting his chest. "That's much better. A woman can hardly be expected to walk on her own two feet when she's being carried about like a sack of grain."

Evelyn's heart soared as the Baron's laughter rang out once more, rich and warm in the night air. He offered her his arm with a gallant flourish, his eyes twinkling with mirth. She slipped her hand into the crook of his elbow, revelling in the solid warmth of him beside her.

As they strolled back towards the manor, Evelyn felt as though she were walking on air. The night seemed alive with possibility, the moonlight casting a silvery glow over everything. She sneaked glances at the Baron's profile, admiring the strong line of his jaw and the way his eyes crinkled at the corners when he smiled.

Their conversation flowed easily, punctuated by comfortable silences. Evelyn found herself laughing more than she had in years, her cheeks aching from smiling so much. The Baron's dry wit and unexpected playfulness delighted her, revealing a side of him she'd only glimpsed before.

All too soon, they reached the manor. The Baron escorted her to the foot of the stairs, his hand warm on the small of her back. As he bid her goodnight, Evelyn's euphoria began to fade, replaced by a creeping sense of dread.

The reality of her situation crashed over her like a bucket of ice water. If the Baron ever discovered the truth about her past, about who she really was... Evelyn's stomach twisted painfully at the thought. She had lied to him, deceived him from the very beginning. How could she ever hope to build anything real, anything lasting, on such a foundation of deceit?

As she climbed the stairs to her room, Evelyn's steps grew heavier with each passing moment. The joy of the evening turned to ashes in her mouth as she realised the terrible truth: if the Baron ever uncovered her lie, she would lose him forever.

Evelyn tossed and turned in her bed, sleep eluding her despite the late hour. The memory of the Baron's kiss lingered on her lips, but it was tainted by the weight of her deception. She couldn't bear the thought of building a life with him based on lies.

As the first light of dawn crept through her window, Evelyn made a decision. She had to know the truth about her situation. Was she truly free, or was the Judge still a threat looming over her future?

With trembling hands, she penned a letter to Amelia, her only link to her past life in London. She chose her words carefully, not wanting to reveal too much, but desperate for information about the Judge's fate.

As she sealed the envelope, Evelyn felt a mix of hope and dread. If she was indeed free, perhaps she could find a way to come clean to the Baron, to build something real with him. But if the Judge still posed a threat...

Evelyn's heart clenched at the thought. She knew what she would have to do. No matter how much it pained her, she would leave the manor, leave the Baron and the girls. She couldn't bear to put them at risk, nor could she resist the growing attraction between her and the Baron.

Chapter 32

Evelyn descended the stairs the next morning, her stomach a tangle of nerves. The weight of her letter to Amelia weighed far more than it logically should as she dropped it into the leather pouch for letters, a constant reminder of the precarious nature of her situation. As she entered the breakfast room, however, her worries momentarily faded at the sight of the Baron.

He looked up from his newspaper, a warm smile spreading across his face. "Good morning, Miss Bane," he said, his voice rich with affection. "I trust you slept well?"

"Good morning, my lord," Evelyn replied, her cheeks warming at the memory of the previous night. "I slept... adequately, thank you."

The Baron's brow furrowed slightly at her hesitation, but he said nothing as she took her seat. A comfortable silence settled over them as they began their meal, broken only by the clink of cutlery and the rustle of the Baron's newspaper.

Evelyn found her gaze drawn to him repeatedly, admiring the way the morning sunlight caught in his dark hair. She longed to reach out and smooth away the slight furrow between his brows as he read, but she kept her hands firmly in her lap. As if feeling her eyes on him, the Baron looked up and met Evelyn's gaze, which made her smile automatically.

The Baron's eyes crinkled at the corners as he smiled back at her. "I must say, Miss Bane, you handled yourself admirably last night. The tenants were quite taken with you."

Evelyn felt a flush of pleasure at his praise, even as guilt gnawed at her insides. "Thank you, my lord. I found them to be delightful company."

The Baron leaned forward slightly, his grey eyes intense. "You've brought a great deal of life back to this house, Miss Bane. I... I cannot express how grateful I am for that."

Evelyn's heart fluttered at his words, even as her conscience screamed at her to confess everything. She opened her mouth, not quite sure what she was going to say, when the door to the dining room opened.

Evelyn's words died on her lips as Julia and Augusta straggled into the dining room, looking as if they'd been dragged through a hedge backwards. Their hair was mussed, and Augusta sported a smudge of dirt on her cheek. Evelyn bit the inside of her cheek to keep from smiling at their bedraggled appearance.

The Baron, to his credit, maintained his composure admirably. He folded his newspaper and set it aside, giving no indication that he'd noticed anything amiss with his daughters' states.

"Good morning, girls," he said, his voice betraying only the slightest hint of amusement. "I trust you slept well?"

Julia mumbled something unintelligible as she slumped into her chair, while Augusta managed a slightly more coherent, "Morning, Papa."

Evelyn caught the Baron's eye, and for a moment, they shared a look of fond exasperation. She quickly averted her gaze, focusing on buttering a piece of toast to hide the warmth spreading across her cheeks.

The Baron cleared his throat. "Now that we're all here, I have an announcement to make."

Evelyn's heart skipped a beat. She glanced up, her eyes widening as she met the Baron's steady gaze. What could he possibly have to announce? Her mind raced with possibilities, each more unlikely than the last.

Evelyn's heart raced as she awaited the Baron's announcement. She watched his face intently, searching for any clue as to what he might say.

"I will be travelling for the next couple of days," the Baron said, his voice steady. "I need to visit some neighbouring estates to discuss shipping crops to bigger cities."

Julia and Augusta's heads snapped up, their eyes widening in alarm. Evelyn felt a pang of sympathy for the girls, understanding their fear of being left alone.

The Baron held up a hand to forestall any protests. "Everything will be fine," he assured them, his gaze shifting to Evelyn. "I trust Miss Bane to watch over you both."

Evelyn struggled to find her breath. The Baron's words, so simple and yet so profound, filled her with a warmth she hadn't expected. To be trusted so completely, especially by a man as guarded as the Baron, was no small thing.

And yet, even as pride and gratitude swelled within her, guilt twisted in her stomach like a knife. She wasn't being fully honest with him. The weight of her secrets pressed down on her, threatening to crush her beneath their burden.

"Thank you, my lord," Evelyn managed to say, her voice sounding strained to her own ears. "I will do my utmost to ensure the girls are well cared for in your absence."

The Baron nodded, a small smile playing at the corners of his mouth. "I have no doubt of that, Miss Bane."

Evelyn lowered her gaze to her plate, unable to meet his eyes. She desperately wanted to be worthy of the trust he'd placed in her. But how could she be, when she was hiding so much?

As the Baron continued to discuss the details of his trip, Evelyn's mind whirled. She knew she should tell him the truth about her past, about who she really was. But the thought of losing everything she'd gained here - the girls, the cottage, the Baron's trust - terrified her.

Evelyn watched as the Baron finished his breakfast, her thoughts still tumultuous. The rest of the meal passed in relative silence, with only the occasional clink of cutlery or murmured request to pass the marmalade breaking the quiet.

As they rose from the table, Evelyn's heart quickened. She knew the moment of the Baron's departure was drawing near, and a strange mixture of anticipation and dread filled her. She ushered Julia and Augusta upstairs to make themselves presentable, then returned to the entrance hall to await their return.

The girls descended the stairs, looking far more put-together than they had at breakfast. Evelyn gave them an approving nod before leading them outside to where the carriage stood waiting. The Baron emerged from the house, his travelling coat buttoned up against the morning chill.

He approached his daughters first, kneeling down to their level. "Now, you two be good for Miss Bane while I'm away," he said, his voice gruff but affectionate. "I'll be back before you know it."

Julia threw her arms around her father's neck, while Augusta hung back, her face a mask of carefully controlled emotion. The Baron embraced them both, pressing a kiss to each of their foreheads before rising to his feet.

As he turned to Evelyn, a sudden breathlessness overtook her. How she longed to bid him farewell as a wife might - to throw her arms around him, to feel the solid warmth of his embrace, to press her lips to his in a tender kiss. But such thoughts were impossible, foolish even.

Instead, she stepped forward, her hands outstretched. "Safe travels, my lord," she said softly, her voice steady despite the tumult of emotions within her.

The Baron took her hands in his, his grip firm and warm. "Thank you, Miss Bane," he replied, his grey eyes searching hers. "I trust all will be well in my absence."

Evelyn nodded, unable to speak past the lump in her throat. She gave his hands a gentle squeeze, allowing herself this small moment of connection before reluctantly letting go.

As the Baron's carriage rolled away, kicking up dust in its wake, Evelyn felt a peculiar sensation settle in her chest. It wasn't merely the ache of missing him, though that was certainly present. No, this was something deeper, more unsettling. A creeping unease that wound its way through her veins, leaving her feeling oddly chilled despite the warmth of the morning sun.

She shook her head, trying to dispel the feeling. It was ridiculous, surely. The Baron would return in a few days, just as he'd promised. There was no reason for this strange foreboding.

Turning to the girls, Evelyn forced a bright smile onto her face. "Well then, shall we head back inside? I believe we were meant to start on geography this morning."

Julia groaned dramatically, while Augusta merely nodded, her eyes still fixed on the spot where her father's carriage had disappeared from view.

"Come along now," Evelyn said, gently herding them towards the house. "I've some fascinating maps to show you of the Americas. Did you know there are mountains there taller than any in England?"

As they walked, Evelyn couldn't shake the nagging feeling that something was amiss. She glanced back over her shoulder, half-expecting to see the Baron's carriage returning. But the road remained empty, stretching off into the distance.

Inside, Evelyn busied herself with setting up the lesson, spreading maps across the table and arranging globes for the girls to examine. Yet even as she spoke of far-off lands and wondrous sights, her mind kept drifting back to the Baron.

What if something happened on his journey? What if he didn't return? The thought sent a spike of fear through her heart. She'd grown far too accustomed to his presence, to the warmth of his rare smiles and the steadiness of his gaze.

Evelyn couldn't shake the feeling of being watched. As she guided the girls through their geography lesson, her gaze kept darting to the windows, half-expecting to see a face peering in at her. The hairs on the back of her neck stood on end, and she found herself constantly glancing over her shoulder.

She tried to dismiss these feelings as mere paranoia. After all, she was alone in charge of the house for the first time since arriving. It was natural to feel a bit unsettled, wasn't it?

"Miss Bane?" Julia's voice cut through her thoughts. "Are you alright?"

Evelyn blinked, realising she'd been staring blankly at the map for several moments. "Yes, of course," she said, forcing a smile. "I was just... lost in thought about the vastness of the Americas."

Augusta raised an eyebrow, clearly not believing her, but said nothing.

Chapter 33

As the day wore on, Evelyn found herself jumping at small noises - the creak of a floorboard, the rustle of leaves outside. She told herself it was simply the girls turning to her more often, seeking guidance and comfort in their father's absence. That explained the constant feeling of eyes upon her, surely?

At dinner, Evelyn was seated at the head of the table, in the Baron's usual place. The empty chair seemed to loom large in her peripheral vision, a constant reminder of his absence. She picked at her food, her appetite diminished by the strange unease that had settled over her.

"Miss Bane," Augusta said suddenly, her grey eyes - so like her father's - fixed on Evelyn's face. "Are you certain you're well? You seem... distracted."

Evelyn managed a wan smile. "I'm quite alright, Augusta. Just a bit tired, I suppose. Nothing to worry about."

But as she lay in bed that night, staring at the shadows on her ceiling, Evelyn couldn't quite convince herself that everything was fine. The feeling of being watched persisted, even in the solitude of her room. She pulled the covers up to her chin, trying to shake off the chill that had nothing to do with the temperature.

Evelyn tossed and turned in her bed, the sheets tangling around her legs as she struggled to find a comfortable position. Sleep eluded her, chased away by the unsettling thoughts that plagued her mind.

Her gaze kept drifting to the window, beyond which she knew the burnt West Wing stood like a silent sentinel. She had never paid it much mind before, but tonight, it seemed to loom large in her imagination. The charred remains of what was once a grand part of the manor now felt like a malevolent presence, watching and waiting.

Evelyn sat up, pushing her hair back from her face with trembling hands. Why hadn't they simply demolished it? The question nagged at her, refusing to be silenced. Surely it would have been easier, less painful, to tear it down and start anew. Instead, it remained, a horrible scar on the face of the manor, a constant reminder of past tragedy.

She slipped out of bed, padding softly to the window. The moon hung low in the sky, casting long shadows across the grounds. In the silvery light, the West Wing looked even more ominous, its blackened walls seeming to absorb the moonlight.

Evelyn shivered, wrapping her arms around herself. She had never felt so acutely aware of her proximity to the burnt wing before. Her room, the closest to that part of the house, suddenly felt exposed and vulnerable. Every creak of the old house, every whisper of wind through the trees outside, set her nerves on edge.

Evelyn froze, her heart pounding in her chest as she strained her ears. There it was again—a faint creaking sound, as if someone were treading carefully on old floorboards. She held her breath, trying to pinpoint the source of the noise. It seemed to be coming from the direction of the West Wing, growing steadily closer.

Her eyes darted to the door of her room, watching for any sign of movement beneath it. The creaking continued, slow and deliberate, now sounding as if it were just outside her door. Evelyn's fingers gripped the windowsill, her knuckles turning white with the force of her grip.

Then, another sensation hit her—the acrid smell of smoke. A gasp escaped her, her breath hitching suddenly. As she whirled around, her gaze immediately falling on her fireplace. But the hearth was cold and dark, not even a hint of embers glowing in its depths. The warm summer night had made a fire unnecessary, yet the scent of smoke hung heavy in the air.

Evelyn's mind raced. Could it be coming from the West Wing? Had a fire somehow rekindled in the burnt-out shell of the building? The thought sent a chill down her spine, memories of the Baron's scarred face flashing through her mind.

The creaking outside her door stopped abruptly, replaced by an eerie silence that seemed to press in on her from all sides. Evelyn stood frozen, caught between the urge to investigate and the paralysing fear that kept her rooted to the spot. The smell of smoke grew stronger, tickling her nose. She tried to convince herself it was her imagination, grown far too active from nerves.

Evelyn took a deep breath, steadying herself against the windowsill. The acrid smell of smoke still lingered in the air, but she pushed her fear aside. She wasn't some wilting lily, cowering at the first sign of danger. She'd proven that already, hadn't she? Running across open fields to warn the Baron of the flood, standing up to him when she disagreed with his methods, fleeing the Judge and seeing his crimes exposed—she was made of sterner stuff than she'd once believed.

The thought of something or someone being in the house, potentially threatening the girls—her girls—filled Evelyn with a sudden surge of courage and determination. She might not be their mother, but she'd grown to care for them deeply in her time here. The idea of any harm coming to Julia or Augusta was simply unacceptable.

Silently, Evelyn crossed the room to the fireplace. Her hand closed around the cool metal of the fire poker, lifting it from its stand with a quiet scrape of iron against iron. The weight of it was reassuring in her grip, a tangible reminder of her resolve.

She padded towards the door, her bare feet silent on the wooden floor. The creaking had stopped, but the smell of smoke remained, a constant reminder of the potential danger lurking beyond her room. Evelyn's heart pounded in her chest, but her hand was steady as she reached for the doorknob.

Evelyn stepped into the hallway, her heart pounding in her chest. The fire poker felt heavy in her hand as she peered into the darkness. Moonlight filtered through the windows, casting long shadows across the floor. The corridor stretched before her, silent and still.

Her gaze was drawn to the door of the West Wing. It stood slightly ajar, a sliver of flickering light spilling out from behind it. Evelyn's breath froze mid-inhale. She'd never been in that part of the house before—it had always been strictly off-limits.

As she crept closer, the acrid smell of smoke grew stronger. Evelyn's mind raced. Surely, if there was a fire, someone would have raised the alarm by now? She pressed her ear to the door, straining to hear. Voices. Faint, but unmistakable. They drifted through the gap, too low for her to make out the words. Evelyn's grip tightened on the poker. Who could possibly be in there at this hour?

She pushed the door open a fraction wider, wincing at the slight creak of the hinges. The flickering light grew brighter, casting dancing shadows on the walls. It looked almost like firelight, but there was something off about it—too steady, too controlled.

Evelyn had never put much stock in ghost stories. She'd always prided herself on her practical nature. But now, faced with the inexplicable, she felt her certainty wavering. The voices continued, rising and falling in a strange, rhythmic cadence that sent shivers down her spine.

She took a deep breath, steeling herself. Whatever was happening in that room, she had to investigate. The girls' safety might depend on it. With trembling fingers, Evelyn pushed the door open wider and stepped into the West Wing.

Evelyn's heart thundered in her chest as she crept down the charred corridor of the West Wing. The acrid smell of old smoke clung to the air, mingling with the musty scent of disuse. Her bare feet made no sound on the blackened floorboards, but every creak of the old house set her nerves on edge.

The faint light grew stronger as she approached one of the empty rooms. Shadows danced on the walls, cast by what seemed to be a single candle or lantern. Evelyn's grip tightened on the fire poker, her palms slick with sweat.

She pressed herself against the wall beside the door, straining her ears. There it was again—the unmistakable sound of movement within. Something, or someone, was shuffling about, accompanied by the occasional rustle of fabric.

Evelyn's mind raced. Who could possibly be in there? A thief? One of the servants? Or something far more sinister? The Baron's scarred face flashed through her mind, and she felt a surge of protective anger. Whatever was happening here, she wouldn't let it threaten the family she'd grown to care for.

Taking a deep breath, Evelyn steeled herself. She couldn't hesitate any longer. In one swift motion, she spun around and shoved the door open with her shoulder.

The hinges groaned in protest as the door swung wide. Evelyn burst into the room, fire poker raised high, ready to strike at whatever danger awaited her.

Chapter 34

A startled shriek pierced the air, echoed immediately by Evelyn's own cry of surprise. As her eyes adjusted, she found herself face to face with Nell, the maid, clad in her stark white nightgown and cap, a shawl thrown haphazardly over her shoulders.

"Nell?" Evelyn gasped, lowering the poker. "What on earth are you doing here?"

Nell's eyes were wide with fright, her hand clutched to her chest. "Miss Bane! You gave me such a fright!"

Evelyn's gaze darted around the room, taking in the single lantern burning on a small table, the lack of any other presence. The acrid smell of smoke still lingered, but now she noticed that the smell was stirred up whenever she or Nell moved.

"Did you hear it too?" Nell demanded, coming forward and clasping Evelyn's hand with her own, clammy and cold.

Evelyn's heart raced as she lowered the fire poker, her mind struggling to make sense of the situation. "What do you mean, Nell? What did you hear?"

Nell's eyes darted nervously around the room, her fingers twisting the fabric of her shawl. "I was just finishing my rounds, Miss Bane, making sure all the lights were out upstairs. That's when I heard it—strange noises, like someone moving about in here."

Evelyn felt a chill run down her spine. She'd heard noises too, hadn't she? Or had it all been her imagination, fuelled by an overactive mind in the Baron's absence?

"I don't know what I heard," Evelyn muttered, not releasing her grip on the poker. She looked about suspiciously, not trusting her own eyes.

Evelyn's gaze swept the room once more, searching for any sign of an intruder. Finding nothing, she turned back to Nell, who still trembled like a leaf in the wind.

"I wouldn't be surprised if the house were haunted," Nell whispered, her eyes wide. "Not with its tragic history."

Evelyn's heart skipped a beat. Here, at last, was an opportunity to uncover the truth about that fateful night. She'd heard whispers and rumours, but nothing concrete. The Baron never spoke of it, and she'd never dared to ask.

"Nell," Evelyn began carefully, lowering her voice to match the maid's hushed tone, "were you here that day? The day of the fire?"

Nell's face fell, her eyes growing distant as if gazing into the past. She nodded slowly, a deep sadness etching itself across her features. "I was, Miss Bane. I'll never forget it as long as I live."

Evelyn felt her breath stutter in her chest. She hesitated, torn between her burning curiosity and the pain evident in Nell's expression. But she had to know. She had to understand what had shaped the Baron into the man he was today.

"Could you... would you tell me what happened?" Evelyn asked gently, reaching out to place a comforting hand on Nell's arm.

Nell drew a shaky breath, her gaze fixed on some point beyond the charred walls of the West Wing. "It was a terrible night," she began.

Evelyn listened intently as Nell's voice dropped to a whisper, her eyes distant with the weight of memory.

"It was such a lovely evening at first," Nell began. "The Baroness was in high spirits, positively glowing. I remember seeing her with the Baron in the hallway, laughing and carrying on like newlyweds. They were so in love, Miss Bane. It was beautiful to see."

Evelyn's heart clenched at the thought of the Baron as a different man, one capable of such open affection. It seemed a world away from the stern, reserved figure she knew.

Nell continued, her voice growing thick with emotion. "The Baroness retired to her room, and the Baron to his study. All seemed well. But then..." She paused, swallowing hard. "The screams started. I rushed out to see what was happening, and the Baroness' room was already engulfed in flames. It spread so quickly, Miss Bane. Like a living thing, hungry and merciless."

Evelyn felt a chill run down her spine, imagining the terror of that night. She could almost hear the roar of the flames, smell the acrid smoke.

"I ran," Nell admitted, shame colouring her voice. "I'm not proud of it, but I ran for my life. The Baron, though... he was magnificent. He charged through the smoke, both girls in his arms. He got them out safely, but..." Nell's voice broke. "He tried to go back in. It took several of the farmhands to hold him back. He fought them like a madman, screaming for his wife."

Evelyn's eyes burned with unshed tears. She could picture it all too clearly - the Baron, wild with desperation, struggling against those who sought to save him from a fiery death. The depth of his love, and the magnitude of his loss, suddenly became painfully clear.

Evelyn listened intently as Nell continued her harrowing tale, her heart aching for the Baron and the tragedy he'd endured.

"He finally broke free," Nell said, her voice barely above a whisper. "The Baron, he... he got back into the house. We all thought we'd lost him too."

Evelyn's breath hitched in her chest, picturing the scene. The roaring flames, the choking smoke, and the Baron's desperate determination to save his wife.

Nell's eyes were distant, lost in the memory. "Then there was this awful crashing sound. A beam had collapsed right on top of him. It broke his ribs, and..." She trailed off, her hand moving unconsciously to her own face. "His face, Miss Bane. That perfect, handsome face. It was... it was terrible to see."

Evelyn felt a pang in her chest at Nell's words. She'd grown accustomed to the Baron's scar, seeing it as part of who he was. But to those who'd known him before, it must have been a shocking change.

"That beam likely saved his life," Nell continued, shaking her head. "But the sight of it... it haunts me still. How his face was permanently altered in such a way."

As Nell spoke, Evelyn found herself silently disagreeing. The scar wasn't a ruin or a blemish. To her, it was a testament to the Baron's courage, his willingness to risk everything for those he loved. It was a badge of honour, of survival against impossible odds. The mark of a man who had faced the worst life could throw at him and emerged, battered but unbroken.

Nell shook herself all over, as if trying to physically dislodge the weight of her memories. Evelyn watched her closely, her mind whirling with the new information. The tragedy that had befallen the Baron and his family seemed almost too terrible to comprehend.

As the silence stretched between them, a thought occurred to Evelyn. She hesitated for a moment, unsure if she should voice it, but her curiosity won out.

"Nell," she began carefully, "if it is indeed the spirit of the Baroness that has grown restless... why now? Why would she be disturbed after years of being at peace?"

Nell's eyes widened at the question, her brow furrowing in thought. "I... I hadn't considered that, Miss Bane," she admitted, twisting her shawl in her hands. "It's true, there've been no disturbances like this before. Not in all the years since..."

Evelyn nodded, encouraging her to continue. She found herself leaning in, eager to hear Nell's thoughts on the matter.

"Perhaps," Nell ventured, her voice barely above a whisper, "Well. Me mam always said that there's only two reasons for a restless spirit."

"Go on," Evelyn encouraged Nell, though she dreaded hearing the rest.

Nell hesitated, looking as if she didn't want to continue. "She said that it was because the spirit either had unfinished business, or...or because something disturbed it in some way."

Nell paused, her teeth flashing out as she chewed on her lip. "I can't imagine what would be disturbing the Baroness after all these years. Nothing's changed that much. Only..." Nell trailed off, shooting a glance at Evelyn and then quickly averting her eyes.

Evelyn felt a flutter in her chest at Nell's words. She hadn't realised the impact her presence had made on the household. "Surely you don't think my being here would upset the Baroness's spirit?" she asked, a hint of incredulity creeping into her voice.

Nell shook her head vigorously. "Oh no, Miss Bane, not at all. Please, I shouldn't have said anything," she said, squeezing Evelyn's free hand once again. "Forget I said it—I shouldn't have. Me mam also always said I had more beauty than brains," she offered with a weak smile.

Evelyn nodded absently, her mind whirling with the implications of Nell's words. She opened her mouth to reply, but before she could utter a sound, a faint noise drifted through the air. Her head snapped up, eyes wide. The sound had come from the direction of her room.

She exchanged a look with Nell, whose face had gone pale. The maid's lips pursed into a thin line, her earlier bravado seemingly evaporated.

"It's nothing, Miss Bane," Nell said, though her voice quavered slightly. "A house this big and old doesn't need ghosts to creak in the wind. It's just... settling, that's all."

Evelyn swallowed hard, forcing herself to nod in agreement. "Of course," she said, proud of how steady her voice sounded. "You're absolutely right, Nell. We're letting our imaginations run away with us."

Together, they made their way out of the West Wing, Evelyn's grip on the fire poker never loosening. As they reached the door, she paused, casting one last glance over her shoulder at the room that had held so many secrets. With a deep breath, she pulled the door shut behind them, the click of the latch echoing in the silent corridor.

Nell turned to her, a wan smile on her face. "I should be getting back to the servants' quarters," she said. "Goodnight, Miss Bane."

"Goodnight, Nell," Evelyn replied, watching as the maid hurried away, her white nightgown fluttering like a ghost in the darkness.

Evelyn made her way back to her room, her heart still racing from the encounter in the West Wing. As she approached, she noticed that the door stood ajar, just as she'd left it in her haste to investigate the strange noises. Moonlight spilled through the window, casting an ethereal glow across the hallway outside her room.

Her eyes drifted down to the carpet lining the wooden floor, and she froze. There, just visible in the silvery light, was a smudge she hadn't noticed before. Frowning, Evelyn leaned closer, struggling to find her breath as she realised it wasn't merely a stain, but a charred spot on the carpet.

She stared at it, her mind whirling. Surely it had always been there, she told herself. It must be a coincidence, a remnant from that terrible night years ago that she'd simply never noticed before. Yet the longer she looked, the more it seemed to mock her attempts at rationalisation.

With a shaky breath, Evelyn straightened and entered her room, closing the door firmly behind her. She threw back the covers on her bed, her movements mechanical as her thoughts raced. When she finally slipped into bed, she placed the fire poker so that it leaned on the nightstand beside her, within easy reach.

Despite her exhaustion, sleep eluded her. Every creak of the old house, every whisper of wind against the windows, set her nerves on edge. Evelyn lay rigid beneath the covers, her eyes wide open in the darkness, the poker a cold comfort beside her. What she wouldn't have given to have the comfort of a warm, solid body next to her in bed instead.

Chapter 35

Evelyn spent the next few days in a state of unease. The Baron's absence left a palpable void in the house, and she found herself longing for his return, not just for the comfort of his presence, but also for the resolution she knew must come.

Nell's words about the Baroness's restless spirit haunted Evelyn's thoughts. She'd never been one for superstition, but the charred spot on the carpet and the strange noises in the night had shaken her more than she cared to admit. Each creak of the old house made her start, and she found herself avoiding thinking of the West Wing entirely.

As she went about her duties with the girls, Evelyn's mind wandered repeatedly to the secret she'd been keeping. The weight of it pressed heavily on her conscience, and she knew she couldn't carry it any longer. The Baron deserved to know the truth about her past, about who she really was.

On the third day of his absence, as Evelyn sat in the library helping Augusta with her Latin, she made her decision. When the Baron returned, she would tell him everything. The thought both terrified and relieved her. She had no idea how he would react, but she knew it was the right thing to do.

That night, as she lay in bed, Evelyn rehearsed what she would say to the Baron. How could she explain her deception without losing his trust entirely? She tossed and turned, the words tangling in her mind like a skein of knotted yarn.

As dawn broke, Evelyn rose, exhausted but resolute. She dressed with care, her fingers trembling slightly as she fastened the buttons of her gown. Today was the day the Baron was due to return, and she was determined to speak with him as soon as possible.

Evelyn descended the stairs, her heart pounding with anticipation. She had steeled herself for a day of waiting, rehearsing her confession over and over in her mind. But as she approached the breakfast room, the sound of familiar voices made her pause.

"Father!" Julia's excited squeal rang out, followed by the scrape of chair legs against the floor.

Evelyn was momentarily breathless. He was back already?

She rounded the corner to find a scene of joyous reunion. The Baron stood by the table, his arms full of his daughters. Augusta, usually so reserved, clung to him just as tightly as her more exuberant sister. The sight made Evelyn's heart twist with a mixture of warmth and longing.

The Baron looked up, catching her eye over the girls' heads. His face, so often stern, softened into a smile that made her knees weak.

"Good morning, Miss Bane," he said, his voice rough with emotion. "I hope we haven't disturbed your routine."

Evelyn shook her head, unable to speak for a moment. She hadn't expected to see him so soon, and the reality of his presence left her momentarily breathless.

"Not at all," she managed at last, moving further into the room. "We're delighted to have you back, aren't we, girls?"

Julia nodded enthusiastically, finally releasing her father. "Did you bring us anything, Father?"

The Baron chuckled, a sound that sent a shiver down Evelyn's spine. "Perhaps," he said, his eyes twinkling with mischief. "But first, let's have breakfast. I've missed Cook's kippers something fierce."

As they settled around the table, Evelyn found herself studying the Baron. He looked tired, with shadows under his eyes, but there was a lightness to him that she hadn't seen before. Their eyes met across the table, and for a moment, the rest of the world seemed to fade away.

Evelyn watched with amusement as Julia and Augusta peppered their father with questions about his journey. Despite the brevity of his trip, the girls' excitement was palpable. Their eyes were wide with wonder at the mere thought of travelling beyond the bounds of their familiar world.

"What were the other estates like, Father?" Augusta asked, her usual reserve giving way to curiosity.

The Baron smiled indulgently. "Not so different from our own, really. Though I must say, Lord Ashbury's library would put ours to shame."

Julia leaned forward, nearly upsetting her teacup. "Did you see any grand balls? Or meet any interesting people?"

"I'm afraid not, my dear," he chuckled. "It was all rather dull business, I assure you."

Evelyn caught the Baron's eye over the rim of her teacup, raising an eyebrow in a look that clearly said, 'I told you so.' She had long argued that the girls needed more exposure to the world beyond their estate, and their eager questions only served to prove her point.

The Baron's lips quirked in acknowledgement of her silent message, a hint of sheepishness crossing his features. He cleared his throat. "Perhaps... perhaps we might consider a short trip to Bath next season. Would you ladies like that?"

The girls' squeals of delight drowned out any response Evelyn might have made, but her triumphant smile spoke volumes. As she watched the Baron's face soften with affection for his daughters, Evelyn felt a warmth bloom in her chest. It was moments like these that made her task of revealing her past all the more daunting, yet all the more necessary.

Evelyn watched the heartwarming scene unfold before her, a bittersweet ache in her chest. As much as she longed to let this moment linger, she knew they had a schedule to keep.

"I hate to interrupt," she said gently, "but we really should begin our lessons for the day."

Julia's face fell, her bottom lip jutting out in a pout. "But Miss Bane, Father's only just returned! Can't we have a little more time?"

The Baron chuckled, his arms still wrapped around his daughters. "Your governess is right, my dears. We mustn't neglect your education."

Julia tightened her grip on her father's waist. "I don't want to let go yet," she mumbled into his coat.

"Well now," the Baron said, his eyes twinkling with mischief, "if you don't release me, I'm afraid I won't be able to reach the presents I brought back for you both."

Augusta's eyes widened, and even Julia's head snapped up at this announcement. Evelyn couldn't help but smile at their excitement, even as a small part of her wondered if she should discourage such bribery. But the joy on the girls' faces was infectious, and she found herself leaning forward slightly, curious to see what the Baron had chosen for his daughters.

Julia reluctantly loosened her hold, stepping back with an expectant look. "What did you bring us, Father?"

Evelyn couldn't help but laugh as Julia and Augusta dashed out of the breakfast room, their excitement palpable. She knew she ought to chide them for their lack of decorum, but the joy on their faces was too infectious to dampen.

"I suppose that gives me a moment to finish my coffee," Evelyn said with a wry shake of her head.

The Baron cleared his throat, a faint flush colouring his cheeks. "Actually, Miss Bane, I think you should join us in the parlour as well." A pause. "Directly."

Evelyn paused, surprised by his invitation. "Oh, I wouldn't want to intrude on a family moment," she demurred, even as her heart quickened at the thought.

"Nonsense," the Baron said, his voice gruff but warm. "You should definitely drink your coffee in the parlour."

Evelyn felt her cheeks grow warm at his words. The idea that he had thought of her during his travels sent a flutter through her stomach. She tried to quash the feeling, reminding herself of the confession she still needed to make.

"That's very kind of you," she managed, her voice steadier than she felt. "I'd be honoured to join you."

As they walked towards the parlour, Evelyn was acutely aware of the Baron's presence beside her. The corridor seemed narrower than usual, and she could feel the warmth radiating from him.

Evelyn followed the Baron into the parlour, her heart fluttering with a mixture of anticipation and trepidation. The girls were already there, bouncing on their toes as they eyed two packages wrapped in brown paper on the side table.

"Go on then," the Baron said, his voice gruff but warm. "Open them."

Julia pounced on her package first, tearing into the paper with unbridled enthusiasm. Augusta approached hers more cautiously, carefully untying the string before unfolding the wrapping.

A gasp of delight escaped Julia's lips as she revealed a ball unlike any Evelyn had ever seen. It bounced with an energy that seemed almost alive, springing back into Julia's hands as if drawn by an invisible thread.

"It's made of real India rubber," the Baron explained, a hint of pride in his voice. "I thought you might enjoy it for your outdoor pursuits."

Julia's eyes shone with excitement. "Oh, Father, it's wonderful! Thank you!"

Meanwhile, Augusta had opened her own gift, revealing a leather-bound collection of sheet music. Her fingers traced the embossed title reverently, a small smile playing at the corners of her mouth.

"New compositions from Vienna," the Baron said softly. "I remembered how much you enjoyed that piece Lady Ashbury sent over last season."

Augusta looked up at her father, her eyes brimming with emotion. "Thank you, Father. It's perfect."

Evelyn couldn't help but smile as she watched the scene unfold. The Baron's choices showed a deep understanding of his daughters' interests and personalities. Julia's ball spoke to her love of physical activity and the outdoors, while Augusta's music catered to her more introspective nature.

The thoughtfulness of the gifts warmed Evelyn's heart, revealing a side of the Baron she had only glimpsed before. It was clear that beneath his gruff exterior lay a man who cared deeply for his children and paid close attention to their individual needs and desires.

Evelyn watched as the Baron's demeanour suddenly shifted. He cleared his throat, his hands fidgeting with the edge of his coat. She'd never seen him look so... nervous.

"There's, ah, one more gift," he said, his voice uncharacteristically hesitant.

Evelyn's brow furrowed in confusion. Surely he didn't mean...

The Baron bent down, reaching beneath the settee to withdraw a large white box. He held it carefully, as if it contained something incredibly fragile. Evelyn's heart began to race as he turned towards her.

"Miss Bane," he said, extending the box. "This is for you."

Evelyn's eyes widened in shock. She stared at the box, then back at the Baron, utterly flummoxed. "For me?" she repeated, her voice barely above a whisper.

The Baron nodded, a faint flush colouring his cheeks. "I saw it and... well, I thought of you."

Evelyn's hands trembled as she reached for the box. "My lord, I... this is too much. I couldn't possibly—"

"Nonsense," the Baron interrupted, his voice firmer now. "Please, I insist."

Evelyn hesitated, overwhelmed by the gesture. She glanced at Julia and Augusta, who were watching the exchange with wide-eyed curiosity. The Baron's eyes met hers, warm and encouraging, and she felt her resolve weaken.

With a deep breath, Evelyn accepted the box, marvelling at its unexpected weight. She placed it carefully on her lap, her fingers tracing the smooth edges of the pristine white packaging. She had grown up surrounded by fine things, had lived in one of the finest houses in London while married to the Judge. However, Evelyn's circumstances had taught her to treasure even the simplest of things.

Moreover, Evelyn couldn't remember the last time someone had given her a gift simply because they had thought of her. It was...well, it was too much, exactly as she had said.

Evelyn's fingers hovered over the box, her heart racing. She glanced up at the Baron, who watched her with an uncharacteristically nervous expression.

"Go on, Miss Bane!" Julia urged, practically bouncing with excitement. "Open it!"

Even Augusta leaned forward, her usual reserve giving way to curiosity. "Please, we'd love to see what Father chose for you."

Evelyn took a deep breath, steeling herself. With trembling fingers, she carefully untied the delicate ribbon and lifted the lid. As she peeled back the tissue paper, a sudden breathlessness overtook her.

The box was filled with the most exquisite fabric Evelyn had ever seen. Rich, dark purple satin cascaded over her hands as she lifted it, the colour reminiscent of a perfectly ripe aubergine. The material shimmered in the morning light, catching and reflecting it in a way that made the fabric seem almost alive.

Evelyn's eyes widened in astonishment. She had never owned anything so fine, not even in her previous life. The quality of the fabric was undeniable, its weight and sheen speaking of its value.

"It's... it's beautiful," she whispered, her voice thick with emotion. She looked up at the Baron, her eyes shining. "My lord, I don't know what to say—where would I ever wear something so beautiful?"

The Baron cleared his throat, his eyes darting away for a moment before meeting hers again. "Well, you see, there's a dressmaker in the village. Not a modiste, mind you, but competent enough. I thought perhaps you might have a dress made."

Evelyn blinked, still not comprehending. "A dress? But why would I need—"

"There's to be a harvest dance," the Baron interrupted, his words coming out in a rush. "At the public assembly rooms. In a week's time." He paused, taking a deep breath. "I was rather hoping... that is, I wondered if you might consider... attending. With me."

Evelyn's heart stuttered in her chest. She stared at the Baron, her lips parted in surprise. The room seemed to fade away, leaving only the two of them in this moment of startling clarity.

"You... you wish me to accompany you to the dance?" she asked slowly, as if she herself didn't understand what she was saying.

The Baron nodded, a hint of uncertainty in his eyes. "If you'd like to, of course. I understand if you'd rather not—"

Evelyn's heart raced as she looked down at the sumptuous fabric in her hands, then back up at the Baron's expectant face. She swallowed hard, trying to gather her scattered thoughts.

"My lord, I... I'm deeply honoured, but I don't think I should attend," she said softly, her voice tinged with regret. "It's hardly proper for a governess to accompany her employer to such an event. People would talk."

The Baron's brow furrowed, a flash of disappointment crossing his features before he squared his shoulders. "Miss Bane, I don't give a fig about what's proper," he declared, his voice gruff but earnest.

Evelyn couldn't help but laugh, the tension in her chest easing slightly. "No, I suppose you don't," she said, her eyes twinkling with amusement. "Not when you're so fond of farmers' hats and muddy boots."

The Baron's lips twitched into a wry smile. "Precisely. And I'll have you know, those hats are exceedingly practical."

His attempt at humour warmed Evelyn's heart, but she still hesitated. "Even so, I'm not sure it would be wise..."

"Consider this," the Baron said, leaning forward slightly. "If you don't attend, I fear we may have a revolt on our hands. The younger farm hands and bachelor farmers would be terribly disappointed. They've been looking forward to seeing you there."

Evelyn's eyes widened in surprise. "They have?"

The Baron nodded solemnly, though there was a mischievous glint in his eye. "Oh yes. I've heard whispers of potential mutiny if you don't make an appearance. We can't have that, can we?"

Evelyn felt a blush creep up her cheeks. The idea that anyone would be eager to see her at a dance was both flattering and slightly overwhelming. She looked down at the fabric in her lap, running her fingers over its silken surface.

Evelyn opened her mouth, her heart racing. "My lord, before I agree, there's something I need to tell you—"

"Oh, Miss Bane!" Julia interrupted, her eyes shining with excitement. "Please say you'll have your dress made! I've never been to a proper dressmaker before. Couldn't I come with you?"

Augusta, usually so reserved, chimed in as well. "I'd like to see how it's done too, if you don't mind."

Evelyn hesitated, torn between her desire to confess and the eager faces of the girls. She glanced at the Baron, who was watching her with an expression of hopeful anticipation. Her resolve crumbled.

"Very well," she said softly. "I suppose I could have a dress made."

The girls' delighted squeals filled the room, and even the Baron's face broke into a rare, genuine smile. Evelyn's heart sank even as she forced a smile onto her face. The weight of her unspoken confession pressed heavily upon her.

Gathering the beautiful fabric in her arms, Evelyn rose to her feet. "If you'll excuse me, I should put this away before our lessons begin."

As she reached the parlour door, the Baron's voice stopped her. "Miss Bane? What were you about to say earlier?"

Evelyn froze, her hand on the doorknob. She turned slowly, meeting the Baron's curious gaze. His eyes were warm, his expression more open than she'd ever seen it. The hope she saw there made her chest ache.

She hesitated, the truth on the tip of her tongue. But as she looked at his eager face, at the girls' excited chatter about the upcoming dance, Evelyn found she couldn't bring herself to shatter the moment.

"I... I'm afraid I can't remember," she lied, forcing a smile. "It couldn't have been important."

That may have been the most significant lie that Evelyn had told in the Baron's house thus far.

Chapter 36

Evelyn sat in the carriage, her heart fluttering with anticipation as they rolled towards the village. She smoothed her hands over the silk of her new gown, marvelling at how the fabric shimmered in the soft lamplight. It had been so long since she'd worn something so fine, so long since she'd had cause to dress up for an evening out.

She glanced across at the Baron, who cut a dashing figure in his evening attire, the white of his waistcoat stark against the black jacket. His usually stern countenance had softened, and she caught him stealing glances at her when he thought she wasn't looking. Evelyn couldn't help the smile that kept creeping onto her face.

"You look... very well this evening, Miss Bane," the Baron said, his voice gruff but sincere.

Evelyn felt a blush rise to her cheeks. "Thank you, my lord. You're too kind."

The carriage hit a bump in the road, and Evelyn's hand instinctively reached out to steady herself. Her fingers brushed against the Baron's, and for a moment, neither of them moved. Then, the Baron's fingers closed around hers, and Evelyn smiled through a blush.

As they neared the village, Evelyn could hear the faint strains of music drifting on the night air. Her excitement grew, pushing aside the nagging guilt that had plagued her these past days. For tonight, at least, she would allow herself to enjoy this moment of happiness.

The Baron cleared his throat. "I hope you'll save a dance for me, Miss Bane," he said, his eyes twinkling with a hint of mischief. "That is, if you're not too busy fending off the attentions of every eligible bachelor in the county."

Evelyn laughed, the sound bright and clear in the confines of the carriage. "I shall be honoured to dance with you, my lord," she replied, her smile widening. "Though I fear you overestimate my appeal."

Evelyn stepped from the carriage, her hand resting lightly on the Baron's proffered arm. The cool night air brushed against her skin, carrying with it the distant sounds of laughter and music. As they approached the assembly rooms, Evelyn felt a flutter of excitement in her chest.

The Baron pushed open the heavy wooden doors, and Evelyn's breath caught in her throat. The room before her was a vision of rustic charm. Candles flickered everywhere, their warm light dancing off the polished floorboards and casting a golden glow over the gathered revellers. The air was thick with the scent of spiced cider and the earthy aroma of freshly harvested wheat.

Evelyn's eyes travelled along the walls, where great stacks of wheat sheaves had been artfully arranged. The golden stalks seemed to glow in the candlelight, creating a backdrop that was both beautiful and deeply rooted in the life of the countryside. It was so different from the grand ballrooms of London, yet Evelyn was utterly enchanted.

"It's beautiful," she murmured, her eyes wide as she took in the scene.

The Baron smiled down at her, a warmth in his gaze that made Evelyn's heart skip a beat. "I'm glad you approve," he said softly. "The harvest dance has always been a favourite of mine."

As they moved further into the room, Evelyn couldn't help but marvel at the simple decorations that adorned every surface. Garlands of autumn leaves and berries hung from the rafters, and bowls of crisp apples dotted the tables that lined the walls. Everything spoke of abundance and joy, a celebration of the land's bounty.

The music swelled, a lively country dance that had couples whirling across the floor. Evelyn watched, captivated by the sight of farmers and their wives, labourers and landowners all coming together in a whirl of movement and laughter. The relief of a bountiful harvest was palpable.

Evelyn paused at the entrance, her fingers working to unfasten the delicate clasp of her lightweight cloak. As she slipped it off, she felt a moment of vulnerability, acutely aware of the eyes that turned towards her. The local dressmaker had worked wonders with the Baron's gift of silk, crafting a gown that was both elegant and understated. Its simplicity only served to highlight the exquisite quality of the fabric, which shimmered like moonlight on water with every movement.

The bodice hugged her figure closely, accentuating her slender waist before flowing into a full skirt that swished softly as she moved. The neckline was modest yet flattering, revealing just a hint of her collarbone.

Evelyn had forgone any elaborate jewellery, choosing instead to wear only a simple pair of pearl earrings that had once belonged to her mother. Her dark hair was piled up on her head with a matching length of ribbon threaded throughout it in a loose style. That was perhaps a little out of date, but made Evelyn feel like a goddess.

As she handed her cloak to a waiting attendant, Evelyn turned to find the Baron staring at her, his eyes wide with an expression she couldn't quite decipher. For a moment, neither of them spoke, the bustling activity of the room fading into the background.

Finally, the Baron cleared his throat, a faint flush creeping up his neck. "Miss Bane," he said, his voice low and earnest, "I fear you have vastly underestimated how appealing you are."

Evelyn felt her cheeks grow warm at his words, a mixture of pleasure and embarrassment coursing through her. She ducked her head, unable to meet his intense gaze. "My lord, you flatter me," she murmured, her fingers fidgeting with the folds of her skirt.

Evelyn was swept up in the lively atmosphere of the harvest dance. The lack of dance cards initially perplexed her, but she soon realised that such formalities held little sway here. Instead of the rigid etiquette she was accustomed to, there was a joyous spontaneity to the proceedings that she found utterly refreshing.

As she whirled across the floor with the Baron, Evelyn couldn't help but laugh at the sheer delight of it all. His strong hands guided her through the steps of a country dance, and she marvelled at how natural it felt to move with him.

"You dance beautifully, Miss Bane," the Baron said, his eyes twinkling.

Evelyn smiled, feeling a warmth spread through her chest. "Thank you, my lord. Though I fear my London dancing master would be quite scandalised by the liberties we're taking with the steps."

The Baron chuckled, a rich sound that sent a pleasant shiver down Evelyn's spine. "I daresay he would. But isn't this far more enjoyable?"

After their dance, Evelyn was partnered with a few other gentlemen. She danced with a jovial farmer whose enthusiasm more than made up for his lack of grace, and a shy young man who blushed furiously every time their hands met.

As the evening wore on, the Baron approached her once more, holding out his hand in invitation. "Miss Bane, might I have the pleasure of another dance?"

Evelyn hesitated, her ingrained sense of propriety warring with her desire to accept. "My lord, we've already danced twice this evening. Any more would be most improper."

The Baron's eyes crinkled with amusement. He gestured around the room with a sweep of his arm. "Look around you, Miss Bane. Does it look as though anyone here would care about such things?"

Evelyn followed his gaze, taking in the scene before her. Farmers and their wives danced with abandon, their faces flushed with exertion and joy. Children darted between the dancers, their laughter rising above the music. Even the village elders, seated along the walls, tapped their feet in time with the lively tunes.

A smile spread across Evelyn's face as she turned back to the Baron. "You're quite right, my lord. I would be delighted to dance with you again."

Evelyn's cheeks were flushed as she and the Baron finished their dance, her breath coming a bit quicker than usual. The warmth of his hand on her waist lingered even as they parted, and she found herself reluctant to step away.

"You look a bit flushed, Miss Bane," the Baron observed, his grey eyes searching her face with concern. "Are you feeling well?"

Evelyn nodded, fanning herself lightly with her hand. "I'm quite alright, thank you. It's just rather warm in here, isn't it?"

The Baron's lips quirked into a small smile. "Indeed it is. Perhaps we might step outside for some fresh air?"

"That sounds lovely," Evelyn agreed, feeling a flutter of anticipation in her chest.

They made their way towards the entrance, the Baron's hand resting lightly on the small of her back as he guided her through the crowd. As they approached the doors, Evelyn could hear raucous laughter and loud voices coming from outside.

Stepping into the cool night air was a relief after the stuffy warmth of the assembly rooms. Evelyn took a deep breath, savouring the crispness of the autumn night. Her eyes were drawn to a group of young men gathered near the hitching posts, their boisterous behaviour making her slightly uneasy.

The Baron seemed to sense her discomfort. "This way, Miss Bane," he said softly, guiding her away from the rowdy group and towards a quieter area of the courtyard.

They walked in companionable silence for a moment, the sounds of the dance fading behind them. Evelyn glanced up at the Baron, noticing how the moonlight softened the harsh lines of his face, making him look younger and more vulnerable than she had ever seen him.

Evelyn reluctantly tore her gaze away from the Baron, tilting her head back to take in the night sky. She felt her breath stutter in her chest at the sight that greeted her. The moon hung low and heavy, a golden orb that seemed impossibly large. Thick clouds drifted lazily across its face, creating an ever-changing tableau of light and shadow.

"Oh, it's magnificent," she breathed, her eyes wide with wonder. The sight stirred something deep within her, a sense of awe at the beauty and vastness of the world. For a moment, all her worries and fears melted away, leaving only a profound appreciation for this simple, perfect moment.

As she gazed upward, Evelyn became acutely aware of the Baron's presence beside her. The warmth of his body seemed to radiate through the cool night air, and she could feel the weight of his gaze upon her. Her heart began to beat a little faster, a mixture of nervousness and excitement coursing through her veins.

Slowly, Evelyn lowered her eyes from the celestial display above, turning to meet the Baron's gaze. The intensity she found there made her breath catch once more. His grey eyes, usually so guarded, now shone with an emotion she couldn't quite name. It was as if he were seeing her for the first time, truly seeing her.

Evelyn's heart raced as she gazed into the Baron's eyes, the intensity of his gaze making her feel both vulnerable and exhilarated. Above them, the heavy clouds began to knit together, bathing them in concealing darkness. Time seemed to slow as he leaned towards her, his hand gently cupping her cheek. She tilted her face upwards, drawn to him like a moth to a flame.

Their lips met softly at first, a tender, hesitant kiss that sent a shiver down Evelyn's spine. It was as if the world around them had faded away, leaving only this moment, this connection. As the initial shock wore off, Evelyn found herself responding with growing ardour, her hands moving to rest on the Baron's broad chest.

The kiss deepened, becoming more passionate as the Baron's arms encircled her waist, pulling her closer. Evelyn's breath hitched in her chest as she felt the solid warmth of his body against hers. Her hands caught on the lapels of his jacket, desperate to pull him nearer.

Without breaking the kiss, the Baron guided her backwards until she felt the cool stone of the building against her back. The contrast of the cold wall and his warm embrace sent a delicious shiver through her body. Evelyn gasped softly as he pressed her gently against the wall, their bodies fitting together perfectly in the shadows.

Her hands moved of their own accord, sliding up to tangle in his hair as the kiss grew more fervent. The Baron's hands roamed her back, pulling her impossibly closer. Evelyn's head spun with the intoxicating mix of desire and the lingering scent of his cologne.

Evelyn felt lost in the moment, her senses overwhelmed by the Baron's passionate embrace. The world had narrowed to just the two of them, the cool stone at her back and the warmth of his body pressed against her. She clung to him, her fingers tangled in his hair, never wanting this exquisite moment to end.

His lips moved from her mouth to trail along her jaw, and Evelyn tilted her head back, a soft gasp escaping her. The Baron's hands tightened on her waist, pulling her even closer, and she felt as though she might melt into him entirely.

Suddenly, a burst of raucous laughter shattered the quiet night. Evelyn's eyes flew open, her heart pounding as she registered the sound of unsteady footsteps and more laughter from the direction of the assembly rooms. Reality came crashing back with brutal force.

Startled, Evelyn pulled back from the Baron, her hands pushing gently against his chest. The loss of contact was like a physical ache, and she hated the sensation of suddenly feeling bereft and exposed.

Her cheeks burned with a mixture of lingering desire and mortification as she remembered where they were and what had just transpired between them. Moreover, she remembered that above all else, she might not have been a free woman.

Evelyn stepped back, her heart racing as she tried to compose herself. She smoothed her hands over her skirts, acutely aware of the Baron's intense gaze upon her. The cool night air did little to calm the flush in her cheeks or the trembling of her hands.

"Miss Bane, I..." the Baron began, his voice husky. He cleared his throat and tried again. "I must apologise for taking such liberties with you. It was unconscionable of me. You deserve far better than to be accosted in the shadows like some—"

"Please, my lord," Evelyn interrupted, her voice barely above a whisper. She raised her eyes to meet his, surprised by the depth of emotion she saw there. "You have nothing to apologise for. Under... under other circumstances, I would never have objected to such attentions from you."

The Baron's brow furrowed, confusion replacing the guilt in his expression. Evelyn took a deep breath, steeling herself for what she knew she must say next.

"In truth, it is I who should be apologising to you," she said softly, her gaze dropping to her hands, which she clasped tightly before her.

The Baron's confusion deepened. "I don't understand, Miss Bane. What could you possibly have to apologise for?"

Evelyn's heart pounded in her chest as she struggled to find the words to explain. How could she begin to unravel the tangled web of her past?

Evelyn's heart raced as she struggled to find the words. The weight of her secrets pressed down upon her, making it difficult to breathe. She knew she had to tell him the truth, but fear gripped her heart like an icy fist.

"My lord," she began, her voice trembling, "there's something I must confess. I... I haven't been entirely honest with you."

The Baron's brow furrowed, his grey eyes searching her face. Evelyn took a shaky breath and continued.

"In my youth, I... I was married." The words tumbled out, each one feeling like a stone in her throat. "And I... I'm not certain, but it's possible that I... I may still be married."

The Baron stared at her, his expression shifting from confusion to disbelief and then to something that looked painfully like betrayal. The silence between them stretched, heavy and oppressive.

Evelyn's heart sank as she watched the emotions play across his face. She longed to reach out to him, to explain further, but she found herself rooted to the spot.

Without a word, the Baron turned on his heel and began to walk away. His shoulders were rigid, his steps purposeful as he strode into the darkness.

"My lord, please," Evelyn called after him, her voice cracking. "Let me explain!"

But he didn't turn back. He didn't even pause. He simply continued walking, disappearing into the night as if he couldn't bear to be in her presence a moment longer.

As if to mirror her anguish, the sky opened up above her. Fat raindrops began to fall, quickly soaking through her silk gown and plastering her carefully arranged hair to her face. It was as though the heavens themselves were weeping for her folly.

Evelyn stood there, alone in the rain, watching the spot where the Baron had vanished. She felt as though her heart might shatter into a thousand pieces, each one washed away by the relentless downpour.

Chapter 37

Evelyn paced the length of her small room, her silk gown rustling with each agitated step. The first grey light of dawn crept through the curtains, casting long shadows across the floor. She hadn't slept a wink, her mind replaying the events of the previous night in an endless, torturous loop.

The Baron's face, so full of hurt and betrayal, haunted her. She could still feel the ghost of his lips on hers, the warmth of his embrace. It was all she could do not to scream in frustration.

Her gown, once a thing of beauty, now hung heavy and damp against her skin. She'd made no effort to change out of it, too consumed by her tumultuous thoughts. Her hair, painstakingly arranged for the dance, now hung in limp, bedraggled strands about her face.

Evelyn paused at the window, pressing her forehead against the cool glass. The grounds of Aylesbury Manor stretched out before her, shrouded in early morning mist. It all seemed so idyllic, so peaceful. How could the world outside remain unchanged when her own had been turned upside down?

She turned away, resuming her restless pacing. Her mind raced, trying to find a way to explain, to make the Baron understand. But how could she, when she barely understood it herself?

The uncertainty of her marital status loomed over her like a dark cloud. She'd thought she'd left that part of her life behind, but now it threatened to destroy everything she'd built here. The home she'd found, the respect she'd earned, the... feelings she'd developed.

Evelyn's hand drifted to her lips, remembering the kiss. For a moment, she'd allowed herself to hope, to dream of a future she'd thought forever out of reach. Now, that dream lay shattered at her feet, as fragile and broken as her heart.

A soft knock at the door startled Evelyn from her reverie. Before she could respond, Nell slipped into the room, her brow furrowed with concern.

"Miss Evelyn? I heard you pacing about and... goodness me, you're soaked through!" Nell's eyes widened as she took in Evelyn's bedraggled appearance.

Evelyn opened her mouth to speak, but found no words. She stood there, a pitiful figure in her ruined finery, unable to meet Nell's gaze.

"Come now, let's get you out of these wet things," Nell said gently, moving towards Evelyn with the quiet efficiency that had become so familiar.

Evelyn allowed herself to be guided to the dressing table, her limbs heavy with exhaustion. Nell's deft fingers began to work at the intricate fastenings of her gown, each touch a reminder of the care and kindness she'd found in this household.

"There now," Nell murmured, easing the damp silk from Evelyn's shoulders. "You'll catch your death if you stay in these clothes."

As Nell worked, Evelyn caught sight of herself in the mirror. She barely recognised the woman staring back at her – pale, dishevelled, with dark circles under her eyes. Was this truly what she'd become?

Nell began to unpin Evelyn's hair, her touch gentle as she worked through the tangles. "Did something happen last night, at the dance?" Nell asked quietly. Evelyn glanced up and saw a quiet curiosity on Nell's face, and felt her own expression crumble. Wordlessly, Evelyn dropped her face into her hands. "Whatever's happened, Miss, it can't be as bad as all that," Nell said softly, pausing to put a comforting hand on Evelyn's shoulder.

Evelyn took a deep, shuddering breath, trying to regain her composure. She lifted her head from her hands, meeting Nell's concerned gaze in the mirror.

"Nell," Evelyn began, her voice barely above a whisper, "how long have you known the Baron?"

Nell's hands stilled in Evelyn's hair for a moment before resuming their gentle ministrations. "Oh, I've been here since before he was married to the Baroness, God rest her soul. Might as well be part of the furniture at this point," Nell said with a lightness that Evelyn envied.

Evelyn nodded, her heart heavy. She hesitated, then asked the question that had been gnawing at her since the previous night. "Is... is the Baron the forgiving type?"

Nell's reflection in the mirror grew solemn. She shook her head slowly, her eyes meeting Evelyn's. "I'm afraid not, Miss. The Baron, he's not the sort of man to forgive a slight easily. Especially not these days, after... well, after everything he's been through."

Evelyn's heart sank, the last flicker of hope extinguishing within her. She closed her eyes, fighting back a fresh wave of tears. The weight of her deception pressed down upon her, crushing any remaining optimism she might have harboured.

"I see," Evelyn whispered, her voice thick with unshed tears. She opened her eyes, staring at her reflection once more. The woman looking back at her seemed a stranger – lost, broken, and utterly alone.

Nell's hands stilled in Evelyn's hair, the last pin set in place. Their eyes met in the mirror, a silent understanding passing between them. Evelyn watched as Nell's expression flickered, caught between her usual cheerful demeanour and a desire to offer comfort. In the end, she did neither.

With a small nod, Nell stepped back from the dressing table. Her footsteps were soft on the squeaking floor as she moved towards the door. Evelyn felt the maid's gaze linger on her for a moment longer, heavy with unspoken words.

The door opened with a quiet creak, then closed again. Nell was gone.

Evelyn let out a breath she hadn't realised she'd been holding. The silence in the room felt oppressive now, pressing in on her from all sides. She turned away from the mirror, unable to bear the sight of her own reflection any longer.

Her gaze fell on the ruined silk gown, now draped over a chair. It seemed a fitting metaphor for her hopes and dreams – once beautiful and full of promise, now sodden and tarnished. Evelyn ran her fingers over the damp fabric, remembering how it had felt to twirl across the dance floor in the Baron's arms.

The memory brought a fresh wave of pain, sharp and insistent. Evelyn wrapped her arms around herself, trying to hold the pieces of her shattered world together. But it was no use. Everything she'd built here, everything she'd come to cherish, was slipping through her fingers like water.

Evelyn moved through the day in a fog, her body going through the motions while her mind remained trapped in the events of the previous night. The girls' lessons passed in a blur, her voice sounding hollow and distant to her own ears as she recited grammar rules and historical dates.

Julia and Augusta exchanged worried glances over their books, their usual chatter subdued. Evelyn caught them watching her with concern, but she couldn't bring herself to reassure them. What could she possibly say?

At luncheon, Evelyn was unable to eat, pushing the food around her plate listlessly. The empty chair at the head of the table seemed to mock her, a stark reminder of the Baron's absence.

As the afternoon wore on, Evelyn found herself drifting to the windows more and more frequently. Her eyes scanned the lane leading up to the manor, hoping to catch a glimpse of the Baron's broad-shouldered figure. Each time she looked, disappointment settled heavily in her chest.

The girls' worried whispers followed her as she moved from room to room, restless and unable to settle. She knew she should focus on them, on their lessons and needs, but she couldn't shake the desperate hope that the Baron would return.

As the sun began to dip towards the horizon, casting long shadows across the manicured lawns, Evelyn stood at the library window. Her fingers worried at the curtain's edge, her eyes fixed on the empty lane. The weight of her secret pressed down upon her, making each breath a struggle.

Her fingers absently traced patterns on the heavy curtains, her mind replaying every moment of the previous night. The warmth of the Baron's embrace, the tenderness of his kiss, the hurt in his eyes when she'd confessed her secret. Each memory was a dagger to her heart, sharp and unrelenting.

So consumed was she by her thoughts that she failed to hear the soft creak of the library door opening behind her. It wasn't until a familiar voice broke the silence that Evelyn realised she was no longer alone.

"Miss Bane."

The Baron's deep voice startled Evelyn from her reverie. She whirled around, her heart leaping into her throat. There he stood, just inside the doorway, his broad frame silhouetted against the dim light of the hallway.

For a moment, Evelyn couldn't breathe. Relief flooded through her at the sight of him, quickly followed by a wave of devastation. His face was impassive, his grey eyes unreadable as they met hers.

"My lord," Evelyn managed, her voice barely above a whisper. She took a step forward, then hesitated, unsure of her welcome. "I... I'm glad you've returned safely."

The Baron remained still, his gaze never leaving her face. The silence stretched between them, heavy with unspoken words and barely contained emotions.

Evelyn's hands trembled at her sides, her mind racing. She opened her mouth to speak, to explain, to beg for understanding if need be. But before she could utter a word, the Baron spoke again.

"We need to talk, Miss Bane."

The stiff, formal tones of his voice sliced at Evelyn as neatly as razors. Gone was any of the familiarity, the lingering looks and gentle look in his eye. It was as if a wall had come up between them, holding rigidly at bay. Wordlessly, the Baron turned on his heel.

Evelyn, feeling despondent and sombre, but not willing to flinch from the consequences of her choices, followed after him.

***

James paced the length of his study, his boots striking a staccato rhythm against the polished floorboards. Though his face remained an impassive mask, his insides churned with a maelstrom of emotions he could scarcely name. He clenched and unclenched his fists, struggling to maintain his composure as Evelyn stepped into the room behind him.

He had to give her credit; she wasn't running from this confrontation. No, she faced him directly, her chin lifted in a gesture that spoke of both defiance and resignation. It was grudgingly admirable, he had to admit, even as anger and betrayal threatened to overwhelm him.

Damn it all, he thought, running a hand through his dishevelled hair. He'd allowed himself to hope, to imagine a future that now seemed as insubstantial as morning mist. The weight of his own foolishness pressed down upon him, making it difficult to draw breath.

James halted his pacing, his back to Evelyn. He could feel her eyes upon him, patient yet expectant. The silence stretched between them, taut as a bowstring.

He opened his mouth to speak, but the words caught in his throat. How could he articulate the tempest raging within him? The betrayal, the disappointment, the lingering warmth of their kiss—it all tangled together in a knot he couldn't unravel.

James turned, intending to face her, but found himself averting his gaze. His eyes fell upon the portrait of his late wife, and a fresh wave of guilt washed over him. He'd allowed himself to care again, to hope for a future he'd thought forever lost. And now...

He tried once more to speak, but the weight of everything left him mute. His jaw clenched as he resumed his restless movement, boots striking the floor with renewed vigour.

Evelyn's voice, soft yet firm, cut through his tumultuous thoughts. "James, please. Hold still and look at me."

Her use of his Christian name startled him. He froze mid-step, torn between the instinct to obey and the fear of what he might see in her eyes. Slowly, reluctantly, he turned to face her.

James shook his head, his grey eyes stormy with emotion. "I can't hold still, Evelyn. If I stop moving, I'll go mad. I've been pacing since..." He trailed off, unable to finish the sentence.

The memory of their kiss, so tender and passionate, flashed through his mind. It was quickly followed by the crushing weight of her revelation. He resumed his restless movement, unable to meet her gaze.

"I've been all across the estate since dawn," he continued, his voice rough with fatigue and barely contained emotion. "I've walked every field, inspected every fence and hedgerow. I've seen the fruits of my labour, the work of years coming to fruition."

He paused by the window, staring out at the rolling hills of his land. The view that had always brought him comfort now seemed to mock him.

"And do you know what I realised?" James turned to face Evelyn, his expression a mixture of anguish and frustration. "It all feels hollow. Empty. What's the point of all this work, all this effort, if there's no one to share it with?"

The words hung in the air between them, heavy with implication. James ran a hand through his hair, marvelling at how quickly his carefully constructed walls had crumbled.

James cut off Evelyn's protest with a sharp wave of his hand. "Don't you see what I'm saying?" His voice was low, tinged with frustration and a vulnerability he rarely allowed himself to show. "All this work, the security I've built—it means nothing if we're living half a life."

The realisation hit him like a physical blow. He braced himself against his desk, his shoulders sagging under the weight of the truth. Evelyn had been right all along, and he'd been too stubborn, too set in his ways to see it.

"I've been so focused on protecting the girls, on building a legacy that would keep them safe," he continued, his voice barely above a whisper. "But what good is safety if they never truly live? If I never..."

He trailed off, unable to finish the thought. James looked up at Evelyn, really looked at her for the first time since she'd entered the room. The anguish in her eyes mirrored his own, and he felt something inside him shift.

"You were right," he admitted, the words tasting both bitter and sweet on his tongue. "All this time, you've been trying to show me what I couldn't see. That there's more to life than duty and obligation. That love, despite its risks, is worth pursuing. You've been saying that my daughters deserve to live a complete life. I didn't know that you were also convincing me of the same thing."

James straightened, a newfound resolve settling over him. He'd spent years building walls around his heart, convinced that they would protect him from further pain. But now he saw those walls for what they truly were—a prison of his own making.

"I've been a fool," he said, his voice growing stronger. "I've let fear dictate my choices, and in doing so, I've denied myself—and my daughters—the chance at true happiness."

James watched as Evelyn's eyes filled with tears, her lips parting as if to speak. But no words came. He felt a twinge in his chest, an urge to comfort her that he quickly suppressed. This was not the time for sentiment.

Composing himself, James straightened his posture and cleared his throat. "I need to know the particulars of your situation," he said, his voice steady and business-like. "I'm a practical man, Evelyn. I require all the information before I can make a decision. I have more than myself to consider—my daughters."

He watched her closely, noting the way she seemed to weigh her options. After a moment, she spoke softly. "I need time to think about your request."

James nodded, relieved that she hadn't outright refused. "Very well," he agreed. "I should like to hear from you, one way or the other, by morning." Evelyn nodded in response gravely, her face settling into resigned lines.

As Evelyn turned to leave, a thought struck him. He called out, halting her retreat. "Wait. There's one more thing I need to know." He paused, steeling himself. "What is your real name?"

He saw her hesitate, her hand on the doorknob. Then, slowly, she turned back to face him. "It's Lady Evelyn Banfield," she said in a small voice, a sorrowful smile on her lips.

James felt his eyebrows rise involuntarily. He had known she was well-born—her manners and education had made that clear—but he hadn't expected this. A lady, here in his home, acting as governess to his daughters. The implications of this revelation whirled through his mind, adding yet another layer of complexity to an already bewildering situation.

James watched as Evelyn slipped out of the study, the door closing softly behind her. The silence that followed was deafening. He slumped into his chair, the weight of the conversation settling heavily upon his shoulders.

His gaze fell upon his two hunting dogs, sprawled lazily across the rug. Their eyes, warm and brown, stared up at him with what he fancied was a mixture of concern and confusion.

"What are you two looking at?" he grumbled, running a hand over his face. "Don't tell me you're living secret lives as well. County magistrates, perhaps? Or are you actually French spies in disguise?"

The dogs, predictably, offered no response beyond a slight tilt of their heads and wagging tails.

James sighed, leaning back in his chair. "No? Nothing to add? Well, at least you're consistent."

He reached for the decanter on his desk, pouring himself a generous measure of brandy. The amber liquid glinted in the fading afternoon light as he swirled it in his glass.

"I thought I knew everything there was to know about running this estate," he mused aloud, more to himself than to his canine companions. "Crop rotations, animal husbandry, land management... I've spent years perfecting it all. But people?" He shook his head ruefully. "It seems I don't know nearly as much as I thought I did."

The brandy burned pleasantly as he took a sip, but it did little to calm the anxiety churning in his gut. What would Evelyn's decision be? The uncertainty gnawed at him, making it impossible to focus on anything else.

James found himself straining to hear any sound from beyond the study door, hoping for some indication of Evelyn's whereabouts or state of mind. But the house remained stubbornly silent, offering no clues to assuage his growing unease.

Chapter 38

Evelyn stirred in her bed, her dreams a tumultuous mix of memories and fears. The weight of her decision pressed upon her even in sleep, and she found herself awake before the first light of dawn crept over the horizon.

With a weary sigh, she rose and slipped on a simple morning dress. Her fingers traced the familiar pattern of her braid, still intact from the night before. For once, she left it as it was, hanging over her shoulder in a cascade of chestnut waves and only tucked a few errant locks behind her ear.

The house was silent as she made her way downstairs, her footsteps muffled by the plush carpets. She paused at the bottom of the stairs, listening intently for any sign of movement. The house was still slumbering, with not even the kitchen maids and hall boys awake yet, so she continued on, her heart pounding with each step.

The kitchen was dark and cool, the hearth long since gone cold. Evelyn fumbled with the latch on the back door, her hands trembling slightly. As it swung open, she was greeted by the soft summer breeze, a sharp contrast to the stuffy warmth of the house.

She stepped out onto the flagstones, breathing deeply in the fresh air. The garden stretched out before her, shrouded in mist and shadow. Evelyn hesitated for a moment, glancing back at the house. It loomed behind her, dark and imposing, holding within it all the complications of her new life.

Taking a deep breath, she stepped forward into the misty garden, leaving the safety of the house behind. The dew-soaked grass dampened the hem of her dress as she walked, but she paid it no mind. Her thoughts were focused solely on what lay ahead, on the decision she had to make.

Evelyn wrapped her arms around herself as she set off across the grounds, her mind whirling with the possibilities laid out before her. The morning air held the first cool kiss of autumn, but she barely noticed, lost in her internal struggle.

As she crested a small hill, she found herself at the edge of one of the estate's sprawling fields. The first rays of sun were slanting across the horizon, making the low mist glow golden, revealing the lush green expanse before her. Evelyn's breath faltered for a moment as she spotted a lone figure in the distance.

It was the Baron, already out and working despite the early hour. He wore only his breeches and boots, with a loose shirt open at the neck, revealing a glimpse of his broad chest. His sleeves were rolled up, exposing muscular forearms as he swung a scythe in a steady rhythm, cutting through the tall grass with determined focus. His face was set, his mouth in a tight line.

Evelyn's first instinct was to turn and flee, to avoid this unexpected encounter. But as she began to pivot away, she found herself unable to tear her gaze from him. It wasn't just the novelty of seeing a nobleman engaged in manual labour.

The Baron's movements were graceful yet powerful, each swing of the scythe precise and controlled. Sweat glistened on his brow, and his dark hair fell across his forehead, unkempt in a way she'd never seen before.

Her heart raced as she watched him, feeling as though she were witnessing something intensely private. Yet she couldn't look away. There was something raw and honest about seeing him like this, stripped of the formal attire and stern demeanour he usually presented to the world.

Evelyn hesitated, her feet rooted to the spot. Then, taking a deep breath, she made her decision. This chance meeting felt like a sign, an opportunity she couldn't ignore. With trembling legs, she began to approach the Baron, her mind racing to find the right words to say.

Evelyn's heart thundered in her chest as she approached the Baron. The swish of her skirts against the damp grass seemed impossibly loud in the still morning air. She watched as the Baron's rhythmic movements slowed, then stopped entirely as he became aware of her presence.

He turned to face her, his expression unreadable. Sweat glistened on his brow, and his chest rose and fell with each deep breath. For a moment, they simply stared at each other, the weight of unspoken words hanging heavy between them.

Evelyn swallowed hard, steeling herself. This was her chance, perhaps her only chance, to lay bare the truth of her past. Without preamble, she began to speak, her voice barely above a whisper.

"My lord, I... I was married once before," she said, the words tumbling out in a rush. "To a man named Banfield. Judge Banfield."

The Baron's eyes widened slightly, but he remained silent, allowing her to continue.

"It was—my life before I was married was not a particularly happy one. I lived in a cage, a beautifully gilded one, but one all the same. My life was decided for me. I played the part of a dutiful daughter," Evelyn explained, her gaze dropping to the ground. "My one moment of rebellion was to choose to marry the Judge. I'd heard rumours about him, the whispers of the ton, but I thought...I thought I could thaw his heart. He was wealthy and powerful, and... That doesn't matter."

She trailed off, memories of those dark days flooding back. When she looked up again, she saw something in the Baron's eyes that gave her the courage to continue.

"He was cruel, my lord. Controlling and... violent." Reflexively, Evelyn pulled at the sleeves of her dress, a habit from years of covering bruises. "A... A friend helped me escape."

Evelyn straightened at that. "No—I will not give you anything less than perfect honesty." Fixing the Baron with an unflinching gaze, Evelyn continued. "My lover helped me to escape. He was a good man, and I am grateful to him. Don't mistake me, it was not a love affair—it was... I don't know what it was, but I was not and am not in love with him, not really. It was thanks to him and his friends and family that I escaped."

Evelyn took a deep breath and wrapped her arms tighter about herself to stop the trembling that she didn't even know had started. "In the end, we exposed the Judge for crimes of bribery and blackmail, and I'm sure a litany of others. I was sent away from London to Richard's Aunt Agnes to be kept from the worst of it. He's a vengeful man," Evelyn explained quietly.

The Baron's eyes hardened at that. Evelyn was lost in her own narrative and realised with a start that the Baron had gone rigid all over, his eyes hardening into flinty points.

"I don't know what became of him after that. I don't even know if I'm truly free of him," she said. Evelyn's voice wavered, but she pressed on, determined to reveal everything.

"I took my aunt's name, became Miss Evelyn Bane. I thought I could leave my past behind, start anew. But I see now that I was wrong to keep this from you. You deserved to know the truth from the beginning. It wasn't to deceive you," Evelyn added hurriedly.

"I just...I just didn't want to be Lady Evelyn anymore. I just wanted to be free, and—and I was so ashamed."

Evelyn's words hung in the air, the silence stretching between them like a chasm. She watched the Baron's face, her heart pounding as she searched for any sign of understanding or forgiveness. But his expression darkened, the scars on his face twisting into a grimace that sent a chill down her spine.

The Baron turned away, his gaze fixed on some distant point beyond the misty fields. Evelyn felt a wave of fear wash over her, dreading his judgement. Yet, beneath that fear, a curious lightness bloomed in her chest. For the first time in months, perhaps years, she felt unburdened by the weight of her secrets.

"My lord," Evelyn ventured, her voice barely above a whisper. "Please, say something."

The Baron remained silent, his jaw clenched tight. Evelyn took a tentative step forward, longing to bridge the gap between them.

"I understand if you're angry," she said. "I can leave, whenever you want. I'd understand, I—"

"Lady Evelyn," the Baron interrupted, his voice low and controlled. He still wouldn't meet her gaze. "I would like time to consider what you've told me. As you requested of me."

Evelyn's words died in her throat. She nodded, even though he couldn't see the gesture. "Of course," she murmured. "I understand."

As she turned to leave, Evelyn felt caught between two powerful emotions. Misery at the thought of losing the Baron's trust and affection warred with the profound relief of finally being honest. She walked away, leaving the Baron alone in the field, her heart heavy yet somehow freer than it had been in years.

Chapter 39

Evelyn returned to her room in a dream-like state, as if her feet were floating. She dressed quickly, steeling herself for whatever the day might bring. As she made her way to the schoolroom, she resolved to focus solely on her charges and their lessons. It was the only way she could keep her thoughts from straying to the Baron and his reaction to her confession.

Augusta and Julia were already seated at their desks when Evelyn entered, their faces bright with anticipation for the day's lessons. Evelyn forced a smile, determined not to let her personal turmoil affect the girls.

"Good morning, ladies," she said, her voice steadier than she felt. "Today, we'll be continuing our study of French literature. Julia, I believe you were to present your analysis of Voltaire's 'Candide'?"

As Julia launched into her presentation, Evelyn felt grateful for the distraction. She listened intently, offering encouragement and gentle corrections where needed. The morning passed in a blur of conjugations, philosophical debates, and historical timelines.

After lunch, Evelyn led the girls in a botany lesson, taking them into the gardens to identify and sketch various plants. The fresh air and focused activity helped to calm her nerves, though she couldn't help but glance towards the manor house occasionally, wondering if the Baron was watching from his study window.

As the afternoon waned, Evelyn set the girls to work on their needlepoint while she reviewed their progress in arithmetic. She threw herself into the task with vigour, checking and rechecking their sums until her eyes ached from the strain.

Before she knew it, the dinner hour was upon them. Evelyn dismissed the girls to prepare for the meal, her stomach churning with a mix of hunger and apprehension. She took her time freshening up, her hands shaking slightly as she smoothed her hair and straightened her dress.

When she finally made her way to the dining room, Evelyn was surprised to find only Augusta and Julia seated at the table. Mrs Turnbell, the housekeeper, was supervising the footmen as they laid out the dishes.

"Where is your father?" Evelyn asked, trying to keep her voice light.

Nell, holding a platter of asparagus steamed in a tall pie crust, ventured an answer. "He departed, Miss Bane. I believe it was quite urgent." Her face was set into a grim expression, which made Evelyn pale.

Evelyn nodded, sinking into her chair. She couldn't decide if she felt relieved or disappointed by the Baron's absence. As she mechanically began to eat, she wondered how long this uncertainty would last; whether she would ever again feel at ease in this house that had so quickly become her home.

Evelyn's heart sank as she watched the girls' faces fall. Julia's lower lip trembled, while Augusta's brow furrowed in a deep scowl.

"He didn't even say goodbye," Julia whispered, her voice thick with hurt.

Augusta pushed her plate away. "He always tells us when he's leaving. Always."

Evelyn forced a reassuring smile, though it felt brittle on her face. "I'm sure it's nothing to worry about, girls. Your father is a busy man with many responsibilities. Perhaps something urgent came up that required his immediate attention."

"No," Augusta said firmly, her grey eyes—so like her father's—fixing on Evelyn with unsettling intensity. "Something's wrong. We can tell."

Julia nodded vigorously. "Ever since yesterday, things have felt... strange. Did you and Papa have a quarrel?"

Evelyn's breath caught in her throat. She hadn't realised the girls were so perceptive. "Of course not," she said, hoping her voice didn't betray her. "What makes you think that?"

Augusta and Julia exchanged a look.

"Is Papa going to send you away?" Julia asked in a small voice.

The question hit Evelyn like a physical blow. It was the very fear that had been gnawing at her since her confession, but hearing it spoken aloud made it suddenly, terrifyingly real.

Evelyn's heart clenched at the girls' words. She took a deep breath, trying to steady herself before speaking.

"Girls, I appreciate your concern, but we mustn't jump to conclusions," she said, her voice gentle but firm. "Your father is a fair and honourable man. Whatever decision he makes will be for the best."

Augusta's eyes flashed with determination. "If Papa tries to send you away, we'll refuse to let you go. We'll... we'll stage a rebellion!"

Julia nodded emphatically. "We'll barricade ourselves in the schoolroom and won't come out until he changes his mind!"

Despite the gravity of the situation, Evelyn couldn't help but feel a rush of warmth at their loyalty. She reached out, taking each girl's hand in her own.

"Listen to me, both of you," she said, her voice soft but earnest. "I'm touched by your devotion, truly I am. But you must always be true to yourselves, no matter what happens."

She squeezed their hands gently. "You are good girls, with kind hearts and bright minds. Never let anyone—not even your father or myself—make you act against your own conscience. Being true to yourselves is the most important thing you can do."

Augusta and Julia looked at her with wide eyes, seeming to absorb her words. Evelyn felt a lump form in her throat as she gazed at these two young ladies who had come to mean so much to her.

"Whatever happens," she continued, "I want you to remember that your father loves you very much, and he only wants what's best for you. And I... I care for you both deeply as well."

The days crept by at a glacial pace, each one heavier than the last. Evelyn found it increasingly difficult to maintain her usual composure around the girls, even as she strove to make their lessons a welcome distraction. Their eyes would dart towards the door at every unexpected sound, causing Evelyn's heart to lurch with a mixture of hope and dread.

On the third morning of the Baron's absence, a letter arrived bearing Amelia's familiar hand. Evelyn recognised the looping script immediately, but couldn't bring herself to break the seal. She set it aside on her desk, telling herself she would read it after lessons were through for the day.

Yet when that time came, the letter remained untouched, almost mocking her with its innocent presence. Evelyn found her gaze drawn to it again and again, until she finally swept it into a drawer, unable to bear its weight any longer.

That night, she tossed and turned, her mind whirling. What if the Baron had decided her secret was too much to forgive? What if he had ridden off, never to return? The thought of being dismissed, of having to leave this place that had so quickly become her sanctuary, was almost too much to bear.

And what of the girls? Evelyn's heart ached at the idea of abandoning them, of leaving them to grapple with their father's decree alone. They were so young, so full of potential—they deserved better than to have their lives upended once more.

Evelyn tossed and turned in her bed, the storm outside matching the tumult in her mind. Thunder crashed, shaking the very foundations of the manor, and flashes of lightning illuminated her room in brief, ghostly bursts. Sleep, it seemed, would continue to elude her.

With a sigh, she pushed back the covers and swung her legs over the side of the bed. The floorboards creaked beneath her feet as she stood, the coolness of them making her shiver. She reached for her dressing gown, wrapping it tightly around herself as another thunderclap echoed through the night.

Her eyes were drawn to the wall that separated her room from the West Wing. In the storm's fury, she could hear the damaged structure groaning and creaking, as if it might collapse at any moment. The sound sent a chill through her, and she found herself backing away from the wall.

"This won't do at all," Evelyn muttered to herself, shaking her head as if to clear away the cobwebs of fear. She needed a distraction, something to occupy her mind until the storm passed or exhaustion finally claimed her.

The library, she decided. A good book would be just the thing to settle her nerves.

Evelyn lit a candle and made her way to the door, pausing with her hand on the knob. The hallway beyond would be dark and full of shadows, she knew. For a moment, she considered staying put, but another ominous creak from the West Wing spurred her into action.

She stepped out into the corridor, her candle casting a small circle of light around her. The flame flickered and danced with each gust of wind that found its way through the manor's old bones. Evelyn moved swiftly, her slippered feet barely making a sound on the thick carpet.

As she approached the library, a particularly loud crash of thunder made her jump, nearly extinguishing her candle. She steadied herself against the wall, her heart pounding in her chest.

Evelyn's fingers trailed along the spines of the books, seeking solace in their familiar textures. The library's musty scent enveloped her, a comforting embrace in the storm-tossed night. Her candle flickered, casting dancing shadows across the shelves.

A title caught her eye: "The Mysteries of Udolpho" by Ann Radcliffe. Evelyn smiled wryly, thinking perhaps a Gothic novel would be fitting for such a night. She plucked the book from its resting place, turning it over in her hands to read the spine.

As she pivoted to face the door, a gasp escaped her, her breath hitching suddenly. There, filling the doorway, loomed a massive silhouette. The figure was motionless, a dark spectre against the faint light from the hallway.

Terror gripped Evelyn's heart. Her mind raced with visions of highwaymen and cutthroats, taking advantage of the storm to prey upon the manor. Without thinking, she let out a piercing scream, her free hand instinctively hurling the book at the intruder.

"The Mysteries of Udolpho" sailed through the air, its pages fluttering as it arced towards the shadowy figure.

The figure ducked swiftly, and Evelyn's heart leapt as she heard a familiar voice curse softly in the darkness.

"I didn't expect much of a welcome in the middle of the night, but throwing a book at me was a bit much, don't you think?"

Relief flooded through her as the Baron stepped closer, the candlelight illuminating his features as he removed his hat. His hair was dishevelled, and his clothes were damp from the storm, but his grey eyes held a glimmer of amusement.

Despite herself, Evelyn let out a laugh that was part relief, part hysteria. The tension of the past few days, coupled with the fright he'd just given her, bubbled up inside her chest and spilled out in a burst of giggles.

"I'm so sorry," she managed between breaths, her hand flying to her mouth to stifle her laughter. "I thought you were a highwayman or worse!"

The Baron's lips twitched, threatening a smile. "I suppose I should be flattered that you think me capable of such daring exploits."

Evelyn felt an overwhelming urge to run to him, to throw her arms around him and never let go. Her body seemed to move of its own accord, taking a step forward before she caught herself. She froze, suddenly acutely aware of her state of undress and the impropriety of their situation.

She clasped her hands tightly in front of her, willing them to stay still. "I... we didn't know when you'd return," she said, her voice softer now, uncertain.

The Baron's expression sobered, and he regarded her with an intensity that made her breath catch. "No, I don't suppose you did," he replied, his tone unreadable.

Evelyn's initial relief at seeing the Baron faded as quickly as it had come. Her heart, which had been racing with fright moments ago, now pounded for an entirely different reason.

The silence stretched between them, broken only by the occasional rumble of thunder outside. Evelyn waited for the Baron to say something, anything, to explain his sudden return or his prolonged absence. But he seemed content just to look at her for a moment, his grey eyes roaming over her face as if committing it to memory.

There was something strange in his expression, a sort of coyness that made Evelyn's skin prickle with anticipation. It was as if he knew something that she didn't, a secret dancing behind his eyes that he was barely containing.

Evelyn swallowed hard, her throat suddenly dry. She opened her mouth to speak, to break the tension that hung heavy in the air between them, but no words came. The Baron's lips quirked into the barest hint of a smile, and Evelyn felt her cheeks flush under his scrutiny.

She clutched her dressing gown tighter around herself, suddenly feeling exposed despite the layers of fabric. The candlelight flickered, casting shifting shadows across the Baron's face, making his expression even more difficult to read.

Evelyn's mind raced, trying to decipher the meaning behind his enigmatic gaze. Had he come to a decision about her future at the manor? Was he preparing to dismiss her, or had he found it in his heart to forgive her deception? The uncertainty was maddening, and she found herself wishing he would just speak, even if it was to deliver bad news.

Evelyn took a deep breath, steeling herself. The tension between them was unbearable, and she couldn't bear another moment of uncertainty.

"My lord," she began, swallowing around a lump in her throat, "where have you been? We've all been terribly worried about you."

The Baron's expression softened slightly at her words. He ran a hand through his rain-dampened hair, seeming to gather his thoughts before responding.

"I apologise for causing you concern," he said, his voice low and gravelly. "It was not my intention to worry anyone."

Evelyn nodded, feeling a small measure of relief at his words. She pressed on, needing to know more. "Is everything all right on the estate? Has there been some trouble?"

"No, no," the Baron replied, shaking his head. "The estate is fine. In fact, I haven't been here at all."

Evelyn's brow furrowed in confusion. "You haven't? Then where...?"

"I've been in London," he said, his eyes never leaving her face. "I went to make some enquiries. And I've come to a conclusion."

Evelyn felt rooted to the spot, like a deer caught in a wolf's gaze. She stared back at the Baron, hardly daring to breathe.

Chapter 40

Evelyn's heart thundered in her chest as she waited for the Baron to continue. Her fingers twisted in the folds of her dressing gown, knuckles white with tension. The air between them felt thick, charged with an energy she couldn't quite name.

"I went to find out what happened to your former... husband," the Baron said, his lip curling in disgust as he spat out the last word. The venom in his voice made Evelyn flinch, though she knew it wasn't directed at her.

She felt her hair stand on end, a chill running down her spine despite the warmth of the room. The Baron's gaze was intense, his grey eyes stormy with emotion. Evelyn was holding her breath, caught between hope and dread.

"And?" she whispered, her voice barely audible over the pounding of her heart.

Evelyn's breath caught in her throat as the Baron stepped closer. His presence filled the room, and she found herself acutely aware of every movement, every shift in his expression.

"From what I initially heard when I asked around London," he began. His voice was low and measured. "It seemed the Judge was simply taken to a convenient green and shot in a duel the moment his crimes came to light."

Evelyn stared at him, her mind reeling. A part of her had always wondered about the Judge's fate, but she'd never dared to ask. Now, faced with the possibility of closure, she felt a strange mix of relief and trepidation.

The Baron hesitated, and Evelyn's heart skipped a beat. She watched as he seemed to weigh his words carefully, drawing out the moment until she thought she might burst from the tension.

Finally, he spoke again. "It appears that wasn't the case," he said slowly. "He was still alive at that point."

Evelyn's eyes widened, her lips parting in surprise. She'd been so certain, so sure that the Judge was gone forever.

Evelyn's heart seemed to stop for a moment, her breath stuttering in her chest. She stared at the Baron, her mind reeling with the implications of his words.

"Does that mean..." she began, her voice barely above a whisper, "does that mean he's still alive now?"

The Baron's expression softened slightly, his grey eyes meeting hers with a mixture of concern and reassurance. "The Judge was alive when he was sentenced to transportation for life to Australia. A number of people had stepped forward to ensure that he was convicted," the Baron said carefully, his eyes never leaving Evelyn's face.

Evelyn's brow furrowed, her mind latching onto the Baron's choice of words. There was something in the way he'd said it, a certain weight to his tone that hinted at more.

"What do you mean?" she asked, her voice gaining strength. "Why did you say it like that?"

The Baron's eyes flickered a little, and Evelyn had the strangest sensation of being toyed with, like a cat with a mouse. Distantly, she wondered if this was a good or a bad thing, that the Baron took the time to torment her.

Evelyn's breath caught in her throat as she processed the Baron's words. Her heart raced, a mixture of fear and hope coursing through her veins. She searched his face, trying to decipher the meaning behind his careful phrasing.

"That's not the end of the story," the Baron said, his voice low and measured.

Evelyn's fingers tightened on the folds of her dressing gown, her knuckles white with tension. She waited, barely breathing, as the Baron continued.

"The crew and other convicts on the ship were not particularly kind to him," he explained, a hint of grim satisfaction in his tone. "It seems the Judge managed to make a lot of people very, very angry."

Evelyn's mind whirled, imagining the scene. She could almost picture the Judge, stripped of his power and influence, surrounded by those he had wronged or their loved ones. A shiver ran down her spine, not entirely from fear.

The Baron's grey eyes met hers, intense and unreadable. "The high seas can be a dangerous place, Evelyn," he said pointedly. "Especially on a ship full of criminals."

The implication hung heavy in the air between them. Evelyn's heart pounded so loudly she was certain the Baron must hear it. She licked her dry lips, struggling to find her voice.

"So you mean," she began hesitantly, her voice barely above a whisper, "that the Judge died on the crossing?"

The Baron didn't answer immediately, merely bobbed his head in a "more or less" gesture. With slow, deliberate movements, he removed his rain-slicked leather overcoat and tossed it on a convenient chair along with his hat.

"It would be easy to assume that he had died on the crossing, given his rough treatment. But no," the Baron said, his eyes twinkling. "He was still very much alive when he landed in Australia. Bruised and battered, I grant you, but still very much alive."

Evelyn sagged, her shoulders slumping as the weight of the Baron's words settled over her. She felt utterly drained, her emotions a tangled mess of relief, disappointment, and lingering fear. The Judge was still alive, still out there in the world. Even if he was on the other side of the globe, the thought made her skin crawl.

She looked up at the Baron, expecting to see sympathy or perhaps concern on his face. Instead, she was startled to see a glimmer of amusement in his eyes, the corners of his mouth twitching as if he were suppressing a grin. The sight ignited a spark of irritation within her, cutting through the fog of her despair.

"Why do you look so damn amused?" Evelyn snapped, her voice sharper than she'd intended. "Do you find my predicament entertaining, my lord?"

The Baron's eyebrows shot up, clearly taken aback by her sudden outburst. For a moment, Evelyn feared she'd overstepped, but then she saw something else in his expression—a flicker of admiration, perhaps?

"I apologise, Miss Bane," he said, his voice softer now. "I assure you, I find no amusement in your suffering. It's just that—"

He paused. Evelyn was leaning forward slightly, hanging on his next words. The Baron's grey eyes met hers, and she saw a warmth there that made her breath catch.

"It's just that I haven't finished telling you the story," he continued, a hint of that earlier amusement creeping back into his tone.

Evelyn's brow furrowed, confusion replacing her irritation. "What do you mean?" she asked softly.

Evelyn watched the Baron intently, her heart racing as she waited for him to continue. His eyes held a glimmer of something she couldn't quite place—amusement, perhaps, or anticipation.

"The Judge survived the voyage and his initial time in Australia," the Baron said, his voice low and measured. "But fate, it seems, had other plans for him."

He paused, as Evelyn was leaning forward, hanging on his every word.

"He died," the Baron continued, "from a snake bite while digging a latrine."

Evelyn blinked, certain she had misheard. "I'm sorry, what?"

"A snake," the Baron repeated, a hint of a smile tugging at his lips. "Apparently, it was a rather nasty species. He didn't last long."

Evelyn stared at him, her mind struggling to process this information. It seemed so... mundane, so anticlimactic after everything she'd been through. A bubble of hysterical laughter threatened to escape her throat.

"So," she said, her voice sounding oddly strangled, "does that mean... am I a widow?"

The Baron's expression softened, his grey eyes meeting hers with unexpected warmth. "Yes, Evelyn," he said gently. "I've never been so happy to tell someone that their husband is dead."

Evelyn felt a rush of emotions wash over her—relief, disbelief, and a strange, giddy sort of joy. She pressed a hand to her mouth, unsure whether she wanted to laugh or cry.

Impulsively, Evelyn threw herself at the Baron, burying her face in his chest. His solid warmth enveloped her, and she felt the rumble of his laughter even before she heard it. His arms wrapped around her, strong and sure, and Evelyn felt a surge of relief and joy so intense it threatened to overwhelm her.

She began to laugh too, the sound muffled against his shirt. It was a giddy, almost hysterical laughter, born of the sudden release of years of tension and fear. Evelyn felt light-headed, as if a great weight had been lifted from her shoulders.

As her laughter subsided, Evelyn became acutely aware of their closeness. The Baron's scent surrounded her—a mixture of leather, rain, and something uniquely him. His hands were warm on her back, and she could feel the steady beat of his heart against her cheek.

Pulling back slightly, Evelyn looked up at the Baron. His grey eyes were twinkling with amusement, a smile playing at the corners of his mouth. The sight of his barely contained mirth sparked a playful indignation in her.

"You!" she exclaimed, swatting his chest lightly. "You tormented me on purpose, didn't you?"

The Baron's smile widened, and he made no attempt to deny it. Evelyn swatted him again, but there was no real force behind it. She was too elated, too relieved to truly be angry.

"It seemed you always enjoyed it so much when you did it to me," he said with a smile.

"I ought to be furious with you," she said, trying and failing to keep a stern expression on her face.

"But you're not," the Baron replied, his voice low and warm.

Evelyn felt her cheeks flush, suddenly very aware of their proximity, and the fact that she was only in a nightrail and dressing gown, her feet bare. But she couldn't bring herself to step away just yet. For the first time in years, she felt truly free, truly safe. And it was all because of the man holding her.

Evelyn reluctantly pulled back to arms' length, her hands resting lightly on the Baron's chest. Her heart fluttered as she looked up at him, a mixture of hope and trepidation in her eyes.

"Does this mean," she asked hesitantly, "that you've forgiven me for lying?"

The Baron's grey eyes softened as he gazed down at her, a small smile playing at the corners of his mouth. He shook his head gently.

"No, Evelyn," he said, his voice low and warm. "I don't forgive you, because there's nothing to forgive."

Evelyn's brow furrowed in confusion, her lips parting to speak, but the Baron continued before she could voice her thoughts.

"You might not have been truthful about your name," he explained. His hands still resting comfortably on her waist. "You never lied, though, about who you really are, deep down."

His words washed over her, and Evelyn felt a warmth blooming in her chest. She searched his face, scarcely daring to believe what she was hearing.

"You revealed your true self in the way you cared for my girls," the Baron continued, his voice filled with a tenderness that made Evelyn's breath catch. "And in the way you heroically saved me that day in the field."

Evelyn felt her cheeks flush at the memory, both from the intensity of that moment and from the Baron's praise. She had never thought of herself as heroic, but the admiration in his eyes made her feel as though she could conquer the world.

Evelyn's heart raced as she gazed up at the Baron, his words washing over her like a warm tide. She scarcely dared to believe what she was hearing, afraid that at any moment she might wake up and find it all a dream.

The Baron's grey eyes held hers, filled with an intensity that made her breath catch. "Evelyn," he said, his voice low and earnest, "I hope enough time has passed for it to be proper for me to ask for your hand, because I can't bear to live without you a moment longer."

A rush of joy surged through Evelyn, so powerful it threatened to overwhelm her. She felt light-headed, giddy with happiness. Without hesitation, she replied, "I don't care about society's rules. I just want to be with you."

The moment the words left her lips, Evelyn realised she was echoing the Baron's own sentiments from the dance. The recognition flashed in his eyes as well, and suddenly they were both grinning like naughty children who had got away with some delightful mischief.

The Baron's smile widened, his eyes twinkling with a mixture of joy and mischief. "Well then," he said, his voice filled with barely contained excitement, "I shall arrange for the banns to be read at once."

Evelyn felt a thrill run through her at his words. It was really happening. After all the trials and tribulations, all the fear and uncertainty, she was finally going to have her happy ending. And not just any ending, but one with a man who truly understood and valued her for who she was.

Evelyn gasped as the Baron pulled a ring from his pocket. It was a delicate silver band with a sapphire setting that caught the light, sparkling brilliantly. With gentle hands, he slipped it onto her finger, and Evelyn felt her heart swell with emotion.

A laugh bubbled up from her chest, light and joyous, only for her to realise that tears were streaming down her cheeks as well. She had never experienced such a whirlwind of feelings before—elation, relief, love, and a touch of disbelief that this was truly happening to her.

As she admired the ring on her finger, a sudden thought occurred to her. "My lord—" she began.

The Baron held up a hand. "James, please."

Evelyn smiled. "Is it proper for me to continue living here while the banns are read? Perhaps I should find lodgings elsewhere for the time being."

The moment the words left her lips, she saw the Baron's expression darken. His brow furrowed, and his grey eyes flashed with a determination that sent a thrill through her.

"I won't hear of it," he said firmly, his hands tightening slightly on her waist. "I've only just found you, Evelyn. I won't be without you again, not even for a moment."

His words filled her with warmth, and she felt her heart soar. She was elated, truly happy in a way she had never been before. And yet, there was something still nagging at the back of her mind.

As she stood there in the Baron's embrace, Evelyn couldn't shake the feeling that she was being watched. She tried to tell herself it was just nerves, a natural reaction to all that had happened in such a short time. But the sensation persisted, a prickling at the back of her neck that made her want to look over her shoulder.

Chapter 49

Evelyn woke early the next morning, her heart light with joy. She dressed with care, fingers lingering on the ring that now adorned her hand. As she made her way down to breakfast, she couldn't help but smile, anticipating the announcement to come.

The dining room was quieter than usual when she entered. Julia and Augusta sat at the table, their faces a mixture of curiosity and concern. The Baron was already there, his expression unreadable as he sipped his tea.

"Good morning," Evelyn said, trying to keep her voice steady despite the excitement bubbling within her.

The girls murmured their greetings, exchanging glances with each other. Evelyn took her seat, acutely aware of the Baron's presence beside her.

As they ate, the silence stretched on, broken only by the clink of cutlery against china. Evelyn could sense the girls' unease, and she longed to reassure them. But she knew it wasn't her place to speak just yet.

Finally, as the meal drew to a close, the Baron set down his napkin and cleared his throat. "I have an announcement," he said, his voice calm but with an undercurrent of something Evelyn couldn't quite place. "I would like to see all the staff in the main hall of the manor after we've finished here."

Julia and Augusta's heads snapped up, their eyes wide. They looked to Evelyn, worry clear on their faces. Evelyn gave them a reassuring smile, hoping to ease their concerns without giving anything away.

As the Baron rose from the table, Evelyn caught his eye. He gave her a small nod, the corners of his mouth twitching upwards ever so slightly. It was all the confirmation she needed that everything was going to be all right.

Evelyn's heart raced as she stood amongst the assembled servants in the main hall. The Baron's presence beside her was a comforting anchor, yet she couldn't help but feel a flutter of nerves as she awaited his announcement. She caught Nell's eye across the room, the maid's sympathetic gaze touching.

The Baron cleared his throat, drawing everyone's attention. "Thank you all for gathering here," he began, his voice steady and clear. "I have called you together because there will be some changes to the household from this point forward."

A ripple of murmurs swept through the assembled staff. Evelyn fought to keep her expression neutral, though her pulse quickened at his words.

"After much consideration," the Baron continued, "I have decided to remarry. There will be a new Baroness in the house again."

Evelyn felt the weight of several gazes upon her, including Nell's, which now held a mix of surprise and concern. She was touched by the maid's evident worry for her wellbeing, grateful for the friendship they had formed.

The Baron paused, his eyes sweeping across the room before settling on Evelyn. "It is someone with whom I have developed a close friendship," he said, his voice softening slightly. "Someone who has brought light into this house and into my life."

With those words, he turned towards Evelyn and offered his hand. Time seemed to slow as she looked up at him, seeing the warmth in his eyes that was usually hidden behind his stern façade. Taking a deep breath, Evelyn placed her hand in his, feeling the strength and gentleness of his grip.

Evelyn felt a wave of relief wash over her as the servants' faces broke into smiles. The tension that had filled the room moments ago dissipated, replaced by a buzz of excitement and genuine joy. She barely had time to register the change before Nell rushed forward, enveloping her in a fierce embrace.

"Oh, Miss Evelyn!" Nell exclaimed, her arms tightening around Evelyn's waist. "I'm so happy for you!"

Evelyn gasped, struggling to draw breath as Nell's enthusiasm threatened to squeeze the air from her lungs. Despite the discomfort, she couldn't help but laugh, touched by the maid's unbridled delight.

When Nell finally released her, she grasped Evelyn's hands in her own, her eyes shining with emotion. "I just know," she said emphatically, her voice thick with conviction, "that you'll be exactly this happy for the rest of your life. You deserve it, Miss."

Evelyn felt her eyes prick with tears at Nell's heartfelt words. She opened her mouth to respond, but before she could, a chorus of excited shrieks filled the air.

"Miss Evelyn! Father!" Julia cried, rushing towards them with Augusta close behind.

The girls threw themselves at Evelyn, nearly knocking her off balance. She stumbled slightly, steadied by the Baron's hand at her elbow, as Julia and Augusta wrapped their arms around her.

"You're staying forever!" Augusta exclaimed, her usual reserve forgotten in the moment of joy.

Julia nodded enthusiastically, her face beaming. "We were so worried—but you're staying!"

Evelyn's heart swelled with love for these girls who had become so dear to her. She hugged them tightly, overcome with emotion. As she looked up, her eyes met the Baron's, and she saw her own happiness reflected in his gaze.

The rest of the day passed in a happy blur for Evelyn. After the announcement, the Baron took her hand and led her out into the crisp morning air. The estate stretched before them, a patchwork of fields and woodlands bathed in golden sunlight.

"I'd like to introduce you properly to some of our people," the Baron said, his voice warm with pride. "They should know the woman who will soon be their new Baroness."

Evelyn's heart fluttered at his words. She squeezed his hand, still marvelling at the feeling of his calloused palm against hers.

They walked together across the grounds, stopping to speak with the gardeners tending to the formal gardens. Evelyn was struck by the easy way the Baron addressed each person by name, inquiring after their families and work with genuine interest.

As they moved on to the stables, the Baron's hand rested lightly on the small of her back, guiding her. The gesture, so simple and yet so intimate, sent a thrill through her.

"Mr Hamish," the Baron called out to the stablemaster. "I'd like you to meet Lady Evelyn, my betrothed."

The older man's weathered face broke into a broad grin. "It's an honour, my lady," he said, bowing slightly. "We're right pleased to have you here."

They continued on, meeting with farm hands and tenants alike. Evelyn was touched by the warmth of their welcome, the genuine joy in their faces as they offered their congratulations.

As the sun began to set, casting long shadows across the fields, the Baron turned to her. "I promise to introduce you formally to more of our tenants soon," he said. "You'll be a wonderful Baroness, Evelyn."

Exhausted but elated, Evelyn retired to her room that night. As she lay in bed, her mind replayed the events of the day: the joy of the announcement, the warmth of the estate's people, and the tender looks the Baron had given her throughout the day.

Evelyn gazed around her room, her eyes lingering on the familiar furnishings. The small writing desk where she'd penned her lessons, the armchair by the window where she'd often sat to read—each piece held memories of her time as a governess. But soon, she mused, this room would no longer be hers.

A warm flush crept up her neck as she contemplated her impending move to the Baron's quarters. She would share his bed, his life, his everything. The thought both thrilled and daunted her.

As she settled beneath the covers, Evelyn's mind wandered to what it might be like to share a bed with a man again. Her experiences with the Judge had been far from pleasant, and her affair with Richard had been a heady thing, but she pushed those memories aside. This would be different. The Baron was kind, gentle when he needed to be, and she'd seen the passion that smouldered beneath his stern exterior.

She imagined the warmth of his body next to hers, the strength of his arms around her. Perhaps he would pull her close in the night, his breath soft against her neck. Or maybe they would wake together in the pale light of dawn, exchanging sleepy smiles before starting their day.

A contented sigh escaped her lips as she nestled deeper into her pillow. For the first time in years, Evelyn felt truly hopeful about her future. As sleep began to claim her, a smile played across her face, her dreams filled with the promise of love and companionship.

Evelyn woke with a start, her heart pounding in her chest. Something was wrong. The air felt thick and heavy, and an acrid smell filled her nostrils. She blinked, trying to clear her vision, but the room remained hazy. It took her a moment to realise that it wasn't her eyes playing tricks on her—her bedchamber was filling with smoke.

Panic gripped her as she sat up, her nightgown clinging to her sweat-dampened skin. The smoke was rolling in beneath the door, accompanied by an ominous flickering light. Fire. The word echoed in her mind, bringing with it a rush of terror.

Evelyn scrambled out of bed, her bare feet hitting the cold floor. She stumbled towards the door, her throat tightening with each breath of the smoky air. Her hand trembled as she reached for the doorknob, praying that she could escape.

But as she turned the handle and pushed, the door refused to budge. Evelyn's heart sank. She pushed harder, throwing her weight against the wood, but it was no use. Something on the other side was blocking her exit.

"Help!" she cried out, her voice hoarse from the smoke. "Is anyone there? Please, help me!"

The crackling of flames grew louder, and the heat in the room intensified. Evelyn's mind raced, searching for a way out. The window—perhaps she could escape through there. But as she turned towards it, she remembered with a sickening jolt that her room was on the second floor. Even if she could open the window, the drop would be dangerous, if not fatal.

Tears stung her eyes as she looked around frantically, seeking any means of escape. The smoke was getting thicker, making it harder to breathe. Evelyn coughed violently, her lungs burning. She couldn't help but think of the Baron's late wife, who had perished in a fire. Was this to be her fate as well?

Evelyn's heart raced as she thought of Julia and Augusta. Their room was just down the hall—were they safe? The thought of the girls in danger spurred her on, and she threw herself against the door with renewed vigour.

"Julia! Augusta!" she cried out, her voice hoarse from the smoke. She pushed harder, feeling the door give slightly. With a final burst of strength, she managed to create a small gap, just wide enough to see through.

"Girls! Can you hear me?" Evelyn called again, desperately hoping to wake them if they were still asleep.

"Don't worry, Miss Evelyn," a familiar voice replied, calm and steady amidst the chaos. "They're safe."

Evelyn's chest tightened suddenly. "Nell? Is that you?"

"Yes, Miss," came the response.

Relief washed over Evelyn, quickly followed by urgency. "Nell, please help me get out. The fire—"

"Now why would I do that?" Nell interrupted, her tone suddenly cold and unfamiliar. "Things are proceeding exactly as I wanted."

Evelyn froze, unable to comprehend what she was hearing. "What do you mean? Nell, please—"

"I'm sorry, Miss Evelyn," Nell said, though her voice held no trace of remorse. "But this is how it has to be."

Evelyn caught a glimpse of Nell's face through the gap in the door. Nell still smiled, her face bright and cheerful as ever, but there was a new, manic light to her eyes that Evelyn had never seen before.

Are you sure? Evelyn asked herself, her mind racing. Have you simply mistaken the warm glow of her friendship for mania?

Evelyn's mind reeled, struggling to process the horrifying reality unfolding before her. The smoke, the heat, Nell's chilling words—it all seemed too terrible to be real.

"Am I still dreaming?" Evelyn asked aloud, her voice trembling with desperate hope. "This can't be happening."

Through the gap in the door, she saw Nell sadly shake her head. The flickering firelight cast an eerie glow around the maid, making her appear almost otherworldly.

"I'm afraid not, Miss Evelyn," Nell replied, her voice tinged with a strange mixture of regret and determination. "This is all too real."

Evelyn stared at her, disbelief giving way to horror as Nell continued.

"You see, the Baron was always meant to be mine," Nell explained, her eyes taking on a faraway look. "I've known it since I first saw him as a girl. But the Baroness got in the way, and then you."

A chill ran down Evelyn's spine as the implications of Nell's words sank in.

"I got rid of the Baroness," Nell said matter-of-factly, as if discussing the weather. "And now, with you gone, the Baron will finally be mine."

Before Evelyn could respond, Nell disappeared from view, leaving her alone with the encroaching flames and thickening smoke. Evelyn's heart pounded in her chest as she realised she was completely trapped, with no way out. Already, flames were beginning to lick at one wall, smoke pouring in from the ceiling.

Desperately, Evelyn threw herself at the door again, trying to call for help, but her throat was too raw and parched to get the words out. She was completely and utterly alone.

Chapter 42

James Ayles, Baron Hastings, jolted awake at the first cry of 'Fire!' His heart hammered against his ribs as he leapt from his bed. The acrid smell of smoke filled his nostrils, and his mind raced with a single, all-consuming thought: his girls and Evelyn.

He burst into the hallway, the heat already oppressive. Smoke billowed through the corridors, obscuring his vision. Servants rushed past him, their faces contorted with fear. James pushed against the tide of fleeing bodies, his eyes searching desperately for his family.

Halfway up the grand staircase, small hands grasped his. Augusta and Julia, their nightgowns smudged with soot, clung to him. Relief washed over him for a brief moment.

'Father, we're all right,' Augusta said, her voice steady despite the chaos.

Julia tugged at his sleeve. 'But Evelyn's still inside! She's trapped!'

The words struck James like a physical blow. His vision narrowed, the world around him fading away save for the path back up the stairs.

'Time to be brave, girls,' the Baron said, pressing a kiss to each of their foreheads. 'Take care of each other. Run to get the steward, and tell him to raise the alarm. Out—now!'

Without a second thought, he turned and bounded up the steps, taking them two at a time. James' lungs burned as he pushed through the thickening smoke. The heat seared his skin, but he pressed on, driven by a force he couldn't name. Fear? Love? Both coursed through him as he raced towards Evelyn's room.

James's heart thundered in his chest, each beat a reminder of what he stood to lose. The thought of Evelyn, trapped and alone, consumed him. He couldn't bear it—not again. Not after everything.

The corridor ahead blazed with angry flames, blocking his path to Evelyn's door. Acrid smoke stung his eyes and burned his lungs, but James refused to yield. He spun on his heel, his mind racing. There had to be another way.

His gaze fell upon the locked door to the West Wing. Without hesitation, he threw his shoulder against it. The wood splintered under his assault, giving way with a groan of protest. James stumbled into the burnt-out shell of his past.

Charred beams and crumbling plaster surrounded him, a grim reminder of the night he'd lost his wife. But now wasn't the time for old ghosts. Evelyn needed him.

James pressed on, navigating the treacherous terrain as swiftly as he dared. His feet found familiar paths through the ruins, muscle memory guiding him where his eyes failed. He ducked under fallen timbers and vaulted over piles of debris, driven by a desperate urgency.

The heat intensified with each step, sweat pouring down his face and back. James coughed violently, his lungs screaming for clean air. But he couldn't stop. Not now. Not when he was so close.

As he rounded a corner, he found what he was looking for: the room that had once belonged to his wife, the Baroness.

James stumbled into the burnt-out room, his eyes stinging from the smoke. The heat pressed against him like a living thing, but he forced himself to focus. Evelyn was close—he could feel it.

His gaze swept the room, memories threatening to overwhelm him. He pushed them aside, zeroing in on the wall that separated this chamber from Evelyn's. To his surprise, it felt cool beneath his palm.

'Evelyn!' he shouted, his voice hoarse. 'Can you hear me?'

No response came, but James refused to give up. His fingers traced the wall, searching for the outline of the old connecting door. It had to be here somewhere—this room had once been his wife's, and Evelyn's chamber her dressing room.

At last, his hand found a slight indentation. The door. James's heart leapt.

'Hold on, Evelyn!' he called out. 'I'm coming!'

He threw his weight against the hidden door, but it refused to budge. Gritting his teeth, James stepped back and slammed his shoulder into it. Pain lanced through him, but he ignored it. Again and again, he hurled himself at the obstruction.

With a resounding crack, the door finally gave way. James stumbled through, coughing as a fresh wave of smoke hit him. He found himself in Evelyn's room, the space filled with choking fumes.

To his right, he saw Evelyn's bed pushed up against the wall, blocking the door he'd just forced open. On the other side of the room, flames licked at the main entrance, trapping them both.

James's eyes swept the room frantically, his heart pounding in his chest. There, by the window, he spotted Evelyn. She swayed on her feet, her hands feebly grasping at the latch. Without a moment's hesitation, James lunged forward, snatching a heavy brass candlestick from a nearby table.

"Stand back!" he shouted, his voice hoarse from the smoke.

Evelyn stumbled away from the window, her eyes wide and unfocused. James swung the candlestick with all his might, shattering the glass. The cool night air rushed in, a blessed relief from the stifling heat.

James dropped the candlestick and reached for Evelyn, his hands trembling as he grasped her shoulders. She felt so fragile beneath his touch, as if she might crumble at any moment. Gently, he guided her towards the broken window.

"Breathe, Evelyn," he urged, positioning her face near the opening. "Deep breaths of fresh air. That's it."

She inhaled shakily, coughing as her lungs cleared. James held her steady, his own breathing ragged. He watched her intently, relief flooding through him as colour slowly returned to her pale cheeks.

Evelyn's eyes focused on him, recognition dawning. "James," she whispered, her voice barely audible above the crackling flames.

Before James could respond, Evelyn threw her arms around him, clinging to him as if he were her only lifeline. He held her tightly, burying his face in her smoke-scented hair. For a moment, the world beyond them ceased to exist. There was only Evelyn, alive and safe in his arms.

James held Evelyn close, savouring the feel of her in his arms. For a moment, the world beyond them ceased to exist. There was only Evelyn, alive and safe.

She pulled back suddenly, her eyes wide with concern. "What are you doing here?"

James opened his mouth to respond, but Evelyn cut him off, her voice urgent. "You need to leave, get out! It's too dangerous!"

The Baron shook his head, his grip on her shoulders tightening. "I'm not leaving without you," he said firmly. "It's my turn to rescue you."

Evelyn's expression softened, a mixture of exasperation and affection crossing her face. "You foolish man," she murmured, but there was love in her voice.

James felt his heart swell as Evelyn placed her hand in his. He gave it a reassuring squeeze, marvelling at how small and delicate it felt in his own rough palm.

"Together, then," he said, tugging her gently towards the broken wall.

They stepped through the opening, into the charred remains of the West Wing. James felt Evelyn stiffen beside him, no doubt taking in the devastation for the first time. He guided her forward, careful to keep her close as they navigated the treacherous terrain.

The heat pressed in around them, and James could hear the ominous creaking of weakened beams above. He quickened their pace, his eyes darting about for the safest path through the ruins. Evelyn stumbled once, and he caught her, steadying her against his side.

"Almost there," he murmured, more to himself than to her.

As they neared the exit, a loud crack echoed through the air. James looked up to see a burning beam falling towards them. Without thinking, he tucked Evelyn beneath himself, curling around her to shield her. The beam caught on a pillar, hovering just feet above them.

"Don't stop," the Baron said, nudging Evelyn forward. Blindly, she reached back and took his hand, and at last, they tumbled out into the night air.

James stumbled onto the front lawn, his lungs burning as he gulped in the cool night air. Evelyn clung to his arm, coughing and trembling beside him. The roar of the fire behind them was deafening, but James could hear shouts and cries from the growing crowd of onlookers.

His eyes swept over the scene, taking in the faces of his servants and nearby farmers who had come to help. Relief washed over him as he spotted Julia and Augusta pushing through the throng, their eyes wide with fear and relief.

"Father! Evelyn!" they cried in unison, rushing towards them.

James felt a surge of protectiveness as the crowd pressed in around them. "Attend to Miss Bane," he ordered, his voice hoarse from the smoke. "She needs air."

A farmer's wife stepped forward, draping a rough woollen blanket around Evelyn's shoulders. James watched as Evelyn's trembling fingers clutched at the fabric, her face pale in the flickering firelight.

To his left, James saw a bucket line forming, men and women passing pails of water with grim determination. Others were dashing in and out of the house, arms laden with furniture, paintings, and whatever else they could salvage from the flames.

James turned back to the burning manor, his ancestral home crackling and groaning as the fire consumed it. He felt torn, knowing he should be leading the efforts to save what they could, but reluctant to leave Evelyn's side.

As if sensing his inner conflict, Evelyn's hand found his. He looked down at her, meeting her gaze. She nodded, a silent understanding passing between them. James felt a swell of emotion in his chest, marvelling at how well she knew him already.

Without a word, James leaned down and pressed his lips to hers. It was a brief kiss, but filled with all the things he couldn't say in that moment - his relief, his love, his gratitude.

As he pulled away, James saw Evelyn gather Julia and Augusta under her arms, holding them close. The sight of them together, safe and whole, gave him the strength he needed to turn back towards the inferno.

***

Evelyn clutched the girls tightly, feeling their small bodies tremble against her. The acrid smell of smoke filled the air, stinging her eyes and throat. Her gaze darted anxiously between the burning house and the men rushing about, their shouts barely audible over the roar of the flames.

Her heart leapt into her throat each time James disappeared into the inferno. She held her breath until he emerged, his broad shoulders straining under the weight of furniture and precious heirlooms. His face was streaked with soot, his eyes wild with determination.

"Papa!" Julia cried out as James vanished once more into the smoke-filled doorway.

Evelyn squeezed the girl's shoulder. "Hush, darling. Your father knows what he's doing."

But even as the words left her lips, Evelyn felt a twinge of doubt. The fire seemed to grow more ferocious with each passing moment, consuming the house with terrifying speed.

A thunderous crack split the air. Evelyn gasped as a portion of the roof caved in, sending a shower of sparks into the night sky. Augusta buried her face in Evelyn's skirts, sobbing quietly.

"Where is he?" Evelyn murmured, scanning the chaos for any sign of James.

The seconds stretched into an eternity. Evelyn's chest tightened, her mind racing with horrific possibilities. She wanted to rush forward, to call out for him, but she couldn't abandon the girls.

Just as despair threatened to overwhelm her, a figure emerged from the billowing smoke. James staggered out, coughing violently, a large gilt-framed portrait clutched to his chest.

Relief flooded through Evelyn, so intense it made her knees weak. She longed to run to him, to throw her arms around him and never let go. But she remained rooted to the spot, holding the girls as they cried out in joy at their father's return.

Evelyn's eyes darted across the chaotic scene, her heart still racing from the terror of the fire. Amidst the flickering shadows and frantic activity, a flash of white caught her attention. There, at the edge of the firelight, stood a familiar figure.

Nell.

The maid's face was a mask of fury and fear as their gazes locked. For a moment, time seemed to stand still. Evelyn's mind reeled, piecing together the horrifying truth. Nell had done this. She had started the fire, endangering not just Evelyn, but the girls and James as well. She glared at Evelyn, a bundle in her arms—either pilfered goods or her own belongings, all wrapped up in a heavy wool cloak.

A surge of rage coursed through Evelyn's veins. Her hands trembled as she gripped the girls' shoulders tightly.

"Stay right here," she commanded, her voice low and urgent. "Don't move a single inch. Do you understand?"

The girls nodded, wide-eyed and confused.

As soon as Evelyn released them, Nell turned and fled, her white chemise stark in the darkness as she raced towards the darkness beyond the estate.

Without a second thought, Evelyn gave chase. Her feet pounded against the damp grass, her lungs burning from the smoke and exertion. She barely noticed the brambles tearing at her nightgown or the cold night air against her skin. All that mattered was catching Nell, making her pay for what she'd done.

"Stop!" Evelyn shouted, her voice raw with anger and desperation. "Nell!"

But the maid didn't slow. She darted between trees, leaping over fallen logs with surprising agility. Evelyn pushed herself harder, ignoring the protest of her muscles. She couldn't let Nell escape, not after she'd put everything Evelyn held dear in jeopardy.

As they raced deeper into the woods, the sounds of the fire and the shouts from the estate grew fainter. Evelyn's world narrowed to the pounding of her heart and the fleeing figure ahead of her. She'd never felt such fury, such determination. This woman had tried to destroy her chance at happiness, had risked innocent lives for her own selfish desires.

Evelyn gritted her teeth and pressed on, gaining ground with each stride. It didn't occur to Evelyn that with every foot she gained, she was getting that much closer to a murderer.

Chapter 43

Evelyn's lungs burned as she raced through the darkness, her feet stumbling over unseen roots and stones. The acrid smell of smoke still clung to her hair and nightgown, a constant reminder of the danger they'd narrowly escaped. But that fear paled in comparison to the rage that propelled her forward, chasing after the woman who had nearly destroyed everything.

The woods were pitch black, the dense canopy overhead blocking even the faintest starlight. Evelyn's eyes strained against the darkness, desperately searching for any sign of Nell. Her heart pounded in her ears, nearly drowning out the sound of her own ragged breathing.

For a terrifying moment, Evelyn feared she'd lost her quarry completely. She slowed, turning in a circle, trying to catch even the faintest rustle of movement. Had Nell veered off in another direction? Was she even still running?

Just as despair began to creep in, a flash of white caught Evelyn's eye. Nell's chemise, stark against the inky blackness. It was only the briefest glimpse, but it was enough. Evelyn surged forward, her determination renewed.

She crashed through underbrush, branches whipping at her face and arms. The pain barely registered. All that mattered was catching Nell, making her answer for what she'd done.

Again, the darkness swallowed everything. Evelyn pressed on, guided more by instinct than sight. Her foot caught on something—a root, a rock, she couldn't tell—and she stumbled, nearly falling. She caught herself against a tree trunk, its rough bark scraping her palms.

Evelyn paused, gasping for breath. She strained her ears, listening for any sound that might betray Nell's location. For a moment, there was nothing but the pounding of her own heart.

Then, just ahead, she caught another fleeting glimpse of white.

Evelyn's voice tore from her throat, raw and desperate. "Nell! Stop this madness at once!"

The maid's laughter floated back through the darkness, mocking and cruel. "Why should I? You don't belong here, my lady. You never will."

Evelyn stumbled forward, her feet catching on unseen obstacles. She could just make out Nell's silhouette ahead, a darker shape against the night.

"The Baron could never truly love a shallow city girl like you," Nell taunted. "You're nothing but a passing fancy, a bit of excitement in his dull life. He'll tire of you soon enough."

The words stung, but Evelyn pushed aside the flicker of doubt they sparked. She'd come too far, fought too hard to let Nell's poison take root.

"You're wrong," Evelyn shot back, her voice steadier than she felt. "At least I've had the good sense to pay attention to the estate's changes. I've learned, I've grown. Can you say the same?"

She drew in a ragged breath, her legs burning with exertion as they continued on, deeper into the night. "Nell, stop! This is madness. You can't run forever!"

As her eyes adjusted to the gloom, Evelyn realised with a jolt where they were heading. The ground beneath her feet had grown softer, more treacherous. They were nearing the edge of the Baron's land, approaching the abandoned canal project. All that remained was a large, murky retaining pond—a dangerous place in broad daylight, let alone in the dead of night.

"Nell!" Evelyn called out again, a new urgency in her voice. "Stop!"

Evelyn's heart pounded as she heard a sudden splash and a panicked cry. Nell had fallen into the pond. Without hesitation, Evelyn pushed forward, her feet squelching in the muddy ground at the water's edge.

In the dim light, she could just make out Nell's thrashing form. The maid was struggling to keep her head above water, weighed down by her belongings and the heavy wool cloak she'd wrapped them in. Nell's arms flailed wildly, sending ripples across the dark surface of the pond.

For a moment, Evelyn froze, her mind reeling. This woman had tried to kill her, had endangered the girls and the Baron. But as she watched Nell's desperate struggle, Evelyn knew she couldn't stand by and let her drown.

Taking a deep breath, Evelyn lowered herself to the ground, feeling the cold mud seep through her nightgown. She inched forward until she was at the very edge of the pond, her arms outstretched towards the floundering maid.

"Nell!" Evelyn called out, her voice steady despite her racing pulse. "Grab my hand!"

Evelyn's arm trembled as she reached out towards Nell, her fingers stretching as far as they could. The cold mud seeped through her nightgown, chilling her to the bone, but she held steady. "Please, Nell," she pleaded, her voice hoarse. "Take my hand!"

Nell's eyes locked onto Evelyn's, and in that moment, Evelyn saw a hatred so deep it made her blood run cold. Even as she struggled to keep her head above water, Nell's lip curled into a sneer, her gaze filled with contempt for the offered help.

Suddenly, the sound of heavy footfalls and laboured breathing broke through the night. Evelyn turned to see the Baron stumbling onto the scene, his chest heaving as he fought to catch his breath. His eyes immediately found Evelyn, relief flooding his features.

"Evelyn!" he called out, rushing to her side without a second glance at the pond. "The girls told me you'd run off after Nell. What in God's name is happening?"

As the Baron crouched beside her, his hand warm on her shoulder, Evelyn saw Nell's expression change. The maid's gaze darted between them, something dark and resigned settling in her eyes. Without a word, Nell stopped her frantic thrashing. Her body went limp, and she slipped beneath the inky surface of the pond, quiet as a sigh.

Evelyn stared at the spot where Nell had vanished, her outstretched hand still frozen in place. The black water rippled gently, then stilled, as if nothing had happened at all. Nell was gone.

Evelyn stared at the dark, still surface of the pond, her mind reeling. The Baron's warm hand on her shoulder anchored her to reality, pulling her back from the edge of shock.

"Evelyn?" The Baron's voice was gentle but insistent. "What's happened? How did you end up out here?"

She turned to face him, her lips parting to explain, but the words caught in her throat. The weight of everything—the fire, the chase, Nell's final, hate-filled gaze—came crashing down upon her. A sob escaped her lips, and she found herself trembling uncontrollably.

The Baron pulled her close, his strong arms enveloping her. "It's alright," he murmured. "You're safe now."

Before Evelyn could gather herself to respond, the sound of running feet and breathless voices broke through the night.

"Father! Miss Evelyn!"

Julia and Augusta burst into view, their faces pale with worry in the dim light. Evelyn's heart leapt at the sight of them, relief washing over her.

"Girls!" she exclaimed, her voice hoarse. "I told you to stay put. It's dangerous out here."

Despite her words, Evelyn was reaching for them, desperate to assure herself of their safety. The girls rushed forward, and she wrapped them both in her arms, holding them tight.

"We couldn't just wait," Augusta said, her voice muffled against Evelyn's shoulder.

Julia nodded vigorously. "We were so worried about you!"

Evelyn closed her eyes, overwhelmed by the love she felt for these children—her children now, in all but blood. She pressed a kiss to each of their heads, her earlier fear and anger melting away in the warmth of their embrace.

Evelyn felt the Baron's strong arms wrap around her, gently guiding her away from the pond's edge. Her legs trembled, threatening to give way beneath her. The adrenaline that had fuelled her chase was rapidly fading, leaving her exhausted and shaken.

"Nell—" Evelyn began, her voice catching in her throat. She couldn't bring herself to finish the sentence, to put into words the horrible scene she'd just witnessed. Instead, she glanced back at the still, dark surface of the pond.

The Baron followed her gaze, his expression crumpling as understanding dawned. Evelyn felt his arms tighten around her, offering silent comfort and support.

Before either of them could speak, Julia's voice cut through the night air. "Father, Miss Evelyn, there's something we need to tell you."

Augusta nodded solemnly beside her sister. "It's about Nell."

Evelyn turned to face the girls, her heart clenching with worry. What more could possibly have happened?

Julia continued, her words tumbling out in a rush. "Nell woke us up earlier. She looked... wrong. Like she was having a terrible nightmare, but awake."

"She told us to run," Augusta added, her voice barely above a whisper. "She said... she said that Miss Evelyn was a monster, and that she was going to hurt us."

"Nell was a liar," Julia interjected, her sooty face creasing into a dour expression. "So we didn't run."

Evelyn felt as though she'd been struck. She stared at the girls in disbelief, her mind reeling. How could Nell have said such things? After everything they'd been through together?

Evelyn's mind reeled as she listened to the girls' words, her heart pounding in her chest. She clutched them closer, as if her embrace could shield them from the horrors they'd witnessed.

"You... you didn't run?" Evelyn asked, her voice barely above a whisper.

Julia shook her head, her eyes wide. "We hid in one of our spots in the hall, behind that tapestry."

Augusta nodded solemnly. "We saw Nell start the fire in the hallway. She was muttering to herself, saying awful things about you, Miss Evelyn."

Evelyn felt the Baron stiffen beside her, his hand tightening on her shoulder. She glanced up at him, seeing the shock and anger warring in his eyes.

Julia continued, her voice trembling. "And then, when she was outside your room, we heard her say something terrible."

For a moment she couldn't breathe. She steeled herself, knowing that whatever came next would change everything.

Augusta's voice was barely audible. "She said... she said that she started the first fire in the West Wing. The one that..."

The girl trailed off, unable to finish the sentence. But Evelyn knew. The fire that had claimed the life of the girls' mother, the Baron's first wife.

Evelyn watched as the Baron's face paled, his eyes wide with disbelief. He turned to the girls, his voice hoarse. "Is this true?"

Evelyn met his gaze grimly, giving the barest of nods to confirm their story. "From the mouths of babes," she said quietly, her heart aching for the pain she saw etched across his features.

The Baron looked utterly rattled, his usual composure crumbling before her eyes. "I... I'd always thought it was a knocked-over candlestick," he said, his voice barely above a whisper. "Or maybe I'd left something too close to the fireplace..." He trailed off, shaking his head in disbelief. "All these years, I've blamed myself. If not for starting the fire, then for not being able to save her."

Evelyn's heart clenched at the raw anguish in his voice. She could see the conflicting emotions warring across his face – devastation at the truth of what had happened, mixed with a glimmer of relief at finally knowing he wasn't to blame.

Without a word, Evelyn took his arm, offering what comfort she could through her touch. On his other side, Julia and Augusta pressed close, their small hands reaching for their father.

Together, the four of them began to make their way slowly back towards what remained of their home. The night air was heavy with the scent of smoke, a stark reminder of all they had nearly lost. But as they walked, Evelyn felt a flicker of hope. They had survived, and they were together. Whatever came next, they would face it as a family.

Epilogue

James surveyed the charred remains of his ancestral home, a mixture of emotions churning within him. The acrid smell of smoke still lingered in the air, mingling with the earthy scent of damp timber and scorched stone. Yet, as he stood amidst the rubble, an unexpected sense of optimism blossomed in his chest.

"It's not as bad as I feared," he murmured, running a calloused hand along a blackened beam. The structure had held firm, a testament to the craftsmanship of generations past. Already, workers bustled about, clearing debris and shoring up weakened sections.

James caught sight of Evelyn across the courtyard. Her hair was gleaming in the morning sun as she directed a group of maids salvaging what they could from the East Wing. A smile tugged at his lips. She'd proven herself more resilient than he could have imagined, her strength shining through in the face of adversity.

As he picked his way through the ruins of the great hall, James found himself envisioning the future. The walls would rise again, stronger than before. The rooms would be filled with laughter once more, not just of his daughters, but of the family he and Evelyn would build together.

"We'll make it grander than ever, my lord," his steward said, appearing at his side with a sheaf of papers. "The insurance will cover most of the repairs, and I've already contacted the best craftsmen in the county."

James nodded, his mind already racing with possibilities. "Good. But let's not simply recreate what was lost. This is our chance to make improvements, to build something that will serve us well for generations to come."

He turned, taking in the full scope of the damage and the flurry of activity around him. It struck him then that this disaster, terrible as it was, had brought his household together in a way he'd never seen before. Servants and tenants alike had rallied to save what they could, working through the night alongside him and Evelyn.

"It's a new beginning," James said softly, more to himself than anyone else. "For all of us."

As if she felt his gaze upon her, Evelyn turned and met James's eyes across the courtyard. Her face, smudged with soot, broke into a warm smile that made his heart skip a beat. She excused herself from the maids and made her way towards him, picking her way carefully through the debris.

James watched her approach, marvelling at how she managed to look both bedraggled and utterly enchanting at the same time. Her hair was coming loose from its pins, and her dress was blackened with soot at the hem, yet she moved with a grace that belied the chaos surrounding them.

"Well, my lord," Evelyn said as she reached him. Her eyes twinkled with mischief. "I suppose no one can say it's improper for me to be married from your house now, as we no longer have one."

James couldn't help but grin at her jest, feeling a surge of affection for this woman who could find humour even in the aftermath of disaster. "I believe you're mistaken, my dear," he replied, his voice warm with amusement. "You're the only one of us who actually has a house right now."

Evelyn's eyes widened, and her face lit up with sudden realisation. "Oh! The cottage!" she exclaimed, as if she'd completely forgotten about the property he'd gifted her. "I can't believe it slipped my mind."

James chuckled, reaching out to brush a smudge of ash from her cheek. "Perhaps we should move our wedding plans there," he suggested, only half in jest. "It would certainly be cosier than this pile of rubble. Or camping beneath canvas," he added, with a pointed look.

"My lord, I cannot believe you would even hint at our living together in sin before we're wed!" she exclaimed, pressing a hand to her heart in feigned outrage.

James felt a warmth spread through his chest at Evelyn's mock indignation. Her eyes sparkled with mirth, belying her scandalised tone. He couldn't help but smile, relishing this playful side of her that had emerged in recent days. "Fear not, my dear," he said, his voice low and tinged with amusement. "I've applied for a special licence, given everything that's happened."

Evelyn's face softened, her pretence falling away. "Oh, James," she said, using his given name in a rare moment of intimacy. "That's wonderful. You know, I've been married before, and I don't want a big society wedding. I just want to be your wife."

James felt his breath catch in his throat. He reached out, taking her hands in his, marvelling at how small and delicate they felt in his rough, calloused palms. "Are you certain?" he asked, searching her face. "Would that truly make you happy?"

Evelyn's eyes met his, steady and sure. "I'd marry you under an apple tree in a potato sack," she declared, her voice filled with conviction. "None of that matters to me anymore. I know what's really important now." She turned to smile warmly at Julia and Augusta, who were engaged in a moment of playfulness. Against all odds, the rubber ball had survived the fire, and they were busy chasing it across the grass.

James felt a surge of emotion so strong it nearly overwhelmed him. He had never imagined finding such happiness again, especially not with someone who understood him so completely. Without a word, he pulled Evelyn into his arms, holding her close as if he could shield her from all the world's troubles.

James watched Evelyn's face carefully, his heart swelling with affection. He couldn't quite believe how fortunate he was to have found such a remarkable woman, one who valued the same things he did.

"Are you certain you don't want anyone there when we marry?" he asked gently, his thumb tracing circles on the back of her hand. "Not even a single soul to witness our happiness?"

Evelyn's brow furrowed slightly as she considered his question. James found himself holding his breath, realising how much he wanted to share this moment with those closest to them. After a moment, a warm smile spread across Evelyn's face, lighting up her eyes in a way that never failed to captivate him.

"Well," she said, her voice soft and thoughtful, "perhaps there is one person I'd like to have there. Someone to whom I owe all of my happiness."

James felt a flicker of curiosity. Who could she mean? He'd assumed her family connections were limited, given what he knew of her past. Could there be someone from her previous life she wanted to include?

"Oh?" he prompted, trying to keep his tone light and free of the sudden anxiety that gripped him. "And who might that be?"

The next book of the series will be available soon. Until then read the Bonus Scene of this book, or my bestselling novel Entangled With The Duke!

Thank you

hank you for purchasing and reading my book. It Means a lot to me and Starfall Publications!

As a token of appreciation, we would like to offer you a 20% Discount on your first order at Starfall's EShop **www.starfallpublicationsbooks.com** using the code **SFKU20** and a Bonus Scene of this book!

Click Here or on the image or Scan the QR Code to gain access 100% for free!

About Starfall Publications

Starfall Publications has helped me and so many others extend my passion for writing to you.

The prime focus of this company has been – and always will be – *quality* and I am honoured to publish my books under their name.

I would like to officially thank Starfall Publications for offering me the opportunity to be part of such a wonderful, hard-working team!

Thanks to them, my dreams – and your dreams — have come true!

Follow Them on Social Media

https://starfallpublicationsbooks.com/

instagram.com/starfallpublicationsbooks/

youtube.com/@StarfallPublicationsHouse

Do you want to influence our next stories and give feedback before it is even published?
Do you post your reviews on Amazon or Goodreads or Bookbub?
Do you share your reads with your friends or followers on Social Media?
Join our Influencers' Group and earn while you read!
https://starfallpublicationsbooks.com/pages/book-influencers

Also by Abby Ayles

Belles of The Ball
Vera At The Ballroom
Olive At The Ballroom
Giovanna At The Ballroom
Esther At The Ballroom
Agnes At The Ballroom

***

The Keys to a Lockridge Heart
Melting a Duke's Winter Heart
A Loving Duke for the Shy Duchess
Freed by the Love of an Earl
The Earl's Wager for a Lady's Heart
The Lady in the Gilded Cage
A Reluctant Bride for the Baron
A Christmas Worth Remembering
A Guiding Light for the Lost Earl
The Earl Behind the Mask

***

Tales of Magnificent Ladies
The Odd Mystery of the Cursed Duke
A Second Chance for the Tormented Lady
Capturing the Viscount's Heart
The Lady's Patient
A Broken Heart's Redemption
The Lady The Duke And the Gentleman
Desire and Fear
A Tale of Two Sisters
What the Governess is Hiding

***

Betrayal and Redemption
Inconveniently Betrothed to an Earl
A Muse for the Lonely Marquess
Reforming the Rigid Duke
Stealing Away the Governess
A Healer for the Marquess's Heart
How to Train a Duke in the Ways of Love
Betrayal and Redemption
The Secret of a Lady's Heart
The Lady's Right Option

***

Forbidden Loves and Dashing Lords
The Lady of the Lighthouse
A Forbidden Gamble for the Duke's Heart

A Forbidden Bid for a Lady's Heart
A Forbidden Love for the Rebellious Baron
Saving His Lady from Scandal
A Lady's Forgiveness
Viscount's Hidden Truths
A Poisonous Flower for the Lady

***

Marriages by Mistake
The Lady's Gamble
Engaging Love
Caught in the Storm of a Duke's Heart
Marriage by Mistake
The Language of a Lady's Heart
The Governess and the Duke
Saving the Imprisoned Earl
Portrait of Love
From Denial to Desire
The Duke's Christmas Ball

***

The Dukes' Ladies
Entangled with the Duke
A Mysterious Governess for the Reluctant Earl
A Cinderella for the Duke
Falling for the Governess
Saving Lady Abigail
The Duke's Rebellious Daughter
The Duke's Juliet
Secret Dreams of a Fearless Governess
A Daring Captain for Her Loyal Heart

Loving A Lady
Unlocking the Secrets of a Duke's Heart

***

German Editions
Vera im Ballsaal
Olive im Ballsaal
Giovanna im Ballsaal
Esther im Ballsaal
Agnes im Ballsaal
Verstrickt mit dem Herzog

***

French Editions
Vera Au Bal
Olive Au Bal
Giovanna Au Bal
Esther Au Bal
Agnes Au Bal
Emmêlée Avec Le Duc

Made in United States
North Haven, CT
04 December 2024